A Breath
of Eyre

A Breath of Eyre

Eve Marie Mont

KENSINGTON PUBLISHING CORP.

www.kensingtonbooks.com

K TEEN BOOKS are published by

Kensington Publishing Corp.
119 West 40th Street
New York, NY 10018

All Kensington titles, imprints, and distributed lines are available at special quantity discounts for bulk purchases for sales promotion, premiums, fund-raising, educational, or institutional use.

Special book excerpts or customized printings can also be created to fit specific needs. For details, write or phone the office of the Kensington Special Sales Manager: Kensington Publishing Corp., 119 West 40th Street, New York, NY 10018. Attn. Special Sales Department. Phone: 1-800-221-2647.

Kensington and KTeen Reg. U.S. Pat. & TM Off.

ISBN-13: 978-0-7582-6948-5
ISBN-10: 0-7582-6948-X

First Kensington Trade Paperback Printing: April 2012
10 9 8 7 6 5 4 3 2 1

Printed in the United States of America

To Ken . . .
wherever you are is my home.

ACKNOWLEDGMENTS

The seed for *A Breath of Eyre* was planted in high school when I read *Jane Eyre* for the first time and fell in love with Jane and Rochester's story. Since then, I have reread the book countless times, and in all those readings, the book has never lost its magic. It is fitting that I am back in high school once again, as a teacher this time, and while I don't have the privilege of teaching *Jane Eyre*, I hope my book might prompt some readers to seek out Charlotte Brontë's original to see what all the fuss is about.

A huge thank you goes out to my multitalented agent, April Eberhardt, for searching for and finding the perfect home for this story; your positive attitude and humor kept me sane, and more important, kept me writing. To my wonderful editor at Kensington, Martin Biro, thank you for having faith in *A Breath of Eyre* and for talking about Emma and Gray like they're real people; your intelligence and insight have made this a much better book. Thanks also to the warm and savvy team at Kensington/K Teen for embracing *A Breath of Eyre* and for doing all in their power to get it into the hands of readers.

Thanks to my friends and colleagues who supported me with early reads, brainstorming sessions, moral support, or just good conversation, especially Ashley Seiver, Barbara Kavanagh, and Taylor and Lisa Klein. A big shout-out to my students for reminding me every day that teenagers are smart, funny, compassionate, complex, and concerned about their world; you provide me with endless material and inspiration.

To the incredible group of young adult and middle-grade writers in the Apocalypsies and the Class of 2k12, thank you for being a community of professionals who truly nurture and support one another. It has been a pleasure taking this ride with all of you, particularly Heather Anastasiu, who read my sprawling mess of a manuscript and gave sound advice on plot and pacing while making me smile.

Thank you to my extended family for their constant love and support; I love you all so much. And a special thanks to my immediate family—Mom and Dad, you filled our house with books and ideas and made me the person I am today; Pete, our infrequent but long phone calls always raise my spirits and my confidence; and Phil, your generosity with your time and advice has made me believe in myself as an author, not just a writer.

Thank you most of all to Ken, "my prop and my guide" throughout this entire journey. Without you, true love would exist only in books.

"... and, best of all, to open my inward ear to a tale that was never ended—a tale my imagination created, and narrated continuously; quickened with all of incident, life, fire, feeling, that I desired and had not in my actual existence."

—Charlotte Brontë's *Jane Eyre*

PART 1

CHAPTER 1

There was no possibility of taking a swim that day. My stepmother had planned a sweet sixteen party, and the guests were about to arrive. I'd told Barbara at least a dozen times that I didn't want a party, but she insisted, saying if I didn't have one, I'd regret it later. And now that the day was here, setting a record for heat and humidity that summer, the only thing I regretted was that we didn't have central air-conditioning. That voice inside my head began to call me, that invisible cord tugging at my chest, drawing me to the ocean. But it was almost noon. The swim would have to wait.

Reluctantly, I threw on a tank top, cut-off shorts, and flip-flops and headed downstairs. The first thing Barbara said when she saw my outfit was, "You're not wearing that, are you?"

I looked down at myself. "It would appear that I am."

"No, that won't do," she said, clicking her tongue and studying me as if I was beyond hope. "Go upstairs, honey, and change into something pretty."

I raised my eyebrow at her, taking in the sight of her dramatic eye makeup and her piles of well-sprayed blond hair. Barbara had been raised in the rich and fertile soil of Georgia, fed a steady diet of debutante balls, diamond jewelry, and Dolly Parton hair. Her favorite color was yellow because "it's the color of sunshiiiine!"

"I'm perfectly comfortable in this," I said. "Besides, it's, like, a gazillion degrees in here."

"Honey, you don't know heat till you've been to Savannah in summertime. Anyway, that's even more reason to dress in something that'll make you feel pretty." Pretty being the end-all-be-all of life. "Gray Newman's going to be here," she sang.

Oh God. Gray Newman was coming to my party. Gray of the soulful hazel eyes that fooled me into thinking he had hidden depths, when really he was just a spoiled rich kid who spent his summers lifeguarding and seducing the sorority girls. At least, that's what I'd heard; we didn't exactly travel in the same circles.

His mother, Simona, had been my mom's roommate in college and later became my godmother, so Gray and I had been thrown together a lot as kids. Since my mom died, we only saw each other once or twice a year when we got dragged to each other's milestone events. The fact that he was going to be here in my house for my party mortified me. I didn't want him to see what a loser I was, to know that I had no friends, that I wasn't popular like he was. The urge to cut and run grew so strong I could feel it in my bones.

Reluctantly, I went back upstairs to change. On a whim, I put on my bathing suit underneath the green-and-white summer dress I'd chosen. I glanced at myself in the mirror and made a quick assessment. Face: too pointy. Hair: too flyaway, and not at all helped by this humidity. Body: too pathetic. I pulled my hair off my neck and scooped it into a ponytail, partly because it was too hot to wear down and partly because I knew it would annoy Barbara. "Ponytails are for horses," she'd say, or some other ridiculous gem of Southern wisdom.

When I got back downstairs, I saw that Aunt Trish, my

cousins, and Grandma Mackie had all arrived together. Next came the neighbors, Bill and Rita, followed by Cassie, a woman I'd made friends with at the real estate office this summer. And yep, that was it. Saddest sweet sixteen party in history.

I went around saying hellos and collecting presents and cards, beginning to hold out hope that the Newmans weren't going to come. But around 12:30, their oatmeal-colored Subaru pulled up in front of our house, and my stomach fell. I watched Gray get out of the car, pick up his little sister Anna, and give her a piggyback ride to the door. Mr. Newman came in carrying an organically grown zucchini the size of a small infant, and Simona held out my present, which appeared to be wrapped in tree bark. They both hugged me, Simona clutching me for so long it was uncomfortable.

"Happy birthday, Emma," she said, tears welling up in her eyes. "You look more like Laura every day." I never knew what to say to this.

Gray squatted down so Anna could dismount, then gave me a slow, uncomfortable perusal, glancing briefly down at my chest, I suppose to see if anything interesting was happening there. It wasn't. Despite nightly pleas to a God I only half believed in, I remained a disappointing five foot three with barely any curves. Gray was even taller than the last time I'd seen him, and he'd definitely filled out. With his close-cropped hair and slightly broken-looking nose, he looked hard and proud, but also sort of haunted—like a medieval saint trapped in the body of a Marine.

Anna ran into me, hugging my legs so I was staring down at her long red hair. "Hey, beautiful!" I said. "You're getting so big."

"I just turned seven," she said.

"And I just turned sixteen."

"I *know,*" she said. "Gray told me, like, a million times."

"So give Emma her present," Gray reminded her.

His voice was deeper than I remembered. A few years at a private school had chipped away at his Boston accent, but a hint of it remained. I found it irritatingly sexy.

Anna handed me a small package and demanded that I open it immediately. "Okay, okay," I said, laughing and making a small tear in one corner. When I pulled off the last of the wrapping paper, I was holding a turquoise leather journal inscribed with my initials. "Wow," I said.

"Do you like it?"

"I love it!"

She broke into an embarrassed smile, and then, mission accomplished, went running off to see if there was anyone to play with. I must have looked a little stunned because Gray felt it necessary to add, "Before you go getting all touched, it was my mom's idea. She remembered you used to write."

"Oh," I said, wanting to slam him into something sharp and hard. Why did guys have to be like this? Was it possible for them to admit they had any feelings other than the sports-induced grunting variety?

"So," he said, "are you still?"

"Still what?"

"Writing?"

"Not so much."

"Why not?"

"I don't know. I guess I haven't been inspired. What about you? Are you still lifeguarding?"

"No."

"Too busy doing keg stands and scoring with fraternity chicks?"

He glared at me, and for a moment, I thought he was going to punch the wall. "I don't do that anymore, Townsend."

"Which one?"

"Either."

I studied his face for traces of sarcasm. Even if he was

being sincere, it was sort of an unwritten rule that Gray and I had to give each other a hard time. When I was five years old and he was seven, I kissed him under the apple tree in our backyard. He responded by giving me a bloody nose. We'd been sparring ever since.

After a few seconds of awkwardly staring at each other, I rolled my eyes and went to join the rest of the party in the kitchen. Everyone was hovering by the whining air conditioner except my poor dad, who stood outside on the deck in front of a hot grill. Why Barbara had planned a cookout for the middle of a heat wave, I had no idea. Grandma Mackie was sitting at the table, sipping her old-fashioned, content to be ignored even though she was probably the most interesting person there. I noticed her drink was getting low, and Grandma didn't like her drinks getting low.

"Can I make you another?" I said.

"A small one," she said. "Just tickle the glass."

"I think you've had enough, Elspeth," Barbara drawled. My grandma was eighty-three years old and had been drinking old-fashioneds since practically World War II. I didn't think one more was going to kill her. "And Emma, you know I don't like you making alcoholic drinks for your grandmother. It isn't appropriate."

"Dad always lets me make them," I said, playing the "real parent" card.

"I know, but he shouldn't. Elspeth, let me get you a nice sweet tea."

"If I wanted tea," Grandma said, "I'd go to the Four Seasons. Right now, I'd like to have a drink at my granddaughter's birthday party." She winked at me, then made a waving motion with her hand, ushering me down to her level. "Who's the David?"

"Who?"

"That beautiful Michelangelo statue," she said, pointing at Gray.

I covered her finger with my hand. "That's Gray Newman, Grandma. You remember. Mom's godson?"

"I don't remember him looking like that," she said, polishing off her old-fashioned. "Delicious." I didn't know if she was talking about her drink or Gray Newman.

My cousins were eyeing him with interest, too. Ashley and Devin were thirteen-year-old twins who resembled the creepy sisters from *The Shining* movie, especially as my aunt insisted they dress in the same outfits. I shuddered to myself and went into the den to make my grandmother's drink. Gray followed me in and watched me from behind, presumably with the intention of making me nervous.

"Quite a party you've got here, Townsend," he said. He always called me Townsend, like I was one of his swim team buddies. "Your parents, my parents, and a bunch of relatives."

"You forgot to mention yourself," I said, "which should make it fairly obvious that I didn't write the guest list." He laughed and nodded an unspoken *touché*. "I told Barbara I didn't want a party."

"You have to have a party on your sixteenth birthday," he said. "But you could have invited some friends. I was expecting a room full of teenage girls."

I was about to tell him I didn't have any friends, but it seemed too naked a statement to make to Gray. Like leaving raw meat out for a wild dog. "So sorry to disappoint," I said, turning away from him and tugging at my necklace. I could feel the heat rising to my face, and I hated myself for it.

"You're not playing this right," he said. "The more people you invite, the more presents you get."

"But there's nothing I want."

"Nothing you want?" he said, feigning shock. "You're not a very good Lockwood girl, are you?"

Lockwood Prep, the school I attended, had a reputation for girls with trust funds and designer wardrobes who received brand-new SUVs on their sixteenth birthdays. Gray was right: I was not a very good Lockwood girl. And he would know. He'd been dating Lockwood's poster girl, Elise Fairchild, for six months. She was as Lockwoodian as they came.

"So," I said, trying to steer the conversation away from me, "this is your last year at Braeburn." Two years ago, Gray's parents had transferred him from Sheldrake, the public school in Waltham, to Braeburn Academy, an alternative school that was all about kumbaya and kindness.

"If I have to sit through one more 'harmonic huddle,'" he said, making made air quotes with his fingers, "I'm gonna impale myself with a drumstick."

"That might be a little extreme," I said, extracting a tiny smile from him. "Have you thought about where you're going to college?" I poured two inches of whiskey into my grandma's highball glass.

"I'm tired of thinking about it, actually." His eyes darted restlessly, like it was paining him to have to talk to me. My mouth went rigid, and I retracted, turtle style. I was thinking of something cutting to say when his cell phone rang. He reached into his pocket and glanced down at the display. "I have to answer this," he said and abruptly left the room.

For some reason, I felt embarrassed and enormously disappointed. What had I expected, for Gray Newman to engage in hostile banter with me for the duration of my party? I stayed in the den for a few minutes so it wouldn't seem like I was chasing after him, then went back out to the kitchen and gave Grandma her drink. Everyone was engaged in conversation, so I stepped outside to see if my dad needed help at the grill.

"Hey, kiddo," he said when he saw me. "Ever eat a tofu dog before?"

"Can't say that I have," I said, smiling.

I sidled up next to him, relishing this brief time alone with my father. For the past few years, we'd grown distant. Well, really, he'd grown distant. He'd be standing right in front of me smiling, but I'd know that his mind was somewhere else. He was a fisherman for the local fleet, handsome in a Gary Cooper way, meaning he could look rugged or elegant, depending on the context. In the middle of summer when his skin was almost bronze, he looked like a weathered lobsterman, but around Christmas when he wore a tuxedo to take Barbara to the Boston Pops, he looked like a movie star. Now, with sweat staining the back of his shirt and a damp, sunburned face, he looked like the browbeaten husband he'd become.

"Why don't you let me finish up out here?" I offered. "Go inside and cool off."

"That's okay," he said. "You're the birthday girl. Go back and talk to your guests."

How could I tell him this was the last thing I wanted to do?

Reluctantly, I went back inside. Nobody seemed to care that I'd returned, so I ended up wandering around the first floor, feeling like I was at someone else's party. In her zeal to keep the chip baskets filled, Barbara stumbled upon me in the living room and seized the opportunity to give me a lecture on feminine wiles.

"What happened to Gray?" she asked in her irritating drawl, her heavily mascaraed eyes wide with alarm.

"He got a phone call."

"Well, honey, take this opportunity to go upstairs and reapply your makeup. Your face is all splotchy and your hair is a disaster. Go now, while Gray is occupied."

I wanted to scream at her, to tell her how awful it made me feel when she looked at me like I was some kind of mutant. Why could I never be good enough for her? Why could I never please her?

It was on days like this that I missed my mother most, even if I could barely remember her. In my mind she was bright and beautiful and wild—an orange poppy or a beautifully plumed bird. Summer mornings, we used to rush down to the beach to go swimming or build castles, and summer nights we'd catch fireflies until it was too dark to see. The ocean was the place where I felt closest to her. I clutched at her necklace—a silver dragonfly with blue and green glass wings—and felt an ache for her that took my breath away.

I had to get out of there. I had to go to the beach and swim—swim until my head cleared, my muscles ached, and my skin went numb—until I couldn't feel anything at all. I knew it would be rude to leave my own party and I'd probably pay for it later, but at that moment, I didn't care. It was almost as if I had no choice.

While the guests were eating their veggie burgers and tofu dogs in the kitchen, I snuck out the front door, determined to walk to the stony beach at the end of our block. The only thing that shook my resolve was seeing Gray Newman sitting on my curb, staring down at his phone like it had just bitten him. I intended to walk right past him and continue with my mission, but he shouted, "Yo, Townsend!"

Startled, I turned around. *Yo, Townsend? Really?*

"Where are you going?" he asked. He looked stunned, like he couldn't believe I was leaving my own party.

"To the opera," I said. My sarcasm was a defense mechanism. Truthfully, acting cool and aloof all the time exhausted me, particularly when the last thing I felt about Gray was aloof. His face hadn't registered my joke, and he was still looking mortally wounded. "Are you okay?" I asked, getting serious for a minute.

His eyes crinkled, like he was working something out in his head. "Yeah, I'm okay," he said. "I just keep choosing the wrong girls."

His face looked so sad and earnest, but I couldn't help feeling a sense of joy at this confession. He stood up and walked over to where I was standing. Barbara's earlier pronouncement about my splotchy face and messy hair echoed through my head, and I felt sweat beading at my temples. Somehow even in the full glare of the sun, Gray managed to look cool and unflustered. "You got a boyfriend, Townsend?"

My face grew even hotter than before. "There's a constant stream of them coming in and out of my house, haven't you noticed? I have to beat them off with a stick."

He laughed out loud, and I was surprised by how good this made me feel. Then he knitted his brow and stared at me. "You know, our schools are, like, five minutes from each other. It's weird that we never see each other."

"Yeah," I said, wondering where he was going with this.

"Do you ever go into town?"

"Waverly Falls?" He nodded. "No, I don't drive, remember?"

"Oh, right. Are you going to get your license soon?"

"Eventually," I said. "My dad's not a huge fan of the idea. He's afraid if I get my license, I'll take off and never come back."

"Is that a possibility?"

"I don't know," I said. "It's tempting."

"You don't like Lockwood, do you?"

I paused before answering. "No, not really." Understatement of the century.

"Why not?"

I couldn't very well say, *Because of people like your girlfriend,* so I just shrugged and said, "I don't belong there."

It was an honest answer, and he gave me an honest response. "I know." I was wondering whether to be offended by this, but I got the sense he'd meant it as a compliment. Then he added, "I don't belong where I am either," and I knew my instinct had been correct.

We stood staring at each other for a few seconds, but instead of feeling awkward like it had before, this time it felt heavy and meaningful. I didn't want to stop looking at him, and then the staring contest grew too intense and I actually felt a little breathless. Finally, because I didn't know what else to do, I said, "Well, I'm going to go now."

"You're really leaving?" he said, his face an open book of disappointment.

"Just going for a quick swim," I said, clutching my necklace. His glance flickered briefly to the pendant, then rose to meet my eyes.

"Be careful, okay?"

"I will. My dad's a fisherman, remember?"

"And my parents own an organic food store. That doesn't make me a vegan."

I laughed and nodded. "I'll be careful."

He smiled, but his face still looked sad. I think it was because his eyes turned down at the ends. "Happy sweet sixteen, Emma," he said. Sincerely. Without a trace of sarcasm.

Feeling a little rattled that he'd called me Emma and not Townsend, I turned toward the beach and felt his eyes on me as I walked away.

The beach was practically deserted. The TV and radio had been airing warnings to stay inside, but there were a few brave souls sitting with their beach chairs in the surf. I took my shoes off and stepped onto the pebbly sand, feeling my feet scald the moment they touched ground. I ran to the water for relief.

The tide was running high, the ocean churning up foam and seaweed. I breathed in deeply, inhaling the briny air as I watched a sailboat skim along the horizon. I imagined it was sailing somewhere exotic: Bermuda, Jamaica, St. Croix. Somewhere with soft trade winds that carried the scent of jasmine and hibiscus. I longed to be on it.

I took off my clothes and waded into the water, feeling its coolness envelop me. After a few more steps I couldn't resist diving in and swimming out a little farther. Once I was out past the breakers, I began a steady and relentless crawl, swimming like I was trying to reach the horizon. My heart was beating fast, but I felt tremendous. Alive. When I finally grew tired, I turned onto my back and let my head float on the water, looking up at a cloudless sky. My ears were underwater, so all I could hear was the magnified sound of my own breathing, hypnotic and soothing.

Somehow I could lose myself in the ocean the same way I could lose myself in a good book. Maybe it was because both involved suspension—a suspension of weight, a suspension of disbelief—a willingness to surrender to something greater than oneself. Cradled by this enormous sea, everything else melted away. I felt alone yet not lonely. I had felt far lonelier back at the house.

Time lapsed in that lazy way it can on the ocean, and after a while, I lifted my head and spun around to get my bearings. I'd never been out this far before, and never on my own. But I didn't panic. I was a strong swimmer, and I liked a challenge. I turned onto my stomach and began swimming to shore, even though I was reluctant to return to my party and face the wrath of Barbara. When I felt my chest tightening, I paused and treaded water to catch my breath. The undertow was strong; I'd barely covered any ground.

I was feeling pretty exhausted already, and my earlier confidence was waning. I resumed my crawl, hoping I had enough energy left to make it back to shore. Cutting through the waves, I kept my eyes closed, praying that I'd open them to see the beach within range. But when I stopped to check, I'd made virtually no headway at all. The realization made me weak with fear. My breathing was ragged, and salt water stung my eyes and nostrils. My muscles burned from the effort of swimming against the tide, and my limbs felt rubbery and slack.

Panic set in as I tried to find the beach through wet eyelashes. My blood was pulsing in my ears as I took in the first few gulps of water, making me choke and sputter. My lungs burned in my chest, and this sent me into a panic spiral. I stopped swimming and did the worst thing I could possibly do: I began to flail. I could feel myself losing control, sinking under, and for one startling moment, I knew I was going to drown. I, Emma Townsend, on my sixteenth birthday, was going to die of extreme stupidity.

I could no longer see the beach, only water and darkness and foam. My brain suddenly went hot, and my mind grew very still and quiet—so quiet that I thought I heard chanting, an angelic chorus of voices calling to me from beneath the sea. I stopped struggling for a minute and floated, surrendering myself to the music. I knew that if I wanted to, I could let the waves overtake me and sink to the bottom to join those voices. It would be so much calmer down there without all this noise and tumult. It might even be peaceful. And I was so tired of fighting. Letting go would be easy.

It was human voices that woke me out of my trance. They were calling out to me, their voices crystallizing as I regained consciousness. One seemed to be calling my name. There was no panic in the voice, only a deep sense of purpose. Hearing it, I knew that I had to keep swimming.

Back at the house, I had told Gray that there wasn't anything I wanted. But that wasn't true. I wanted to go to Paris. I wanted to write a novel. I wanted to fall in love. I wanted so many things.

Buoyed by this revelation, I mustered all my remaining strength and resumed my swim toward shore, letting the voices guide me. I don't know where this surge of energy came from—adrenaline, survival instinct—but I was swimming now with a power I didn't know I had. The tide had carried me so far down the beach that I could see the lighthouse blinking out on the point. Just below it, the shoreline jutted out into the ocean like a bent arm, the tip curving toward me like a miraculous hand.

I swam with singular determination, my arms burning,

lungs heaving, knowing I couldn't stop. Not until my palms felt hard sand. As I neared the shoreline, I got caught in the heavy surf. Water came crashing over my head, spinning me under the water, dragging my back and legs along the rocky bottom. I clawed my way along the ocean floor and let the water barrel over me, so long as it was moving me closer to shore. Finally, a mammoth wave tossed me onto the sand, where I collapsed, sputtering water out of my nose and mouth and opening my eyes to the silhouette of my saviors, the beacon of the lighthouse flashing behind one of them like a halo.

CHAPTER 2

The next thing I remember was waking with the feeling that I'd had a terrible nightmare. I lay in the darkness for a few minutes, feeling my heart race as I remembered that it had really happened. I had almost drowned. And now I was lying safe in my bed and couldn't remember how I'd gotten here.

Thunder rattled the windows, and I sat up, feeling pain seize through my limbs. My body hurt everywhere. As I swung my legs over the side of the bed, I was fairly sure somebody had doped me up with some heavy-duty painkillers. I felt woozy and weak and could barely stand, let alone walk. Feeling drunk, I stumbled to the window and opened it, feeling cool air rush in, along with a fine mist that coated my face. Rainwater was pooling all over the yard and racing down the gutters, making a whooshing sound that exhilarated me.

I stood staring out the window for several minutes, trying to remember what had happened. Vaguely I recalled someone standing over me at the beach, asking me questions. One of my saviors had called 911. And even though it defied logic, I couldn't help but believe that the person standing over me with the halo behind her head had been my mother.

As I watched rain pummel the house, I half remembered

lying in a hospital room as guests from my party came in and out, looking down at me with worried expressions. But their faces were vague in my mind, silhouettes from a surrealist painting. I wondered if maybe I'd dreamed them.

Feeling faint and shivery, I decided to take a hot shower. I stood under the spray for half an hour, letting the water massage my sore muscles and calm my nerves. I threw on a T-shirt and my coziest pair of pajama pants, then headed downstairs to get something to eat. I felt ravenous. As I rounded the corner of the living room, I heard hushed voices coming from the kitchen.

"She's been so reckless lately," Barbara was saying. "She's getting more and more like Laura every day."

"Don't say that," my dad said. "You didn't know her."

"But you told me that was what she was like at the end. Withdrawn. Erratic. Irresponsible."

"It was more complicated than that. She was very, very sick."

There was a pause, followed by more whispering. "Maybe that's what's happening to Emma. She is sixteen. A lot of these illnesses manifest themselves in adolescence."

"She's sixteen, period, Barbara. It's a difficult age."

"An age when she should start acting like a responsible adult. Don't you think it's odd that she has no friends? That she doesn't go shopping or socializing like other kids? She seems very, very . . . troubled."

Another pause, during which I wondered how my father was going to respond. Finally, in a voice so quiet I could barely hear him, he said, "I wouldn't say she's *very* troubled." *Way to defend me, Dad.*

"All she did all summer long was mope around the house. She complained incessantly about having to work at the real estate office, as if I wasn't doing her a favor by giving her some practical job experience to put on her transcript. All I can say is thank goodness she goes back to school next week. Let someone else worry about her for a change."

Barbara's words stung, but my father's silence hurt even more. How could he let her talk about me that way? And what had she meant about my mother's "erratic" behavior? Or me getting sick?

I felt betrayed by them both, and more alone than I'd ever felt. I was about to go back upstairs when I noticed a package sitting on the floor by the bookcase. It must have been overlooked the day before amidst all the commotion. I bent down to pick it up and recognized the tree bark wrapping paper. Simona's gift.

I took it upstairs to my room and tore off the paper. The card inside read: *Happy Birthday, Emma! This was your mother's favorite book in college. I hope you adore it as much as she did. With love, Simona.*

The book had a worn leather spine and marbled covers. I cracked it open, smelling decades of must and age and wear. Turning to the title page, I read: *Jane Eyre. An Autobiography. Edited by Currer Bell. Harper & Brothers, Publishers, New York, 1848.* It was such an early copy that Charlotte Brontë hadn't even used her own name.

I had always wanted to read *Jane Eyre,* but for some reason, I'd never gotten around to it. For me, reading a book is an experience I like to savor. While I'm in the world of a story, the characters become more real to me than the people in my own life. If I'm having a bad day, I look forward to coming home and rejoining my friends on the page.

Last summer, I'd read every Jane Austen novel, beginning with *Northanger Abbey* and ending with *Persuasion. Sense and Sensibility* had been my favorite because I'd always wished for a sister. The summer before, I'd read Dickens— *David Copperfield, Oliver Twist,* and *Great Expectations*— but I'd never gotten that feeling of coming home with Dickens.

Pip and Estella never felt like my friends, not like Lizzy Bennet or the Dashwood sisters.

I looked down at the copy of *Jane Eyre* and ran my hand across the cover, feeling the years of the book's existence fill me up with a sort of longing, a wanderlust to travel into its pages. And since I had nowhere else to go and the rain seemed like it would never stop now that it had started, I turned to page one and began to read.

The book was about a young orphan named Jane who lived with her Aunt Reed, a selfish woman who treated her horribly and punished Jane by sending her to the red room where her uncle had died. I flipped the pages breathlessly to find out about Jane's banishment to a boarding school and her abuse at the hands of the evil Mr. Brocklehurst. I grieved for Jane when a typhus epidemic killed her best friend and when her beloved teacher, Miss Temple, had to move to another school. I stopped reading right after the chapter when Jane accepted a position as governess of Thornfield Hall. The rest would have to wait until I was back at school.

I had been dreading my return to school for weeks. In some ways, Lockwood was similar to Jane's boarding school. Sure, ours was for rich kids instead of orphans, and we certainly had better teachers and better food. But in some ways, Lockwood felt like a prison to me, full of rules and bells and social hierarchies that oppressed and confused me.

Lockwood was a little under an hour's drive from Hull's Cove, but it might as well have been another world. In Hull's Cove, the dominant color was brown—old fishing boats, crab traps, hemp nets, lobster pots, seafood shacks. Even the water looked sort of brown. But as we drove farther away from the coast and got off the Massachusetts Turnpike, it was all misty air and rolling hills and farms broken up by stonewalls so they resembled green patchwork quilts.

My dad and I didn't talk much on the ride. He was still angry with me about the swimming incident. That last week of my summer break, I'd had to endure multiple lectures about the dangers of the ocean. Being a fisherman, he had been fanatical about water safety all his life. He'd warned me dozens of times never to go swimming alone, never to go swimming during riptide, never to get complacent just because we lived near the sea. I didn't even try to argue because I knew he was right.

I rested my head against the window as we meandered through some low hills and passed by ponds and meadows, briefly entering the town of Waverly Falls, which sat on a river straddled by a red covered bridge. The landscape grew denser as we passed the state forest, woods on all sides and the smell of evergreen in the air. When we came out of the woods and onto Oakwood Lane, the East Gate of Lockwood Prep emerged in the clearing like some golden gate into an enchanted country.

But that was where the enchantment ended. The campus was built on old plantation lands once owned by Thomas Danforth, the deputy governor who sentenced nineteen innocent people to hang during the Salem Witch Trials. As we drove along the main drive into school with its canopy of overhanging trees, I felt a choking sensation in my chest and a knot in my stomach as if I were awaiting a sentence of my own.

The first time my dad and I visited the campus, those trees had reminded me of footservants greeting the arrival of some forgotten princess. I suppose that was the idea—to reinforce the sense of entitlement and privilege one would feel if one came here—but it only served to remind me how much I didn't belong.

The school was admittedly impressive with its banks of stately oak trees and sloping green fields, its cobbled walkways and nineteenth-century stone façades. But the sight of it now made me queasy. My father parked in the visitors' lot, and we hoisted my suitcases from the back of his station wagon and walked slowly toward the dormitory. This was my least favorite part of the year, the first day when all the girls thronged the hallways in giddy reunion, giggling and whispering, turning up their stereos to share recently discovered music, crashing into each other's rooms to speculate on what the new year would hold.

I knew I was getting a new roommate this year. In his infinite wisdom, our headmaster, Dr. Overbrook, always housed the scholarship recipients together so everyone would know who was attending Lockwood by the grace of charity rather than privilege. My roommate from last year, Becky Fulton, would not be returning because Elise Fairchild had seen to it that her life here was a living hell. Granted, Becky was not the typical prep-school girl; she wore fuzzy cat sweaters and dangly cat earrings and went to church every day, lecturing the girls on the consequences of smoking and drinking to their immortal souls. But that didn't give the other girls an excuse to torture her. Her parents had to pick her up in the middle of finals because she'd had a breakdown right in the middle of our history exam.

My new roommate was named Michelle Dominguez, and apparently, she'd been farmed from the local public school as a last-minute replacement for Becky. Dr. Overbrook had told my father she was some kind of science whiz and that he was counting on me to make Michelle feel welcome. I hoped Michelle wouldn't be disappointed to find I had no connections whatsoever around this place. In fact, with Becky no longer here, I feared I might be the next logical target for Elise Fairchild and her hellish minions.

When I opened the door to my room, it was clear that Michelle had already arrived, although she wasn't there at the moment. She had claimed the bed on the left side, where I'd slept last year, and some of her clothes were scattered over it. I couldn't help but notice that most of them were red. She had already hung some things on the wall—a map of the constellations, a poster of Degas's racehorses, a postcard of Albert Einstein sticking his tongue out. On her dresser sat two framed photos, side by side. One was of a woman on horseback wearing a red riding jacket, her dark hair tucked inside a riding cap. The other was of a distinguished-looking man with thick gray hair and big white teeth.

My dad watched me unpack my clothes in the dresser and make my bed, but I could tell he just wanted to leave. Goodbyes made him uncomfortable. Later he stood in front of me in the hallway, trying to find a graceful way to make his exit. My dad had never been particularly touchy-feely, but when I was a kid he'd at least let me sit on his lap after dinner or give me a hug before bed. But I honestly couldn't remember the last time he'd touched me. The fact that we were not hugging at this iconic hug moment loomed over us like a giant neon sign.

He stood playing with a tag that had fallen off my suitcase. "Do you have everything you need?" he said.

"I think so."

"Vitamins? Tylenol? Lifetime supply of Pop-Tarts?"

"B-complex. Advil. Brown Sugar and Cinnamon. Check."

"Okay, well, I'm gonna head off, kiddo."

"Okay."

He made a slight move toward me, and I braced myself for contact. But he ended up only squeezing my arm. "Be good."

"Always."

I watched through my window as he exited the dorm and shuffled to his car, hands in his pockets. When I thought about the chasm that had opened between us, I felt like it might swallow me up.

Something rustled behind me. I whipped around to see a girl who could only be Michelle carrying in bags from the school bookstore. I tried to muster up all my roommate enthusiasm.

"Hi. You must be Michelle. I'm Emma, your roommate."

Duh.

"Michelle," she said, not offering me her hand. It seemed no one wanted to touch me today.

She was a few inches taller than me and athletically built, with thick dark hair that fell in waves well past her shoulders. Her face was long and thin, the color of caramel, dominated by wide-set green eyes. While her expression was flat and resigned, her eyes looked rebellious.

"Was that your dad who just left?" she said.

"Yeah. He doesn't like to hover, thank God. Are your parents still here?"

"No. My aunt dropped me off hours ago."

We stood in silence, staring at the walls, trying to think of something to say to each other. "So, you like Degas?" I said.

"His horses, not his ballerinas."

"Oh." We continued standing and staring. "Is that your mom?" I asked, pointing to the photo on the dresser.

"Yeah."

"She's pretty. She's a rider?"

"Was a rider."

"And that's your dad?" I said, pointing to the other photo. She snorted at me like I was a moron. "That's Carl Sagan."

"Oh." Long, awkward silence during which I felt like a complete idiot. "So . . ."

"So . . ."

"I guess I'll finish unpacking."

Michelle gave me a look that implied, *do whatever you want.* She seemed self-contained, like there was no room inside her for anyone else. She put on a set of headphones and lay down on her bed with her back to me, bouncing her head rhythmically to the music. Not exactly what I'd hoped for in a new roommate.

I couldn't wait for classes to begin just so I'd have a reason to leave the room. On Monday, we had a half day during which we ran through our schedules on a twenty-minute rotation so we could meet our new teachers, receive our books, and get our first week's reading assignments. Michelle and I kept our distance that first week, as much as that was possible when you lived in the same room with someone. We were cordial, but we didn't exchange schedules or gossip or watch late-night TV like the other roommates did. We didn't go to the dining hall together and come back with our pockets full of cookies and free bagels. And we didn't even commiserate over all the work Lockwood teachers piled on. Michelle liked to listen to her headphones while she did her homework, and I liked to study at the library on Old Campus.

Lockwood's library was magnificent—an enormous Gothic structure that looked like something out of an Edgar Allan Poe story: three stories tall with an imposing stone façade and the notched roof of a fortress. Birds nested up there, so there was the constant sound of crows, adding to the Poe-like atmosphere. Rows of knotty oaks ran behind it, and the steeple of the chapel could be seen peeking through the trees a little farther down the lane. A big round tower flanked the north side; it reminded me of the tower where Hamlet sees the ghost of his father. Many years ago, the tower had been turned into a reading room with transom windows at the top to let the light in. It was the best place on campus to study, surrounded by ancient trees, watching the leaves fall above you.

By the end of that first week, I was exhausted from running between Old and New Campus, carrying a backpack full of heavy textbooks, and trying to make sense of all the daunting syllabi. The second week was even worse. I was already struggling in my French class. I was taking French II, so I had to endure the humiliation of being lumped with the freshmen, and even they seemed miles ahead of me. Probably because they spent six weeks in Paris every summer and had personal French tutors.

Our teacher, Madame Favier, was comfortingly plump with a short pouf of gray hair and enormous eyeglasses that made her look like an owl. I'd find myself looking at her and thinking, "Hoo? Hoo?" and imagine her replying, "En français, Emma. C'est *Qui? Qui?*" I understood the verb conjugations and memorized the vocabulary just fine; it was the speaking part that got me. My pronunciation was terrible. Whenever I was asked to read a passage aloud, I'd stumble through it like I had marbles in my mouth.

Music class was just as degrading. Many of the students had taken private piano and voice lessons since childhood. Elise had been christened a music prodigy when she was seven years old and sang like an angel. She was also gorgeous—slender with unfairly big boobs, long buttery blond hair, and the most amazing wardrobe of cashmere sweaters, expensive tweed skirts, and knee-high boots that made her look like a 1960s film goddess. Everything about her was soft and feminine and lovely, which made it all the more astonishing when you found out she was a mean-spirited, soul-crushing wench.

Unfortunately, she was in every afternoon class with me. European History was my least favorite. Last year's history teacher, Mr. Morris, had been young and funny and innovative, but he'd been fired for "taking liberties with the curriculum." The headmaster, Dr. Overbrook, had taken over the class temporarily. He was middle-aged, short, paunchy, and balding. His one unique attribute was the birthmark on his forehead that looked like Edvard Munch's *The Scream*. When he was at the front of the classroom, I had to resist the urge to slap my palms against my cheeks and howl.

History had never been my strong suit anyway. I just couldn't make myself care about all those dates and wars and battles and religious edicts. But with Overbrook at the helm, it became even more intolerable. We were studying nineteenth-century Europe that year, focusing on the themes of Imperialism and Revolution. During Friday's class, Michelle surprised us all by challenging Overbrook after he made an insensitive remark about third world countries being backward.

"Just because a country is third world," Michelle said, "doesn't mean it's backward. My country, Haiti, is the only country in the Western Hemisphere to have had a successful slave revolution. But we lack the goods and infrastructure you would require to call it a civilized nation. Oppression by dictators and foreign occupation have made political autonomy there all but impossible. America has had its military in Haiti and other developing countries for centuries, and I think it does more harm than good."

Overbrook glowered at her. He generally discouraged discussion and debate. *History is about facts, not opinions,* he always said. He cleared his throat.

"Excuse me, Ms. Dominguez, but the presence of American military in *your* country is the only reason Haiti has any roads, hospitals, houses, or infrastructure at all. America has been the salvation of countries like yours all over the world. Just because you disapprove of the politics that have prevented your native country from thriving does not make the U.S. a tyrant. The very system you condemn makes it possible for the rags-to-riches tales of so many of our most successful American leaders. Those of us lucky enough to live in this country recognize that it's the greatest country on earth and are thankful for the opportunities we've been afforded here. I would think that as a daughter of immigrants you might agree."

Elise snorted and gave her friends a knowing look, and they all sniggered like morons. Elise's roommate Amber Stone was a miniature poodle version of Elise, cuter and smaller but impeccably trained. Jess Barrister was tall and cross-country skinny with a long face and a withering stare. And Chelsea Anderson was the ugly one they kept around to make themselves feel better. Her father also co-owned the Boston Celtics, which made her quite popular among guys, and therefore, socially useful.

Michelle continued, undaunted. "I *am* grateful to live in a country that allows me an education and a home and food on my table. What I'm saying is, we shouldn't be so narrow-minded as to think that our government and way of life are the only ones that work. Or that they're necessarily the right ones. Especially when we see daily how this country abuses the very freedoms we have by victimizing and oppressing other cultures."

Overbrook strolled to the door, twirling a piece of chalk in his hand. "Oh, yes, everyone is a victim in Ms. Dominguez's philosophy. My dear, you're going to have to accept the fact that this world is about survival of the fittest. Kill or be killed. The law of the jungle is the law of man."

"But we aren't animals—" Michelle said.

"Enough, Ms. Dominguez. I've grown tired of this pointless debate."

"You didn't let me finish."

He scowled at her and raised an index finger. "You are finished."

"But—"

"Ms. Dominguez, please step into the hallway."

Michelle flinched briefly, then stood up and walked out the door, shutting it quietly behind her. I admired her for standing up for her beliefs, but I worried where it might get her, fearing it would be far worse than the outside of Overbrook's classroom.

Physics came next. Mr. Sarkissian was an adorable man with curly red hair and a slight lisp. Students could always get him off topic by mentioning time travel. Today, he was talking about Einstein's theory of relativity, saying some scientists believed time travel might be possible during our lifetime.

"Time isn't linear like people think," he said. "It's fluid, like my coffee." He held up his glass mug, then dropped a sugar cube in it. "Stir a spoon through it, and the cube gets twisted, just like time can be twisted. One day, we'll be able to use light to twist time and send particles backward or forward at will. They're already doing it at the subatomic level."

Michelle raised her hand. "Do you think humans might be able to go back and change the past?" she said.

Sarkissian rubbed a hand through his curls, coaxing them around his ear. "Not exactly," he said. "I don't think we'll be able to change what's already happened, but I do think we might be able to start a new path. Grow a new branch in the space-time continuum." As comforting as this idea was, I didn't think we'd ever be able to change the past. In life, there were no do-overs.

After Physics, I barely had time to grab a bagel at the dining hall before running down to the stables for Equestrian class. The instructor, Ms. Loughlin, had chosen Elise to be her assistant that year, and I knew Elise was going to lord it over the rest of us. That afternoon, Ms. Loughlin was telling us about the Interscholastic Equestrian Championship coming up in the spring.

"If you're thinking of competing," she said, "you'll need to start training now. But you have to qualify first. There's a written test in November and open tryouts in December. I know some of you have your own horse, but the school will lend out horses for training and competing as long as you qualify." Michelle's face lit up momentarily, and I wondered if she was thinking of entering.

"I've competed in I.E.C. every year," Elise told us, flipping that silky column of hair behind her, "and I placed second last year. My mother says this is my year. For those of you who have never competed before, I'll warn you that it's very expensive—seventy-five hundred for entry fees and another thirty-five hundred for special training." She looked directly at Michelle, and the warm light in Michelle's face went cold.

Eleven thousand dollars? That kind of money was pocket change for most of these girls, but for Michelle, it was an impossibility. On our way back to Exeter, I ran to catch up with Michelle.

"Sometimes you can get a sponsor," I said, trying to match her stride.

"What?" She glanced at me briefly but didn't slow her pace.

"A sponsor. For the competition. Someone willing to pay your training expenses. You looked like you were thinking of trying out."

"Well, I wasn't." Her glare implied that I should mind my own business.

Last period of the day was Brit Lit with Mr. Gallagher. I'd had Gallagher last year for Freshman Composition, and he was my favorite teacher at the school. I don't know exactly why I worshipped him. Maybe it was the way his forehead loomed so large and noble, like his brain held all the wisdom of the world. Or the fact that he could recite "Kubla Khan" from memory. Or how his hair looked dark and wild, like it wanted to fly off his head. Rumor had it that he and his wife had separated, and sometimes when I was the first one in the classroom, I'd find him wiping off his eyeglasses, looking like he'd just been crying. He was dark and melancholy and brooding, like some dashing hero from a nineteenth-century novel.

That afternoon, he was telling us about our big research project for the year. We were to choose a classic novel from a list of nineteenth-century British authors and read at least fifty pages of it by Monday. This was on top of the Samuel Johnson essays he'd assigned for Wednesday. The class uttered a collective groan. It was last period on Friday with two minutes to the bell, and Gallagher had just dashed dozens of plans for shopping excursions to Boston, sailing trips to the Cape, and parentless parties with pot and beer.

"Now, come on, you knew this year was going to be a challenge," he said. "You will be writing a research paper

based around a thesis that is critical in nature. This will not
be a book report. You'll actually have to read this time." The
class forced some weak laughter, and Mr. Gallagher raised
one of his jutting eyebrows. "Do you know what I mean by
'critical'?"

I glanced up at the clock, willing the second hand to move
faster. As much as I adored Gallagher, I lived in mortal terror
that he might call on me some day, as I'd recently come to believe that my voice made me sound like a cartoon rodent. Besides, if there was any hope of him returning my affections,
the chances were far greater if I kept my mouth shut.

"How about you, Ms. Townsend?" Gallagher said, con-
firming my fears.

"Um, critical," I said, buying some time by repeating the
word. "Critical means . . . using criticism to prove your point?"
I knew this was a feeble answer, but honestly I couldn't speak
intelligently in front of someone as good-looking and intimi-
dating as Mr. Gallagher.

"I suppose that's true," Gallagher said, to my relief. Public
flogging wasn't his style. "But I was hoping for something a
bit more . . . incisive. How about you, Ms. Fairchild?"

"Critical," Elise said in a breathy voice. "I don't know
what you're looking for by way of a definition, but I know
I'm an expert at it." The class laughed, spurring her on.
"Being critical is judging something, like what someone's
wearing, for example. Because it's so . . . trashy and awful,
you can't believe anyone would be caught dead in it." She
turned around in her seat, her eyes boring into Michelle's red,
off-the-shoulder sweater as her mouth curled into a smirk
that reminded me of the Grinch's evil smile that keeps going
and going until it takes over his entire face. Amber gave Elise
a dainty fist bump, and Jess and Chelsea both laughed under
their breath.

Mr. Gallagher ran a hand through his flop of dark hair.
"That'll do, Ms. Fairchild," he said. "But let me remind you,

a critical thesis doesn't have to be negative. It simply must take a stand. And sometimes in the face of majority opinion, that's a difficult thing to do. I will be asking some of you to submit your papers to the Middlebury Essay Symposium, held this spring. The deadline is January, so you'll want to finish your drafts by December."

And with that, the bell rang, and the ghastly week came to an end.

Everything was a competition at Lockwood. Sports, academics, music. If you were good at something, you better believe some teacher would be hounding you to enter a competition. And if someone else was good at the same thing you were good at, watch out. On the other hand, if you were mediocre at everything, people ignored you, and sometimes that was better.

I watched as students pulled out their cell phones, affixing them to their ears as if reattaching their limbs. "If he thinks I'm reading fifty pages this weekend," Elise said, "he's crazier than I thought. Hasn't he ever heard of SparkNotes?"

Amber laughed absurdly and pulled four Blow Pops from her purse, passing them out to Elise, Jess, and Chelsea, and popping one into her mouth. Michelle's eyes fluttered in disgust.

"What's your problem?" I heard Elise say, and my stomach lurched down to my kneecaps. But Elise wasn't talking to me; she was talking to Michelle. Becky Fulton's departure must have left a vacuum in the power system, and somebody had to fill it. "Girls," Elise said, "the new girl must be lesbo, because she can't stop staring at us."

They all launched into cackling hysterics and walked out of the room with their inner arms linked together, their outer arms juggling Prada purses and iPhones and Blow Pops, like they were some kind of hideous, social-climbing octopus. Michelle bit her lip, looking for the first time like that hardened exterior of hers was about to crack. She left before I could say anything.

I waited in the classroom long enough to be sure the ferocious foursome had gone, then glanced up to find Gallagher staring at me. It was a perceptive look, a look that suggested he could see right through me. I picked up my books and fled the room like it was on fire.

CHAPTER 3

I crossed the quad at a run, then headed down the hill to the stables, hoping to spend some time with Curry. Last year, that horse had been my only friend. Curry whinnied when he saw me, so I climbed the slats of his pen and gave him a firm nuzzle along his neck. "How you doing, baby? You miss me?"

Curry was the mellowest of the horses, with a sweet, compliant disposition and a desire to please. That was why Ms. Loughlin used him to train beginners. He was so gentle I sometimes forgot he weighed over a thousand pounds and could knock me flat with one careless toss of his head. Elise kept her own horse at the school, a sleek black Arabian named Odin. Odin was cruel, just like his owner. I'd heard that horses sometimes take on the personality of their trainers; if the trainer uses a prod and a bit in the mouth, the horse becomes hardened and mean and only responds to fear and pain. While I felt sorry for Odin, I still avoided him. He didn't respond well to strangers and had been known to bite and kick when the mood struck him.

I sat down on one of the hay bales and took out my journal, its bright turquoise color putting me immediately in a better mood. I couldn't help but think about Gray Newman, too, how he'd been so quick to remind me that this journal was his mother's idea, not his. In my experience so far, all high school boys were immature and shallow, even the ones with soulful hazel eyes.

So I transferred my thoughts to a more worthy subject: Mr. Gallagher. Now here was a real man—mature, intelligent, and sexy in that brooding poet way. Like Keats or Byron. I imagined him in one of those billowy white shirts, his strong legs encased in leather breeches. Not a bad image, really.

Why had his wife left him? And what was she like? What had made Gallagher fall in love with her? And in what universe did I think he would ever look at me and see anything other than an unremarkable teenage girl?

I jotted down all the things I admired about him and contemplated writing a poem, maybe even a sonnet. I'd never tackled a sonnet before, but it seemed like the perfect form for a poem about one's English teacher. I was completely immersed in the task when I heard a strange noise coming from the loft. At first I thought it was birds—last week I'd discovered a swallow's nest in the eaves—but the sound was deeper and more guttural. I couldn't tell if it was laughter or crying.

Setting my journal down, I made my way up the ladder, peering over the edge to find Michelle sobbing in the straw. It was such a personal, intimate moment that my first instinct was to climb back down and pretend I hadn't seen her.

Then she looked up at me with fierce eyes. "What do you want? You want a piece of me, too?"

"No," I said, shaking my head. I finished climbing and went to sit down next to her. "What's wrong?"

"Do you really not know?" she said. Of course I did. This place was toxic.

I sat in silence, wondering what I could say to make her feel better. "You realize they're all a bunch of spoiled brats with nothing better to do than mess with everyone else's lives. Why do you even care what they think?" I said. But I knew why she cared. It was impossible not to.

"How do you stand it?" she asked with an abruptness that startled me. "These people. This school. Being here on scholarship and having everyone look down on you?"

"I stand it because I have no choice," I said. "My dad and stepmom want to make a young lady out of me. Even though I haven't met anyone here I'd consider a young lady."

Michelle laughed and wiped her eyes with her sleeve. "They think they're so superior just because they have money. I don't know why I left my old school."

"Why did you?" I asked.

"That's the funny thing. Lockwood approached me. Someone from the school board contacted my guidance counselor and said there was an open scholarship here and that my grades qualified me. My guidance counselor told me if I wanted to go to MIT, I should take the money and run. So I did. But I don't know if it was worth it. I feel like I sold my soul, you know? I hate the students, and the teachers aren't much better."

"Gallagher's all right, don't you think?" I said defensively.

"At least he's not bad to look at. I like that he's letting us do some actual research. What book are you going to read for your project?"

"I'm thinking of *Jane Eyre*."

She shook her head. "I haven't read it. What's it about?"

I tried to summarize what I had read so far. "At first, there's all this tension between Jane and Rochester since they're from different worlds, but then they get to know each other, and they realize they're more alike than they thought." I was getting excited just talking about it. "There are these long passages where all they do is stare at each other in the firelight and talk, and you know they're falling in love even though they won't admit it to themselves." Michelle looked at me like I was pathetic, which I totally was. "Anyway, I'm not finished yet, so I don't know how it ends. What about you? Which book did you choose?"

"*Frankenstein.*"

"Really?" I said, scrunching up my face. I hadn't read *Frankenstein,* but it seemed pretty dark and morbid. "Why?"

"I like that it explores the possibility of bringing people back to life. Cheating death. My mother died. In case you hadn't heard."

I was shocked she'd shared something so personal with me. "How did she die?" I asked.

Michelle's eyes widened in surprise. "You know, it's weird, but hardly anyone ever asks me that. They just say sorry and get all funny and quiet. It's like they're afraid it's contagious."

"I know what you mean," I said. "My mom died, too."

Michelle's face brightened for a moment, like she was happy to hear it. I knew she was only expressing relief at having found someone who might understand what she was going through. "When did she die?" she asked.

"Eight years ago." It amazed me how that knot of pain kept coming back, even all these years later. "What about yours?"

"Last year. She was thrown off a horse while riding. Broke her pelvis and died three days later." She said the last four words with a bubble of grief in her throat. "I haven't been able to ride since."

"So you used to ride?" I said.

"Since I was six."

"I thought serious riding was just for the elite of the school, not for us charity cases."

Michelle gave me a bitter smile. "My mother grew up in Haiti, riding horses on the beach. When she came to the States, she worked as a maid for this wealthy family, and the husband sort of . . . took a liking to her. He let her ride his horse on weekends. Among other things." My eyes popped when I caught her meaning. "Yeah, well, when his wife found out, my mom got fired. She had to move in with my aunt, and after she had me, she worked three jobs so I could have every opportunity she didn't have. For some reason, it was really important to her that I learn to ride."

"And what happened to the guy? To . . ."

"My father? I have no idea. He used to send my mother a check every month, but she'd always refuse them. Now he sends them to my aunt. She claims she doesn't know who he is or where the checks come from, but I think she's just afraid I'll go looking for him. Which I won't. If he's such a coward that he won't acknowledge his own daughter, I don't want to know him. If it were up to me, I'd send the checks back just like my mom did. But my aunt needs the money. She just started her own business."

My eyes roamed to the floor, then back to her. "If it was so important to your mom that you learn how to ride, why don't you compete?" I asked. "I'm sure she would want you to."

"Not gonna happen," she said, shaking her head.

"Why not? You could probably place."

"After what happened to my mom, I can't do it."

"Look, I almost drowned this summer at the beach, and I've been scared to swim ever since. But I know I'll get over it eventually. And you will too."

"Even if I wanted to, my aunt has forbidden me from riding. She thinks it's too dangerous. Besides, how would I get the money?"

"Aha," I said, grinning. "So you were considering it?"

"No, I wasn't."

"Yes, you were. I saw that glint in your eye when Loughlin mentioned it."

"Let's just drop it," she said. "I don't ride anymore, and that's that. You lost your mother, so you of all people should understand."

I did understand, but I still thought it was sad that death could paralyze a person like it had Michelle. Like it had my father.

We were sitting in silence when we heard footfalls on the loft ladder. I was scared we were going to get in trouble for being here, but Michelle looked ready for a fight. She stood up, took a step forward, and peered over the edge.

Slowly a brown head emerged, followed by a lanky body dressed in a Gumby T-shirt, cargo pants, and Converse sneakers. It was a boy—a rather cute boy—with soft brown eyes fringed with darker brown lashes and messy hair that flopped charmingly onto his forehead. His shirt had little flecks of hay stuck to it, and his pants were filthy. "Oh, hey," he said. "There *are* people up here."

"Yeah, there are," Michelle said. "Who the hell are you?"

"Sorry," he said, brushing his hands off on his pants and reaching out to shake her hand. Michelle refused to take his hand, possibly on the grounds that it was dirty or possibly because he'd offered it. "I'm Owen. Owen Mabry." The way he said it sort of reminded me of 007 saying, "Bond. James Bond."

I shook his hand since Michelle wouldn't and introduced myself. He smiled, and two enormous dimples emerged.

"What are you doing here?" Michelle asked, finally.

"I work here. I go to school at Braeburn."

"Oh," Michelle said, "you're a Braeburn boy. I've heard about you guys."

"And I've heard about you Lockwood girls. That doesn't mean I believe everything I hear. Actually, I thought you were going to be Elise Fairchild," he said.

"You know Elise?" I asked. An unwelcome vision of Gray Newman and Elise popped into my head, giving me an irrational shudder of jealousy.

"Yeah," Owen said. "She and her friends come here to smoke."

"I know," I said. "I used to see them here last year."

"They think they're alone, but I hear everything they say."

Michelle narrowed her eyes, like she was sizing him up to see if she could trust him. "If you go to Braeburn," she said, "why do you work here?"

"Braeburn doesn't have an equestrian center, so I work here and Overbrook lets me ride for free."

"You ride?" Michelle said. Owen nodded. "Hey, you said your name was Mabry. Is that the same Mabry who invented the Blue Flame?" Blue Flame was the electronic reader everyone was buying that year.

"Well, not me personally. My dad did."

"So your family's, like, loaded."

"Don't hold it against me."

"It's hard not to when a millionaire takes one of the few jobs on our campus when some of us actual Lockwood students could use the money," Michelle said.

"I'm sorry," he said. "I didn't think Lockwood girls needed the money any more than I did. If it makes you feel any better, I'm trying to save up to go to Europe. Just because my dad's loaded doesn't mean he'll buy me whatever I want. He only pays for the things he thinks are worthwhile. Piano lessons, math tutors . . . entrepreneurial camp." He said the last two words like they tasted sour in his mouth.

"Entrepreneurial camp?" Michelle said.

"I know, right? My dad thinks I'm going to end up like my older brother. MBA from Harvard, 3.9 GPA, blah blah blah. He hopes I take over the business some day. He hasn't quite accepted the fact that I don't want to go into business."

"What do you want to do?" I asked.

He glanced at me thoughtfully. "I don't know—join the Peace Corps maybe. Or roam the country singing songs like Woody Guthrie." We both gave him blank stares. "Don't tell me you don't know who Woody Guthrie is."

Michelle shrugged her shoulders.

"He's only my personal hero and the greatest folk singer who ever lived. 'This Land is Your Land' ring a bell?"

"Oh, yeah," we both said.

"He used to travel around with farmers during the Depression, singing folk songs to give them hope. And he had this really tragic life. He lost a sister and a daughter in a fire, his father drowned, and his mother was put in an insane asylum."

"And this guy's your hero?" Michelle said.

"Well, him and Bob Dylan. If I could write songs like Dylan, I'd die a happy man."

"Oh, so you're a hippie?" Michelle said.

"I draw the line at Joan Baez," Owen said, laughing. "But yeah, I wish I'd gone to Woodstock. I'm not ashamed to say it."

We hung out for another half hour or so, talking about our music tastes. Michelle said she liked classic rock—the Beatles, the Who, the Stones. This was true, but more often than not when I came back from class, Michelle was listening to Rihanna, Lady Gaga, or Timbaland, sometimes even dancing in her bathrobe. I could tell she was trying to impress him.

I told them I'd been listening to a lot of British bands lately—Coldplay, Snow Patrol, A Silent Film. "Ahh," he said. "Emma's crushing on the Brit boys."

"Guilty as charged. I have a pretty big soft spot for Chris Martin."

"Why do girls always fall for the sensitive, brooding guys?" he said.

"Because they think they can fix them," Michelle said. "Not me. Give me an insensitive asshole any day of the week. I enjoy beating them into submission."

Owen chuckled. "How about a perpetually nice American boy?" he said. "I don't stand a chance, do I?"

"I don't know," Michelle said. "I've never tried one before." A charged look passed between them, and I wondered how long it would be before Michelle and Owen hooked up.

We decided to leave the stables when it got dark, but the afternoon spent with Owen seemed to have broken some chinks in the wall that stood between Michelle and me. All through dinner, we continued chatting about music and movies and other normal roommate topics.

Later that night, we sat on our beds reading excerpts from James Boswell's *Life of Samuel Johnson,* which Mr. Gallagher insisted on calling Boswell's *Johnson,* making the class erupt into fits of immature giggles. Michelle made some crude joke lamenting the length of Boswell's *Johnson,* and I threw my pillow across the room at her. She responded by tossing her book at me. My hand darted up to shield my face.

"Hey, I don't want your *Johnson,*" I said.

"Get enough *Johnson* on your own?"

"You're disgusting," I said, laughing in spite of myself. I tossed her book back to her and saw my necklace drop onto the bed. "Look, you broke my necklace."

"Here, give it to me and I'll fix it," she said, reaching across our beds. I handed the necklace to her, feeling naked without the weight of it on my chest. "The clasp is loose," she said. "I'm gonna bend it back in place, but it should hold for a while. This is gorgeous, by the way."

"Thanks."

She held the dragonfly up to the light and inspected the markings. "Do you know what this pattern is?"

"I think it might be Celtic or something. It was my mother's. Her family came from Scotland."

She passed the necklace back to me. "You never told me what happened to your mom. How she died."

I refastened the necklace and let the pendant drop onto my chest. "She had a bad heart," I said. "I was only eight when she died."

"That must have been hard. Losing your mom so young."

"Yeah, but in a way, I think it'd be worse to lose her now."
Michelle bristled, like she'd gotten a sudden chill. "I'm
sorry," I said. "We don't have to talk about this."

"No, it's okay. I brought it up." She picked up the photo
of her mom from her dresser and brought it over to my bed.
"You've probably wondered what's with all my red clothes,"
she said. I tried to pretend the thought had never crossed my
mind. "Come on, don't say you haven't noticed. It's weird, I
know. It's just, red was my mom's favorite color. We buried
her in her red riding jacket. So red is sort of like . . . my talis-
man. When I'm wearing red, I feel like no harm can come to
me. Like my mom's protecting me. Does that sound stupid?"

"No," I said. "It doesn't sound stupid at all."

All this time, I'd been thinking Michelle was about science
and reason, facts and figures, but there was a side to her that
believed her mother was watching over her from beyond the
grave. I had spent half my life feeling abnormal and broken,
like I was missing some puzzle piece that made everyone else
complete. But if someone as cynical as Michelle believed a
red sweater could bring her closer to her mom, then maybe I
could find my own way of reaching my mother. I tugged on
my necklace and uttered a silent prayer to her, hoping I hadn't
waited too long to try and find her.

CHAPTER 4

The stables quickly became our go-to place to do homework or talk or just to get away from the girls in the dorm, since Elise and her twisted little cult had commandeered the lounge. Owen became a frequent visitor, and I began looking forward to seeing his face pop up over the loft ladder. His dimpled smile was so warm and sincere I found myself trying to be funny around him just so I could bear witness to its glamour.

One day we were hanging out, Michelle doing math homework, me writing in my journal, and Owen messing around on his guitar, doing his best to distract us. He never seemed to have any schoolwork.

"Emma?" he said, like he was about to ask me a favor. "Let me read something from your journal."

"Um, how about no?"

"Come on. I've shown you some of the songs I wrote."

"That's different."

"How is it different?"

"It just is."

He stretched his lanky arms over his head and whined. "It's such a tease to watch you scribbling away in that thing and not know what you're writing about."

"It's not as fascinating as you think," I said. "In fact, it's pretty awful."

"Don't feel bad," Michelle said. "She won't show me either."

"I won't show anyone!" I said.

"Why not?" Owen asked.

"It's too embarrassing."

"If you don't share your writing, what good is it?" Michelle asked. "Come on, show us something. One little poem. One teensy-weensy little rhyme?"

I laughed. "No way," I said. "You'll make fun of me."

"We promise we won't," Owen said, putting his pinkie out and making Michelle do a pinkie swear. He gave me an endearing smile and mouthed the word "Please."

I sighed loudly. Something about Owen's face made him seem utterly trustworthy. "Okay, I'll let you read something on one condition."

"What?" Michelle said.

"You take the written qualification test."

Michelle shot daggers at me with her eyes.

"Qualification test for what?" Owen asked.

"For the equestrian competition in West Springfield," I said. Michelle pursed her lips together, trying to squelch her anger.

"You ride?" Owen said.

"Used to," she said. "Long story."

"Well?" I said, dangling my journal in front of her. "What's it going to be?"

After several seconds of consideration, she said, "Fine. But only the qualifying exam. I can still back out after that."

"Fair enough."

Reluctantly, I leafed through my journal, looking for anything acceptable to share. I found a poem I'd just started a few days before, called "From the Dark Bower." The title was an allusion to a Countee Cullen poem I'd read last year called "From the Dark Tower," a sonnet about the frustration black America felt as they struggled to survive the racism of the 1920s. My poem didn't come close to Cullen's in terms of structure or imagery or eloquence of language, but I sort of liked it anyway.

"I'm only sharing this with you guys because you pinkie swore," I said, smiling at Owen and handing Michelle my journal.

"Aren't you going to read it to us?" she asked.

"I'd rather die, thanks."

I closed my eyes and covered my face with my hands, cringing at the prospect of hearing my own words read aloud. Michelle stood up and cleared her throat, then proceeded to read. The first line sounded too loud and dramatic, but once she settled into the poem, she found the right rhythm and tone:

> "You laugh at us from your ivory tower
> As we sit below in our earthen bower.
> You hurl epithets from golden roofs,
> Fling arrows from atop golden hooves.
> Sticks and stones may break our bones,
> But words . . . ah, words alone
> Can slice through bone.
> We try to turn the other cheek—
> You know not what you do or speak.
> And yet we hate your petty din;
> We feel our patience wearing thin.
> One day you'll find our cheeks won't turn;
> The golden rule we soon shall spurn,
> Until this lesson you do learn—
> Those who burn us soon will burn."

Michelle and Owen sat silent for a moment. And then we heard clapping coming from below, followed by obnoxious laughter.

Owen was the first to peer down, and Michelle and I followed. Elise, Amber, Jess, and Chelsea were standing at the foot of the loft stairs giggling. The sickly sweet stench of marijuana wafted upward.

"What do you want, princess?" Owen asked.

"Nothing, stable boy," Elise said. "We were just enjoying Michelle's enlightening poetry. What ever was she talking about, girls? It sounded like she was threatening us."

"The poem wasn't about you," Michelle said.

"I particularly like the line, 'Sticks and stones may break our bones.' Highly original."

"Shut up, Elise," Owen said. "Why don't you go back to killing brain cells?"

"Oh, that's the pot calling the kettle black. Get it?" she said. "Pot?" The other girls threw their heads back and screamed as if this was hilarious, and Owen rolled his eyes. Elise walked to the stall where Odin stood and gave him a pat. "So, Michelle, I hear that in addition to being a marvelous poet, you're going to try out for the equestrian competition."

"Where'd you hear that?" Michelle said.

"I have my spies."

"So what if I am?" she said.

"It's just that Odin and I have been riding together for five years. We practically share a brain when we're in the arena. Do you own a horse?"

"Of course not," Michelle said.

Elise snorted, and Odin echoed her, stamping his hoof on the ground. "If you're just starting to work with a horse this fall, it's going to be tough to get in sync with him by the competition in May."

"I'll take that into consideration," Michelle said. I smiled to myself. Elise's taunts would only make Michelle more motivated to compete.

"Well," Elise said, sighing dramatically, "we'll leave you three to your rhyming couplets. Bye, Owen." She winked up at him, and Owen looked like he wanted to jump down and throttle her. *How can Gray Newman be dating this girl?*

Michelle's jaw was rigid. "I didn't think I could hate her any more than I already did."

"Why didn't you tell her it was my poem?" I asked.

"What's the point? Let her think it's mine if she wants to. She hates me anyway. No need to drag you into it."

"Now the critical question is, are you going to kick her ass in the competition?" Owen asked.

Michelle frowned. "I don't have a horse. I don't have money for training."

"I might be able to help you there," Owen said. "Let me talk to my dad."

"Oh, right. Just run to Daddy."

"He's trying to help, Michelle," I said. "Can you lay off the sarcasm?"

Michelle pouted. "Sorry. Defense mechanism." In that way, Michelle and I were very much alike.

"My dad likes finding causes," Owen explained. "It's good for tax breaks."

"But he hasn't met me yet," Michelle said.

Owen shrugged. "That can be remedied. I'm sure he'll agree to sponsor you if I offer something in return."

"Like?"

"Entrepreneurial camp?" I said.

Owen laughed and nodded. "Exactly."

We promised to meet again next Friday, same time, same place. As Michelle and I walked back to the dorms, I suggested she talk to Loughlin about training with Curry. She nodded distractedly while a smile played at her lips.

"Want to let me in on the joke?" I said.

"Hmm?"

"Are you aware that you're smiling?" Her mouth peeled into an exaggerated frown. "Come on. Tell me what you were thinking about."

"Nothing."

"Fine, whatever," I said, well aware that I was using the two most lethal words in a girl's arsenal.

"All right, I was just wondering . . . I mean, well . . . what do you think about Owen?"

I glanced over at her and smirked. "He's a sweetheart."

"I know that, but do you think he's . . . cute?"

"He's adorable."

"He's not really my type."

"What's your type?"

"Tall, muscular. A little bit . . . smoother."

"So Owen's kind of goofy," I said. "Admit you like him anyway." If her skin had been any lighter, I'm certain she would have blushed. "And admit that he likes you."

"He does not."

"Oh, no, I'm sure he offers to help everyone raise ten thousand dollars."

"He was just being nice."

"Michelle, a guy opens a door for you, he's being nice. A guy asks his dad to sponsor some girl he's never met before in exchange for spending eight hellish weeks with some tight-wad Future Business Leaders of America, that's a big crush."

She waved me off like I was talking nonsense, but I could see her turning possibilities over in her mind. A twinge of emotion washed over me, and it wasn't until we got back to the dorm that I recognized it for what it was: jealousy. Not because I liked Owen, but because I wanted to feel that kind of excitement, that thrill of romantic promise. Mr. Gallagher was smart and sexy and mysterious, everything I wanted in a man. He was my Rochester. But like Rochester, he was ir-refutably out of reach.

While Michelle could call Owen if she wanted or ask him out for coffee, I could only be with Gallagher in my dreams. And sometimes dreams weren't enough.

CHAPTER 5

On Halloween, Gallagher took us to the library to do some research for our projects. Everyone was restless and anxious because we knew there were only fifty minutes separating us from a weekend of Halloween festivities. The temperature had dropped twenty degrees seemingly overnight. We all clutched our jackets around us as we made our way to Old Campus, dry leaves scudding across the pathways and crunching beneath our feet.

We followed Gallagher up the massive oak staircase and into the main hall of the library, feeling dwarfed by the tall mullioned windows that lined the walls. Michelle and I claimed a long table by the windows, where we spread out our books and notes so you could barely see the surface. I pulled out my notebooks and articles and began sifting through them, trying to find a good place to begin. As Michelle searched the stacks, Gallagher called me to his table to conference about my paper.

I approached him like Dorothy making her way down the corridor to see the great and powerful Oz. I'd been so busy these last few weeks that I hadn't been able to finish reading *Jane Eyre*. I think a part of me was reluctant to finish because I'd stopped reading at such a high point. Jane had just agreed to marry Rochester despite their vast difference in age and position, and I almost wished the book could end right there. The fact that there were still a hundred pages left made me nervous.

I sat down across from Gallagher, catching a faint whiff of his evergreen cologne. My palms began to sweat, and my tongue dried up.

"*Jane Eyre,*" he said, a sigh in his voice. "Did you know it was one of my favorites?" His eyes were hooded, lovely and deep. My chest grew tight. "It's achingly romantic, isn't it?" All I could do was nod.

The book *was* achingly romantic. I got a pang in my chest just thinking about it. Briefly I recalled the scenes in which Jane and Rochester got to know each other, their chemistry palpable, their dialogue sizzling. But as I stared across at Mr. Gallagher, willing my tongue to speak, I couldn't think of a single thing to say, let alone something witty and charming that would make him love me forever.

But what if he saw beyond my awkwardness and knew what was in my heart? What if our age difference didn't matter to him? Nor the fact that he was my teacher? Rochester had been Jane's employer, and that hadn't kept them apart. What if Mr. Gallagher returned my feelings but couldn't express them because, well, because it was illegal?

God, I was such an idiot.

"So, Ms. Townsend," Mr. Gallagher said, ripping me out of my foolish daydream. "Tell me more about your thesis."

With a nervous bubble in my throat, I explained that I wanted to do a feminist interpretation of *Jane Eyre,* showing how Jane was a role model for Victorian women. I quickly ran through some of the reasons: she was determined and self-sufficient, she never used beauty or sexuality to gain favor, she made her decisions based on moral principles even when they went against her own desires. I stopped talking and waited for him to say something, feeling his eyes appraise me in a way that made my heart pound.

"That sounds promising," he said, "if a little safe." My heart sank. So much for undeniable chemistry. "Emma, you're one of the best writers in this class. But I'd really like you to work on your voice." *Great,* I thought, *he thinks I sound like a cartoon rodent, too.* "By voice, I mean that intangible quality that makes a person's writing come alive. When the reader feels like the writer is speaking directly to him. Last year, your papers were a bit . . . conventional. Don't get me wrong, they were well-written, organized, and full of sophisticated ideas and insights. But you need more confidence and passion. I want you to own every sentence."

I knew what he was talking about. It was what I loved about Jane. She spoke her mind with such self-assurance and conviction. Mr. Gallagher's eyes lingered on mine a moment too long, and prickles of heat erupted along my neck and face. "I do hope you'll consider submitting your paper to the symposium," he added.

"I will. If it's any good," I said. He smiled as if this were a foregone conclusion, and I walked away, feeling the tremendous pressure that comes with being told you are good at something.

When I got back to the table, I tried sorting out my materials amid the mess we had made. That's when I noticed my journal was missing. I'd stupidly left it sitting out with my other notebooks. I dashed to the stacks to see if Michelle had inadvertently picked it up.

"Are you sure you had it with you?" she said.

"I always have it with me."

"You think someone took it?" she asked, and I shrugged helplessly. "Don't worry, we'll find it."

"Find what?" I heard a voice say from over by the circulation desk. "Are you looking for this?" Elise stood with her friends gathered around her, holding my journal in her hands like a trophy. My mouth fell, and the acid in my stomach began to roil. "Hey everybody, did you know Michelle was a poet? And if you all gather round, I'll read you some of the highlights," she said, flipping to a page she'd already marked.

The other girls clapped and snickered and fawned. I was about to say something, to claim the journal as my own, when Michelle grabbed my arm and squeezed. Her eyes blared a warning. Before I could act, Elise was reading my poem in her most practiced silky voice. She read the final lines slowly, tauntingly: "'The golden rule we soon shall spurn, until this lesson you do learn—those who burn us soon will burn.'" I felt as though all the clothes had been stripped from my body. "That sounds like a threat, don't you think, Mr. Gallagher?"

Mr. Gallagher came over, wondering what all the commotion was about. "What sounds like a threat, Ms. Fairchild?"

"Michelle Dominguez seems to be making threats against the student body in her journal. And look, she's even written a poem about you!"

Oh my God. Elise had read the sonnet about Gallagher. I wanted the floor to swallow me whole. Either that, or for Elise's head to spontaneously combust. Gallagher approached Elise and took the journal from her. Fear and humiliation took over my body. "Ms. Fairchild, that's enough for today," he said. "Now why don't you all go back to the dorms?"

"But Mr. Gallagher, don't you care that—?"

"Ms. Fairchild, go now before I change my mind." His voice was stern, his expression grim.

"Fine," she said. "I was just trying to help." She flipped her hair and gathered her books from the table, giving us her patented malicious grin. "Trick or treat," she said to us just before leaving.

I glanced at Michelle, whose face was oddly devoid of expression. After everyone else had gone, Gallagher went from table to table, shoving in chairs and making a terrible racket.

I sat down at the table with Michelle and bit my lip. She still had that vacant look in her eyes. "I'm so sorry," I said. "I should have told everyone it was mine."

"I didn't want you to," Michelle said. "Why do you think I grabbed your arm?"

"But, Michelle—"

"I'm serious, Emma. Don't make your life miserable over this. It's no big deal."

When he had restored relative order, Gallagher took a seat next to Michelle and closed his eyes, his lashes leaving long shadows on his cheeks. He laid the journal in front of her, still open to the page that held my sonnet.

"What's all this about?" he said.

"If you haven't noticed," Michelle said, "Elise doesn't like me very much. She stole my journal so she could humiliate me."

"Listen," he said. "I know Elise did this to embarrass you, and it was very wrong of her. But I'm going to ask you not to retaliate."

"Revenge isn't my style, Mr. Gallagher."

"The poem seems to imply otherwise."

"It's just a poem. It's not real."

He sighed, looking exasperated. A thick lock of hair fell onto his forehead. "It's just, Elise Fairchild . . ."

We both knew what he wanted to say. Elise Fairchild was big money. He was powerless to punish her. And even if he did, she'd have her father's cavalry of lawyers here in a heart-beat, rescinding thousands of dollars of endowment money that funded the very scholarships we had.

"Those girls will always be poison because they've been given everything they've ever wanted," he said. "You two have had to work for what you've gotten. Elise is threatened by that. You've earned your spot. Elise bought hers. Does that make any sense?" We nodded. "I hope you two can put this behind you and manage to have a happy Halloween, despite it all."

"Thanks, Mr. Gallagher," Michelle said. He smiled faintly, and Michelle and I got up and headed for the stairs.

I was speechless. Michelle was the most courageous person I'd ever met. I envied her ability to stand there and take the consequences for a poem I had written. Why hadn't I said something? Done something? Sometimes it felt like I was sleepwalking through life, reading lines from a script instead of making conscious choices. I wanted to be strong like her.

"Michelle—" I began to say as we came out into the cool October air.

"I don't walk to talk about it, okay?" she said, passing the journal to me. "Keep that thing under lock and key from now on."

"I'm so sorry," I said.

She shook her head. I thought she was too angry to respond, but then she blurted, "Let's do something, for God's sake!"

"What do you mean?"

"Go somewhere. Live a little. If I don't get out of this place, I'm going to explode."

"But where do you want to go?" I asked.

She got a mad gleam in her eye and exclaimed, "Braeburn!"

CHAPTER 6

All the way back to the dorms, I tried to talk Michelle out of sneaking to Braeburn, but I felt like I owed her something.

"Come on, it'll be fun," she said. "Owen told me Braeburn's having a big bonfire tonight."

"Really? You think they'll have a drum circle and make us tie-dye our clothes?"

"At this point, I don't care if they sing 'Hare Krishna' and dreadlock my hair. I need to get away from these Lockwood bitches. And let's wear costumes. Get out of our own skins for a change. It's Halloween!" Her mood was suddenly effervescent, and I found myself won over by her enthusiasm.

We rummaged through our closets in search of costumes, but I couldn't find anything promising, just boring sweaters, faded jeans, and bland T-shirts. Michelle emerged from her closet with a ruffled red blouse and a pair of red leggings. "Sexy devil," she said. "What do you think?"

"Slutty."

"Perfect." She twirled around, holding her outfit to her rib cage and flashing a mischievous smile.

I picked through my paltry wardrobe and settled on a simple black dress with a white collar. Barbara had bought it for me to wear to her niece's wedding last year. I slipped it on and turned to show Michelle.

"What are you going as, a nun?" she said.

"Very funny. I was thinking Wednesday Addams."

"Oh, right," she said, nodding. "You actually look a little like her. Let me do your braids."

After we finished dressing, we set out into the night, heading down the hill toward the stables. It was only seven o'clock, but it was already dark out. Most of the girls were taking the path to the Commons, where Student Council was hosting a chaperoned Halloween party, but no one seemed to notice we were headed in the opposite direction. When we reached the woods, Michelle took out her flashlight.

"I talked with Nicole Manning," she said. "She and Blake were the ones who got caught last year. She said the path is pretty worn down. Apparently, guys from Braeburn sneak here all the time. They tied yellow markers on the trees to guide people."

"There's one," I said, pointing midway up the trunk of a tree to a little flicker of fabric. We entered into the brush, slowly making our way deeper into the woods and trying to stay on the makeshift path. Michelle's flashlight cast a small pool of light ahead of us, but everything else disappeared in the gloom. Wind whipped through the trees, making the trunks heave and whine. The largest trees, twisted and gnarled with age, looked like giant goblins.

When we got to the log that lay between the banks of the stream, my stomach clenched. The water wasn't that deep here, but the currents could be really strong. Ever since the incident this summer, I'd been acutely aware of water's power and its indifference to my survival.

Michelle crossed the log with ease and stood waiting for me on the other side. "Come on, slowpoke!" she shouted.

I could barely see ahead of me. The woods were inky dark.

I remembered how the Puritans who once lived here believed this wilderness was the devil's territory. During the witch trials, a few of the condemned escaped and followed the Old Salem Road all the way to these woods, where they hid in a network of caves somewhere on the Danforth plantation. I couldn't help but imagine the spirits of those escaped souls lurking behind me, waiting for the moment I fell into the water and drowned so they could enter my body and take over my human form.

Cautiously, I sidestepped along the log until I was poised over the deepest part of the stream. The water whooshed below my feet, hypnotizing me, fixing me in place. Michelle's voice woke me out of my daze.

"What's taking so long?"

"You're not helping!" I said.

The log jiggled, and I froze, crouching down and clutching the log. In her impatience, Michelle had come back across to fetch me. She reached down and took my hand, then lit the rest of the way with her flashlight. I tried not to look down as she guided us safely to the other side.

For another twenty minutes, we trudged across pine needles and fallen leaves until we heard the sounds of music and the crackling of a great fire. We emerged from the woods into an overgrown meadow that led to the football field of Braeburn's campus. Some kids were making out on the bleachers as we passed, so we followed the noise and the smoke up the hill to a large parking lot, where an enormous fire was blazing, lighting up the sky.

Michelle pointed to a figure strumming a guitar by the bonfire, surrounded by a few other guys. It was Owen. He was wearing a pin-striped suit and tie with a fedora and singing some old blues song.

"You made it!" he said when he saw us, launching into an intentionally off-key version of "A Little Help from My

Friends." He had this big, goofy grin on his face that made me want to hug him.

"Who are you supposed to be?" Michelle asked.

"Robert Johnson. You know, the blues legend?"

"I know who Robert Johnson is," Michelle said, laughing. "I just didn't recognize you because you're so . . . so . . ."

"So white?"

"Exactly."

"I may be white, but I've got the blues in my soooooul," he crooned.

Michelle and I cracked up. "What have you been smoking?" she asked, laughing.

"Sadly, nothing," he said. "Come meet some of my friends."

He introduced us to some guys—a surfer type named DJ or TJ, a very small freshman named Benjamin, and an extremely good-looking guy named Flynn.

Despite her issues with the girls at our school, Michelle had no such problems with guys. She flocked to them, and they responded in kind. Her exchanges with Owen's friends were easygoing and tinged with flirtation. I, on the other hand, went mute in the presence of boys.

Owen sat at the center of our group, his face golden in the firelight so he looked like a tiny sun, all these other boys shining in his orbit, trying to catch a little of that warmth. Owen had a lightness about him, a magnetism that drew people in. Unlike Gray, Owen fit in here at Braeburn, harmonizing perfectly with its guitar-strumming, karma-loving vibe.

TJ and Benjamin were cordial—well, more than cordial to Michelle—but Flynn didn't seem particularly interested in getting to know us, and after a while he got up and went off in search of beer or drugs or who knows what. Owen just smiled and continued to play his music. We sang with him as he played "Cross Road Blues," then a medley of Beatles songs, ending with a hilarious folk cover of Guns N' Roses'

"Sweet Child o' Mine." Michelle sat next to Owen, so close that she kept brushing against his leg and shoulder.

We chatted and joked by the warmth of the fire, letting the buzz of the night spread through us. The parking lot was packed with cars, kids tailgating even though chaperones were supposedly patrolling the lot, sniffing out alcohol and drugs.

"Any chance of getting a drink?" Michelle said. "You know, to warm up."

"A few coolers are floating around," Owen said. "You want to check it out?"

Moments later, Michelle, Owen, and I were standing at the back of some guy's convertible, slurping wine coolers like they were Gatorade. At first I said no, but Michelle gave me a disapproving look, and Owen just laughed as if to say, "What's the big deal?" So I relented. The wine cooler tasted sweet, like berry Kool-Aid, and after a few sips I felt nice and warm and mellow inside, so mellow that when the owner of the convertible asked if I wanted another, I said yes. Michelle had another, too, and we all laughed at something Owen said, and I felt fine, really fine, as if everything was right in the world. After another drink, I felt so fine that when Gray Newman appeared in front of me, I had no desire to walk away from him.

"Is that Townsend?" he said. "At a party? Shouldn't she be in her room with her head in a book or something?" He was wearing jeans and a crisp white shirt with the sleeves rolled up. The light from the fire turned his skin a surreal bronze color.

"I'm having fun," I said. "Is that okay with you?" My voice sounded different to my ears, husky, like I was getting a cold.

"It's perfectly okay," he said.

"You're not drinking?" I asked, surprised to see him empty-handed.

He shook his head. "So, what made you decide to come to Braeburn? I've never seen you here before."

"It was Michelle's idea."

"You weren't hoping to see me?" he said.

I pushed some hair behind my ear, trying to hide my blush with my hand. "Believe it or not, I don't spend my days thinking about you."

"Just your nights, then," he said, arching an eyebrow. A shiver ran the entire length of my body. "Are you cold?" he asked, looking concerned.

I said no, rubbing my hands together anyway. "How's Elise?" I asked out of some perverse desire to ruin the moment.

He narrowed his eyes like he didn't like that question. "I don't know," he said, looking at the ground and shuffling a leg in his jeans. "We're not together anymore."

"Really?" Cartwheels danced across my rib cage. "You broke up with her?"

"Actually, she broke up with me."

Now it was my turn to raise an eyebrow. "Why?"

"She got bored with me."

"Bored? With Gray Newman, party animal?"

"Reports of my reputation have been greatly exaggerated," he said, laughing. He cocked his head to see if I believed him. "In the end, we just weren't compatible."

"Oh, come on," I said. "You two were the golden couple—rich, popular, good-looking."

"Well, I guess those things just aren't enough." He got that sad far-off look in his eyes, and I felt bad for having brought the subject up. But then his lips curled into a teasing smile. "So," he said, "you think I'm good-looking?"

I wanted to wipe that cocky grin right off his face. "Well, you're not my type, but I'm sure *some* people find your looks interesting."

He pretended to clutch a knife in his heart. "*Interesting?* That's the kiss of death. Why don't I just call you nice?"

"I am nice."

"I know you are," he said, his gaze burning a hole through me.

"But you don't like nice girls."

"You've got me all wrong, Townsend."

"Do I?" We stood there in a face-off mode, me grabbing my necklace and willing my face into a challenging sneer. He was trying to conceal a smile.

"Take a walk with me, Townsend," he said. I eyed him suspiciously. "Come on, it's just a walk. You act like you're afraid of me."

"I'm confused by you," I said. "Not afraid."

I glanced over at Michelle, who was talking to some guy I didn't know. Owen glanced in my direction and opened his mouth as if to say something.

It was just a walk with an old family friend. So why did I feel so nervous? Gray dipped his head in an unspoken question—*are you coming?* I nodded and followed him away from the fire and the crowds toward one of the school buildings, dark now but for a single floodlight illuminating the side entrance.

"So, talk to me," he said, continuing to move us farther away from the crowd.

"About what?"

"About anything."

"How about you tell me what you want to know."

"All right," he said. "Tell me about your necklace." He stopped walking and reached across to touch the pendant. When his finger brushed my skin, I stopped breathing.

"It was my mother's," I said, hearing my voice shake.

"Oh, yeah. I knew I'd seen it before." He bent his head to inspect it, his eyes at my level. I dropped my own because the

moment felt too heavy, too real. I was staring at the top button of his shirt when I saw a glint of silver. "Hey, you're
wearing something, too." I reached out and barely grazed his
collarbone with my knuckle. He drew open his shirt to reveal
a pair of dog tags.

"My uncle's," he explained. "He died in Cambodia when
he was nineteen. My dad tells me I'm a lot like him. I wish I'd
known him. My dad and I don't really get along, but I have a
feeling me and my uncle would have. My dad just thinks I'm
a screwup."

"My dad thinks the same thing."

"Your dad thinks I'm a screwup?" he said.

"No, no," I said, laughing. "He thinks I am."

Gray regarded me quizzically. "He couldn't possibly.
You're, like, the goody-two-shoes, straight-A student. My
mom told me you have over a 4.0 G.P.A. with all those hon-
ors classes you take."

"How does she know that?"

"Apparently your dad brags about you when you're not
listening." I suppressed a smile. "We refer to you as Miss Perfect around the dinner table."

"Believe me, I'm not perfect," I said, flattered that they
talked about me at the dinner table. "Barbara thinks I'm
troubled. My dad doesn't even like me anymore. I'm just so
tired of trying to please everyone. I'm tired of being good all
the time."

He stopped walking and focused on me. "Don't under-
estimate good. There are times I'd give anything to be good."
His face clouded over, like some awful memory had just
caught up with him. I wanted to say something to make him
feel better, but I didn't know what. When he turned to face
me, he looked like he wanted to tell me something.

"What is it?" I said.

"Nothing. It's just . . ." His voice trailed off, and he bit the inside of his cheek. For a moment, his eyes held on to that vulnerability, and then they flickered with a mischievous glint. "It's hard to take you seriously in those braids, Townsend."

I glanced down at my costume. "I know. I feel so stupid. Nobody else dressed up."

"Don't feel stupid," he said. "You look adorable." He tugged gently on one of my braids, and my heart soared. One little compliment, and I was getting all soft around the edges.

"Michelle was the one who—" I started to say, and before I could finish my sentence, his hands were cupping my cheeks and he was leaning in to kiss me.

Whoa. I couldn't believe that this mouth, usually set in a cocky sneer, could look so serious, or so sexy. And I couldn't believe how much I wanted him to kiss me.

And then I remembered. This was Gray Newman, a guy with a reputation for doing just this—seducing girls with his dark looks and smooth ways. As if snapping out of a daze, I pushed him away before his lips made contact.

"What's wrong?" he asked, genuinely puzzled. This had probably never happened to him in his life.

"I just remembered."

"What?"

"This is wrong. This isn't how it's supposed to happen."

I'd always imagined my first kiss being in the middle of a meadow under starlight. Rochester kissing Jane under the tree after he'd proposed to her. A scene from a romantic novel. Not standing drunk with Gray Newman at the side of a building.

"How is it supposed to happen?" he said, putting his hands gently on my shoulders. He didn't look angry, merely curious. I pushed him harder this time, almost shoving him. It was starting to drizzle, and I suddenly felt very cold. I wanted to be home. I wanted to be back in my dorm, alone, safe in my bed. "This is payback for when you were five, isn't it?" he said, a smile curling at his lips. "You've been waiting ten years for me to try to kiss you so you could give me a bloody nose. Go ahead. I've broken it once already."

"Shut up," I said. I knew he was only teasing me, but the truth was, I was mortified. I'd finally been given the opportunity to kiss someone, someone I found maddeningly attractive, and I'd blown it. With the magical moment lost and my buzz quickly dissipating, I felt a little dizzy. I began to walk away, not wanting him to know I'd gotten drunk off three wine coolers.

"Come back, Townsend," he called after me. "I was only joking."

But I kept walking until I could no longer hear the sound of his voice. Some foolish part of me wanted him to chase after me, apologize on his knees, beg forgiveness. But he'd done nothing wrong. I was just an immature girl who'd had too much to drink.

I made my way back to the parking lot, stanching tears and looking for Michelle. The rain was picking up, and people were gathering up their things. A rumble of thunder echoed above.

"Emma!" Michelle said when I found her. "Where were you?" I blinked smoke out of my eyes and shivered. "Did something happen?"

"No. I just want to leave."

Owen sprang up and put a hand on my shoulder. "Are you okay?"

"I'm fine," I lied.

"It's late," Owen said. "Let me walk you guys back." He packed up his guitar and slung the case over his shoulder.

We made our way across the meadow and entered the woods. As we walked, the storm intensified around us. Thunder rattled the trees and shook the ground. A streak of jagged lightning flared just ahead of us, sending us all to the ground.

When we reached the stream, I froze. Owen offered to follow behind me and make sure I didn't fall. With his hand on my waist to steady me and Michelle's flashlight illuminating my steps, somehow I made it across. Together, we followed those little yellow markers like bread crumbs until we arrived back at the stables. The horses neighed and whinnied inside, frightened by the storm. I had a sudden wish to crawl inside Curry's pen, climb atop him, and fall asleep on his warm, sleek fur. I turned in the direction of the barn.

"Emma, where are you going?" Michelle said.

Owen leaned his guitar case against his leg and put his jacket around my arms. He tried to steer me back to the path that led to the dorms, but I was beyond reason. "I want to sleep with Curry," I said. Owen's sleepy brown eyes filled with concern.

Thunder boomed again, louder this time, like a freight train hurtling past. I squeezed my eyes tight, and the blackness in front of my eyelids became cloudy and began to spin. Another terrible sound tore through the air like something being ripped apart, like the fabric of space and time.

A brilliant stab of light flashed before my eyes, and I gripped my chest, electricity surging into my heart and through my veins. Sensation washed over me in waves—first pain, then agony, then a sort of blissful calm until the bright light flickered and faded, and the world went suddenly black.

PART 2

CHAPTER 7

I woke with my hand wrapped tightly around my mother's necklace, so tightly that when I uncurled my fingers, it left nail marks on my palm. I sat up too quickly then felt the pain. A throbbing in my head and a pasty taste in my mouth like sour berries.

Where was I? Horses, the smell of hay, the lumpy ground. The stables. The previous night came back to me in a humiliating flash. Gray Newman. The almost kiss. The drunken walk through the woods. The storm.

I lay back down and groaned. My head had never felt this bad before. Everything around me seemed to be covered in burlap. *This must be what a hangover feels like,* I thought. *And I can't believe Michelle and Owen just left me here!*

I tried sitting up, feeling that awful vertigo again. Water. All I wanted was water. Swaying a little, I stood up, brushed myself off, and walked over to Curry's stall. He greeted me like he always did, bending his head down to let me rub his muzzle.

"What a crazy night," I said to him. "Give the girl three wine coolers, and she's wasted."

Feeling faint with thirst, I walked to the stable door and pushed it open. It had stopped raining, but the sky was the color of lead and filled with storm clouds. The trees glistened with rainwater. Even though it would have been quicker to head up the main path back to the dorms, the path through Old Campus would be dead this time of morning. I'd be less likely to run into anyone who might witness my walk of shame.

I turned to trudge up the path, my legs feeling like wooden blocks beneath me. The campus looked surreal, like I was viewing it through a kaleidoscope. I unwound my braids and swept my hair into a simple ponytail. It was no longer Halloween, and I didn't want to look any more ridiculous than I already felt. When I reached the library, I hesitated for a moment and stared up at its façade. It looked strange to me—larger and more ominous, leached of its color.

A woman appeared at the main door. I sighed gratefully when I saw it was only Madame Favier, with her reassuring gray pouf of hair and owl glasses.

"There you are," she said. "You must be so tired. I'm afraid you've had a tedious journey. We expected you yesterday." She came down the stairs and shook both of my hands like we'd never met before. "Oh, you poor thing, your hands are chilled to the bone. I'm Mrs. Fairfax, of course. Won't you come inside?"

Mrs. Fairfax? But she was Madame Favier. Was this some kind of joke? She turned around and gestured for me to follow her into the library. "And what do you think of Thornfield?" she said when we got to the main door.

"Thornfield?" I said, staring up at the library's walls. Madame Favier had clearly lost her marbles.

"It is a pretty place," she said, "but I fear it will be getting out of order, unless Mr. Rochester should take it into his head to come and reside here permanently. Great houses and fine grounds require the presence of the proprietor."

"Mr. Rochester?" I repeated, more confused than ever. Where had I heard these lines before? They were so familiar. Familiar because I had just read them a few weeks ago. They were lines from *Jane Eyre*.

"Yes, Mr. Rochester. The owner of Thornfield," she said. "Did you not know he was called Rochester?"

I was about to laugh—this was all so ridiculous. And then a little girl came running up the hill, stopping by our side. I almost shouted "Anna!" because she looked so much like Gray's little sister, but her red hair was in ringlets, and she wore an old-fashioned smock dress. She didn't seem to recognize me.

"Good morning, Miss Adèle," the false Mrs. Fairfax said. "Come and speak to the lady who is to teach you, and to make you a clever woman some day." Adèle. Rochester's French ward in *Jane Eyre*. Things were only getting weirder.

"C'est là ma gouverante?" the girl said, pointing at me—*Are you my governess?* I opened my eyes wide and bit my lip. I was afraid to speak.

"Come on inside," the woman said. "You are tired."

I followed her up the stairs in a daze. Was this some elaborate joke the entire school had drummed up to mess with me? Like *Punk'd*, but for awkward sophomores instead of celebrities? Somehow I couldn't quite see Madame Favier going along with something like that.

Once I stepped inside the library door, my stomach fell out from under me. The interior of the library had been transformed to look like a well-furnished country estate. We were standing in the long hallway that used to be the main floor of the library, now lined with sinister-looking portraits where school banners had once hung. A large bronze lamp dipped from the ceiling, and thick dark drapes covered the windows, making everything look Gothic and sinister. A cold sweat prickled along my neck.

Okay, maybe I was still asleep. After all, this wasn't the first time I'd felt a blurring of the lines between my dreams and my conscious world. I just had to pinch myself and I'd find myself back in bed, still hungover, but at least not crazy. The thing was, it didn't feel like a dream. And when I pinched myself, seven times just to make sure, nothing happened.

I followed Madame Favier or Mrs. Fairfax—whatever her name was—through a large kitchen and into a smaller servants' area, where a woman in a black dress and apron set some breakfast down in front of the little girl. The girl turned to me suddenly and uttered a familiar phrase: "Mademoiselle—Comment appelez-vous?" *What is your name?*

Before I could reply "Emma," some inner force prompted me to say, "Jane Eyre." I almost laughed when I said it.

"Aire? Bah!" the girl said, then proceeded to prattle on completely in French. I hoped she wasn't saying anything important, because I was only catching about every fourth word. Mrs. Fairfax made me a cup of tea, which I cradled in my hands and sipped very slowly as I glanced around the place.

Mrs. Fairfax was giving me instructions on tutoring Adèle, and it was almost as if I could predict every word she was going to say. Like we were rehearsing a play, and I'd memorized everyone's lines, not just my own. And just as I'd naturally given my name as Jane Eyre, the surroundings were feeling more and more familiar as I sat there, memories of the bonfire and Michelle and Gray fading away like the echo of a voice I'd already forgotten.

When we finished our breakfast, Mrs. Fairfax took us to the library where I would be working with Adèle. I stood mute while she went over the procedures for the day. She had a formal way of speaking, and I didn't want her to think I was uncivilized. "I know you must be awfully tired, Miss Eyre, but perhaps you can occupy Adèle for a short time while I finish my chores, and then I will show you the house."

I nodded obediently, and she left me alone with the child. For a moment I stared at the girl cluelessly, wondering what on earth to do with her. She looked up at me expectantly. But then, just as before, the answer came to me without any conscious thought.

"Voulez-vous lire avec moi?" I asked, the French rolling off my tongue like I'd been speaking it my whole life. The girl nodded happily, and we chose a few books from the cabinet and sat down on a plush sofa to begin reading. I wasn't sure how much she understood, but I read to her robotically while my mind wandered. *This has to be a dream,* I thought. Because I felt too comfortable in this skin, like I'd just slipped into someone else's story. *Wake up,* I told myself. *Wake up!*

But nothing around me changed. Adèle sat watching me with a mixture of curiosity and impatience. My voice kept steady, but inside I was freaking out. What if it was worse than a dream? What if I was the one who'd lost her marbles?

Before I finished our final book, Mrs. Fairfax returned as promised to take me on a tour of the house. "House" was too modest a word for the three-story mansion with grand oak stairways and lavish rooms filled with antique furniture and endless hallways. When I ran my finger across a wooden table to make sure it was real, Mrs. Fairfax clicked her tongue.

"You won't find any dust. The rooms are quite tidy. Though Mr. Rochester's visits here are rare, they are always sudden and unexpected. I thought it best to keep the rooms in readiness."

She went on to tell me about her "master," how he traveled widely and was away much of the time. As she spoke about him, she brought me up to the third story. Here, it was dim and echoey, with narrow corridors and small dark bedrooms that smelled of age and decay.

"Does anyone sleep up here?" I asked.

"No, certainly not. Though if a ghost inhabited Thornfield, this would surely be his haunt."

I shuddered and followed her up a very steep and narrow staircase into the attic. We ascended a ladder that led through a trapdoor to the roof, so we were now standing out on the battlements, looking out on the whole expanse of the campus. I surveyed the grounds: the lawn, the woods beyond, and the horizon bounded by sky. It was a stunning view. There was just one problem. Aside from the stables, there was not another building in sight. No dorms. No classrooms. No parking lots either. No pathways. No playing fields. Just uninterrupted grass and trees as far as the eye could see.

I had to be dreaming! It was the only explanation that didn't involve me being committed to the local funny farm. All I had to do was tell myself to wake up, and I'd be released from this incredibly vivid fantasy, right? I shook my head and closed my eyes tightly, but when I opened them, the image before me remained. And, I realized, Mrs. Fairfax had left me alone on the battlements.

Feeling my pulse race, I descended back through the trap-door and down the ladder, though I could hardly see since my eyes hadn't adjusted to the dark. When I got back to the long corridor of the third floor, I glanced down at the rows and rows of closed doors and thought, for some reason, of skeletons hidden within.

And then I heard a laugh. An unpleasant, cackling laugh. When I paused to listen, the laughter stopped for an instant, then it began again, louder and more sinister. It seemed to echo in every room of the house.

"Mrs. Fairfax," I said. "Did you hear that?"

She did not seem alarmed. "One of the servants, very likely. Perhaps Grace Poole. I often hear her laugh. She sews in one of these rooms. Grace!" she called.

A nearby door opened, and a servant came out, a fat woman with weathered features and a tight, grim mouth. I thought I caught a whiff of alcohol on her breath. "Too much noise, Grace," said Mrs. Fairfax. Grace flared her nostrils and shot me a look that froze my blood, then curtsied to Mrs. Fairfax and returned to her room.

We retraced our steps and found a meal waiting for us in the parlor. It wasn't until I sat down that I realized how hungry I was. The food was nothing special—boiled potatoes and some rare meat in gravy, but I cleaned my plate. Servants came quietly in and out, clearing dishes and lighting candles. After I'd eaten, I felt a peculiar calm settle over me. I closed my eyes for just a moment and leaned back in my chair.

Mrs. Fairfax said, "You have been traveling all day. You must be tired. Let me show you to your bedroom. I've had the room next to mine prepared for you."

She led me to the second floor and showed me to my room, furnished with a four-poster bed, a dresser and vanity, and a washstand with a water pitcher and basin. After she left me for the evening, I closed the door and fastened the latch.

Finally alone, I sat on the bed and tried to make sense of the day. I wanted to call someone, text someone, e-mail someone, but my cell phone was missing and the house didn't have electricity, let alone a computer. Did people at Lockwood even realize I was gone? Had Michelle and Owen called the police to organize a search party? Or were they hiding in the next room, laughing their asses off?

The possibilities made my head hurt. Unable to think anymore, I poured some water from the pitcher into my palms and splashed my face, using the collar of my dress to dry off. All I wanted to do was lie down on that bed and fall asleep, surely to wake up in the morning and find myself back in my dorm room. I opened the closet, which was filled with simple dresses, a coat and some shawls, and a few bonnets on the top shelf. Not a T-shirt or pair of sweats in sight. I rustled around until I found a thin white dress that looked like a nightgown and slipped it on, relieved to find that it fit perfectly.

I desperately needed to find a bathroom. Did they even have bathrooms here? I was a little alarmed when I noticed a chamber pot sitting under my bed. I knew what it was for but had no idea how to use it.

Picking up the lit candle by my bed, I opened the door that led into the corridor, now cold and dark as a tomb. I knew Mrs. Fairfax's room was just next to mine, but there were three other doors off this hallway alone. Maybe one led to the bathroom. I walked past Mrs. Fairfax's room and tried the next door. Locked. I continued to the end of the corridor and tried another, which was locked as well. On my return trip, I tried the final door, and the latch clicked. A small shaft of light broke into the hallway.

I felt like I was an actor in a horror movie, walking by candlelight through a haunted house. At this point in the movie, the audience would be yelling at the screen, "Don't go in there! Don't go in there!" I laughed at my own paranoia and then, almost as if I'd conjured a ghost with my imagination, footsteps pounded overhead.

I froze, and then the footsteps began rattling down the stairs. Without thinking, I ran down the hallway and back into my room, locking the door behind me and blowing out my candle. I crouched by the door, listening for sounds outside. All I could hear was my own labored breathing.

My heart was pounding. And I still needed a bathroom. I considered venturing back into the dark hallway, now possibly occupied by a pissed-off ghost. And then I glanced at the chamber pot. It was no contest.

Later, I crawled into bed and drew the blankets tight around me, laying my head on the crunchy pillow. I couldn't remember having ever felt this alone or terrified. Surely this was all a dream—a long, elaborate, highly realistic dream spurred by too much reading of *Jane Eyre*. I would wake in the morning in my own bed at Lockwood, safely restored to my normal world.

The only thing that saved me was a mind-numbing fatigue. After some tossing and turning, I finally fell asleep clutching the only meaningful object I'd taken with me from my real world: the dragonfly pendant.

CHAPTER 8

When I woke the next morning, I opened my eyes, hoping to see the digital LCD of my alarm clock staring back at me or Michelle's lanky body in the bed across from mine. I longed to hear some girl's radio blasting hip-hop or maybe the sound of an airplane flying overhead. Better yet, the hiss of a shower spraying hot water, thanks to the miracles of modern plumbing. But when I opened my eyes, I saw the high ceilings and ornate bedclothes of Thornfield. My heart sank, and dread overwhelmed me.

I climbed out of bed, almost falling since the bed was much higher than the one in my dorm room, and felt my feet land on a freezing floor. Stumbling over to the vanity, I washed my face and underarms in the basin on the washstand, then opened the closet. Boring black and gray dresses as far as the eye could see. I considered putting on my Wednesday Addams dress, but it smelled faintly of berry wine cooler, and I was afraid that another whiff might make me sick.

That old woman and little girl I'd met yesterday would be expecting Jane Eyre to come downstairs. I couldn't help but wonder what had happened to the real Jane. If I was here in her place, where was she? Was she sleeping in my bed, looking into my closet, wondering how a modern girl wears her hair? I dismissed the idea as ridiculous, but a small part of me panicked at the thought of being stranded here.

I chose one of the dark dresses from the closet and eased it over my body. The material was coarse and uncomfortable and there was a row of buttons in the back that took me a year to fasten. The neckline was high and tight, making it difficult to breathe. I found my rubber band from the day before and managed to secure my hair in a makeshift bun.

When I was finally dressed, I looked at myself in the mirror. My hair needed a good washing. I'd also need a pair of tweezers soon or I'd be sporting some serious eyebrows. I had to admit, though, I did look a little like a nineteenth-century governess—plain and serious and old-fashioned.

This was ridiculous. What was I doing here? Was I being punished for something? Or had I, in some way, asked for this?

I thought back to my state of mind these past few months. I didn't fit in at school. I didn't fit in at home. Barbara didn't approve of me. My father didn't talk to me. My love life was hopeless. I had often wished for some escape from it all. Was this some twisted answer to my prayers?

I knew I had to get back to the stables to see if I could find a clue, anything that might explain why I was here and how I could get back. Grabbing a shawl from the closet, I left my room, walked down the hallway and stairs, and let myself quietly out the side door. The sun was barely over the horizon, pouring diffuse light over the lawn. I guessed it was before seven o'clock.

I passed through the garden behind the house, noting its similarity to the garden behind the Commons Building on campus. The same pathways and beds of seasonal flowers, the same fountains and antique sculptures. Off in the distance was the giant two-hundred-year-old chestnut tree, which had been marked with a plaque designating it as historic. When I circled the tree this morning, though, I could find no sign of the plaque. The wind rustled through its leaves, which seemed to whisper something strange and otherworldly and meant just for me. Shivering, I pulled the shawl around my shoulders and headed for the stables.

I was relieved to see Curry, who nickered when he saw me. And then I wondered, was this even Curry? Madame Favier was no longer my French teacher; she was Mrs. Fairfax. And Anna was no longer Gray's sister; she was Adèle. Was Curry one of Rochester's horses now? He still seemed like Curry to me—sweet and docile with that earthy, leathery scent I'd come to love. But I wasn't sure of anything anymore.

"Who are you?" I said to Curry, patting him on the head. "Are you still my boy? And more to the point, am I still me? Or am I crazy?"

Curry sneezed and shook his head, which made me laugh. Not exactly the answer I was hoping for. I wandered around the stables for half an hour, looking for any signs of my old life. Maybe there was a door I could walk through and find myself back at Lockwood. Maybe the loft held the key. I climbed up and looked around but found only hay and swallows. Their cheerful warbling turned to nervous chitter at my arrival. I quickly descended the ladder and left them in peace.

Feeling frustrated and none the wiser, I returned to the house. Mrs. Fairfax was waiting for me at the front door. "What, out already?" she said. "I see you are an early riser."

"Not usually," I said.

"Breakfast is ready."

I followed her into the kitchen and tried to pretend everything was normal, that this was just an ordinary turn of events for me. But inside my mind was swimming. Breakfast was a lukewarm porridge, and I ate it absently, knowing I had to keep up my strength. But what I would have given for an Egg McMuffin or a Pop-Tart.

When we finished breakfast, Mrs. Fairfax led us into the library and handed me a language primer so I could work on

Adèle's English. And this became our routine. We spent the mornings working, took a break for lunch, then resumed our lessons in the afternoon, and met for dinner around six o'clock. It was all very tedious and repetitive. After dinner, I took to walking the grounds, searching desperately for something that might lead me back to my old life.

I had thought I wanted to get away from school—from the competition, the cruelty, the constant stress and noise. But now I found myself missing it, longing for some signs of life around this place, hoping to run into a familiar face. Michelle. Owen. My father. Gray.

No. I wouldn't let myself think of him. The emotions were still too raw, my humiliation too recent. *What must he think of me after that pathetic display on Halloween?* I thought. *Or worse, does he even think of me at all?*

Adèle was the one element that kept me sane during my first weeks at Thornfield. She was spoiled and clearly starved for attention, but that suited me fine. We told each other funny stories and made up jokes, and all the while, her English improved, and so did my French. But once Adèle went to bed, the nights were long. I couldn't get over the dimness of the rooms, the constant cold, the eerie quiet that descended over the house, broken only by the wind howling across the moors. I would sit by the fire with Mrs. Fairfax, reading while she sewed. I must have read every book on those bookshelves, even tried some of the French ones. But eventually reading grew dull, and I longed to do something active.

I was infinitely bored. I missed Michelle. And Owen. And pizza. And electricity. I wanted to watch bad reality television with Michelle and make fun of the contestants. I wanted to sneak off campus and meet cute boys. I wanted to go for a bike ride and gossip over coffee in Waverly Falls.

Unfortunately, Mrs. Fairfax wasn't the best company. She insisted on speaking formally all the time and often corrected me when I lapsed into casual conversation. Over those first few weeks, I learned how to play my part well so as not to arouse her suspicion or criticism. Our evening exchanges usually went something like this:

"So, Miss Eyre, how are you progressing with Adèle?"

"Very well, thank you."

"My, but the weather has been cool of late."

"Yes, it has."

"I do wonder when the master shall return."

"As do I."

The master. She meant Rochester, and I had almost forgotten about him. Funny, since he'd been my favorite part of *Jane Eyre*. And yet, as I tried to recall the details about him, I found myself unable to remember what he looked like. Or when I would meet him. The thought that it might be soon made the prospect of staying at Thornfield a little less intolerable.

One morning when I was feeling particularly churlish, I went downstairs to find Mrs. Fairfax and Adèle in the kitchen. Mrs. Fairfax's face nearly collapsed when she saw me. "Why, Miss Eyre, your hair is absolutely wild." My hand instinctively flew to my head. I'd forgotten to pin it up. "Why, you look like . . . a sorceress."

"I'm sorry," I muttered, trying not to laugh. I didn't know why my hair was such a big deal. Clearly, there was no one here except an old woman and a little girl. What did they care what my hair looked like?

Dutifully, I went back upstairs, annoyed by Mrs. Fairfax's constant rules of propriety. I was so weary of the same clothes, the same books, the same lessons, the same walks, the same conversations, day after day after day. I sat down at the vanity and hastily pulled my hair back in a bun. My dress was chafing my neck. I was dying to throw on a T-shirt and jeans, a pair of Converse.

Irritably, I yanked at the collar of my dress. With one particularly fierce tug, my mother's necklace came flying off, throwing the dragonfly pendant free. A cold wind overtook me then, almost as if the windows had all been thrown open at once. Panicked, I crouched down on all fours and scoured every inch of that floor looking for the pendant, but I couldn't find it anywhere.

When I stood up, I felt light-headed. My hand went instinctively to my chest, the way it always did when I was nervous or sad. But my neck was bare. I had lost my dragonfly necklace, the last relic of my mother's.

I sat down at the vanity and felt like crying. I knew so little about my mother, about the woman who'd given birth to me. But I knew that I missed her presence, her vitality, even all these years later. After she died, my father had become a shell of a man until he met Barbara in grief counseling. With her in the house, he gradually came back to life, but he was different, like one of those people who survives a coma but comes back with a completely new personality. A few weeks before he proposed to Barbara, he gathered up my mom's belongings—her clothing, her sketches and books, the photos of the two of them from various vacations—and put them in boxes in the attic. He said it was out of respect for Barbara; he wanted her to feel at home in our house. But I never bought that excuse. I think secretly he was relieved not to have to deal with the memories anymore, to have a reason to hide them away.

After that, he rarely spoke of her, rarely reminisced with me about all the fun times we'd had together as a family, but instead closed himself off—from her and from me. Sometimes I think he resented me for reminding him too much of her. Now, as always, I longed for a way to reach him. Somehow, I was always trying to reach my father. But I realized, just as I had no cell phone or computer to reach anyone from my old life, I had no magic wand that would bring me closer to my dad. And now I had lost the one link tying me to my mother.

Heartbroken, I glanced in the mirror and was shocked by what I saw. It was not Emma, high school sophomore, staring back at me. It was Jane. I can't describe the feeling that washed over me, but in that moment, with my necklace gone, I had nothing left to keep me grounded, nothing to maintain my shaky hold over reality. And so I surrendered myself to the fantasy.

I went back downstairs, hair appropriately tamed, and did exactly what was expected of me for the rest of the day. And the day after that. And all the days to follow. There was no question of rebelling, no thoughts of finding my way back home. Thornfield was my home.

And while the days were still a bit monotonous, each felt a little more satisfying than the last. I grew to love the mornings tutoring Adèle, the afternoons strolling through the garden on my own, the evenings reading by the fireplace with Mrs. Fairfax. I got used to the quiet, the solitude, the time spent in my head.

As the days grew colder and the nights grew longer, my former life at Lockwood simply faded away. When I got up in the morning, I was no longer surprised to find myself in a guest room at Thornfield instead of a dorm room. When I saw Mrs. Fairfax, I did not stop and think, *This is Madame Favier, my French teacher.* Lockwood ceased to exist for me, the way school retreats so quickly from one's mind during the summer vacation. Teachers and schoolmates simply faded from consciousness, replaced with the characters of *Jane Eyre,* more real to me now than reality itself.

Once I had given in to this new life, three months went by as quickly as if they were three weeks. But there was something curious about the passage of time, something insubstantial in my understanding of it. I felt like one walking through a dream, no longer controlling my own actions, but rather allowing larger forces to control me. I woke in my room each day and cheerfully rose to my closet to choose something to wear from the rows of plain frocks and shawls. They were my clothes now. I was Jane. Her words and thoughts came to me like the rehearsed lines of a play.

A part of me knew that if I gave myself over to this world completely, I'd be in danger of losing myself, losing my own thoughts and words to Jane's. It would be so easy to do. My one way of combating this was to write. Even in the chill of winter, I'd walk out along the battlements, creating stories and adventures in my head. I began inserting the mysterious Mr. Rochester into these tales, and in my mind, he took on mythic proportions; he was the dashing hero of my most passionate fantasies. His fictional adventures fed my imagination. Sometimes when I returned to my room to write the stories down, for a brief moment I'd remember some other man, a boy really, who had once held my heart. I'd try to pin down a memory of him, but it always flew from my mind the moment I tried to grasp it.

CHAPTER 9

One afternoon in January, Mrs. Fairfax had begged a day off for Adèle, who was sick with a cold. I agreed, but I knew I would go mad stuck inside the house all day with nothing to do. It was a fine, calm day, and I was tired of sitting in the library reading. Mrs. Fairfax had just written a letter that was waiting to be posted, so I volunteered to carry it to town.

I set out on the moors, pulling the flaps of my cloak tight against my chest. The ground was hard, and the air was bitterly cold, so I walked quickly. The road went uphill all the way to town, and I was out of breath, so I sat down on a fence rail to rest. From my seat I could look down on Thornfield, the only object in the valley below, its woods rising against the west. I stayed until the sun began to dip behind the trees, then continued on, worried I wouldn't make it home before dark. The darkness descended quickly here, and an eerie fog was creeping in from the moors, shrouding everything in a gray mist.

I was coming around a bend in the lane when I heard a rhythmic tramping and a metallic clatter, the sounds of a horse approaching. I stood to the side of the road to let it go by, feeling a twinge of fear as I waited for it to appear through the fog, dimly recalling some Halloween tale about a headless man on horseback. I half expected to see a ghostly apparition on a black horse crashing through the night.

Just after I heard a rush under the hedge, an enormous black-and-white hunting dog flew past my legs. It ran on ahead, and the horse and rider followed close behind. My eyes followed the rider, who was no headless horseman, but a traveler dressed in black. He passed, and I went on a few steps in the opposite direction, turning only when I heard a sliding sound, followed by a heavy thud and a shout.

"What the—?" the man called out, forcing me to turn and go back.

The horse had slipped on a sheet of ice, trapping its rider beneath its heaving flanks. Seeing his master on the ground, the dog began barking and came bounding back to me, nipping at my cloak, begging me for help. I ran quickly to the man, who was struggling furiously to get out from under his horse.

"Are you hurt? Can I help?" I said. "What can I do?"

"Just stand on one side," he said, cursing as he rose, first to his knees, then to his feet. The horse began groaning and attempting to stand while the dog continued barking. "Down, Pilot!" the man said, stooping to feel his foot and leg to see if they were broken. Apparently something hurt, because he cursed again and went to lean against a tree.

"If you're hurt, I can get someone from Thornfield," I said.

"Thank you. I have no broken bones, only a sprain." Again he stood up and tried his foot, grunting.

I could see him clearly now. He seemed to be in his mid-thirties, of average height, with broad shoulders and a dark face with a heavy brow. Even in the dimness, I observed that he was quite handsome. Once he'd determined that all was in working order, he glanced up and, seeing me standing there, waved me on with a dismissive flick of his hand.

"Are you sure you're all right?" I said.

"I should think you ought to be at home," he said. "Where do you come from?"

"From below. I can run over to town for you if you want. I'm going there to mail a letter anyway."

"You live just below? Do you mean at that house with the battlements?" he said, pointing to Thornfield. I nodded. "Whose house is it?"

"Mr. Rochester's."

"Do you know the man?"

"No, I've never met him."

"He is not resident, then?"

"No."

"Can you tell me where he is?"

"I'm afraid I can't."

"And you are—" He stopped, running his eye over my dress, puzzled to decide who I was.

"I'm the governess."

"Ah, the governess!" he said. "Deuce take me, if I had not forgotten! The governess!" In two minutes he rose, and his face expressed pain when he tried to move. "I cannot commission you to fetch help," he said, "but you may help me a little yourself, if you will be so kind."

"Of course."

"I must beg of you to come here." He laid a heavy hand on my shoulder, and leaning on me, limped to his horse, which had struggled to its feet and stood, head down, beside the path. Having caught the bridle, the rider sprang to his saddle, wincing as he made the effort. "Now," he said, "just hand me my whip."

Once I handed it to him, he dug his spurs lightly into the horse's sides, and the horse started and reared, then they bounded away, the dog following after them. I watched their silhouettes for a moment, then continued into town. The incident had occurred and was gone. Gone, except for the face of the man, which stayed with me. It was one of those darkly rugged English faces, and it seemed somehow familiar. I was thinking about that face when I entered town and slipped the letter into the letterbox. I was still considering it as I walked down the hill and headed back toward Thornfield. Where had I seen this man before?

When I arrived at the house, I heard the clock strike six. A warm light glowed from the parlor, so I went in and saw a fire in the grate, but no Mrs. Fairfax. Instead, sitting upright on the rug was the black-and-white hunting dog I'd just seen on the lane. "Pilot," I said, recalling the name the man had called him. When the dog approached to sniff me, I gave him a pat on the head, and he wagged his tail happily.

Mrs. Fairfax entered then, and I asked her whose dog it was. "He came with Master," she said. "Mr. Rochester—he is just arrived."

"Mr. Rochester is here?"

"Yes, he is in the dining room, and Miss Adèle is with him along with the surgeon, for Master has had an accident. His horse fell, and his ankle is sprained." She hurried out to give orders about tea, and I went upstairs to take off my things.

So, that was Mr. Rochester. I was a little annoyed that he hadn't revealed his identity out on the lane. Then again, the rich could afford to trifle with whomever they pleased. I knew I would probably not see him again that night. Surely he would be tired from his journey and would go to bed early. I was tired myself, unaccustomed to walking four miles out in the cold. I changed into my nightgown and crawled into bed, summoning the image of Rochester's face to my mind as I tried to go to sleep. Why did I feel I knew the man? Was it possible we had met before?

And why did I feel as if an entire world of memories was drifting farther and farther out of my reach and if I didn't retrieve them soon, they might be lost to me forever?

CHAPTER 10

Thornfield was no longer a silent place. It now echoed with knocks and footsteps and bells and voices. Adèle was preoccupied and could not attend to her lessons. She kept running to the door and looking over the banisters to see if she could catch a glimpse of Mr. Rochester, speculating about what presents he had bought her on his travels.

One afternoon was wild and snowy, and we passed it in the schoolroom. At dark I allowed Adèle to put away her books and run downstairs. It seemed Mr. Rochester had concluded his business for the day.

A moment later, Mrs. Fairfax came into the room. "Mr. Rochester would be glad if you and your pupil would take tea with him in the drawing room this evening," she said stiffly. "You should change your frock now to the gray one with the satin trim."

"Is it necessary to change?" I said.

"Yes, you had better. I always dress for the evening when Mr. Rochester is here."

I thought this was a bit strange; what did Mr. Rochester care what one of his employees was wearing? But I climbed the stairs to my room, and, with Mrs. Fairfax's help, replaced my dress. As she fastened the last button at my neck, she turned me around, looking me over. "You want a brooch or a necklace," she said.

I explained to her that I had lost the only necklace I owned, and a peculiar sensation crept over me as I tried to lock onto the fragment of a memory. Mrs. Fairfax left the room and returned with a pearl brooch and fastened it to my collar.

When we arrived at the drawing room, two candles stood lit on the table, and another glowed on the mantelpiece. Basking in the light and heat of the fire lay Pilot and Adèle. Pilot's tail thumped on the ground when he saw me. Half-reclined on a couch was Mr. Rochester, his foot supported by the ottoman. The fire shone full on his face.

I recognized him from the night on the lane—the broad eyebrows, the square forehead, the sweep of wild black hair that looked as if it wanted to fly off his head. Again, I had the feeling I'd met him some time before.

"Here is Miss Eyre, sir," said Mrs. Fairfax.

Mr. Rochester made no sign that he'd heard her. He bowed his head, not taking his eyes from the fire. "Let Miss Eyre be seated," he said. Something in his manner seemed to suggest his haughty indifference to me.

Tea was poured, and Mrs. Fairfax motioned for me to take it to him, so I handed the cup to Mr. Rochester, who drank his tea and spoke only to Adèle. I began wondering why he'd invited me to the drawing room at all.

"Come to the fire," he said suddenly after the tea tray was taken away. I sat in the chair opposite him while Adèle played with Pilot. Mrs. Fairfax sat off to the side with her sewing. "You have been in my house three months?" he said, not looking at me directly.

"Yes."

"And you came from . . . ?" I hesitated to answer. I couldn't quite remember. "You are an orphan," he said. "You have no family here?"

I reflected for a moment. "None."

"And who recommended you to me?"

Thankfully, Mrs. Fairfax came to my rescue. "She advertised, and I am daily thankful for it. Miss Eyre has been an invaluable companion to me, and a kind and careful teacher to Adèle."

"Don't trouble yourself to give her a character," said Mr. Rochester. "I shall judge for myself. She began by felling my horse. I have to thank her for this sprain." I glared at him then, wondering what on earth I had done to deserve this hostility. After all, I was the one who had helped him back onto his horse. "Miss Eyre," he went on, "what skills do you have? Can you play pianoforte?"

"I'm afraid not."

"But you write. Adèle showed me some stories this morning, which she said were yours. Fetch me your journal, if you can vouch for its contents being original."

I glowered at the back of his head, then went to fetch my journal from the library and handed it to him. He read slowly, pushing a handful of hair off his forehead every now and then. I couldn't tell from his expression what he thought.

The longest story I'd written was about a little bird who thought she was an angelfish because of her brightly colored feathers. The other birds were jealous of her and told her if she tried to fly, she'd fall. So she was content to float on the water all day long until a large black bird came and stole her beak. Without a voice to call him back, she had no choice but to fly after him. At first she flew beautifully, but when she remembered the warnings of the other birds, she grew terrified and fell, careening into the ocean. She tried to flap her wings underwater, but met only with resistance. She wasn't a fish after all. If drowning was to be her fate, she knew she must stop fighting and accept the inevitable. But as soon as she stopped panicking, she rose effortlessly to the surface. Having tested her wings and proven they were flightworthy, the bird took to the air again, chasing after the black bird and retrieving her beak. Her voice and confidence now restored, she spent the rest of her life soaring through the air, singing her story to anyone who would listen.

"Were you happy when you wrote this story?" Mr. Rochester asked when he had finished.

"I was . . . absorbed in the task, so yes, I guess you could say I was happy."

"And you felt satisfied with the result of your labors?"

"Far from it. I imagined something far greater than my abilities could realize."

"It does show some skill," he said. "But it's a peculiar story for a young girl to write. There you sit, so small and sedate, so mouselike and quiet. But here, on the page, there is life. Your story seems to have a voice of its own." I felt a blush creeping up my cheeks as he passed the journal back to me. Then he said in a very abrupt manner, "It is nine o'clock. What are you about, Miss Eyre, to let Adèle sit up so long? Take her to bed."

Insulted, I curtsied, receiving a cold bow in return, and led Adèle from the room. *What an arrogant man,* I thought. And how stupid was I to have felt elated because he complimented my writing.

When I saw Mrs. Fairfax the next day, she asked me what I had thought of the master. "He's very moody," I said, feeling anger course through me again. I could have said far more, but I checked myself. Anyone could see that Mrs. Fairfax worshipped Mr. Rochester.

"No doubt he may appear so to a stranger," she said, "but I am so accustomed to his manner, I never think of it. He is used to making demands and having them done without question. You might think of addressing him as 'sir,' as I have always done." I resisted the urge to roll my eyes. "Besides, if he has peculiarities of temper, allowances should be made."

"Why?" I asked.

"Partly because it is his nature—we can none of us help

our nature—and partly because he has painful thoughts to harass him."

"What kind of thoughts?"

"Family troubles, for one thing. He broke with his family, and now for many years he has led an unsettled kind of life. I don't think he has ever been resident at Thornfield for a fortnight together, and, indeed, no wonder he shuns the old place."

"Why?"

"Perhaps he thinks it gloomy."

She admitted his reasons were a mystery to her, and that what she knew was chiefly from conjecture. I wanted to ask her more, but it was evident that Mrs. Fairfax wanted me to drop the subject entirely.

For several days I saw little of Mr. Rochester. In the mornings he seemed occupied with business, and in the afternoon, gentlemen from the neighborhood called and stayed to dine with him. When his sprain was well enough, he rode a great deal and generally did not come back till late at night.

One evening after his company had left, he called for Adèle and me. Upon our arrival in the dining room, he gave Adèle a doll, telling her to amuse herself elsewhere and asking me to sit in the chair next to him.

"Don't draw that chair farther off, Miss Eyre," he said. "Sit down exactly where I placed it—if you please, that is. Confound these civilities! I ought to be at liberty to attend to my own pleasure. Miss Eyre, draw your chair still a little farther forward; you are yet too far back."

His bossy, domineering tone had returned, but I reminded myself of what Mrs. Fairfax had said. He was accustomed to people obeying his every word. I did what he asked, even though I resented his expectation of obedience.

A large fire flickered and crackled in the hearth, filling the room with warmth as frozen rain beat against the panes. Mr. Rochester looked different than before, not quite so stern, much less grim. There was a smile on his lips, and his eyes sparkled, probably from all the wine he'd had. He was in an after-dinner mood, relaxed and friendly, but still a bit imposing in his look. The glow from the fire cast him in light and shadow so his face emerged in planes like a great slab of granite. His dark eyes seemed to change in their depths like the ocean, some spots deep and cool, others lighter and full of warmth.

"You examine me, Miss Eyre," he said. "Do you think me handsome?"

A direct question. Before I could think, I gave him a direct answer. "No."

He laughed heartily. "By my word, there is something singular about you," he said. "You look so quaint, quiet, grave, and simple, as you sit with your hands before you, your eyes bent on the carpet. But when one asks you a question, you rap out a round rejoinder, which, if not blunt, is at least brusque."

"Sir," I said, trying to backpedal. "I'm sorry. I should have said that beauty is in the eye of the beholder."

"Beauty in the eye of the beholder, indeed! And so, under pretense of softening the previous outrage, you stick a sly penknife under my ear! Go on, what fault do you find with me? I suppose I have all my limbs and all my features like any other man?"

I couldn't help but laugh. "Mr. Rochester, forgive me. I didn't mean to offend you."

"Does my forehead not please you?" he went on, a sly grin playing on his lips. He lifted up the waves of hair that lay over his brow. "Now, ma'am, what kind of brow is this?"

"A noble one, I'd say."

"There again! Another stick of the penknife. Noble I may have been, once upon a time, but Fortune has beaten it out of me." He rose from his chair and stood, leaning his arm on the marble mantelpiece of the fireplace. I stared at his profile.

There was something undeniably striking about his looks, some force that made it difficult to look away.

"I am disposed to be gregarious and communicative to-night," he said. I was waiting for him to continue, but he just stared at me, his eyes dark and penetrating. "Therefore, speak," he said.

I opened my mouth in disbelief. "I am not a dog, sir. But I'll be happy to talk with you if you give me a topic of conversation."

He made a grumbling noise, trying to decide if I was being impertinent. "You are quiet, Miss Eyre. Stubborn perhaps? Annoyed. Ah, that is it. Miss Eyre, I beg your pardon. The fact is, I don't wish to treat you like an inferior. That is, I claim only such superiority as must result from twenty years' difference in age. I desire you to have the goodness to talk to me a little now, and divert my thoughts, which are galled with dwelling on one point—cankering as a rusty nail."

"But how do I know what will interest you? Ask me questions, and I'll do my best to answer them."

"Then, in the first place, do you agree with me that I have a right to be a little masterful, on the grounds that I am old enough to be your father, and that I have roamed over half the globe while you have lived quietly with one set of people in one house?"

"It all depends on how you've used that time and experience," I said.

"Promptly spoken. The truth is, I was thrust onto a wrong tack at the age of one-and-twenty, and have never recovered the right course since." Some awful thought seemed to grip him, and he ground his teeth and went silent. I wanted to change the subject, so I asked him how he had come to be Adèle's caretaker.

In a rather amused tone, he told me of his adventures in Paris, where he'd had an affair with a beautiful French dancer named Céline Varens. He thought he was in love with her. But Céline betrayed him by taking up with another man. Some years later, he received word that Céline had abandoned a baby girl, claiming she was his. The child was destitute. "I took the poor thing out of the slime and mud of Paris and transplanted it here to grow up clean in the wholesome soil of an English country garden. Mrs. Fairfax found you to train it, but now that you know it is the illegitimate offspring of a French opera girl, you will perhaps think differently of your post and protégée."

I shook my head. "You call Adèle 'it' as if she were some animal you'd rescued and put inside a cage. She's a little girl. And her background is not any fault of her own. She knows neither of her parents and has never known any real affection. I shall love her even more than before." He looked startled by my words. "Sir," I added sheepishly. And then he laughed as if my passionate nature amused him.

"Ah, Miss Eyre, I envy your peace of mind, your clean conscience. I am not a villain—you are not to suppose that— but I am a commonplace sinner who feels the dreaded sting of remorse. And remorse, Miss Eyre, is the poison of life."

"Is it too late to turn your life around?" I asked, meeting his eyes.

"I could reform, but since happiness has been irrevocably denied me, I have a right to get pleasure out of life, and I will get it, cost what it may." For a moment, I felt certain he was going to cast me out of the room like he had the other night, so I rose from my chair.

"Where are you going?" he said, clearly displeased.

"To put Adèle to bed. It's past her bedtime."

He brusquely gestured for me to sit back down, but I remained standing. "You are afraid of me now," he said.

"I am confused by you, sir. Not afraid."

"You are shy and reserved with me, unsure yet of my character. I think you will learn to be natural with me in time. I see you as a curious sort of bird in a cage, a vivid, restless captive. Were you free, you would soar cloud high like the bird from your story." I smiled at him softly, then said good night. Pilot followed me out of the room, and I suspected Rochester's eyes did as well.

As I lay in bed, I began wondering how Mr. Rochester felt about me. Despite his initial gruffness, I could feel him softening toward me. He seemed to enjoy our little chats, and I had to admit, they were growing on me, too. I got the sense that perhaps we were more alike than at first we seemed— two lost souls trapped in a gloomy mansion together—one haunted by a past he could not relinquish, the other haunted by a past she could not remember.

CHAPTER 11

That night as I lay in bed dissecting my feelings for Mr. Rochester, I heard a noise above me and sat upright. I wished I had kept my candle burning; the night was so dark. But soon after, the sound died. I tried to sleep again, but my heart was racing. The clock down the hall struck two. Just then it seemed as if someone rattled the doorknob.

"Who's there?" I said. Silence.

All at once I remembered it might be Pilot and sighed in relief. I crept out of bed and went to the door, but when I opened it, the hall was empty. I forced myself to lie down again and began to feel the pull of sleep when I heard a demonic laugh—low and deep—and seemingly coming from the keyhole of my door. Before long, steps retreated up the hallway and toward the third-story staircase. I heard a door open and close, then all was quiet again.

I had heard that same laughter on my first day here, when Mrs. Fairfax had taken me on a tour of the house. She had blamed a servant named Grace Poole. Thinking it impossible to stay by myself any longer, I put on a shawl and went to get Mrs. Fairfax. I opened the door with a trembling hand, surprised to find the air in the hallway filled with smoke. Something creaked down the hall—it seemed to be Mr. Rochester's door. Smoke was rushing out from it in a cloud. I ran down and opened the door, immediately choking from the fumes. The stench of burning fabric filled the air. The curtains were on fire, tongues of flame were darting toward the bed, and Mr. Rochester lay stretched motionless, in a deep sleep.

"Wake up! Wake up!" I cried. I shook him, but he only murmured and turned; the smoke had stupefied him. I rushed to his basin filled with water, heaved it up, and drenched the burning side of the bed. Though it was dark, I knew Rochester had woken because I heard him cursing under his breath when he found himself lying in a pool of water. "What the—!"

"Sir, there's been a fire. Get up. You're soaked."

"Is that Jane Eyre?" he demanded. "What have you done with me? Have you plotted to drown me?"

"Somebody has plotted something. Get up."

Following this, I snatched a rug from the hallway, and Mr. Rochester and I used it to beat back the flames until we finally succeeded in extinguishing the fire.

In the moonlight, I could see him standing beside the bed surveying the damage, half the mattress blackened and scorched, the sheets drenched. "What happened? Who did this?"

I briefly told him what I knew—the strange laugh, the steps ascending to the third story, the smoke in the hallway, the smell of fire that had brought me to his room. He listened very gravely.

"Remain where you are till I return," he said. "Be as still as a mouse. I must pay a visit to the third story. Don't move, remember, or call anyone."

I was confused but did what he asked. A very long time elapsed as I listened for some noise but heard nothing. It was cold in the room, and I was growing weary. I was at the point of leaving when a light gleamed on the wall, and I heard footsteps in the hall.

He entered the room, finally, looking pale and sad. "I have

found it all out," he said, setting a lit candle down on the washstand. "It is as I thought."

"How?" He made no reply, but stood with his arms folded, looking at the ground. "There is a woman who sews here," I said, "called Grace Poole. Was it her?"

He nodded gravely. "Just so. Grace Poole—you have guessed it. Meantime, I am glad that you are the only person, besides myself, acquainted with the precise details of tonight's incident. Say nothing about it. Now return to your own room. I shall do very well on the sofa in the library for the rest of the night. It is near four, and in two hours the servants will be up."

"Good night, then," I said, turning to go.

"What!" he said. "Are you quitting me already, and in that way?"

"You said I should go."

"But not without taking leave. Not without a word or two of acknowledgment and goodwill. Why, you have saved my life! Snatched me from a horrible and excruciating death! And you walk past me as if we were mutual strangers! At least shake hands." He held out his hand, and I gave him mine. He took it first in one, them in both his own. "You have saved my life. I have a pleasure in owing you so immense a debt." He gazed at me in the dim light, and I felt a flush of warmth from his intense stare. "I knew," he said, "you would do me good in some way, at some time. I saw it in your eyes when I first met you."

Strange energy was in his voice, strange fire in his eyes. For a moment, I thought he might kiss me, and the prospect made me blush and pull away. Still he held on to my hand. At last he relaxed his fingers, and I turned and fled the room. Back in my chamber, I lay in bed but never thought of sleep. I could still feel the warmth of his fingers on my palm.

I both wished and feared to see Mr. Rochester the next day. I wanted to hear his voice again, yet feared to meet his eyes. Something had transpired between us last night, that much was certain. During the early part of the morning, I waited to see him. But the morning passed as usual, and nothing happened to interrupt the quiet course of Adèle's studies.

Soon after breakfast, I heard some of the servants in Mr. Rochester's room, exclaiming about the danger of leaving candles burning at bedtime and lamenting the condition of his bedclothes. No one suspected I'd had any hand in his rescue.

When I passed his room later that afternoon, I saw that everything had been restored to complete order. I peered in to see if perhaps Mr. Rochester was there, but instead, I saw a woman sitting on a chair by the bedside, sewing rings to new curtains. Grace Poole.

What was she doing here? If she had tried to kill Rochester last night, why wouldn't he have fired her on the spot, or better yet, dragged her out of the house himself? Here she sat with total impunity, quietly intent on her sewing.

"Good afternoon, Grace," I said.

"Good afternoon," she replied.

"I see you've set everything back to normal." She only nodded. "Can I ask you a question? Did you happen to hear a strange laugh in the middle of the night?"

"No, miss," she said. "Did you?"

"Yes," I said, irritated by her show of innocence.

"And you did not think of opening your door and looking out into the gallery?" she asked. She appeared to be cross-questioning me.

"No," I said. "I bolted my door."

"It would be wise to do so from now on," she said without looking up from her sewing.

"I thought I heard footsteps. On the third floor. In the middle of the night." Still she said nothing. "The footsteps came down the stairs and stopped right outside my door. Are you sure it wasn't you?"

"There are many servants who sleep on the third floor," she said. "Perhaps one of them had a nightmare." I could tell I wasn't going to get anywhere with her.

Feeling frustrated and a little afraid of her, I left and went down to the parlor to find Mrs. Fairfax, who was busy preparing Adèle's dinner. She greeted me and gazed out the window. "It is fair today," she said. "Mr. Rochester has a favorable day for his journey."

"Journey? Is Mr. Rochester going somewhere?" I said, not attempting to conceal the disappointment in my voice.

"He is gone already, to Mr. Eshton's place ten miles on the other side of Millcote. I believe there is a party assembled there."

"Do you expect him back tonight?"

"No, nor tomorrow either. I should think he is very likely to stay a week or more. Mr. Rochester is so talented and so lively in society, that I believe he is a general favorite—the ladies are very fond of him. Mrs. Eshton and her three daughters are very elegant young ladies, and there are the Honorable Blanche and Mary Ingram—most beautiful women, I suppose. Last time they were here, Miss Ingram was considered the belle of the evening."

"Miss Ingram?"

"A fine woman, well endowed with a fine bust, a long graceful neck, brilliant eyes. And then she had such a fine head of hair, so becomingly arranged."

"And you say she was admired?"

"Yes, indeed; and not only for her beauty, but for her accomplishments. She sings, draws, speaks French fluently. On the whole she would make a fine match for our Mr. Rochester."

A fine match for our Mr. Rochester?

Adèle came in, and the conversation turned to other things, but my spirits had plummeted. Last night in his bedroom, I had been harboring silly fantasies that I was a favorite of Mr. Rochester's. Now I realized how stupid I had been. He was my boss, and I was his employee. He may have felt some friendly affection toward me for saving his life, but that was all.

A week passed, and no news arrived of Mr. Rochester. Ten days, and still he didn't return. I went on with my day's business, but I couldn't concentrate. I missed him. Why did a girl's happiness always seem to depend upon a man? Why couldn't I be content with the quiet, peaceful existence I'd carved out for myself? Wishing and hoping for romance and adventure would only get me into trouble.

All the same, when Mrs. Fairfax told me that Mr. Rochester and his entire party were to return to Thornfield that week, my body thrummed with anxiety and excitement. Early that week, the house went into a state of frenzied cleaning and preparation. Adèle ran quite wild in the midst of it. The party was expected to arrive on Thursday afternoon in time for dinner at six.

When Thursday finally came, Mrs. Fairfax was the first to spot Miss Ingram approaching on horseback. Moments later, a joyous stir could be heard in the hall—gentlemen's deep voices and ladies' accents and distinguishable above all, the voice of Mr. Rochester. I couldn't help but feel as giddy as Adèle at his return. Hidden behind a column in the hallway, I watched as a parade of elegant guests in brightly colored riding costumes passed through the foyer. I tried in vain to figure out which one of them was the famous Miss Ingram, but they all wore riding hats. I stayed hidden as they went upstairs, their cheerful laughter echoing through the gallery. I listened as they discussed plans and finally parted ways to go to their rooms to change for the evening.

Wondering where Adèle had gone, I sought her upstairs in the schoolroom. There she was, peeping through the schoolroom door, waiting for the guests to emerge in their finery. When they did finally assemble in the gallery, looking haughty and elegant, Adèle exclaimed in her thick French accent, "What beautiful ladies! Oh, I wish I might go to them! Do you think Mr. Rochester will send for us after dinner?"

"No, I don't," I said. "Mr. Rochester has other things to think about." But I had been wondering the very same thing myself.

I told Adèle stories for as long as she would listen, and then for a change I took her out into the gallery to watch. The hall lamp was lit now, and it amused her to look over the balustrade and watch the servants passing backward and forward. As it got later, piano music issued from the drawing room. Adèle and I sat down on the top step of the stairs to listen. When the clock struck eleven, I looked down at Adèle, whose head leaned against my shoulder, her eyes waxing heavy. I took her up in my arms and carried her off to bed.

The next morning as Adèle and I had our breakfast, Mrs. Fairfax leaned over to me and said, "You will see Miss Ingram this evening. Mr. Rochester requested you to accompany Adèle to the party."

Later that afternoon, I put on my finest dress of violet satin with lace trim. I pinched my cheeks for color, then went to fetch Adèle, and we headed downstairs together. There were eight guests in the drawing room, and I spotted Rochester at the other end of the room. My eyes were drawn involuntarily to his face—that square brow, those deep eyes and strong features. It was true he was not conventionally handsome, but he had become beautiful to me. I had not intended to love him. I had tried not to. But now that I'd finally admitted to my feelings, it was too late. He was in love with Blanche Ingram.

I had the sense that I'd met Blanche before, felt I knew that glossy golden hair, that superior smile, the arched brow, and the full lips that erupted in haughty laughter at anything Rochester said. After observing her for some time, I confirmed what Mrs. Fairfax had told me—Miss Ingram played the piano proficiently, sang angelically, and spoke French with fluency and a good accent. There was no doubt she was a beautiful and accomplished woman.

I watched her with Rochester, too, saw the way her hand brushed his arm when she spoke, how she whispered things so he would have to lean in close. She seemed manipulative and vain, a social climber only interested in Rochester's wealth and position. Could he really love this woman?

It was agonizing to have him so near, yet not be able to talk to him. Why had he requested my presence if he was only going to ignore me? Jealousy crept into my heart like water inside a stone, freezing and breaking it into little pieces.

CHAPTER 12

The party lingered on for days, and rumors of an impending engagement put an end to all my foolish hopes.

"Do you really think Miss Ingram is the right match for the master?" I asked Mrs. Fairfax one morning at breakfast.

"But of course! In what way could she be lacking? She would be the very thing to make our Mr. Rochester happy."

I chewed my lower lip absently and went to pour myself some tea. *The very thing to make him happy?* If anything, Miss Ingram would make Mr. Rochester more miserable than he already was. Underneath her delicate façade lurked a shark, a creature swimming coldly in pursuit of wealth and social prestige.

It was later that day that Rochester took a rare break from his duties as host and went out riding alone. I took the opportunity to study Miss Ingram in his absence. Not once did I hear a kind or selfless word from her. When Adèle hopped up on the window ledge to look out for Rochester's return, Miss Ingram frowned and said, "You tiresome monkey! Who perched you up in the window to give false intelligence?" She cast on me an angry glance, so I removed Adèle and shuttled her away.

Rochester was still gone when a strange man arrived at the door that evening just before the dinner hour. Mrs. Fairfax greeted the man at the door and led him in to join the party. His manner was polite, and his accent struck me as somewhat unusual. Adèle and I went upstairs to prepare her for bed, and it wasn't until after dinner that I saw the man again. He seemed quite at his ease among the party, but something disturbed me about him. Who was he, and why had he come here? What was his connection to Rochester?

By late evening, I had been waiting so long for Rochester's return that my restlessness led me outside to meet his horse.

"Jane," he said, looking pleased to see me as he dismounted his stallion. "How is the party? Come with me! Let me hear what they said about me in my absence."

I wanted to mirror his jovial mood, but the stranger's arrival was still bothering me. "Sir, are you aware that a stranger has arrived since you left this morning?"

"A stranger!" he said, putting an arm around me as he led me inside. "I expected no one. Did he give his name?"

"His name is Mason, and he comes from the West Indies. From Spanish Town, in Jamaica, I think."

Mr. Rochester was standing near me. He had taken my hand, and as I spoke, he gave my wrist a convulsive grip. The smile on his lips froze. "Mason. The West Indies," he repeated, his face growing pale as ash.

"Do you feel all right?" I said.

"Jane, I've had a blow." He seemed to stagger.

Quickly, before anyone else could see his reaction, I led him into the library, where we sat down on the sofa. Holding my hand, he rubbed it and gazed at me with the most troubled expression. "My little friend," he said. "I wish I were alone with you on a quiet island, where trouble and danger and hideous recollections were forever removed." Flattered as I was, I worried for him. He was not himself. He turned and gazed at me earnestly. "Jane, if all these people came in and spat at me, what would you do?"

"Turn them out of the room if I could."

He half smiled. "You would not leave me?"

"No, I'd stay."

"To comfort me?"

"Yes, to comfort you."

He seemed suddenly in better spirits. "Jane, if you would, go now into the dining room, step quietly up to Mason, and whisper in his ear that Mr. Rochester wishes to see him. Show him in here, and then leave us."

I was angry and hurt that his authoritarian tone had returned. He was capable of switching from tenderness to gruffness at a moment's notice. But I left to find Mason in the dining room. Miss Ingram glared at me as I bent over to speak to Mr. Mason, but his speedy departure from the room gave me an excuse to leave as well. I brought the stranger to the library and excused myself. Mr. Rochester did not even say good-bye.

I couldn't sleep at all that night, replaying the events of the evening over in my mind. Who was Mason? And why had his presence filled Rochester with such dread? There were so many things I didn't know about Rochester.

I don't know how long I lay there like that, but the silence in my room was split by a sharp cry that ran from end to end of Thornfield Hall. It had come from the third story, I believed in the room just above my bedroom ceiling. My heart stopped as I heard a struggle and a voice shouting, "Help! Help!"

Though horror shook my limbs, I threw on some clothes and ran from my room into the hallway. The guests had all gathered there, terrified. They ran to and fro, crowding together. Just then the door to the third floor opened, and Mr. Rochester emerged into the hallway, a candle in hand. Miss Ingram ran to him and seized his arm.

"What has happened?" she said.

"All's right!" he cried. He looked wild, his black eyes darting sparks. Calming himself, he said, "A servant has had a nightmare, that is all. Now then, I must see you all back into your rooms." And so, with some coaxing and commanding, he managed to get them all back to their bedrooms. I didn't wait to be ordered back to mine. I went to stand by the window, looking out at a dull moon, shivering from the cold.

Moments later, a cautious hand tapped at my door. "Are you up?" I heard. It was Mr. Rochester. I exited my room quietly and saw him standing in the hallway, holding a candle. "I need your help. Come this way and make no noise."

I followed as quietly as a cat. He glided along the hallway, opened the door to the third floor without a sound, and climbed the stairs. At the top, we stopped in the dark, low corridor in front of a door.

"You don't turn sick at the sight of blood?" he said.

"I don't think so."

He turned the key and opened the door, and I heard a snarling sound, almost like a rabid dog. Mr. Rochester went forward to the inner room. Laughter greeted his entrance, Grace Poole's goblin laugh. After a moment, he came back out and closed the door behind him.

"Here, Jane!" he said, leading me to the other side of a large bed, which concealed in its curtains an injured man. Rochester held the candle over him, and I recognized him as the stranger, Mason. I saw, too, that his shirt on one side and one arm was soaked in blood.

Mr. Rochester fetched a basin of water from the washstand, dipped in a sponge, and moistened the man's face. Mason groaned. "I shall have to leave you in this room with this gentleman for an hour," Mr. Rochester said. "Or perhaps two. You will sponge the blood as I do. You will not speak to him on any pretext, nor you to her, Mr. Mason." Again the poor man groaned. "Remember! No conversation," he said, then left the room hurriedly.

No conversation? Questions flooded my brain. What crime had taken place in this mansion? What mystery that broke out first in fire and now in blood, at the deadliest hours of night? And what did this man, Mason, have to do with it all? Why had Rochester asked me not to speak to him, nor him to me?

Finally, regardless of the consequences, I said, "Sir? Mr. Mason, can you speak?" I gave him a sip of water. "Can you tell me what happened?"

"She bit me," he said, though he seemed delusional. "She sucked my blood. She said she'd drain my heart."

"Who? Grace Poole?" He was unable to continue, though he tried. "Calm yourself," I said. "Try not to get upset. You've lost a lot of blood."

I found his story difficult to believe. How could Grace Poole, a woman with the calm presence of mind to sit sewing while I questioned her about her whereabouts during the fire, have the audacity to bite a man's chest? But I had to know if this was true. I knew I was risking everything I'd worked for so far at Thornfield—my position as governess and any affection I might have gained from Rochester—but I got up from the chair beside Mason and crept to the door. All seemed silent on the other side. I knocked lightly, expecting to hear a renewal of that growling from before. Footsteps padded quietly to the door, then stopped.

"Who's there?" I heard. It was the voice of Grace Poole. She sounded calm and self-possessed.

"It's Jane Eyre," I said.

"Go away. If you know what's good for you, go away from this house and never return."

"Please," I said, "you must tell me what's going on. Please, open the door, Grace."

Silence fell behind the door, then the footsteps retreated. Eventually, I resumed my post next to Mason, feeling spent and confused. The night lingered and lingered. Finally, Mr. Rochester returned with a surgeon in tow.

With Mason now in the surgeon's care, Mr. Rochester dismissed me. I walked, trembling, back down the third-story stairwell with no thought of returning to my bedroom. It was half past five, and the sun was on the point of rising. I tiptoed down to the kitchen and let myself out the side door. In the courtyard I saw a carriage, horses already harnessed and stationed outside. Mr. Rochester and the surgeon appeared shortly thereafter, holding Mason. They assisted him into the carriage, and the doctor climbed in behind him.

"Take care of him," Mr. Rochester said. "And keep him at your house till he is quite well. I shall ride over in a day or two to see how he gets on."

Before the carriage left, Mason stuck his head out the opening and said with the little strength he had left, "Let her be taken care of. Let her be treated as tenderly as may be." He seemed on the verge of crying.

"I do my best, and have done it, and will do it," Rochester answered as the chaise drove away.

I was about to turn back when Rochester noticed me by the door and called my name. "Come, Jane, where there is some freshness for a few moments," he said. "That house is a dungeon."

He walked down a path into the garden, fruit trees lining one side and flower borders on the other. The sun was just rising, its light shining down on the path.

"You have passed a strange night, Jane, and it has made you look pale. Were you afraid when I left you alone with Mason?"

"I was afraid of Grace coming out of the inner room."

"But I had fastened the door. I should have been a careless shepherd if I had left a lamb so near a wolf's den, unguarded. You were safe."

"Will Grace Poole still live here?"

"Oh, yes, don't trouble your head about her."

"It seems you're hardly safe while she stays."

"Never fear—I will take care of myself. Here, Jane, sit down."

Mr. Rochester took a seat on a bench, leaving room for me. He sighed, exhausted. "Jane," he began, "suppose you were no longer a girl, but a wild boy indulged from childhood on. Imagine yourself in a remote foreign land, and conceive that there you commit a capital error, one whose consequences must follow you through life and taint all your existence. You take measures to obtain relief, but still you are miserable. You wander here and there, seeking happiness in pleasure. You come home after years of voluntary banishment and make a new acquaintance. You find in this stranger much of the good and bright qualities which you have sought for twenty years. You feel better days come back, higher wishes, purer feelings. Is the sinful, but repentant man justified in daring the world's opinion, in order to attach to him forever this gentle, gracious creature?"

I felt a curious squeezing in my heart as I contemplated whether the "gentle, gracious creature" he was talking about could be me. I observed him for some sign, but words seemed caught in his throat. Then he said, "You may have noticed my tender penchant for Miss Ingram. Do you think . . . do you think if I married her, she would make me happy?"

The bindings squeezing around my heart now cinched tightly so I could barely breathe. Miss Ingram was the gentle, gracious creature? And he believed she could make him happy? I was so consumed with envy and heartache that I stood up and began walking back toward the house.

"Jane, Jane!" he said, and I glanced back hopefully. "There are my guests! They cannot see us together out here. Go in by the shrubbery."

I turned and fled, trying not to cry. Wiping foolish tears off my cheeks, I made my way up the stairs to my room and found Grace Poole standing outside my door. She was holding something in her hand, inspecting it. When she saw me, she froze like she'd been caught stealing. Her fingers closed over the object, which only made me want to see it more.

"What is that?" I said. "Is it mine? Have you taken something from my room?"

"No, miss. I found it in the hallway. A mere trifle."

"Show me," I demanded, and by some miracle, my voice sounded authoritative, and she obeyed.

Her hand opened to reveal a small pendant in the shape of a dragonfly. Familiarity and emotion washed over me as I studied the markings, the patterns made by blue and green glass on silver. "That is mine," I said.

"I found it—"

"I will take it now!" I said with a firmness that shocked me.

She handed over the dragonfly, and I quickly entered my room, bolting the door behind me. There was nothing in the room to comfort me; everything reminded me of the nights spent sleepless thinking of Rochester's face, the mornings spent dressing for him, hoping he would notice me and pay me a kind word. I wanted to go far away from here, to a place where I wasn't inconsequential, where my most prized possession was not called a trifle, where I meant something to someone.

I walked over to the vanity and found the chain from my necklace and carefully slid the dragonfly on it, then fastened it around my neck, feeling the weight of the pendant return to my chest. When I looked in the mirror, I reeled backward with shock and recognition. For it was not Jane who stared back at me, but another girl. A girl I'd almost forgotten.

Her name repeated in my head like an echo, and then faces came flooding back to me, their names slowly returning to my consciousness: Michelle, Owen, Dad, Barbara, Grandma. I tried to call out to them, but their images hovered in front of my eyes yet out of reach.

I knew that I was connected to each and every one of

them, and I had to find my way back. Clutching the necklace, I prayed to my mother for assistance. If anyone could help me now, it was her. I cried her name and wept and fought with my memories to sort out the truth from the fantasy. All that had happened here at Thornfield—my position as governess, my friendship with Mrs. Fairfax and Adèle, my love for Rochester—it was all illusion. My true destiny lay somewhere else.

Mother, please, help me! Help me fight my way back. I don't want to be here anymore. I want to live my own life. I want to go to Paris. I want to write a novel. I want to fall in love. I want so many things.

Miserable and exhausted beyond measure, I crawled into bed, hearing the sound of my name repeat over and over again in my head, two syllables, so rhythmic and comforting they sounded almost like a heartbeat.

PART 3

CHAPTER 13

I thought the pulsing sound in my ears was my own heart-beat, but it was too high-pitched, too mechanical. I tried opening my eyes but felt like a baby mouse prying his eyes open for the first time, awaiting a harsh and terrifying world.

When my vision sharpened, I saw that I was in a hospital room, hemmed in by metal rails with tall machines on either side of me, humming and beeping steadily, presumably keeping me alive. I heard someone stirring beside me and turned to look, but my movements were restricted. I panicked. I tried to say something, but all that came out of my mouth was a moan. Oh God, I couldn't speak.

"Emma?" a voice said. "Emma, Emma!" My father's face appeared above me, tearstained and pale. I tried to reach for him, tried to say just one word, but I couldn't speak or move. "Doctor, she's awake! Dr. Gupta!" my father shouted, jumping to his feet and running out of the room.

Where am I? And where did my father go?

A few minutes later, he returned with a woman in a white lab coat. She was small and dark and disconcertingly young. She examined my eyes and said in a tiny little voice, "Emma, can you hear me?"

"Yes! Yes!" I wanted to shout, but I could only utter a gasp.

"What's wrong with her, Doctor?" my father said. "Why can't she speak?"

"It's not unusual. I told you there might be complications." The tiny doctor took my father aside and whispered something, but I could hear her plainly. "Paralysis. Brain damage. We'll need to wait and see."

Paralysis? Brain damage? There is absolutely nothing wrong with my brain!

I tried to shout again and felt exhausted by the effort. My father came back to my bed and seized both of my hands. "Emma, you're awake, that's all that matters. And I'm here." Tears filled his eyes. "Can you hear me? Do you understand me?"

I focused all of my power into nodding, just once, and it seemed to do the trick because my father dropped his head down onto my chest and broke down, crying. I began crying, too. It had been so long since he'd touched me, and now he was embracing me. When he lifted his head, tears were streaming down his cheeks.

"She can hear what I'm saying, Doctor," he said. "She just can't answer." I tried to say something again, anything to reassure my dad I was back, but the intense concentration was too much. I felt myself being sucked back into sleep.

I slept frequently over the next few days, waking for brief stints, during which doctors and nurses crowded around me with miniature flashlights and equipment, prodding and poking me until I fell asleep again. My father was worried, but the doctor assured him excessive sleep was normal for someone coming out of a coma. It took time to readjust to waking life.

Here is what I learned over the next few days. I had not been struck by a car, and I was not paralyzed. I had been struck by lightning. Yes, I was one of the two thousand people struck by lightning each year, approximately sixty-five of whom would die from their injuries. I had been flown by helicopter to Children's Hospital. They didn't think I was going to make it. Survival rates for coma patients are usually less than 50 percent, especially for people who lose consciousness for more than a few hours. I had been in a coma for three weeks. I had forgotten how to walk and talk. And I remembered no lightning storm at all and nothing from the time I was under; in fact, the last thing I remembered was getting dressed in my Wednesday Addams costume on Halloween.

Doctors came in and out of my room constantly, but I slept through most of it. Little blips of their conversations entered my subconscious, phrases like "external stimuli," "Glasgow Coma Scale," and "frontal lobe activity." But my lucid moments were few and far between.

After a few days, I was able to stay awake for longer periods. Dr. Gupta came to speak with me, calling it the first of her "cheerleading sessions." It was going to be a long road to recovery, she warned, but I was making phenomenal progress already. My MRI was normal, I had no permanent paralysis, no skull fracture, no brain damage. All in all, I'd been extraordinarily lucky.

"I'm sure it's quite frustrating that you can't remember anything about the accident," she said. "But temporary amnesia is quite common after a trauma like this. Don't worry. The memories are still there. You just need to retrieve them. Re-teach yourself. You will walk and talk again."

After a week, I was allowed to have visitors, but I still couldn't talk very well. My father stayed with me every night, refusing to go home. Barbara and Grandma Mackie came the day after Thanksgiving and brought some stuffing and cranberry sauce, even though I couldn't eat solid food. The smell was comforting all the same.

Michelle and Owen visited that Sunday. It was good to see my friends again, to hear their voices filling the stale hospital room with lively gossip and Lockwood drama. Owen sat on the edge of my bed, wearing a T-shirt with a cartoon piece of

bread and a dialogue bubble that read: *I'm toasted!* Michelle
seemed agitated and chatty, pacing around the room like a
wild animal. In my groggy state, she was making me dizzy.
She filled me in on our Halloween excursion to Braeburn and
its aftermath. Dr. Overbrook had blamed Michelle for the in-
fraction, sentencing her to fifty hours of community service,
which she was completing five hours at a time at a women's
shelter in Waverly Falls.

"One more incident and I'm expelled," Michelle said.
"But you were absolved completely. Overbrook said I put
undue influence on you, and you were not responsible for
your own actions." I wanted to apologize to her for the in-
justice of it all, so I tried to reach out my hand, and Owen
grabbed it. "Hey, your fingers are moving," he said. "That's
good. That's real good."

"You didn't tell her the really exciting news," Michelle
said, an edge of sarcasm to her voice.

"Oh, yeah," Owen said. "Michelle's going to compete in
the riding championship! My dad's company is sponsoring
her."

"So, basically," Michelle said, "I'm indebted to Owen and
his father for, like, the rest of my life."

"That's not true and you know it," Owen said.

"Whatever. It's fine." Michelle fidgeted with the sash of
the window. Something seemed off between them, but I didn't
know what. "Oh my God, I almost forgot to tell you!" she
said, grabbing the bouquet of flowers from the windowsill
and bringing them over to my bed. "Guess who these are
from?"

"She can't guess," Owen said. "She can't speak. Just tell
her."

"Gray Newman." She brought over the flowers—enormous rainbow-hued Gerbera daisies that didn't look real.
The card attached said, *All Naturals*. I wanted to tell Michelle
that the flowers were probably Simona's idea, not Gray's.

Just like my journal. "He came to visit you," Michelle said. "He seemed really worried."

"Worried he was going to get in trouble," Owen said. "How many wine coolers did he make you drink that night?" I tried to shake my head. Owen had the wrong idea. "There's something about that guy I don't trust."

"What do you mean?" Michelle said.

"I don't know, I've heard some bad things. Emma's too good for him."

"You never told me what happened between you two on Halloween night," Michelle said. "When you came back from that walk, you seemed upset. Of course, you probably don't remember now. The doctor told us you have temporary amnesia. How cool is that? It's like something from a movie. I still can't believe you got struck by lightning. . . ."

She kept prattling on, but suddenly I wanted them gone. I was overwhelmed, tired, starved for sleep. I didn't want to think anymore or talk to people or deal with all this light and noise. Fortunately, the nurse returned and told Michelle and Owen that visiting hours were ending. I watched my friends leave with relief.

Even though I couldn't remember what had happened to me while under the spell of the coma, I often felt a force calling me back to slumber, back to whatever twilight world I'd lived in for those weeks. Images loomed on the horizon of my brain of peaceful meadows and crackling fires and of something larger and more powerful, something vague and frightening but also exciting. I was desperate to remember.

Sleep seduced me for those first few days, pulling me under again and again and releasing me for only hours at a time. But by the following week, I was feeling more energetic. I had regained the ability to speak, and this gave me motivation to stay up for longer periods. Maybe if I began to talk, I'd start remembering what had happened to me.

Feeling motivated by this prospect, I began working with a

physical therapist to retrain my muscles, and by the end of the second week, I was out of the wheelchair and conversing with the staff. The doctors were amazed by my rapid recovery. Apparently, I had been an 11 on the Glasgow Coma Scale, a score that made it probable I would survive and make a full recovery, but likely that I would sustain some permanent physical and cognitive impairments. However, the doctors weren't seeing any evidence of this. In fact, I was speaking normally and had transferred to crutches by the beginning of the third week. Dr. Gupta said it usually took months of recuperation before a coma patient could walk and talk on her own, but my body seemed to be working overtime to restore all my functions.

"You're an interesting case study," she said. "You were in a coma for three weeks, but you showed extraordinary activity in your right frontal lobe. We usually don't see that."

"What's the right frontal lobe?" I asked, my voice still sounding strange to my ears.

"It's the part of your brain responsible for creativity and imagination. It's very rare for it to be so active during a comatose state. We're all very curious what was going on in there while you were under," she said, tapping the side of my head.

Despite some reservations, Dr. Gupta decided to release me after only three weeks of recovery in the hospital. Although I was fit enough to leave, she wanted me to make up any schoolwork from home and not return to Lockwood until after the winter break. That way, my dad and Barbara could keep an eye on me and make sure I didn't have a relapse.

The next few weeks were rigorous as I made up the work I had missed, worked on my *Jane Eyre* essay, and met with the physical therapist. Since life for a fisherman is slow in the winter, my dad had picked up some construction jobs and was gone five or six days a week. Barbara had offered to work from home so she could look after me. I tried to stay out of Barbara's way, but she insisted on checking up on me about every five minutes, cell phone attached to her ear, big hair bouncing, phony smile gleaming. I couldn't wait to get back to school.

Michelle called every few days to keep me up to date on my assignments and all the Lockwood gossip. The one person she didn't mention was Owen.

Finally I asked her, "What's the deal with you and Owen? Don't you like him anymore?"

"It's not a question of like," she said. "He's just so . . . immature. He's always hanging out with that kid Flynn, who I really can't stand, and he doesn't have any idea what he wants to do with his life. He actually thinks he's going to roam around Europe with his guitar after he graduates. I mean, come on. Grow up already."

"Hey," I said, "just because you're on the fast track to MIT and a career in astrophysics doesn't mean the rest of us have it all figured out."

"I know," she said. "It's not just that. I'm uncomfortable with this whole training thing."

"What do you mean? It's so nice of Mr. Mabry to sponsor you."

"Yeah, but you know I don't like owing people."

"I'm sure Owen doesn't see it like that."

"It just makes me feel like I'm indebted to him in some way. Like I'm his charity case."

I knew what she meant, but sometimes the chip on Michelle's shoulder was so big it blinded her from seeing a good thing for what it was.

In mid-December, I had a follow-up appointment with Dr. Gupta. My dad and Barbara had been acting strange around me for the past week, but I'd written it off as pre-Christmas jitters. When we arrived at Dr. Gupta's office, it seemed my intuition had been right.

While we were talking, a middle-aged man in a tweed sports coat and khakis entered the room, introducing himself as Dr. Reese. He took a seat by us and smiled at me. Something about his face reminded me of a fish. "The reason I brought Dr. Reese here today," Dr. Gupta said, "is that your parents have expressed some concern about your mental health."

"My mental health?" I looked at my dad, whose eyes were fixed firmly on the floor.

"I'm sorry," Dr. Gupta said, smiling kindly. "I know that term must be a little alarming. It's just that after a traumatic experience like the one you've had, many people become depressed and start exhibiting uncharacteristic behaviors in order to cope."

I turned to my father. "Have I been showing uncharacteristic behaviors?" I asked.

"No, honey," Barbara said. I hated that she was answering for him. "We're just worried about you. Since you've woken from the coma, it's like you're a different person. You seem empty and disconnected, like you're all locked up inside yourself."

I felt like a wounded zoo animal, with four adults staring at me from outside the bars. "I'm fine," I said. "It's just, I miss my friends. I want to get back to school." That wasn't entirely true. I had been feeling empty lately, like something was missing. Something I couldn't put my finger on.

"I'd like to schedule an appointment with you," Dr. Reese said.

"And you're . . . a psychologist?" I said.

"A psychiatrist."

"So you think I might be depressed or something?"

"Not necessarily," he said. "There's a stigma associated with psychiatric therapy, but believe me, it's very common. All I want to do is talk to you. Get a sense of how you've been coping since the accident. You might find it liberating to talk to someone about your experiences."

"But I don't remember anything."

"The therapy might help."

"Are you going to hypnotize me?"

"No, nothing like that. Sometimes, in the act of talking, memories come back. Think of this as another step in your recovery. Just like you need physical therapy to help you regain your physical balance, you need mental therapy to help you regain your mental balance." I glanced at my father for support, but his eyes were still cast downward.

This was Barbara's idea, I knew it. She wanted desperately to find something wrong with me, to prove that I really was "troubled." I was so tired of my father taking her side, of him not standing up for me. And even though I was feeling pressure from all fronts to buckle under, I refused to consent to an appointment. Not yet, not when I'd barely had time to make sense of things myself. I certainly wasn't going to talk to some stranger about it.

Then again, my father was the one I really wanted to talk to, and he'd been a stranger to me for years.

CHAPTER 14

Grandma Mackie came over on Christmas Eve, and we all sat by the tree, drinking eggnog and listening to Christmas carols and trying to act festive. Barbara made dinner: butternut squash soup, citrus-rubbed pork loin, and garlic mashed potatoes. What actually ended up on the table were four bowls of orange sludge, blackened hockey pucks, and some piles of white potato-flavored paste. My dad and I gritted our teeth and moved our food around our plates so it looked like we had eaten.

That night I couldn't sleep—either residual effects of believing in Santa Claus or the fact that I was still starving. I got out of bed and went downstairs to make myself a snack, nearly screaming when I turned on the light and saw my grandma at the table.

"Laura?" she said. She'd been sitting in the dark with a drink, staring into space.

"No, Grandma, it's me, Emma."

"Oh." Her eyes were cloudy, almost opaque.

"What are you doing?" I said.

"Thinking." I studied her face. There was something distant and disturbing about her expression. "She just left the house and walked right into the ocean," she said, muttering to herself.

"What?"

"It was her birthday."

"Grandma, are you talking about me? About the time I went swimming last August?"

She wouldn't answer, but she seemed like she was going to cry. "I should have stopped you," she said finally.

"Grandma, you couldn't have stopped me. You didn't even know I'd gone." A tear escaped onto her cheek. "Grandma, look. I'm here now. And I'm fine."

"I should have stopped you," she said again, and I wondered just how many old-fashioneds she'd had. "I should have listened. We never talked. I didn't know."

"You didn't know what, Grandma?" She stared at me, like she was recognizing me for the first time, and I felt a little frightened for her. Grandma had always been a bit eccentric, but her behavior now verged on full-blown senility.

"I didn't know how sad you were," she said.

"I'm not sad, Grandma."

"I never asked." She looked down at the table, lost in her thoughts.

"Come on, let me take you back to bed," I said. I helped her up from her chair and took her back to the den and got her situated on the pullout couch. Then I kissed her good night, made myself a Pop-Tart, and took it upstairs to my room.

The whole conversation left me feeling unsettled. I didn't want to lose my grandmother to dementia. There were few enough people in the world who really knew me and understood me. If my grandma stopped recognizing me, I didn't know what I'd do.

The rest of Christmas week was unbearable, as I was still feeling pretty listless and empty. And despite wanting to be mature, I continued to hold a grudge against my dad for allowing Barbara to steamroll him about the psychiatrist. Thankfully, the Newmans came to visit on New Year's Day, giving us a welcome distraction from the humorless drama playing out in our home. I was nervous about seeing Gray again, especially as Michelle kept telling me that something had happened between us that night at the bonfire, something I couldn't remember.

"Oh, sweetie," Simona said when I met her at the door on crutches. "Look at you. How are you feeling?"

"I'm all right," I said.

She came inside and gave me a big hug. When she released me, I lost my balance for just a moment. Gray caught me by the elbow and propped me back up. I smiled shyly, feeling awkward in his presence.

"Simona, thanks so much for the flowers you sent to the hospital," I said, testing out the theory I'd had. "They were—"

"I didn't send flowers," Simona said. I looked at her, perplexed.

"Gray did!" Anna said. "I helped him pick 'em out."

"Oh," I said, glancing at Gray, whose face was infuriatingly impassive. "Well done. They were beautiful."

"Hey, Em, can I try your crutches?" she said, already bored by the flower discussion.

I sat down on the sofa and handed my crutches to Anna, who placed them under her arms and tried to walk. She ended up just dragging them behind her like faulty wings. Gray picked her up and placed her on my crutches so she was dangling by her armpits. "Ouch," she said. "Crutches hurt." Gray and I laughed.

Simona joined my parents in the kitchen, and Gray turned to me and smiled strangely. He seemed a little nervous too.

"How are you feeling?" he asked.

"Everyone keeps asking me that. I guess I'm fine. It's just this stupid walking thing that's a problem."

"Do you want to practice on the beach?" Anna asked, looking very earnest.

"No, thanks."

"Why not?" Gray said.

"Um, because it's January."

"It's not that cold out," Anna said.

I looked down at her hopeful face, unable to come up with a good excuse. "All right, I guess. Let's go for a walk."

I didn't really feel like sitting around the table drinking coffee and listening to Barbara blather on about the real estate market anyway. Lately, she'd been obsessed with her new project, which involved tearing down the old cottages on Cedar Point and building an upscale condo community. I could already hear her telling Simona, "I thought of the perfect name, Mansions on the Mer. Isn't that fabulous?" I popped my head in the dining room and told them we were taking Anna for a walk on the beach. Simona smiled at me, but Barbara didn't even skip a beat in her story.

It wasn't exactly warm outside—forty degrees at most— and the sun was trying to burn its way through a thick layer of clouds. I loped along next to Gray on my crutches while Anna ran on ahead of us. I felt a little self-conscious since neither of us was saying anything. When we got to the end of the block, Anna was already scrambling over the dunes. Gray followed me as I hobbled onto the beach.

The water and sky were virtually the same silver color, and the ocean looked so wild and dangerous I couldn't imagine ever wanting to swim in it again. At the same time, the roar of the surf and the smell of salt water made me a little giddy. I'd been cooped up inside the house for far too long with virtually no contact with the outside world.

Anna was playing that game where you stand as close to the surf as possible, then run away when a wave sweeps in. Gray sat farther up the beach, and I stood with my back to him, staring out at the fuzzy horizon, thinking back to that sailboat I'd watched last summer. I turned around to find him staring at me.

"Come sit," he said, patting the spot next to him.

"I'm not a dog," I said.

"I wasn't implying that you were," he said, laughing. "I just want some company." I shrugged my shoulders and hopped over to where he was, attempting to sit down next to him, but falling onto him instead. He laughed as I tried to recover.

"See why I didn't want to sit down?"

"I thought you just didn't want to sit next to me."

"You're right." I gave him a teasing smile.

And then at the same time we both said: "Cooties."

"Jinx!" I said, making him laugh.

It felt good to be on the beach with him, joking and laughing like we were kids again. He must have been feeling nostalgic, too, because he said, "Hey, do you remember those play dates we used to have when we were little?"

"Yeah."

"Our moms would always try to get us to play together, but you'd always be off climbing a tree or reading a book. I'd ask if I could play with you, and you'd shriek and run away."

"I didn't trust you."

"You didn't trust me?" he said, making a falsely indignant face.

"Well, you did punch me in the nose."

"True," he said, chuckling and looking down at the sand. "And what about now? Do you trust me now?"

"I don't know yet."

He glanced over at me, his eyes narrowed. "You don't think much of me, do you?"

I weighed my next words carefully. "I know you have a history."

"A history of what?"

"Of being a player."

"Ancient history," he said. He turned his gaze toward the

water and clenched his jaw. "I'm not who you think I am, Townsend."

I squinted up at him, blocking out the sun with my hand. "Why do you care what I think of you anyway?"

"I don't know. I guess I want you to like me."

My heart swelled. "I do like you," I said, my voice faltering. "It's just, we're so different."

He turned to face me, touching my wrist for a second, then pulling away like my skin had burned him. "You really think we're that different?" he said.

"Yeah, I do."

"Why?"

"Because I spend my free time with my head in a book, and you . . . spend your free time with your head in a beer bong."

"Not fair," he said, laughing. "I told you, I don't do that anymore."

I rolled my eyes. "Come on, Gray, I've heard the stories."

"That's all they are, Townsend. Stories. You believe too much in stories."

A memory surfaced suddenly: Gray standing over me, bending down to look at my necklace. The heat from his body had felt like fire. His lips had been inches from mine. He was about to kiss me, and . . . oh God. I had pushed him away, hadn't I? Why had I done that? I would have given anything for him to try and kiss me now.

"Hey, do you remember the last time our moms took us to Six Flags?" I said.

"Yeah." He got a sad look on his face, possibly remembering that it was the last time he saw my mother alive.

"I was finally tall enough to ride the roller coaster."

"Barely."

"Shut up!" I said, laughing. He turned to me and smiled, and I noticed how unusually green his eyes looked.

Gray and I had sat in the first car of the roller coaster, our moms right behind us in the next car. I remembered that nervous thrill I'd felt as we approached the top, the clicking sounds marking the increments of our ascent. I had looked over at Gray right before we reached the summit, and he'd grabbed my hand for just a second as we crested the peak, right before my heart lurched up into my throat.

I looked down at the sand now and saw that our hands were almost touching. All I'd have to do was move mine two inches.

"Your mom was so cool," he said.

"You remember her?"

"Of course."

"Because sometimes I feel like I'm forgetting her. I can't even remember her funeral. Isn't that strange?"

"Not really. You were pretty young when it happened."

"Do you remember it?"

"I remember that my mom read a poem. Something about not being sad that someone had died. But she was crying the whole time she read it."

We both fell silent. I liked that Gray knew how to be quiet with me. "Well, they were like sisters," I said.

"I used to wish they were," Gray said. "I used to wish that we all lived together, your family and mine."

"Really?"

For a minute, I imagined what it would have been like to grow up in Gray's house, to eat meals with his family around the kitchen table, to roll down that enormous hill behind their house, to help Anna with her homework, to watch Gray walking shirtless through the hallway at night. Whoa. Bad idea.

"My parents seemed so much happier when your mom was around," he said. "Like she made them forget they were supposed to be fighting all the time. Your mom made everyone smile."

I nodded. "She did make people smile," I said. "But there were other times. Times when she could be so sad. Times she didn't want to be with anyone, including me." *Where did that memory come from?*

"But everyone has times like that," Gray said. "Times when you need to get away from the world. When you think they'd all be better off without you." I snuck a glance at him, and his eyes had gone wistful again. "Like your sweet sixteen party," he said.

"Oh, thanks so much for bringing that up. A day that will live in infamy."

"No, seriously," he said, trying not to laugh. He was attempting to make a point. "You were having one of those moments then. Why else would you have decided to leave your own party?"

"I don't know. I was just feeling . . . sad." I studied his expression, trying to guess what he was thinking.

"Don't you think that's a strange way to feel during your birthday party?"

"What are you, my shrink now?"

"No, it's just I understood how you felt. I was worried about you. When I found out what happened at the beach, I kept wanting to call you to make sure you were all right, but I never did." *Damn it. Why didn't you?*

"Why didn't you call, Gray?" I asked, emboldened by his unexpected intimacy.

He looked out to the water, squinting. "I don't know. I guess I felt like I had no right."

"No right? You've known me your entire life. If anyone had the right, it was you."

He nodded glumly. "And then I saw you again. On Halloween."

"Another fond memory. Actually, it's not even a memory. I can barely remember that night." I drew a circle in the sand with my finger, feeling a fresh wave of humiliation.

"You really don't remember anything?"

"Only what people have told me," I lied, tugging on my necklace. "Why, what's your version?"

He inhaled deeply. "Well, you came to the bonfire with your friend Michelle, and you guys were hanging out with some Braeburn hippies."

I laughed. "And . . . ?"

"And then you and I went for a walk. . . ."

"And . . . ?"

He looked over at me, and for the first time, Gray Newman seemed a little flustered. He bit the inside of his cheek. "And then, nothing," he said. "You told me you wanted to leave, and then you went running back to that Owen guy."

"He's not 'that Owen guy,' and I'm pretty sure I didn't go running back to anyone."

"You kind of did. You guys seemed pretty tight that night."

"We're friends, that's all. And he's not a hippie. He's a really nice guy."

"I'm sure he is," he said, irritation in his voice.

"You'd like him if you got to know him." Gray didn't respond to this, just looked straight ahead grinding his teeth.

Then he said, "Is he taking you to the Snow Ball?" and I almost choked. *Gray Newman knows about the Snow Ball?*

"No. Why would you think that?"

"I don't know. Seeing as he's such a nice guy and all."

"Like I said, we're just friends. Besides, he's got a thing for Michelle."

Gray rubbed his hands together and blew warm air onto them. It had gotten colder in the last half hour, and my legs were feeling damp from the sand. "It's just, I thought I might see you there. I'm going with Elise."

"Elise?" My voice had gone high and cartoon-like again. I adjusted it and said very calmly, "I thought you two broke up."

"We did. We're just going *as friends*." He emphasized those last words, teasing me.

"Well, good for you."

"Really?" he said, looking disappointed.

"Yeah. It's good that you can be mature about these things."

"Hmm."

"What?"

"I don't know. The whole 'going as friends' thing is tricky."

"What do you mean?"

"I mean, once you've been with someone, it's almost impossible to think of them as just a friend."

"Oh, right," I said. *Once you've been with someone.* What did that mean anyway? Had Gray slept with Elise? The thought made me nauseous.

All I could imagine was Gray dancing with Elise at the Snow Ball, her head on his shoulder, his hands running through her hair, any thoughts of being "just friends" a distant memory for them both.

"It's getting cold," I said. "We should be getting back."

"Already?" He looked surprised. Then his jovial mood disappeared entirely. "Where's Anna?" His voice was deep and urgent.

"I don't know. She was here just a minute ago."

He bolted up from the sand and spun around. I scrambled onto my crutches and watched as he ran to the water's edge, peering out in all directions. Frantically, he began calling her name, scanning the beach for any sign of her. I was searching, too, but a misty haze had settled over the beach, obscuring our vision.

Gray's face went pale. He was sick with worry. "Anna!" he was screaming. "Anna!"

"It's okay," I said, trying to reassure him. "She can't have gone far. We'll find her."

At that moment, I saw a flicker of pink far down the beach. Gray ran toward the form, and I followed behind as quickly as I could move. When Anna reached us, she was obviously upset and completely out of breath. Gray lit into her like I'd never seen him.

"Goddammit, Anna!" he shouted. "Don't you ever walk off like that again! You scared the hell out of me."

Anna looked like she was about to cry. I took her under my arm and hugged her. "It's okay," I said, patting her back.

"I was chasing a dog," she said breathlessly. "I didn't know I went so far. And then I didn't see you, and I got scared."

"It's all right, you're here now," I said.

Gray's eyes were burning. Anna looked up at me, her lower lip quivering. We watched as Gray stalked off the beach, muttering to himself, and followed him at a safe distance. Anna's disappearance had cast a pall over the entire afternoon, and Gray's fleeting happy mood seemed to vanish along with the last of the sunshine.

The Newmans didn't stay long after that; the forecast was predicting snow, and Simona wanted to get a jump on the storm. From my bedroom window, I watched the snow fall—first in flurries, then in fat flakes that stuck to the ground. By ten o'clock, there were four inches on the ground. The world outside looked like a giant snow globe.

And I was the tiny figure stuck inside, waiting for my moment to escape.

CHAPTER 15

After winter break, my dad and I picked up Michelle at her aunt's place on our way back to Lockwood. Michelle's aunt Darlene lived in a section of Boston that was sort of a "Little Haiti"—lots of Haitian restaurants and churches and businesses. Darlene invited us up to her apartment for coffee and put out an elaborate tray of pastries from Bec d'Or. Pronounced like "back door," Bec d'Or was Darlene's bakery, named for the golden sweet potato rolls she baked in the shape of birds' beaks. The name was also a play on words because to enter the shop, you had to walk down an alley to get to the back door.

We all sat down in the living room, and Darlene put out a rich butter cake made with rum, pineapples, and pecans, along with a tray of sweet potato crepes that were so good I couldn't stop eating them. Since my crutches were in plain view, conversation inevitably turned to my accident, and my father filled in Darlene on all the gory details.

"You're lucky to be alive, child," she said. And then she squinted at me. "You wear a dragonfly on your neck?"

My eyes dropped to my chest. "Oh, yeah. It was my mother's." I pulled the pendant out to show her.

"It's beautiful," she said. "You know, the dragonfly is the essence of the crossroads."

"The crossroads?"

She nodded. "The dragonfly lives in two realms. It lives underwater first, then it climbs out of the sea and takes flight. Some say it contains the spirit of our loved ones." Darlene moved closer to inspect the design. "It looks like Papa Legba's vévé, no?" she said to Michelle.

Michelle rolled her eyes. "Aunt Dar, Emma doesn't believe in voodoo."

"Voodoo?" my father said, looking half-alarmed, half-amused.

"My aunt practices Haitian folk magic," Michelle said.

"Not magic," Darlene said. "Religion."

"If you say so," Michelle said.

"What's a vay vay?" I asked.

"Vévé," Darlene corrected me. "It's a symbol used to attract the loa, or the spirits, back to earth. It acts as a beacon. Your dragonfly looks like Papa Legba's vévé. Papa Legba stands at the spiritual crossroads. He speaks all human language, and he opens and closes the doorway to the dead."

"So he's like a god?" I said.

"More a spirit guide. But you'll know him if you see him. He wears a brimmed hat and carries a cane, and he always has his dog with him. Legba loves his dog." She issued a deep, throaty laugh, like she was remembering an old family friend who amused her.

Michelle frowned at my dad and me apologetically. "My aunt believes Papa Legba can communicate with the dead and bring us in touch with our ancestors. She claims to have spoken to my mother through him."

"I have," Darlene said, clicking her tongue. "Michelle has no faith. That's why she never sees her mama. But I see Marie. I talk with her all the time."

"Yeah," Michelle said, rolling her eyes. "Apparently they fight about me."

Darlene rolled her eyes in the same way Michelle had.

"Her mama wants her to ride again, but I say no. I already lost a sister to the horses. I don't want to lose you, too."

"But you always said Mama watches over me," Michelle said, challenging her aunt.

"And she does. But she can only protect you from the evil things of her world, not of this one. I'll bet Emma's mama gives her protection from the evil things, too. Were you wearing that necklace when you had your accident?"

I looked up, surprised that the conversation had shifted back to me. "Oh, you mean when I got struck by lightning? Yeah, I was."

"See, that's your mama's way of protecting you," she said. "It wasn't your time to die. You keep that necklace close, you hear?"

When we left Darlene's apartment, Michelle apologized again, embarrassed by her aunt's superstitions. My dad seemed mildly unsettled by the whole discussion, but I was fascinated.

"So you don't believe any of it?" I asked Michelle.

"It's just a lot of hocus pocus about gods and spirits. You know I'm not a religious person. Science is my religion."

I wasn't a religious person either, but I wanted to believe.

The next two months at Lockwood crawled at the pace of a prison sentence. Things felt strained between Michelle and me, almost like they had at the beginning of the year. But we both kept busy, Michelle with her equestrian training and community service at the shelter, me with my schoolwork.

But school was a huge adjustment for me. Everything on campus seemed too intense, the colors too saturated, the noises too amplified. My thoughts were drowned out in a constant barrage of TV, radio, and inane chitchat over cell phones. I was in a constant state of sensory overload. I longed to get away from the teeming hallways, the crowded classrooms, the competition and cattiness. But of course, I couldn't walk, and therefore, couldn't escape.

Somehow, I managed to finish a draft of the *Jane Eyre* essay for the symposium and e-mailed it to Mr. Gallagher for feedback. And while I thought the paper had achieved the voice Gallagher was looking for, I wasn't entirely happy with my thesis. Yes, Jane was a strong female role model, a heroine to be admired for her character and integrity. But something about the ending of the novel wasn't sitting right with me. Jane and Rochester got their happy ending, but it came at the expense of several other characters. I couldn't help but think that if I'd been in Jane's place, I might have done things differently.

As the weeks went on, I couldn't get *Jane Eyre* out of my head. Thornfield haunted my dreams. At night, I walked the moors, seeking solitude. Pilot followed me down dark hallways, and Mrs. Fairfax hovered over her sewing by the firelight. Adèle joked with me in French, and Mr. Rochester called to me like a lover. I'd wake up in the middle of the night, sweat-soaked and agitated, feeling the dream ebb away from me and missing it profoundly, wishing I could live in that world instead of my own.

One day in French class, we were reading excerpts from Baudelaire's poetry, and Madame Favier asked if anyone would like to read "L'albatros" aloud to the class. Before any other hands went up, I got the strongest conviction that I could do it.

Madame and the rest of the class stared at me in astonishment when I volunteered and continued gaping as I read the lines flawlessly, *in French*. Not only was my pronunciation perfect, but I understood every word. The poem was about an albatross caught by some sailors who made fun of him because his wings were too large to allow him to walk properly. Baudelaire compared the albatross to the poet, once elevated by his own ideas and words, now exiled on earth as an object of ridicule and scorn.

Madame stood silent for several moments after I finished

reading, then clapped her hands. "Incroyable!" she said. "C'est presque parfait." *Almost perfect.*

But as my mental agility was surging, my physical agility was plunging. The weather had turned bitterly cold, and the campus was icy. I felt so unsure of myself on my crutches, like a newborn foal getting used to its legs. At times, it seemed like I didn't belong in my own skin, like I was wearing a body that didn't fit me anymore.

On my way to English class on Wednesday, I slipped on a patch of ice. I was struggling to right myself when a large shadow appeared overhead. I looked up to see Mr. Gallagher's figure looming above me.

"I fell," I said, stupidly stating the obvious.

"I can see that," he said, stooping down to help me up. "Where's your other half to help you?"

"Michelle? She's coming from gym." Our phys ed elective had switched from equestrian studies to swimming for second term. Thankfully, I was being excused on account of my legs. That, and the fact that I didn't know if I'd ever swim again.

"Let me carry your book bag," he said, smiling, as we walked together to class. "How are you adjusting back to school, Emma?"

"Fine," I lied.

He reached down and drew something out of his messenger bag. "I had a chance to read your essay," he said, tapping the front page. "Very impressive."

"Really?"

"It surprised me, actually. Almost like it had come from a different place inside you. You usually sit so quietly in class, never speaking. But here, in your essay, there's this powerful voice. There is *life*."

When he punched that last word, I got the strongest sense of déjà vu, so powerful that I stopped in my tracks. "Is everything okay?" he said, pausing on the path beside me.

Where had I heard those words before? *There you sit, so small and sedate, so mouselike and quiet. But here, on the page, there is life.* I examined Gallagher's face—the noble brow, the dark eyes, the wild hair. Oh my God.

A blast of icy wind roared past me, and my time at Thornfield came back to me in one wild rush. I almost lost my balance from the torrent of memories. "Emma, are you okay?"

"What?" I said, shaking my head.

"Maybe I should take you to the infirmary. You look unwell."

"No, I'm fine, I'm fine," I said. "I've already missed too much class."

He took my arm and helped get me going on my crutches again, and I limped beside him in a daze. All the memories were suddenly back—my stunned arrival in the stables, meeting Adèle and Mrs. Fairfax, the strange laughter on the third floor, the party with Miss Ingram, the fire, Mr. Mason. And of course, Mr. Rochester. Standing next to me now was my Mr. Rochester, in the flesh.

"Here we are," Mr. Gallagher said as we arrived at the classroom.

"Thanks," I muttered, still feeling rattled.

"My pleasure." He took my hand in his and held it for a few seconds—gripped it, actually—then released.

I hopped to my seat, placed my crutches on the floor beneath my desk, and tried to catch my breath. Michelle arrived about ten minutes late. Elise glared at her as she slipped into the seat next to me. I handed Michelle my notebook so she could see the notes she'd missed. Gallagher was introducing a new unit today.

"The Gothic novel," he said, "aims to evoke terror through its use of an eerie setting and supernatural occurrences. A classic example would be Ann Radcliffe's *The Mysteries of Udolpho*. Radcliffe introduces readers to the Byronic hero, a brooding male character with a mysterious past who plays foil to the shy, respectable heroine. Another example is Char-lotte Brontë's *Jane Eyre*. Emma is reading it for her research paper. Do you want to tell the class how it fits the Gothic mode?" he asked, staring directly at me.

"Sure," I said, spurred on by a newfound confidence. "*Jane Eyre* is about a young, penniless orphan who becomes a governess for a mysterious man named Rochester. She moves into his mansion on the moors and falls in love with him. But she doesn't know that he hides a terrible secret on the third floor." Some of the girls snickered at the dramatic premise. "The novel is full of eerie settings, evil omens, hid-den secrets and terrors, all conventions of Gothic literature."

"Thank you, Emma," he said, winking at me. I was sur-prised he'd called me Emma and not Ms. Townsend. "Proba-bly the most famous Gothic novel is the one we're about to begin today: Mary Shelley's *Frankenstein*." Muffled groans filled the classroom. "I know what you're thinking," he said. "You're picturing some tall green monster with bolts through his neck, grunting 'Fire bad, fire bad!'" A few girls laughed. "But Frankenstein isn't a monster; he's a scientist who makes a creature out of used body parts, all in an effort to push the limits of science. Dr. Frankenstein believed he could bring the dead back to life. *Frankenstein* is essentially a novel about the dangers of excessive pride in the face of nature.

"Now, Mary Shelley came up with the idea while on vaca-tion with some friends in Switzerland. Lord Byron challenged each guest to write a ghost story, and *Frankenstein* was Shel-ley's contribution. We know Shelley was inspired by the experiments of Galvani, who used artificial electricity to re-animate a frog's body parts. Shelley had surely read Galvani's treatise and thought it might be possible to use electricity to reanimate the human body and bring the dead back to life. Sounds implausible, I know, but who among us knows what's truly possible?"

He paused just long enough for Elise to say, "Why don't

you ask Emma? She's come back from the dead." I waited for the inevitable laughter, the cowardly encouragement from her peers, but when I looked around, nobody seemed to think it was very funny.

"Ms. Fairchild—" Mr. Gallagher began, about to caution her.

"No, it's okay," I said, turning to face Elise directly. "I think some form of reanimation might be possible. We all know doctors use defibrillators to jump-start a heart when it stalls. So why couldn't a giant dose of electricity have other supernatural effects? I don't necessarily believe in reanimating the body like Dr. Frankenstein does, but I do believe death isn't the end. Nature doesn't destroy matter, so why would it destroy the soul? It must go on in some other form."

Mr. Gallagher got a philosophical twinkle in his eye. "'There are more things in heaven and earth, Horatio, than are dreamt of in your philosophy,'" he said, winking at me again. *What was that about?* Blood rushed to my cheeks, and I glanced to my left to see if Michelle had caught it. "In the end, Shelley was dealing with some universal questions about humankind's place in the universe. Man often believes in his dominion over nature and all of creation. But every once in a while, nature has to kick our ass to show us who's boss."

Everyone was laughing when the bell rang, and no one even complained when Gallagher assigned us the first hundred pages of *Frankenstein* to read for next week.

"Gallagher seemed pretty fond of your response about reanimation," Michelle said as we walked out of the classroom.

"What do you mean?"

"I saw him winking at you."

I blushed. "Oh, don't be stupid."

"Weird that he didn't ask me about it, seeing as *Frankenstein* is my research topic. But I guess *I* didn't get struck by lightning."

I glared at her, incredulous. "What's with you lately?" I said, quickly losing my temper. "Do you think I enjoyed getting struck by lightning and being in a coma for three weeks?"

She glared back at me, and we walked the rest of the way in silence. When we came to the path that led to the stables, I remembered Owen was supposed to be working.

"Do you want to go see if Owen's at the barn?" I asked. I didn't really feel like going back to the dorm alone with Michelle.

"I guess," she muttered, like she was doing me a favor.

When we got to the barn, Owen was just finishing cleaning the stalls. "Owen!" I said, galloping over to him. I threw my arms around him while my crutches fell to the ground. Hugging him felt like coming home.

When he pulled away he said, "Wow, you look great."

"Thanks. I wish I could say the same for you." His hair was sticking up all over the place, and his clothes were filthy as usual. He looked so very . . . Owen.

"You really have the most terrible taste in T-shirts," Michelle said. Today's said, *Never turn your back on a cactus* and had an image of three menacing-looking cacti.

"Nice to see you, too, Michelle," he said.

Since I was on crutches, we couldn't very well go up to the loft to hang out, so Owen and I sat down on some hay bales while Michelle went to say hi to Curry. I had never seen Curry so excited to see anyone. His ears perked up at the sound of her voice, and his tail swished against his pen. He nickered as she climbed up to pat his nose, then dropped his head and closed his eyes as she stroked him, looking like he was in some kind of heavenly horse trance.

Owen asked how my physical therapy was going, and I told him my doctor thought I only had another few weeks on crutches. "And how about the amnesia?" he said. "Are you remembering anything?"

"Actually, can I tell you guys something weird?"

"Sure," Owen said. "I love weird."

I told them both about the rush of memories I'd just experienced on the path with Gallagher and filled them in on the details of my *Jane Eyre* dream. They listened with rapt expressions. It felt so good to finally tell someone who wasn't getting paid to listen.

"Cool!" Owen said when I finished my story.

"But that's not the weirdest part. You know how French used to be my worst subject? Well, it turns out I'm fluent now."

"What do you mean, *fluent?*" Michelle said.

"Je peux parler français aussi bien que tu peux," I said with the perfect accent. *I can speak French as well as you can.*

Michelle's jaw dropped. "No. Way."

"Oui."

"Actually," Owen said, "I've heard about stuff like this."

"Instantaneous language acquisition?"

"No, lightning strike survivors. They can get special powers after their accident—photographic memory, telekinesis, the ability to communicate with the dead."

"Oooh, spooky," Michelle said in a melodramatic voice.

"Nothing about jumping into the plot of the book they're reading and becoming the main character?" I said.

"No. But if you really believe you lived Jane's life, reading and speaking French every day, it's not outlandish to think you'd come back fluent, is it?"

"I don't know," I said. "It's pretty out there."

"It's awesome! You're, like, a superhero."

"Did you say Mr. Gallagher was your Rochester?" Michelle asked.

"Yeah, and Madame Favier was Mrs. Fairfax. And, ugh, Elise Fairchild was Blanche Ingram." My stomach sank at the sound of Elise's name because I'd just remembered Gray was taking her to the Snow Ball.

"Hey," I said. "Not to change the subject, but what do you guys think about the Snow Ball?"

Michelle groaned. "That it's a stupid tradition, and I wouldn't be caught dead going."

"I think," Owen countered, "that despite its uninspired name, it could be fun. I went my freshman year and had a blast."

"You went your freshman year?" Michelle said. "With who?"

"Bree Harmon. She graduated two years ago."

"You went with a senior when you were a freshman?" Michelle said. She sounded a little jealous.

"Yeah, Emma's not the only one who falls for the older type." He punched me playfully in the arm. "You know what we could do?" he said, as if reading my mind. "Go together, the three of us?"

"As in a threesome?" Michelle said. "Your schoolboy fantasy?"

"That's not what I meant. I mean, go as friends."

"Yeah," I said. "It might be fun to get dressed up."

"Come on, Michelle. You'll get to see me in a tux," Owen said, waggling his eyebrows. "This could be a once-in-a-lifetime opportunity. What do you say?"

We both looked at her hopefully. "But I don't have a dress."

"So we'll go shopping," I said.

"I have no money."

"I'll buy you a dress," Owen said.

"No!" She spat out the word, and Owen recoiled. "If I agree to go, I'll buy my own dress."

"Maybe we can take the train to Boston next weekend and go shopping at some of those consignment stores in Back Bay," I offered. She shrugged, like I was twisting her arm.

"Excellent," Owen said. "It's a date. A double date." He grinned, revealing his dimples.

"I'm going to take Curry out for a ride," Michelle said abruptly.

We both stared at her. "Right now?" I asked.

But she was already inside Curry's pen, saddling him up. Moments later, she led Curry out of the barn and trotted him out to the riding ring, running him through some exercises—circles and serpentines and small jumps. After months of training together, they made it look effortless.

"What's with her lately?" I asked Owen once she was out of earshot. "She seems so angry all the time."

"I don't know. I guess she's dealing with a lot. The training's been rough on her, and she's been working with all these single mothers at the homeless shelter. I think it's dredged up some old feelings. She's been talking about finding her father."

"Really?" I felt crushed that I didn't know this.

"She needs something right now. Something I can't give her."

I stuck my lip out in sympathy and put an arm around him. He sighed and let his head drop momentarily onto my shoulder. "If it makes you feel any better, she hasn't been very nice to me either," I said.

"She's just jealous."

"Jealous? Of what?"

Owen twisted his mouth like he was trying to understand it himself. "Probably all the attention you've been getting since the accident."

"Believe me, I don't want any of it."

"I know. But sometimes I think Michelle wouldn't mind trading places with you."

I scrunched my face and turned my attention to the riding ring, watching Michelle and Curry glide over a fence like they were flying. I glanced down at my own legs that couldn't even remember how to walk. "Why on earth would Michelle want to trade places with me? She's brilliant, gorgeous—"

"So are you," he said unexpectedly. I thought I saw the faintest flush in his cheeks. He bit his lip and stared down at the ground.

I cocked my head and looked at him again, seeing Owen in a very different light. Since I'd come out of the coma, I'd had this nagging feeling I'd been trying to ignore, but now it felt so obvious. And if my hunch was true, it explained the tension I'd been feeling from Michelle.

I peered across the riding ring and watched Michelle bring Curry to a sudden halt, yanking on his reins harder than usual, yanking like someone who feared she might be losing her grip.

CHAPTER 16

"That color would look great on you," I said, pointing to a cranberry red strapless gown with a knee-length skirt. We had taken the commuter train into Boston, where we found a consignment shop that sold cocktail and prom dresses, all for under fifty dollars. "Try it on."

"What about you?" she said, scanning the aisles. "I'm picturing Audrey Hepburn in *Roman Holiday*. Sweet and innocent." She rummaged through the racks, choosing an off-white satin dress with an empire waist and a chiffon skirt. I held up a black velvet dress with a matching scarf. "Uh-uh," she said, shaking her head at my selection. "This one. Trust me."

We went into the dressing room, which had large unflattering mirrors and no drapes or doors. I leaned my crutches against the wall and changed carefully, somehow managing to get the Audrey Hepburn dress over my head. Michelle secured the row of fifteen tiny buttons on the back, then moved me so I was in the center of the mirror. She drew my hair behind me and wound it into a bun, then held it there while I studied myself in the mirror. It was a strange transformation. I looked like a ballerina or a Russian princess.

I sighed, thinking of Gray's broad swimmer's body and what it might look like straining against a tuxedo jacket. I was so angry with myself. On Halloween, he had almost kissed me. And I had fled, like I always did when things got too real for me. I preferred my love at a distance—a crush on a teacher or, better yet, on a fictional character. And now it was too late. I'd pushed Gray right into Elise's arms.

Michelle and I made our purchases, then took the Red Line to Aunt Darlene's. When we emerged from the subway and onto the street, the neighborhood seemed right in the middle of a Mardi Gras celebration. Most of the restaurants had colorful signs boasting food and festivities, and the famous Mardi Gras beads dangled from bare tree branches everywhere. As we passed a Caribbean restaurant, the scents of citrus and grilled meats wafted out the door. My stomach grumbled.

We walked up to Darlene's second-flood apartment, and she greeted us warmly with hugs and repeated pleas for us to sit down and relax. We took off our coats and settled in the living room, the smell of fresh baked bread in the air.

Darlene had made us nonalcoholic Cremas, which tasted like coconut milk shakes. She also brought out some pumpkin fritters and fried plantains as appetizers. I scarfed down two fritters and three plantains while Darlene asked us about school, boys, everything. Michelle and I could barely answer one question before she'd ask another.

"Aunt Dar, slow down," Michelle said. "It's only been a month since you've seen me."

"And you," she said, looking at me. "You still on those crutches?"

"I can't seem to get my balance back."

"Well, you had quite a spell, sleeping away all that time. You need to let your waking self catch up with your dreaming self." I liked Darlene's way with words—it was almost like poetry.

"Why don't you tell Darlene about that dream you had?" Michelle said.

"What dream?" I said, giving Michelle the evil eye.

"You know, the one when you were in the coma."

Darlene fixed her eyes on me, obviously curious; there was no escaping it. "It's silly," I said. "I dreamed that I became the main character of the book I was reading, *Jane Eyre*. I was staying in this huge mansion, working for an older man and teaching his little girl English. And there was this strange woman who worked there—she had this evil laugh—and she tried to burn the house down. It sounds crazy, but it felt so real at the time. It felt like more than a dream."

Darlene leaned forward, resting her elbows on her knees. "Dreams are very powerful. The loa come to you in your dreams."

"The loa. Spirits of the dead, right?"

She nodded. "Sometimes they need to speak to you. Tell you something from the other side."

"It's weird that you say that, because I've been thinking there was something I was supposed to learn there, but I came back too soon."

"Oh, so you want to go back now?" she said.

"I don't know. Sometimes I do."

Darlene watched me intensely. "Emma, I'm gonna give you a way to invite that dream back."

"Aunt Dar," Michelle said. "The last time she had the dream, she was in a coma for three weeks. I don't think she should try to go back."

"If the girl has unfinished business, she needs to go," Darlene said, smiling. "I'm just going to give her a way to open the door again." She went to a set of drawers in the dining room and extracted a small card and handed it to me. "This is Papa Legba's calling card. You call on him, and he'll show you the way."

I flipped the card over in my hands. On one side was Papa Legba's symbol; on the other, an incantation. The words were in French, but I translated them easily: *Father Legba, open the door for me. Father Legba, open the door to let me pass through. To pass truly, loa, I give thanks to you.*

"Is it dangerous?" I said. "To pass back through the door?"

"It depends what's on the other side," Darlene said, laughing. "You keep Papa Legba happy, and you'll be safe." She touched my necklace and shook her head. "He likes rum and Coke and a good cigar after dinner. And you bring a toy for his dog. He'll take care of you." She laughed again, then moved on as if she'd forgotten all about this otherworldly talk. "You hungry?" she said. "I'm gonna fix dinner."

She walked out to the kitchen, and Michelle moved next to me. "Emma, don't mess with this stuff. You don't understand it."

"I thought you didn't believe in it."

"I don't, but it's kind of like God. I don't believe in him either, but he still scares me." The fear in her eyes made me wary. But I dismissed her concerns. I was certain I'd never go back to Thornfield.

After a feast of Haitian dishes, we watched some revelers outside on the streets forming a makeshift parade, playing rhythmic music with lots of chanting and drums. While we walked back to the T stop that night, the neighborhood seemed alive with color and music. I was sad to leave. Lockwood was a lonely place. I suddenly remembered how happy I'd been at Thornfield, how Mrs. Fairfax and Adèle had treated me like family, how Mr. Rochester had shown me such kindness and introduced me to the promise of love. I missed them all so much.

What if Thornfield was the place I truly belonged? What if Lockwood was the real dungeon, a place where I would never thrive, would never stop being a shy, helpless creature trapped by her own insecurities, hopping about on crutches instead of soaring?

We got back to school at nearly eleven o'clock and crawled into our beds without talking or watching TV. I felt the psychic pull of the dream drawing me in, so seductive that I couldn't wait to fall asleep in the hopes that I might return to it. I tucked Papa Legba's card under my pillow, too scared to recite its verses just yet, but reassured to know it was there if I ever needed it.

CHAPTER 17

For the most part, things returned to normal between Michelle and me. Every now and then, I'd catch her looking at me with a hint of resentment, wondering what I had done to bring it on. But then my fun and feisty friend would return, and the two of us would go back to being partners in crime.

The night of the Snow Ball, Owen was coming to pick us up in his father's car at seven. I was finally off my crutches and was looking forward to a night of dancing. Michelle and I both showered and stood in front of our mirrors, combing our hair, moisturizing, perfuming, applying makeup. The Snow Ball was the only major social event open to underclassmen, so we were determined to make the most of it.

Michelle put on a mix of dance songs and jazz, which only intensified my mood of nervous anticipation about seeing Gray. I knew it was foolish to get excited about seeing him—did I have to remind myself he was coming with Elise Fairchild?

"Can I give you an updo?" Michelle said.

"A what?"

"You know, pin your hair up so you look like Audrey Hepburn?"

"Yeah, right," I said.

"You don't have to pretend to be so modest all the time," she said. "You know you're pretty."

I most definitely did not know this. In fact, whenever I looked in the mirror, I was vaguely disappointed. There was nothing ugly about my face, but there was nothing exceptional about it either. My features were too small, my coloring pale with little contrast provided by my lips, and my face was, in general, too pointy. No, I did not look at myself and think the word "pretty."

"I'm not pretending to be modest," I said.

"Sorry. It's just, sometimes the whole 'innocent ingénue' thing gets old."

"What 'innocent ingénue' thing? You're the one who wants me to look like Audrey Hepburn. That's the only reason I bought this stupid dress with all these stupid buttons."

She looked mildly hurt, as she'd been the one to pick out the dress, but her insinuations were making me irritable. "If you don't like the dress, why don't you wear mine instead, and I'll wear yours?" At first I thought she was kidding, but then she shoved her dress at me. "Here. Try it on. See what you think."

"Michelle—" I pleaded, but she'd already snatched my dress and was throwing it over her head and squeezing into it. We wore about the same size, but Michelle was taller and had bigger breasts, so the dress that had looked so demure on me fell just above her knees, showing considerably more leg, and the tight-fitting bodice gave her Renaissance-era cleavage. She spun her hair up into a bun, then secured it with a silver clasp and turned to face me.

"Well?" she said.

"You look really . . . elegant." She looked like a slutty bride.

She nodded toward her red dress, implying I should try it on. Reluctantly, I slipped it over my body and slid my feet into my heels, turning to face Michelle.

"Isn't it cool to be someone else for a change?" she said. "You look really sexy in that." I wondered if she was lying, too. "Hang on a sec." She ran to her dresser and grabbed a few safety pins, then did some tucking and pinning in the back of the dress so my bodice was as tight as hers. "There," she said. "Perfect. But you can't wear those shoes anymore. And we're going to need to change your makeup."

By the time Michelle had finished with me, I did feel like a different person. She had transformed my pale little face into something warm and glowing. My lips were wine-colored to match the dress, and my eyelids were lined with smoky shadow. My hair fell in loopy curls around my shoulders like a mane. I almost didn't recognize myself.

Michelle's cell phone rang, and she looked out the window to see Owen in the parking lot, waving from his father's shiny silver car. We giggled at the sight, then grabbed our coats and headed out. The dorm hallway reeked of perfume. Girls were running around half-dressed, some with curling irons in their hair, others frowning at runs in their stockings. I felt like Cinderella awaiting her pumpkin carriage and her prince, even though a part of me knew that when the spell wore off, I'd be left in rags.

Outside the air was cold and dry, the kind that makes your lungs hurt when you breathe. Michelle and I stood shivering, white puffs of air wafting from our lips.

"You two look amazing!" Owen said, coming around to open the door for us. He was dressed in a black tux, his hair slicked back to look like a 1920s idol, like Nick Carraway or Rudolph Valentino. He stared at us and shook his head, seeming genuinely flustered by our presence. It was strange to realize we had this power over men if we chose to use it.

I let Michelle get in the front, opening the back door myself. "No, no," Owen cried. "Allow me." I waited for Owen to open the door, then gingerly crawled into the back. The interior of the car seemed cavernous and luxurious, particularly compared to my father's battered and fishy-smelling station wagon. I smoothed my hands along the plush seats.

When Owen turned the ignition, romantic piano music filled the car, and he turned back to me and smiled. "Here we go," he said, pulling away from the dorm and taking us for a drive around campus. "Michelle, there's a bottle of champagne under your seat."

"Emma can open it," she said, finding the bottle and handing it back to me.

I had never opened a bottle of champagne before, but I carefully unwound the wire cage around the cork and shook it ever so slightly as I'd watched my father do countless times on New Year's Eve. "Don't shake it too much," Owen said. "I don't want it spilling all over my dad's car."

I nudged the cork a little and directed it toward the back of the car, where it flew off, popping against the back windshield with a satisfying thwack.

"I'm such an idiot," Owen said. "I forgot glasses."

"No problem," I said. I slumped down in my seat in case any chaperones were making their way down to the Commons and took a sip. It tasted sharp and sweet, and I laughed as the bubbles went up my nose.

"Miss Innocent guzzling champagne from the bottle?" Michelle said. "I never thought I'd see the day."

She was really starting to piss me off, but I handed the bottle back to her and watched as she brazenly chugged half the bottle.

"Damn, Michelle," Owen said. "Save some for us."

She wiped her mouth with her hand and passed the bottle to Owen, who pulled the car under a bank of trees and took a small sip. "Come on," Michelle said. "You can do better than that."

"I'm driving," he said.

"Yeah, less than half a mile. Come on." He tipped the bottle back and took another sip. "You guys are no fun," Michelle said.

I was so tired of Michelle accusing me of being too innocent that I swiped the bottle from Owen and took a huge swig. The buzz went straight to my head. A minute later, I felt tingly and magical, blissfully optimistic, as if anything could happen.

Owen made a couple of circuits around the campus while we polished off the champagne, and by the time we parked in the lot behind the Commons Building, we were all feeling giddy and euphoric. Michelle leaned against Owen and teased him about his hair, and Owen's eyelids started to droop, making his eyes look even sleepier than usual. At one point he turned and smiled at me, his dimples transforming his face.

When we got out of the car, Michelle stumbled a little, and Owen caught her arm. "Hey, I thought I was the lame one here," I said.

Michelle looked at me and started to laugh. "You, my dear, are incredibly lame. You write poetry and have a crush on your English teacher."

Owen shot me an apologetic look. "Michelle, let's go inside and get you some water."

"I don't want water!" she said. "I want more champagne!" Her voice carried across the parking lot.

Other guests were arriving now, dressed in suits and tuxes, gowns and cocktail dresses. Once inside the Commons Building, we checked our coats and entered the ballroom. The planning committee had done a beautiful job with the decorations, making the conference room nearly unrecognizable. Panels of sheer organza fabric camouflaged the drop ceiling, and drifts of fake snow were piled around the perimeter of the room. Twinkly icicle lights hung at varying heights throughout the room, making it feel like we were in a real winter wonderland. The first thing I did after taking in the scenery was scope around for Gray and Elise. I didn't find them, but I did see Mr. Gallagher and Madame Favier standing by the refreshments table.

Michelle tugged on my arm and pointed, quite unsubtly, at Gallagher. "Look," she said. "Mr. Rochester's here. Do you think he'll dance with you? Will Mrs. Fairfax approve?" She erupted into horrible, uncontrollable laughter.

"Michelle," Owen said. "Shut up. He'll hear you."

"So what?" she said. "He should know that dear Emma has a crush on him. He probably still thinks that stupid journal was mine."

"What's your problem?" I said.

Michelle stood upright, straightening her dress as if she'd just realized what a bitch she was being. "Sorry," she said. "I'm just joking."

Owen took each of us on one arm, and we walked over to the photography booth where we posed for our picture. The photographer had Owen sit on a stool and made Michelle and me crouch down as if we were each whispering sweet nothings into his ear. It was all vaguely humiliating, but we tried to have fun even though nobody seemed to be enjoying themselves very much.

"Do either of you want to dance?" Owen said.

Michelle shrugged her shoulders, but I could tell she wanted to. "Take Michelle," I said. "I'm going to sit for a minute."

"You sure?" Owen asked. "All three of us can dance."

"Um, no thanks," I said.

I watched as Owen led Michelle to the dance floor. The DJ was playing a hypnotic song about the ocean. It only served to make me feel even more sorry for myself as I recalled that afternoon Gray and I had spent at the beach.

As if that memory had summoned him, Gray was suddenly standing in the doorway, Elise by his side. They strode in, surrounded by an aura that made everyone stop and stare. Gray looked tall and broad-shouldered in his tuxedo, and his face had that air of sadness to it underneath the sheen of bravado. Elise was casually elegant in a black, backless floor-length gown. Her blond hair was perfectly straight and hung like a drape against her rail-thin back. I felt tacky and foolish in Michelle's dress, and suddenly my makeup, my hair, everything seemed wrong.

I was also embarrassed to be sitting by myself like some pathetic wallflower, so when the song ended, I walked out to the dance floor. Michelle and Owen were standing apart now, and Michelle's mouth was set in a rigid line. When she saw me there, my face going three shades of pink, she spun her head around and spotted Gray and Elise by the door.

"Gray's here with Elise?" she said, her eyes taking in what a gorgeous couple they made. "So that's why you wanted to come tonight."

I bit my lip and made a sheepish expression. "I don't want him to see me all alone," I said. "Is there any way I can cut in? Just for one song, and then you can have him back."

"What am I, your boy toy?" Owen said, laughing.

"He's all yours," Michelle said, leaving without so much as a glance back.

"Is everything okay?" I asked once she was gone.

"Yeah, Michelle's just an ugly drunk."

He put his arms delicately around my waist as I wrapped my arms around his shoulders. I had never stood this close to Owen before. He smelled crisp and clean, like a forest. It was strange to be dancing with him, particularly as we were trying our hardest not to let our bodies come into actual contact, knowing Michelle was watching from the sidelines.

While we danced, I couldn't stop looking for Gray. At one point, I turned back to Owen, whose face looked hurt. "So what do you see in him?" he said.

"Gray?"

"No, in the other guy you've been giving yourself whip-lash over."

I gritted my teeth. "Sorry," I said, feeling guilty.

"You obviously like him," he said. "I'm just trying to fig-ure out why nice girls always fall for . . . bad boys."

"Gray's not as bad as you think," I said, and he raised a skeptical eyebrow. "I've known him since I was five years old, and we've always been complete opposites. So we never really took the time to get to know each other. I think we were afraid that if we did, we might actually find out we're more alike than we think."

"So, it's that whole Spencer Tracy–Katharine Hepburn thing?" he said.

"What do you mean?"

"You know, the love-hate relationship."

"Maybe. I don't know." Gray had entered the dance floor with Elise, and when I saw his eyes searching in our direc-tion, I buried my head into Owen's shoulder.

He let me stay that way for a few seconds, then said, "It's okay if you use my shoulder. It feels nice."

I glanced up at him. His face looked heartbreakingly earnest and a little flushed. I quickly pulled away.

"I'm feeling a little . . . warm," I said. "Do you mind if we sit this one out?"

"Sure," he said. "I've served my purpose."

I felt terrible, like I'd used him and he knew it. Ever the gentleman, he took my hand and escorted me off the dance floor.

When we got back to Michelle, Owen sat down next to her and tried to pull her out of her foul mood, but she refused to look at him. It felt like we were all treading on a thin sheet of ice and that at any moment, the whole thing could crack, sending us into frigid waters.

I turned to find Gray and Elise in the crowd and forced myself to watch them dance. It was strange—I knew I should have been jealous, but there was something in Gray's posture and in the distant look in his eyes that made me think he didn't really want to be here with Elise. He gave the impression of someone playing a role, an actor.

"Why don't you tell him how you feel?" Owen said, nodding to the dance floor.

"I think I'd rather die, thank you," I said.

"He might surprise you."

"You're one to talk," Michelle said in clipped syllables.

"What?"

"You know what I'm talking about," she said. "Tell her. Tell Emma what you told me."

"Michelle, I don't think this is the time."

"Come on, you were just telling Emma to bare her feelings to Gray, so what better time to—?"

"Michelle, you're drunk," Owen said.

"Oh, no, unfortunately I'm sober. And if you don't tell her, I will."

Owen stared at her, his mouth agape like he couldn't believe this was happening. "Why are you doing this, Michelle?"

"Oh, right, I'm always the bad guy." She stood up and scowled at him. "Not only do I have to accept your father's charity, but I have to deal with this, too? Do you have any idea how this makes me feel?"

People were staring now. Gray and Elise were staring. I felt helpless, like everything was spinning out of control.

"Michelle, you don't owe me or my father anything," Owen said. But she was crying now. I wanted to hug her, to talk some sense into her, but I knew I was the last person she wanted to comfort her right now. Owen tried to put an arm around her to console her, but she shrugged him off. "Michelle, let me take you back to the dorm."

"No!" she shouted. "I want to be alone."

She walked away from us, lurching into a run as she got closer to the door. Owen ran after her. I didn't know what to do. This entire ugly scene had taken place in full view of the entire student body of Lockwood. I was moving toward the door, determined to catch up with them when I heard a gravelly voice behind me.

"Let them go," the voice said. I turned around and saw Mr. Rochester, in all his brooding glory. I felt a sudden rush of emotion that nearly knocked me off my feet as I took in his rangy physique, his untamed hair, the stunning planes of his face. I had to remind myself that this was Mr. Gallagher, my English teacher, not the romantic figure of my wildest dreams, not the fictional character I'd saved from a burning bed.

"They're my friends," I managed to say. "I should go with them."

"Don't worry," he said in a gentle but authoritative voice. "They'll work it out on their own."

He was probably right. I'd already gotten in the way once tonight. I cursed myself for having cut in on Michelle and Owen, for letting my fragile ego get the best of me.

Mr. Gallagher put a firm hand on my back and led me back into the hall. It was all I could do not to collapse into his arms crying. He led me to a chair and got me a soda, then sat down across from me. "Do you want to talk about it?" he said. I was stifling tears, and I knew if I tried to speak, the dam would break. I shook my head and took a sip of soda.

Mr. Gallagher noticed a tear that had escaped. He reached out gently to catch it with one finger, then took an old-fashioned handkerchief out of his jacket pocket and offered it to me. Madame Favier stood by the refreshment table, lips pursed, watching us with her arms crossed.

I wiped my face with the handkerchief, then shook away any lingering tears. "Thank you," I said. "I'll be fine."

"Yes, you will be," he said, bending his head down to inspect my face. "Life is confusing at your age. Nothing makes any sense, and everything seems so vital and important. Very little of it is, in the big scheme of things. It isn't until you get to be my age that you'll have any real regrets." He got a far-off look in his eyes that reminded me of Rochester. I wondered if his regrets had anything to do with the reason his wife left him.

I saw Madame striding toward us, to intervene I suppose, but just before she reached us, Gray Newman appeared above me, his eyes fixed on Gallagher. He had taken off his jacket and tie so he was wearing only his tuxedo vest over a crisp white shirt. Standing over us, he looked large and menacing. His eyes radiated malice.

"You okay, Townsend?" he asked as Madame Favier watched on, curiosity seeping from her every pore.

"I'm fine," I said, feeling terribly embarrassed.

Mr. Gallagher stood up and extended a hand to Gray. "Ben Gallagher," he said. "Emma's English teacher."

Gray paused a moment, then accepted Gallagher's hand, reluctantly. He then extended the same hand to me. I was confused. Did he want me to shake hands with him?

"Will you dance with me, Emma?" he said. I swallowed loudly, shocked that he'd used my first name. Even more shocked that he'd asked me to dance.

Gallagher got a sheepish look on his face, like he'd just realized he was superfluous. I was still sitting there, stupefied, so Gray took my hand, bringing me to my feet and leading me onto the dance floor.

I felt that familiar urge to cut and run, to flee and run back to my room and crawl under the covers. The DJ was playing a haunting song with lyrics about the sun and the sky, about gravity. And I was drawn like a satellite around Gray's orbit.

He didn't tiptoe around me like Owen had but grabbed me by the waist and pulled me close, so my body was thrust against his chest. His neck smelled warm and spicy, like the beach at nighttime. I could barely move.

He guided me slowly back and forth, one hand placed

firmly on the small of my back, the other warm and dry around my right hand. "What's with Professor Snape?" he said, breaking me out of my trance.

"Who?"

"You know, Mr. Gallivant, or whatever his name is."

"Gallagher," I corrected him.

"Whatever. When he touched your face, I wanted to kill him."

"He's harmless," I said.

"Oh, really? He's a teacher, for God's sake. What's he doing touching you? If I was your father, I'd kick his ass."

"Kind of you to be so protective," I said. "But I can handle myself."

"Really? 'Cause it looked like you were going to fall into his arms if I hadn't come over and rescued you."

I leaned away from him. "So that's what this is? A macho attempt to rescue me?"

"No. It's a dance, Townsend. You know, feet moving, body swaying to music?" Just for fun, he tried to dip me, but I wasn't prepared and staggered. "Sorry," he said. "Bad move."

"Go easy on me," I said. "I'm still shaky on my feet." His cologne wasn't helping matters. "Where's your . . . date?" I said.

"She ditched me."

"No, really," I said.

"She did. She and her friends went outside to smoke."

I peered at him skeptically. His eyes appeared almost gray in the dim light, and his jaw looked like a piece of granite. My eyes drifted to his lips, those seductive lips. I really wanted him to try and kiss me again. I promised myself I wouldn't pull away this time.

"What if Elise comes back and sees you dancing with me?" I said, but he just smiled. His teeth gleamed, and I caught a whiff of peppermint. "She hates me," I said. "If you really want to rescue me, you should let me go."

"Why would I want to do that?" he said, pulling me even closer. His leg brushed against my hipbone, and my legs turned to butter. The rational part of my brain kept warning me to walk off the dance floor before Elise came back, but every other part of my body was making it impossible to leave. I drew my eyes from his face and turned to lay my head against his chest. I could feel his heartbeat thrumming against my ear, and my heartbeat responded in kind, crashing fast and hard against my rib cage.

His shirt had fallen open at the collar, and I wanted to bury my head in the warm hollow of his neck. His hands gripped my hips, while his lips grazed my hair. Every nerve ending was on full alert. I was intoxicated by the moment, by the promise of something I'd only ever imagined before. I lifted my head and peered up at him, and his head leaned forward so our faces were inches away, so close I could feel the heat of his breath on my forehead. And just as my lips were floating up to meet his, about to forge some cosmic collision of lust and frustrated desire, the song ended and segued into a mind-numbing techno beat. Abruptly jerked back to reality, I looked past Gray's shoulder to see Elise Fairchild stalking toward us in rhythm to the music.

"Oh my God," she said when she saw I was the one Gray had been about to kiss. "You?" I felt foolish instead of triumphant. "Typical that you'd ditch me for Little Miss Innocent," she said. "Trying to atone for your sins?"

"What are you talking about?" Gray said.

"Guess who I was just talking to outside." She shoved her way between us and grabbed Gray's arm. "Dan Brockman. You remember him, don't you? From Sheldrake?" Gray's face went pale, and he looked like he was going to be sick. "He's here with Amber. And he told me a very interesting story about you."

Gray's eyes shifted from me to Elise and then back to me. "Emma," he said, his voice nearly cracking. I stared back, expectant, but he didn't go on.

Without warning, he broke through the crowd and moved swiftly away from us, heading for the lobby. Elise glared at me for a moment, then turned to catch up with him. I was left standing in the middle of the dance floor, listening to the pulsing beats of the dance song, wondering what the hell had just happened.

I followed them to the lobby, quickly retrieved my coat from the coat check, and stumbled out into the frigid winter air. I knew Sheldrake was the school Gray had attended before Braeburn, but who was Dan Brockman? And why had Gray reacted so violently to his name?

I walked down the Commons stairs and went to stand beneath the enormous chestnut tree, trying to decide what to do. Gray's deep voice shattered the silence. "Emma."

"Gray?" I turned, startled to see him standing next to me.

He grasped my arm and stared into my eyes. "What would you do if someone told you something awful about me?" His voice was trembling.

I shivered and took his hand. "I guess I'd want to know what it was."

"But I mean, would you assume the worst?" he said, pulling my hands into prayer position and then rubbing against my knuckles with his palms. "Would you automatically believe what people told you?"

"No," I said. "I'd let you tell me, and then make up my mind. Why?"

He shook his head like he was expelling some horrible nightmare. "I just wish we were alone on the beach again, like that day in January." His eyes seared into mine, and his mouth hung half-open like he was about to say something more.

And then Elise and Amber and two guys I'd never seen before came out on the patio, all of them abuzz with anticipation. Something was about to go down. One of the guys descended the stairs so he was standing directly in front of us, his body language issuing a challenge to Gray. His eyes studied me briefly then dismissed me.

"Gray," he said, nodding.

"Dan," Gray said, breathing white vapor into the frigid air.

So this was the mysterious Dan Brockman. There was nothing in his appearance to suggest why his name had given Gray such a shock.

I stood in silence, trying to sort it all out, and Elise strode toward me. "Why are you still here?" she said. My eyes flickered to Gray to see if he'd defend me, but he seemed paralyzed by Dan's presence.

"I was just leaving," I said, turning to go. Whatever was about to happen, I didn't want any part of it. And Gray clearly wanted no part of me. I glanced back at him one last time, hoping he'd come to his senses or tell me what was going on, but he wouldn't look at me. Disgraced and disappointed, I began walking down to the stables, forcing myself not to cry.

I was such an idiot. So Gray Newman had danced with me. So we seemed to have a moment out there on the dance floor. Big deal. It obviously meant nothing to him. Saving face in front of his friends was far more important than sparing my feelings. As my pace quickened, I let the tears fall, feeling a rush of adrenaline and emotion. By the time I reached the bottom of the hill, my face was streaked with tears, my eyes blurry from crying, so much so that I could barely take in the sight before me. Plumes of smoke were coming from the barn. It looked almost cozy at first, like smoke billowing out of a chimney.

But then I came to my senses and realized something was very wrong. The air was hot and charged with static. I shook my head, wondering why everything around me seemed coated in a thin film of gray. As I got closer, I could hear the horses snorting and stomping. And I could hear something else—a low roar, like the sound of wind over the moors. Without thinking, I flew to the double doors and opened them, setting free pillars of black smoke that charged at me like wild horses. Heat as I'd never felt slammed against my body like a living thing, and a magnificent golden light filled the night sky.

The horses reared and neighed wildly, the sound of their panic over the hiss and snarl of fire jolting me to action. "Help!" I called at the top of my voice. "Somebody, help!"

The flames were a fiery wall, a hot tidal wave advancing toward me. I pressed through the heat and the smoke and began unlatching the gates of the pens, ducking my head under my arm to keep myself from choking. Some of the horses bolted right past me as soon as the gates swung open, but others reared back, afraid to move. I didn't even think about what might happen once they were loose; all I knew was I had to get them out of the burning barn.

Curry was squealing and pawing the ground with nervous hooves. I wished I had Michelle's ability to calm him because he refused to come out of his pen. Much as I wanted to save him more than the others, I couldn't stop. I continued through the rows, releasing horse after horse, feeling sickened by the smoke and the acrid smell of burning hay. I threw myself to the ground for a moment to take a deep breath, crouching there and gulping air like a fish starved of water.

When I stood, the flames on the far side of the barn had grown ten feet high and were crawling their way up to the loft. Once the hay there ignited, the loft would collapse, crushing all the remaining horses. I didn't have much time. I began screaming again, for help, for life. Black smoke poured into the stalls. I moved forward, ramming into that wall of heat again.

When I got to Odin's pen and released his latch, he shot out like a dart, knocking me backward. My head hit the ground with a thud, and pain sliced through my body. I tried to sit up but I couldn't move. I could barely see—the smoke felt like acid on my eyes. I could still hear the screaming of the horses, their panicked neighs, and the thunder of their hooves as they ran off in terror. But I couldn't do anything for the others.

At that moment, I wanted to be anywhere but here. I couldn't bear waking to the sight of a scorched barn and the charred remains of dead horses. A flood of words came into my head, words I'd memorized but had never spoken aloud. I recited them now, forcing my mind to focus on Thornfield, on Adèle and the study where we'd spent so many days playing and laughing. On Mrs. Fairfax and Pilot and the cozy nights spent in the parlor. On Mr. Rochester.

Father Legba, I prayed, *open the door for me. Father Legba, open the door to let me pass through. To pass truly, loa, I give thanks to you.*

I repeated the refrain until the words stopped making sense, because all my senses had gone dim. A warm wave spread over me, and instead of fighting it, I let it wash through me, giving myself over to the wondrous tide of a deep and drifting sleep. The wave carried me aloft through the doorway of flames and continued its relentless course until it finally slowed, depositing me onto a strange but familiar distant shore.

PART 4

CHAPTER 18

I woke to the sounds of horses and the smell of hay. For a moment, I panicked, expecting licks of fire and pillars of smoke all around me. But when I opened my eyes, I knew exactly who and where I was. I was Jane again, and I was back at Thornfield.

It had worked! Papa Legba had let me through. This time, the journey to Jane's world had not been jarring and terrifying; it had been like slipping into a warm bath—comforting, reassuring. I was so relieved to be back. My brain would not allow me to dwell on the horror I'd just experienced. Lockwood already seemed very far away. All I could think about now was Rochester and how much I'd missed him.

I ran to the barn doors, which opened onto a brilliant day. I had but one path to walk, one lawn to tread, and I might see Rochester again. The fields and gardens looked so different than the last time I'd been here. It was spring now, and the hedges were full of roses. As I glanced up at the façade of the mansion, I caught a glimpse of Grace Poole standing on the battlements where I had once stood. She was peering out with a hand held over her eyes, staring straight at me.

I hurried my pace, approaching the walled garden where Rochester and I had sat to discuss his engagement to Miss Ingram. I was startled to find him there again, sitting on the same bench with a book and a pencil in his hand. Every nerve in my body came unstrung. I hadn't expected to react so strongly to seeing him again.

Much as I wanted to run to him, I couldn't speak to him, not yet. I attempted to sneak into the side entrance so I could go upstairs and change out of my dress, but he spotted me as I passed behind him.

"Hello!" he cried, putting down his book and his pencil and rising to greet me. "There you are! Come over here, you wicked sprite!" I approached him shyly, as if we were meeting for the first time. "Jane Eyre? You look like a dream to me. What the deuce have you done with yourself this last month?"

I was back from somewhere. But where had I been? Slowly I recalled this part of the story—Jane's Aunt Reed had taken ill, and Jane had gone back home to tend to the woman who had tormented her as a child. I was supposed to be returning from her funeral. But I was still wearing Michelle's red dress—hardly funeral attire. I drew my coat closed and buttoned it full to the top.

"I have been with my aunt, who is dead."

"A true Janian reply! I am sorry for your loss, but did you forget all about me in your absence?" His words seemed to imply he had missed me. "You must see the carriage, Jane, and tell me if you don't think it will suit Mrs. Rochester exactly."

And then all of my illusions shattered on the spot. Mr. Rochester's smile warmed me slightly but did not take away the sting that he was still planning on marrying Blanche Ingram. "Jane, go up and stay your weary feet. You must be tired."

His look was so sincere, his comment so kindhearted that something hard inside me crumbled, and I said, "Thank you, Mr. Rochester, for your great kindness. I am strangely glad to be back. Wherever you are is my home—my only home." I hastily walked away so he couldn't see the tears in my eyes.

Little Adèle was wild with delight when she saw me, and

Mrs. Fairfax received me with her usual friendliness. We had a pleasant reunion, sipping tea and catching up, and the day waned cheerfully. That evening I shut my eyes against the future and stopped my ears against the voice that kept warning me of near separation and grief.

Over the next few days, nothing else was said about Rochester's marriage. There were no trips back and forth to Ingram Park, and no preparation seemed to be taking place for such an event. I began to hold out hope that the match was broken, that rumors of marriage had been mistaken, or that Rochester had changed his mind. Never had he called me more frequently to his presence, never had he been kinder to me, and never had I loved him so much.

The next day dawned sunny and clear. The fields around Thornfield were shorn, the roads white and baked, the trees in their prime. After a full day of collecting strawberries, Adèle went to bed early, and I took advantage of my momentary freedom to stroll the gardens outside. To my surprise, Rochester was out there as well with his head bent low amid the flowers, staring at something that had caught his interest.

I wasn't sure if he'd registered my presence, but then he called to me without turning, "Jane, come and look at this fellow. Look at his wings. He reminds me rather of a West Indian insect." I stood behind him and examined the insect, startled to find it was a blue and green dragonfly, its colors more brilliant than anything I'd seen. "One does not often see so large a dragonfly in England. There! He is flown." The insect flew away, and I felt stirred by the moment, like a spark inside me had been lit. I clutched my dragonfly pendant and felt a rush of emotion.

"Come," he said. "Walk with me." Automatically, I began to follow him down the path, trying to drown out the voice inside my head that was telling me to run. "Jane," he said as we walked in the direction of the giant chestnut tree, "Thornfield is a pleasant place, is it not?"

"It is."

"You must be somewhat attached to the house."

"Yes, I am."

"And though I don't comprehend how it is, I perceive you have acquired a degree of regard for that foolish little child, Adèle, too, and even for that simple dame Fairfax." I nodded and laughed. "You would be quite sorry to part with them?"

"Of course."

"Pity," he said, sighing. "No sooner have you got settled in a pleasant resting place than a voice calls out to you to rise and move on."

"Must I move on?" I asked. "Must I leave Thornfield?"

"I believe you must, Jane. I am sorry, but indeed you must."

"Then you are going to be married?"

"Exactly. Precisely. You have hit the nail straight on the head. In about a month I hope to be a bridegroom," he said. "And I have already found a new situation for you. You'll like Ireland, I think. They are such warmhearted people there."

"Ireland?" I felt crushed and betrayed. "But it is such a long way off from—"

"From what, Jane?"

"From England and from Thornfield and—"

"Yes?"

"From you." I said this almost involuntarily, and despite wanting to remain strong, tears gushed out. "It's a long way," I said again, wiping my eyes.

"It is, to be sure, and when you get to Ireland, I shall never see you again, Jane." He stood behind me, his hands hovering above my shoulders as if he wanted to comfort me. "We have been good friends, Jane. Have we not?" he said, his hands finally coming to rest on my shoulders.

"Yes," I muttered, trying to stem more tears from falling.

"And when friends are on the eve of separation they like to spend the little time that remains to them close to each other. Come, we will sit here tonight, though we should never more be destined to sit here together." He sat down and took my hand, bidding me to sit next to him. "It is a long way to Ireland, and I am sorry to send my little friend on such travels. I sometimes feel as if I had a string somewhere under my left ribs, tightly and inextricably knotted to a similar string situated in some quarter of your little frame. And if two hundred miles or so of land comes between us, I am afraid that cord of communion will be snapped. And then I've a nervous notion I should take to bleeding inwardly. As for you—you'd forget me."

"I wouldn't," I blurted out. I couldn't repress what I felt.

"You cry, Jane, because you are sorry to leave Thornfield?"

"I am sad to leave Thornfield," I said. "I love Thornfield. But I love it because I have known you here, Mr. Rochester, and I don't want to leave you."

"Why must you?"

"As you've said, because you are marrying Miss Ingram. Because of your bride."

"My bride! What bride? I have no bride!"

"But you will have," I said.

"Yes, I will. I will." He ground his teeth.

"Then I must go. You have said it yourself."

"No, you must stay!"

I was confused, and my heart was full. Emotions swirled in a torrent. "I tell you I must go!" I said. "Do you think I can stay to become nothing to you? Do you think because I am poor and plain, I have no heart? I have as much heart as you! And if God had given me some beauty and wealth, I should have made it as hard for you to leave me as it is for me to leave you."

"It is as hard!" said Mr. Rochester, grabbing me in his arms and pressing his lips to mine. Momentarily, I gave into the kiss, soft and tender at first, then more insistent.

I wrangled away, angry with myself for indulging my feelings, for indulging his, which could not be trusted. "You don't love me," I said.

"I do. I offer you my hand, my heart, and a share of all my possessions."

"You're playing a game with me."

He shook his head violently. "No! I'm asking you to pass through life at my side—to be my second self, and best earthly companion. Jane, will you marry me?" he said.

Joy and disbelief swept through me like a wave. "I can't! You have Miss Ingram."

He scoffed and took both my hands in his, like we were making a joint prayer. "What love have I for Miss Ingram? None, and that you know. What love has she for me? None, except that which she has for my wealth and property. I would not—I could not—marry Miss Ingram. You, you strange bird, I love as my own flesh. You, Jane. I must have you for my own. Jane, accept me quickly. Say, Edward—say my name—Edward, I will marry you."

"Yes, Edward," I heard my voice say. "I will marry you."

He drew me to him again and kissed me deeply, and for a moment, I forgot all sense, felt nothing but sensation through every nerve of my body. A violent gust of wind tore through us, almost separating us by force. The chestnut tree under which we sat groaned.

"We should go in," I said. "It's beginning to rain."

A vivid spark of lightning streaked above, and I sprang from the bench and began running toward the house. The rain rushed down, and Rochester followed behind. We were soaked as we entered the foyer, and the clock struck three times. I thought of Cinderella, recalling how the termination of the magical spell had left only a poor girl in rags. My hand reached for my necklace, and at that moment, it was as if a silent alarm tripped inside me. Rochester tried to kiss me again, but I tore myself away.

"What is it, Jane?" he said.

I couldn't speak. Finally I said, "This is wrong. This isn't how it's supposed to happen."

He laughed and drew me to him. "This is exactly as it's supposed to happen. Jane, be still. Don't struggle so like a wild, frantic bird."

I tried to recall where I had heard these words before. And then I remembered. Those were the words Rochester spoke to Jane in the book after proposing to her. And in the book, the moment had been magical, transcendent. The only problem was, I wasn't Jane.

Didn't I have words of my own? My heart was a turbulent riot, torn between surrendering to Rochester and remembering something it had buried deep within itself. When Rochester tried to kiss me once more, I pushed him off and fled to my room. There, I threw off my wet garments and collapsed onto the bed in turmoil.

Wasn't this what I had wanted all along? To have someone love me unconditionally? To know I belonged to someone, heart and soul?

Yet there was a part of me that was fleeing the idea. Did I love this man, or did I simply love the idea of being swept up in a passionate romance? I had said yes to him, recklessly, but now every part of me was rebelling against that choice. Could I really marry Rochester and live at Thornfield for the rest of my life? Or did I have my own story to finish? A story that was only just beginning?

The wind blew all night and thunder crashed, fierce and frequent as the lightning that flickered outside. Mr. Rochester came to my door three times during the storm to ask if I was safe, but I couldn't answer him. I couldn't face him. That night as I lay trying to sleep, I listened to the wind wail across the battlements and the storm assail itself against the house. At one point, I rose and moved to the window just in time to see lightning strike the great chestnut at the foot of the orchard. It was split right in two.

CHAPTER 19

The next morning I rose and dressed, pondering what had happened the day before and wondering if it had all been a dream. I could not be certain until I had seen Mr. Rochester again. While arranging my hair, I examined my face in the glass. Who was this girl who looked back at me? Was it Jane? Or Emma? I felt the answer lay somewhere in these gloomy walls, but I didn't know where to find it.

I went downstairs in a mood of trepidation. Mr. Rochester was in the parlor, and he called me when he heard my steps in the foyer. "Jane, come and bid me good morning," he said.

When I entered, he did not remain on the chair, his leg sprawled on the ottoman, hardly meeting my eye like he once had, but sprang from his chair and embraced me, kissing me tenderly. "Jane, you look truly pretty this morning. Is this my pale little elf?"

"I am just Jane."

"Soon to be Jane Rochester," he added. "Do you hear that?" I did, and I couldn't quite believe it. The feeling it sent through me stung like fear. "You blushed, and now you are white, Jane. Why?"

"Because it all seems so strange."

"Yes, Mrs. Rochester," he said. "And we shall be enormously happy together."

"It seems like a fairy tale or a daydream."

"Which I can and will realize. This morning I wrote to my banker in London to send me certain jewels he has in his keeping. In a day or two I hope to pour them into your lap."

"I don't want jewels. I would rather not have them."

"I myself will put the diamond chain round your neck and clasp the bracelets on these fine wrists and load these fingers with rings."

"No, no! Don't treat me like a princess. I'm an ordinary girl."

"You are a beauty in my eyes, and I will attire you in satin and lace, with roses in your hair. This very day I shall take you in the carriage to Millcote, and you must choose some dresses for yourself. I will cover my little sparrow's head with a priceless veil."

"And then I will look just like your Miss Ingram."

"She was never my Miss Ingram."

"Though you made her think it," I said.

"Well, I feigned courtship with Miss Ingram because I wished to render you as madly in love with me as I was with you. I knew jealousy would be the best ally I could call in for the furtherance of that end."

I bristled at his confession, though it flattered me as well. "It's a disgrace. Did you even consider Miss Ingram's feelings?"

"Her feelings are concentrated in one—pride, and that needed humbling. Were you jealous, Jane?"

"Never mind, Mr. Rochester."

"I love the fire in your eyes when you are vexed with me. Now be my good little girl. Go to your room and put on your bonnet. I mean you to accompany me to Millcote this morning."

I didn't want to go shopping, and at the moment, I couldn't remember why I loved Rochester. Even after our engagement, he still treated me like a little pet rather than his equal. He instructed me to be a good little girl, and I was tired of being good. The truth was, I didn't wish to be married to Rochester, but I wasn't sure how to extract myself from the promise I'd made.

I went upstairs to get my bonnet, and when I came back down, Mrs. Fairfax was sitting at the kitchen table. Seeing me, she made an effort to smile, but could not.

"I feel so astonished," she began. "I hardly know what to say to you, Miss Eyre. I have surely not been dreaming, have I? Sometimes I half fall asleep when I am sitting alone and fancy things that have never happened. Now, can you tell me whether it is actually true that Mr. Rochester has asked you to marry him? Don't laugh at me. But I really thought he came in here five minutes ago and said that in a month you would be his wife."

"It's true," I said, my voice empty of feeling.

"Have you accepted him?"

"Yes," I said, though I could barely believe it myself.

She gaped at me. "I could never have thought it. He is a proud man—all the Rochesters were proud. He, too, has always been called careful. But he means to marry you?" She shook her head, bewildered. "I really don't know. Equality of position and fortune is often advisable in such cases, and there are twenty years of difference in your ages. He might almost be your father. Is it really for love he is going to marry you?"

But the real question she might have asked was, is it really for love that I was going to marry him? Perhaps she was more right than she knew in saying he might be my father. I'd heard of such things happening—young girls falling for older men because they provided safety and security, or they replaced a paternal love that had been missing in the girls' lives. Was this the reason I had fallen for Mr. Rochester, a man who called me his "little sparrow" and expected blind obedience?

Mrs. Fairfax continued. "You are so young, and so little acquainted with men that I wish to put you on your guard. It is an old saying that 'all is not gold that glitters,' and in this case I do fear there will be something found to be different to what either you or I expect. I hope all will be right in the end," she said, "but believe me, you cannot be too careful. Try and keep Mr. Rochester at a distance. Distrust yourself as well as him."

I did distrust myself. In fact, I had no sense of who my true self was anymore. Happily, Adèle ran in. "Let me go! Let me go to Millcote, too!" she cried. "Mr. Rochester won't let me, though there is so much room in the new carriage. Beg him to let me go, mademoiselle."

"I will, Adèle," I said. "I will."

The carriage was ready, and servants were bringing it round to the front. Rochester was pacing the pavement, Pilot following him back and forth. I convinced Rochester to allow Adèle to accompany us to Millcote, though he seemed cross about it. The hour spent shopping was a misery. Mr. Rochester made us go to a silk warehouse where I was forced to inspect dozens of samples. Adèle was in her glory, prancing about, holding up multicolored silks to her face like she was an Arabian princess. I hated the ordeal, but Rochester insisted we choose one. Eventually, I handed the task over to him, but he chose such a gaudy and expensive silk that I finally persuaded him to choose a plain one. A similar thing happened with the veil. He chose an elaborate one covered in pearls and gilt and lace, and I made him give it back and replaced it with the simplest one of cream chiffon. Finally we went to a jeweler's shop. The more he bought for me, the more my cheeks burned.

As we got back in the carriage, I felt exhausted, like a doll Adèle had spent all day dressing up in play clothes. Rochester couldn't understand why the day hadn't pleased me.

"You needn't look so glum," he said. "You are going to be the most beautiful bride that ever lived."

"No, I won't be. And I don't like this flattery. I don't want to feel like someone I'm not. If you're not careful, I'll wear the old black frock I came here in and walk down the aisle looking like I'm in mourning."

"Very well," he said, smiling as if my anger amused him. "You have made your point." We were now approaching Thornfield. "Will it please you to dine with me tonight?" he asked as we reentered the gates.

"No, thank you."

"And why not, if I may inquire," he said, barely concealing the anger in his tone. I had found, since our engagement, he expected even more obedience from me than when I'd been his employee. It made no difference to me that he had grown up accustomed to having his orders obeyed. If I was going to be his wife, he would have to learn how to treat me like an equal.

"I've never dined with you before," I said, "and I see no reason why I should now."

When we went inside, he stormed into the parlor. Pilot followed him in, and I heard a clinking of glassware that no doubt meant he was pouring himself a drink. I took my newly acquired jewelry and veil and went upstairs. Adèle wished to follow me into my room to revel in my new acquisitions, but I was too tired and needed to think.

That night, I was so exhausted I fell asleep immediately, though I did not sleep tranquilly. In fact, I dreamt that night that Thornfield Hall was a dreary ruin. What remained of the building was nothing but a wall, very high and very fragile-looking. In my arms, I carried a child wrapped in a shawl. I knew I couldn't leave the child, no matter how tired my arms grew. We wandered through the remains together, stumbling over ruins.

In the distance, I heard the gallop of a horse. I was sure it was Rochester, so I climbed up the wall, eager to catch a glimpse of him from the top. But the stones rolled from under my feet, and the child clung round my neck in terror and almost strangled me. At last I reached the top. I saw Rochester and his horse as a speck, getting smaller every moment. A gust of wind blew so strong I could no longer stand. I sat down on the ledge just as Rochester turned on the road. When I bent forward to take one last look, the wall crumbled and the child rolled from my lap. I reached out for her, lost my balance, and woke right before my body hit the ground.

I had woken because of a noise in the room. It sounded like a rustling coming from the closet. "Pilot, is that you?" I said.

Of course no one answered, but I thought I saw a ghostly form by the closet. I rose in bed, breathless, and the blood ran cold in my veins. The apparition held something in its hands, and then I heard a tearing sound. Throwing my legs to the side of the bed, I watched the wraithlike figure disappear into the hallway. After catching my breath, I bent down to inspect a white shape on the ground, only to find it was my wedding veil. It had been torn in two.

I got out of bed and opened the door with a trembling hand. Something creaked down the hallway. It was not Rochester's door this time, but the door to the third floor, which had been left slightly open. Without thinking, I crept down the hallway and entered the stairwell. I tiptoed up to the third floor, no longer feeling any fear, even as I recalled the night I had followed Rochester up these stairs to see Mr. Mason, who had claimed someone tried to bite his heart out.

I kept on until I found myself at an iron door, the one that had separated me from the truth that night long ago. I knocked on it now without any reservation or fear.

"Who is it?" I heard. It was Grace Poole's voice.

"It's Jane," I said.

"Go away, I beg you."

"You must let me in. Tell me who is there with you."

"Go away!" she hissed.

"If you don't let me in, I'll wake Mr. Rochester and tell him you came to my room and tore my wedding veil. He'll surely turn you out for that."

Silence fell in the space between us, and I heard what seemed to be the clattering of several dead bolts unlatching, as if this were the cage of some wild beast. Grace opened the door a crack and peered out to make sure I was alone. "Come in," she said. "Be quiet."

We were in the tower. The round room was dark but for one candle on a bed stand, and there were no windows. Other than the feeling of coldness from the stone walls, the room was ordinary with a bed, dresser, and vanity. In fact, it looked very much like my own. I noticed a pair of eyes in the corner. As my own eyes adjusted to the dark, I saw that the person crouched there was a woman.

"Who is that?" I said.

"That is Bertha. Mr. Mason's sister."

"Mr. Mason's sister? Is she the one who . . . bit him?"

"Yes."

"Is she mad?"

Grace sighed. "I have calmed her tonight with some valerian root tea."

"Why is she here? Is she the one who tried to kill Rochester in his bed? Is she the one who—"

"Shush," Grace said. "You ask too many questions. I will tell you what you need to know."

I knew Jane had never been to this room, had never met Bertha face-to-face. I feared what I had done to Jane's fate in coming here. But my curiosity as Emma far outweighed any sense of loyalty I felt to Jane's story.

Slowly, Grace told me Bertha's tragic history. Rochester had fallen in love with her exotic beauty, and in his folly, he'd brought her all the way from Jamaica to England, like some rare West Indies prize. A lovely insect to trap under glass. Unaccustomed to the English climate and the loneliness of life on the moors, Bertha grew despondent. Rochester was away much of the time, and the cold, bleak winters left her lonely and depressed. She craved sunshine and water, friendship and love.

"I thought she'd be better once the child came along, but when she lost the baby, she fell into such despair I thought she'd tear her heart out. She moaned like a wild beast day and night, and nothing would console her. That was when the master restricted her to the attic under my care."

"Lost the baby?" I said. "Do you mean Bertha was pregnant?"

"Yes," Grace said. "This was a long time ago. I took pity on her then. But now she has gone too far, trying to set fire to his room and sneaking into yours to tear your veil. Mr. Rochester will certainly turn me out for my negligence. But if I leave her, she will have no one. No one in this world." Grace Poole, who had always appeared so stolid and unflappable, seemed genuinely distressed.

"How can he keep her up here?" I said. "Surely she needs help. She needs the care of doctors and specialists."

"Mr. Rochester cannot risk it. After all, she is his wife. That is why he keeps her here. The master thinks to marry you. He would not be able to if people knew the truth." I fell mute. Mr. Rochester had imprisoned his wife in the attic because she was depressed? No wonder she'd gone mad! What kind of man could do this to his wife? And what kind of woman would agree to marry this man, knowing the truth?

I lifted the candle from the bed stand and approached the corner cautiously, like one approaching a wild animal, half believing it might attack, but suspecting the creature was more afraid of me than I was of it. Beneath the glow of the flickering candlelight, I saw a face that stopped me cold. The woman was not yet middle-aged, covered with grime, her long dark hair matted into rope-like pieces and tangled webs. Yet even beneath the dirt and mass of hair, I recognized the face.

She seemed to recognize me as well and inched forward. She was wearing a white dress, which though dirty and torn, looked like a wedding dress. I knew her face like I knew my own. It was my mother's face. My two worlds converged in a moment, and I nearly stopped breathing.

"Emma?" the woman said.

My mouth fell. "How—?" I couldn't go on. Finally, I said, "Grace, why did she call me that?"

"Emma was the name she was going to christen the child, had it lived."

I knelt down beside the woman and reached out my hand. At first she stared at me warily like a dog who's been beaten too many times and doesn't trust the hand that feeds it. Grace watched us fearfully, then stood by the fire in awe as the woman took my hand. We stared into each other's eyes. She clutched my hand to her chest, and the two of us fell to the floor, clutching each other, sobbing. When we finally pulled away, she searched my face with her hands, fixing on my necklace. She gently lifted the dragonfly from its perch on my neck and leaned down to kiss it.

I was not Jane, after all. I was Emma Townsend. And this was not Bertha. This was my mother. Like Aunt Darlene had said, the spirits were giving me a chance to speak with my mother through the dream. My mother had something important to tell me.

"What can I do?" I said to Grace.

"You can help her escape," Grace said.

"But how?"

"You and she shall leave this place under cover of darkness. Before the wedding is to take place. It must be soon."

"What about Rochester?" I said. Yet in that moment, I knew I would never marry Rochester. I did not love Rochester.

Perhaps Jane had loved him and could forgive him for this, but I could not.

I did worry what would happen to Jane if I left, if I changed the ending of her story. But it didn't matter. Like Mr. Sarkissian had said in physics class, we cannot change what's already happened, but we can start a new path. Grow a new branch in the space-time continuum. That's what I would have to do. Write a new chapter in Jane's story.

"Pretend all is well," Grace said. "When the plan is arranged for your escape, I will send word with a servant. She shall be ready."

I kissed my mother's cheek, and with a promise to return, fled to my room, knowing I would never sleep.

CHAPTER 20

Over the next few days, I went through the motions of wedding preparation, though my heart and mind were full of other plans. Mrs. Fairfax had gotten over the shock of my engagement to her master, and she and Adèle helped me attend to all the arrangements. My dress had arrived and was hanging in the closet, sheer and white. Every time I saw it, it reminded me of my mother's form floating through my room in the middle of the night. She was the one who'd torn my wedding veil. She'd been trying to warn me.

Rochester told me to pack my trunks for the honeymoon, and I did so, knowing full well the trunks would never arrive at their intended destination. As resolved as I was, still I had doubts. I was experiencing an ordeal of struggle, caught between two paralyzing states. At times, I looked at Rochester after he had smiled or kissed me and thought maybe I could forgive him like Jane had. Maybe I could tell him I knew his secret, and we could endeavor together to get my mother the help she needed. But then I thought of her imprisonment in that dungeon for all those years, and my feelings of affection and forgiveness disappeared.

I did not return to the tower during those nights of preparation, out of fear that I would be discovered and our plan would be ruined. I thought ceaselessly about my mother. The night I'd met her, she had not seemed insane, yet she *had* tried to murder Rochester in his sleep, just as she'd bitten Mr. Mason's chest. But was she really mad? And wouldn't any of us go mad if we were faceless to the world, invisible, voiceless, imprisoned in stone with no blue sky, no ocean, no fire but that which burned within us?

On the night of the planned escape, I sat on my bed waiting for the hours to pass. I even drifted off to sleep once or twice. At one point, I had a dream that I was standing on the beach at Hull's Cove as a little girl. I lifted my head to the sky and saw storm clouds, high and dim, and a moon breaking through them. The moon kept descending until it fell into the ocean itself, transforming into a white human form. A woman emerged from the waves and spoke to me. Actually, she whispered: "My daughter, flee temptation."

"Mother, I will," I said. And she turned around, walked back into the waves, and disappeared into the dark mirror of the ocean.

I woke with a start, worried I had slept too long. It was still night, but summer nights are short, and I knew we had to go. I had packed some clothing in a small trunk, along with a cloak and a purse containing twenty shillings. I tied on my bonnet and shawl and stole from my room.

In terror, I wound my way up the stairs to the third floor. I knew what I had to do, and I went through the motions mechanically. Grace opened the door before I knocked. My mother was waiting with a small trunk of her own, which she dropped as soon as she saw me so she could embrace me. I struggled not to cry and put a finger to her lips to remind her we must be silent. I shook Grace's hand and nodded, noticing she had tears in her eyes.

We carried our trunks downstairs, where I went to the kitchen and packed us some water and bread for the journey. I met my mother at the side door, which we passed through and shut softly behind us. Dawn was already glimmering in the yard. I took my mother's hand and we began to run with our small trunks in tow, passing through the gates of Thornfield, leaving it behind forever.

Beyond the fields about a mile off lay a road, which stretched in the opposite direction of Millcote. We walked in that direction, neither of us knowing where it would take us. We walked till after sunrise until our shoes were wet with dew. A weakness extending to my limbs seized me, and at one point I fell. My mother reached down and helped me stand. When we met the road, we rested a while under the hedge until we heard the wheels of a coach. I stood up and lifted my hand, and the coach stopped. I asked where it was going, and the driver named a place a long way off, where I hoped Mr. Rochester had no connections. I told him I had only twenty shillings, but he agreed to take us anyway. We climbed inside the coach, and it rolled on its way.

After driving for several hours, the coachman set us down in a town called Whitcross. We paid him all we had, so now we had no money in the world. Whitcross was not quite a town, more a crossroads in the moors, with waves of mountains framing a valley far beyond. Even though it was now midday, we saw no passengers on these roads. The terrain seemed wild, the heather growing deep on the surrounding slopes.

We waded into the heather, knee-deep in its dark growth. Wearily, we walked in search of shelter. After a few hours with no sign of civilization, we found a mossy granite crag and sat under it for cover from the sun. I passed some water to my mother, and she drank greedily. Now that we were resting, I noticed that Grace had combed my mother's dark hair and pinned it neatly off her head. She was dressed in a simple black frock. She did not look crazy at all; in fact, she looked just like me.

Hunger pangs gnawed at my stomach, and I knew my

mother must be hungry, too. I broke off a piece of bread and handed it to her. As we ate silently, I noticed the sky was deep blue and already contained a few stars. Night would fall shortly. For tonight, we would have to sleep here.

Beside the crag, the heather was very deep, so we lay down in it, our feet buried in the dusky pink blooms. I folded my shawl over us both and tucked my bonnet under our heads as a pillow. We lay on our backs with our eyes to the stars.

My mother rolled onto her side to look at me. "Did you ever meet a person and feel a physical tugging, as if some string connected you to her, pulling your own soul toward hers?"

I knew what she meant, and Rochester had known it, too. It was the unseen connection that made us love certain people. "Yes," I said, remembering dimly a boy who stood on the other side of a great ocean, a boy with hazel eyes and strong swimmer's arms.

"When I lost my baby," she said, "I felt a snapping of something inside me so profound it caused me physical pain. I thought I'd never recover. When you walked into my chamber that night, I felt as though the cord had been mended. I felt whole in a way I could not explain. You were a stranger to me, and yet, you were as familiar to me as my own skin."

"I felt the same way," I said. "I lost my mother when I was very young. When I saw you, I felt she'd come back to me."

She sighed. "I am glad we found each other," she said. "But do not entertain hopes that this will end well for me."

"What do you mean?" I said, turning on my side to look at her.

"That same tug I felt when I saw you pulls at me now, yet it pulls me in the opposite direction. It pulls me toward destruction rather than redemption."

"So fight against it," I said.

"I am trying, but it feels as though this night with you is

not real. This is all a dream. I am just a dream." She'd been living so long as a prisoner that the very glimmer of freedom must have felt unreal to her.

"You are not a dream," I said. "You're real." I reached over to pinch her, and she winced.

"Am I? How long does one have to be invisible to the world before she disappears completely? Fades into the walls of the attic? Maybe I'm just a ghost after all."

"No," I said. "You are not a ghost. You're a mother and a wife—a woman with a past, present, and future. You have an existence beyond those walls now. You're free!"

She sighed. "Emma, you cannot change what happens to me. My destiny was sealed the moment I agreed to marry Mr. Rochester. I knew I would not be suited for marriage, but I had no voice to say no. My father had arranged the marriage when Rochester was a young man. He may have believed he was in love with me then, but the truth is that he married me for my dowry. He had been cheated of his inheritance, and he knew the only way to protect his estate was to marry for money. I allowed thoughts of romance to cloud my judgment. When first I saw him, I thought he was a knight on horseback who would save me from my dull and obscure existence. I thought he was my savior. I let him make promises to me and take me away from everyone I loved. But once in his home, I became his prisoner. As a daughter, I'd been a servant to my father, and after marriage, I became a servant to my husband. I don't know that I have ever felt true love and affection from anyone."

"You have it now," I said, grabbing her hand.

"Yes, but you cannot stay with me. The longer you stay here, the harder it will be for you to leave. You must go back where you belong."

Again I felt that inner turmoil, two tides pulling me in opposite directions. "I don't know where I belong," I said. "But I'm here with you now. And I can help you."

She sat up, her face lit by moonlight. "You cannot save me, but you can save your friends," she said, her voice scaring me with its intensity.

"I don't have any friends," I said, thinking with a lump in my throat about my father and Grandma Mackie, about Michelle and Owen, about Gray. Their faces came to me vividly now, and I felt that ache my mother had talked about, a physical tugging that caused me internal pain.

"You are not alone," my mother said.

"Then why do I feel so lonely?" I asked.

"Because you don't know how strong you are. You are far stronger than you believe."

"I'm not strong. Every time things get difficult, I run away. That doesn't take courage."

"One day you will learn what true courage is. It is not always in the dramatic gesture or the daring rescue. Sometimes it takes courage to run away, especially when you must run from the one you love. You left Thornfield, even though you loved Mr. Rochester. You are stronger than I ever was."

"But you had no choice!" I said. "You couldn't leave!"

"There were times . . ." Her voice trailed off, and I suspected she was fighting tears. "There were times I could have left, but I never had the strength. Something always made me stay. A force as strong as gravity."

"But you did leave," I said. "We did. We left him for good."

"Yes, you are right," she said, taking my hand. We lay back down, and I yawned. Fatigue had overtaken me like a drug. "Sleep now," she said. "You will need your strength."

I didn't think I'd be able to sleep, but she began singing a lullaby, and I felt a stirring inside me as if I'd heard this song many times before.

> "Love, to thee my thoughts are turning
> All through the night

All for thee my heart is yearning,
All through the night.
Though sad fate our lives may sever
Parting will not last forever,
There's a hope that leaves me never,
All through the night."

She wrapped her arms around me, and we fell asleep in that bed of heather, lying beneath the moon like a mother and daughter from some dark and wondrous fairy tale, a tale I feared would not end happily.

CHAPTER 21

I woke to a groaning stomach. Feeling an unfamiliar ache in my neck, I turned over and opened my eyes. Panic seized me until I remembered the events of last night and how I had come to be here. I rubbed the sleep out of my eyes and focused on the foreign terrain. A mist hovered over the moors, and sunlight was creeping through hazy clouds. I spun around in search of my mother and saw an empty spot where she'd slept. Maybe she'd gone up to the road to flag down a carriage.

I scrabbled up to the road and scanned in all directions. Where was my mother? A horrible thought struck me, of marauders coming in the night and kidnapping her. But why would they take her and not me? I roamed the area in search of her for almost an hour, calling her name until my voice was hoarse. She was gone, her trunk missing, too. Then it occurred to me—she hadn't been kidnapped at all; she'd left of her own free will. And I knew where she'd gone: back to Thornfield.

When I returned to the spot where we'd slept, I found a note pinned to my trunk. It said: "Do not ever forget who you really are, and how valuable you are to those who love you."

With tears in my eyes, I gathered my things and set out in

search of her. I followed the road away from the sun and kept to the path a long time, stopping only when fatigue over-powered me. The valley on my right was full of pasture and cornfields and woods. A stream zigzagged through the fields, and civilization seemed near. I turned in the direction of the pastures and walked for about a mile until I heard a church bell chime.

I would go to this church and inquire about getting a carriage back to Thornfield. Surely someone there would help me. I walked another half mile until I came to a tiny village that looked like it had been built right into the craggy mountainside, the houses all huddled together with smoke plumes streaming from their chimney tops. At the bottom of the hill stood a lonely church, whitewashed and plain. I proceeded toward it in the hopes of finding a kindly minister who might direct me to the nearest inn and tell me how I might rent a carriage back to Thornfield.

I entered the tiny church through its simple wooden door and walked down the central aisle to the altar. There was no sign of life in the church, but the smell of incense lingered. I crept into one of the pews and sat down, wondering what to do. I had not been raised in a religious household, although my father did believe in giving thanks and asking forgiveness.

Now I said a simple prayer for help. I didn't know who it was intended for—was I praying to a great Christian God to send me a guardian angel? Was I praying to Papa Legba to guide me back through the door between worlds? Or was I praying to the Universe to help me find the path of my own destiny? I didn't know, and I didn't care. I just knew I couldn't make it on my own.

After several minutes, I felt faint with hunger and thirst. I had to find some food and drink before continuing. I stood up, grasping the back of the pew in front of me, feeling my head spin. A wave of nausea overpowered me, and I ran out of the church and into the graveyard that lay beyond, getting sick in some hedges that lined the perimeter. I felt a little better then, but still dizzy and flushed. I wiped my hand across my forehead, which felt warm and clammy. I glanced up at a sky of brilliant blue—unreal-looking, magical. I'd never seen a sky so blue. All I wanted was to float straight up and be cradled in one of its billowy clouds.

I crawled on the ground for a moment and then stopped, unable to go on. I laid my head down on the grass, feeling its green coolness soothe me. When I opened my eyes, I was staring at a headstone, overgrown with weeds, its engraving faded from years of weather. Crawling closer, I read its inscription: *To Laura, loving mother and wife. May you rest in the peace you could not find in life.*

Laura. My mother's name. This could be no accident. The gods were sending me a message, though I didn't understand it yet. I tried to get up and resume my search for her, but I stumbled on a rock and fell. Something warm oozed from my temple, and I suddenly felt calm and very sleepy.

My recollection of the next three days and nights is dim. I know I was in a small room in a narrow bed. I took no note of the lapse of time, of the change from morning to noon, from noon to evening. I observed people entering and leaving the room, heard them call each other by different names, even understood for the most part what was said about me, but I was incapable of answering. A servant, Hannah, was my most frequent visitor. Two girls about my age came in less frequently and whispered worried phrases at my bedside. I think their names were Mary and Diana.

A man came once, examined me, and said my fevered state was the result of reaction from excessive and protracted fatigue. He pronounced it needless to send for a doctor since there was no disease. I think he was the girls' brother, and they called him "Sinjun."

After several days, I felt better, and by the end of the week, I could speak, move, rise in bed, and turn. The family who had rescued me was named Rivers, and the brother they called Sinjun was a minister at the church. I recalled that in *Jane Eyre,* Jane had stayed with the Rivers family at Moor House and had become one of their own. She had taken a position as a teacher at a local school, had become dear friends with Diana and Mary, and had even been proposed to by the minister, whose real name was St. John. It was here at Moor House that Jane would learn of her inheritance of a great sum of money from her uncle, which would make her, for the first time in her life, an entirely independent woman. All this good fortune awaited me if I stayed.

But I could not stay. My mother had told me: *Sometimes it takes courage to leave.* It would have been so much easier to stay with these people, to feel part of a family who would grow to love me, to wait for the inheritance that would free me from want and need. But this family was part of a storyline that no longer belonged to me. I had torn myself from the pages of Jane's story the night I had escaped from Thornfield with my mother. I had to go back and find her.

I left Moor House as soon as I was well, thanking the family for their pains and promising to return when I was able, knowing I'd never see them again. St. John gave me money for the fare, and by four o'clock that Saturday I stood at the crossroads in Whitcross, waiting for the arrival of the coach that would take me back to Thornfield. It stopped when I beckoned, and I entered the carriage, feeling like the messenger pigeon flying home.

The journey took over six hours. When we came upon the lane where I had first met Rochester and Pilot, I asked to get out of the coach and paid my fare. I walked that familiar lane, stopping at the fence to recall Rochester's horse clattering along the lane, Pilot appearing suddenly in the hedge, the crash on the ice, my rescue of Rochester. But instead of feeling a quaint nostalgia, I felt a wave of fear as I approached the house, intensified by a low roaring noise coming from beyond the hill. When I crested it, my fears were confirmed: Thornfield was a mass of flames.

I began running down the hill and felt heat pulsing from the building. The stones were groaning like they were alive. As I approached, I saw my mother on the battlements, her dress billowing, her long black hair streaming against the flames. Mr. Rochester emerged onto the roof behind her and called out her name.

I ran to the bottom of the building and called up to her as well. "Mother," I screamed. "Mother!"

She ignored Rochester's pleas and peered down at me. I thought I saw a glimpse of tender regret on her face. Rochester ran toward her, arms outstretched, and she yelled something I could not hear, then threw herself off the roof. I watched as this dark-plumed thing descended, wings outstretched, then shielded my face to avoid seeing her smash against the stones. I ran to the spot where she'd fallen, screaming wildly.

Suddenly, there was a great crash. The building seemed to heave and shudder. Servants dashed madly across the lawn. Walls collapsed, and the stone battlements where Mr. Rochester stood began crumbling.

I ran in after him, heading to the stairs. Smoke surged through the stairwell, and I held my palm to my mouth to shield my nose and lungs. I arrived on the third-floor corridor just in time to see a massive beam crash down from the ceiling, striking Rochester on the side of the head. I ran to him. A gash by his left eye was bleeding profusely.

"Mr. Rochester, I'm here," I said. I took off my cloak and pressed it against his temple. "Are you all right?"

"I cannot see, but I must feel, or my heart will stop and my brain burst." He groped for me, and I seized his wandering hand. "Her very fingers!" he cried. "Is it Jane?"

"It is," I said. I couldn't help but cry at this unexpected reunion.

"Jane Eyre! Jane Eyre!" he shouted, then sputtered from the smoke. "It must be a dream."

"It's not a dream," I said, stroking his head.

"Oh, Jane. I tried to stop her," he said, losing all composure. "I tried to save her. I'm so sorry. I tried—"

"Quiet," I said. "Don't trouble yourself."

Some men had entered the hall and stood waiting to place Mr. Rochester onto a stretcher. One came up behind me and said, "The engines have arrived from Millcote. The building is not sound. We must leave immediately. A carriage awaits Mr. Rochester."

"We must go, Mr. Rochester," I said.

"I am Mr. Rochester again? Please, call me Edward."

"All right, but Edward, we must leave now."

"Kiss me before we go," he said. "Embrace me, Jane."

And because I knew I'd never see him again, I pressed my lips gently to his, then swept his hair from his brow and kissed his wound, too. He suddenly seemed to rouse himself. "It is really you, Jane? You are come back to me, then?"

I couldn't crush him with the truth. "I am, Edward. I am."

In the real story, Jane would come back to her Rochester, and she would forgive him for his transgressions. Finding him blind and enfeebled, she would agree to be his nurse, his guide, and his best earthly companion. All would end well for them, and Bertha's death, while tragic, would allow them the happiness they could never have had while she was alive.

But my story had yet to be written. I held his hand as the men loaded him onto the stretcher, and he clung to me until the last. I stood in the hallway crying and choking until someone found me and led me downstairs and out of the burning house.

I walked to where my mother lay, all her life extinguished. I had come back for her. I had tried to save her. But I couldn't. Why was I unable to change her ending?

I pulled myself away from the carnage and toward cleaner

air, and that's when I saw smoke rising from the stables beyond. The fire was spreading to the barn. I set off in a run.

As I got closer, I could hear the horses snorting and stomping. And I could hear something else—a low roar, like the
sound of wind over the moors. Without thinking, I flew to
the double doors and opened them, setting free pillars of
black smoke that charged at me like wild horses. Heat as I've
never felt before slammed against my body like a living thing,
and a magnificent golden light filled the sky.

The horses reared and neighed wildly, the sound of their
panic over the hiss and snarl of fire jolting me to action.
"Help!" I called at the top of my voice. "Somebody, help!"

The flames were a fiery wall, a hot tidal wave advancing
toward me, but I pressed through the heat and the smoke and
began unlatching the gates of the pens, ducking my head
under my arm to keep myself from choking. Some of the
horses bolted right past me as soon as the gates swung open,
but others reared back, afraid to move. I didn't even think
about what might happen once they were loose; all I knew
was I had to get them out of the burning barn.

When I got to the pen that held Mr. Rochester's best stallion, I released the latch, and he shot out like a dart, knocking me backward. My head hit the ground with a thud, and
pain sliced through my body. I tried to sit up but found I
couldn't move. Blood pounded in my ears, and my heart
thudded in my chest. Suddenly my heart seemed to stand
still, as if it had been jolted by an electric shock.

A realization swept through me. I was going to die here in
this barn on the same night my mother had died. I hadn't
been able to save her; why should I be able to save myself? I
clutched my chest, feeling like this was going to be my last
moment here on earth. Fumbling, I grabbed hold of my necklace.

I thought of Papa Legba's refrain, but I knew it didn't hold
the key to my fate. In fact, it never had. The key had always

been within me. I felt two tides pulling me, one toward life, the other toward death. I closed my eyes and felt an overpowering urge to surrender to the tide that was drawing me out toward the wide blue sea—a brilliant turquoise ocean sparkling under a full moon. I knew there was a shore at the other end of that ocean, and that if I let myself go to it, my mother would be there waiting for me. How I longed to give in and let myself go, to stop fighting against this relentless tide.

Then I thought of the words my mother had written for me. *Do not ever forget who you really are, and how valuable you are to those who love you.* I had to fight harder. I had to get back to the ones who loved me. To the ones I loved. I could hear their voices in the distance, calling to me. One seemed to be saying my name. Some inner force propelled me across the water toward that voice with a power I didn't know I had.

I fought madly against the current, swimming with all of my strength away from the open sea that threatened to drown me. I swam and swam toward that single voice, arms burning, breath ragged, until I felt certain I was going to make it. Just a little farther. My mother's advice came to me again from across the vast distance of that other shore: *You are far stronger than you believe.* It gave me the strength to keep swimming, to fight against the current until a hand reached out for me.

I gripped this hand and let it pull me to safety. A halo of light shone behind the one who had saved me.

I heard the voice again, repeating my name. My true name. *Emma.*

PART 5

CHAPTER 22

I woke with my hand inside someone else's. "Emma?" a familiar voice said. "Emma, wake up."

I knew I was in a hospital before I even opened my eyes. There is a smell particular to hospitals, a mixture of disinfectant and sterilizer with an undercurrent of illness. But then a warm face came down toward mine, and I smelled something else. Citrus and spice. The beach at nighttime. I peeled my eyes open, and they fell on Gray's face, blurry at first and surrounded by a circle of light, then clear and miraculous—his haunted eyes and usually sarcastic lip, now grim with worry.

"Emma?" he said when he saw my eyes open, felt my hand stir beneath his. His voice was deep and trembling.

"Gray," I mumbled. I could speak! He leaned over and touched my face tenderly. "Where am I?"

"Hopkins General." They'd taken me to the local hospital this time, not the children's hospital in Boston. That was a good sign.

"What happened?" I asked, my voice weak.

"There was a fire. The stables. I found you, but you wouldn't wake up."

"How long?" I muttered. "How long was I out?"

"Three days."

Only three days. Not three weeks. "And the horses? Curry?"
I said, trying to sit up and nearly falling out of the bed.

"Calm down," he said. "They're fine. They all escaped,
but they were rounded up and put in temporary housing.
You saved them. You saved them all."

I slumped back down on my pillow, relieved. Gray stood
up and moved toward the door.

"No!" I said. "Don't go."

"I'm just getting the doctor. I'll be right back, I promise."
He came back and squeezed my arm. The pressure was so reassuring it warmed my entire body.

I tried moving my arms, my legs, my head. They all responded obediently. After a few moments, Gray returned
with a doctor I didn't recognize. He was young and mild-
looking, and he smiled as soon as he saw me.

"Well, hello," he said. "I'm Dr. Richter." I watched as my
own hand rose to meet his. "Oh, good," he said. "Everything
seems to be in working order."

"What's wrong with me?" I said. "Why do I keep blacking
out?"

"We're not sure yet," the doctor said. "We spoke to your
doctor at Children's Hospital. She says it may be a residual
effect of the lightning strike. The fact is, we just don't know
that much about lightning-strike survivors. We're going to
have to run a few more tests."

"Great," I said sarcastically.

The doctor laughed. "Well, you're definitely lucid," he said.

Gray returned to my side, and I tried to sit up again. "Is it
okay if I raise the bed?"

"That should be fine," the doctor said. Gray used the buttons on my bed to raise me up halfway.

"Where's my dad?" I asked.

"I told him I'd stay with you," Gray said. "He hadn't slept
in two days. And it's after midnight."

I remembered the nurses at Children's Hospital being kind

of strict about visiting hours. "Aren't visiting hours over?" I asked him.

"What, you want me to go home?" Gray said.

"No, I just—"

"Sometimes we allow parents, spouses, and significant others to stay after visiting hours," the doctor said. "If they promise to behave." He winked at Gray. "I'm going to go call your parents and tell them the good news. You two hang tight."

He left the room, and Gray leaned in close. "I had to tell them I was your boyfriend. I hope you don't mind."

"No," I said. How could I mind? And then because it was all so astonishing and wonderful, I laughed. The sensation felt utterly foreign to me. I realized I had not laughed much during the past few weeks.

Thornfield had not been a happy place. I recalled Rochester's proposal, the shopping trip to Millcote, the discovery of my mother in the attic, our escape to the moors, the fire at Thornfield. It all felt like it had taken place over many weeks, but Gray said it had only been three days. The expression on Gray's face was entirely new to me. If I had to describe it, I'd say it was grateful. I felt grateful, too.

"Your voice pulled me out," I said, feeling woozy.

"What?"

"I heard you calling my name," I said. "While I was under, you were saying my name, weren't you?" He bit his cheek, and then Gray Newman actually blushed. "It worked," I said. "I could hear you somehow. I swam toward your voice."

"You swam toward my voice? What are you talking about, Emma?"

"Nothing. Never mind. I'm a little out of it." Because that was impossible, right? I couldn't have heard Gray's voice while I was unconscious. And yet, I was pretty sure I had.

"You sure you're okay?" he said. "You did bump your head pretty bad."

"I'm fine." I lifted my hand to my temple and felt the bandage that covered my wound. "I've really only been here for three days?"

"Yep."

"It felt like so much longer."

He stared into my eyes, a crease forming over his brow. "I know. I've been here every night."

I fell silent. Gray Newman had kept vigil by my bedside for three nights in a row? "Why?" I said.

"I was worried about you. After you left the dance that night, I went down to the stables and found you passed out on the ground."

"What happened with Elise?"

"Elise?"

"And that guy Dan? Who is he? And what happened with . . . ?" I desperately wanted to ask him all these questions, to try and understand the events of that night, but I felt so tired I could barely hold my head up.

"Relax," he said, taking my hand in his. "We can talk about all this later."

I allowed myself to fall back against the pillow while Gray stretched his hand over my forehead, gently pushing some hair off my face. I must have drifted back to sleep because when I opened my eyes, my father and Barbara were there. My dad had circles under his eyes, and his hair was sticking up in all directions.

"Emma," he cried, running to my side and hugging me.

Barbara was crying, too. "Oh, sweetie, we were so worried."

"Dad, it's okay. I'm okay."

"You can talk!" he said. "Oh, thank God."

He kept saying my name over and over again while Barbara stood next to him looking overwrought. After about ten minutes, Gray said he was going to leave. I didn't want him to, but I'm sure he felt awkward standing there while my parents showered me with attention. We wouldn't be able to talk anymore anyway.

As he was about to leave, I called his name, and he stopped in the doorway. "Thank you," I said. "For everything."

He smiled modestly. "You're welcome, Emma." He lingered for a moment, and I tried to memorize the look in his eyes, the sound of his voice when he'd said my name. And then he was gone.

Dr. Richter returned the next day, and I had to undergo another battery of tests. Just like last time, my tests came back normal. He said they wanted to keep me a few days longer for observation, but if all went well, I'd be released by the weekend.

Gray visited several nights that week, and he always brought games for us to play—Battleship and Boggle, Mastermind and Sorry. A strange hush came over the hospital at night. Hardly any doctors and nurses were bustling around, the lights in the hallway were dim, and it felt almost intimate in the room, like the normal rules of life no longer applied.

On Friday night, Gray set up his laptop with some good music (he'd complained earlier about the crappy AM-FM radio in the room), and he took out some playing cards for poker. I'd never played poker before, but Gray taught me the rules for five-card stud and daytime and nighttime baseball.

"In daytime baseball, most of your cards are out in the open for your opponent to see," he said. "But in nighttime, your hand is only revealed at the very end. Which do you want to play?"

I narrowed my eyes at him. This seemed like a test. "Daytime," I said, and he laughed as if he'd expected as much.

"What's so funny?" I said.

"Nothing."

"You prefer nighttime baseball, don't you?"

He flashed a sexy smile. "I don't like to give my secrets

away." He shuffled dexterously and dealt us three cards each. "Threes and nines are wild," he said.

"Wild?"

"It means they can be any card you want them to be."

I studied my hand. Two nines and a king. My lip curled ever so slightly, and I realized I was a terrible poker player already. Gray dealt us each a fourth card, face-up. Mine was an eight; his was a jack.

"Let's play for questions. The winner gets to ask questions of the loser, and the loser has to answer honestly."

"Oh, like in Truth or Dare."

"Exactly. Except it'll just be Truth. Poker Polygraph."

He lay down another card for us both. By the third round, Gray's hand looked pretty pathetic. But he kept raising the bet anyway. We were already up to five questions. When he tried to raise the bet to seven questions, I folded.

Then came time for the reveal. He was grinning, and I didn't know why. When he fanned his cards out, I didn't see any discernible pattern. Then I realized that was exactly the point.

"You jerk," I said. "You have nothing!"

"Yeah, well, sometimes nothing can be a real cool hand," he said, doing a fairly decent *Cool Hand Luke* impersonation.

"I thought you had something really good."

"It's called bluffing, Emma. You should try it some time."

"I'm terrible at this," I whined, tossing my cards back at him.

"No, you just have too many tells."

"Tells?"

"Things you do that give you away. Like, when you got those nines, the right side of your mouth went up, and I knew you had a good hand. Then when I tried to up the stakes, you tugged on your necklace, and I knew you were going to fold."

"Really?"

"Yeah, you always tug your necklace when you're nervous."

"Great, you know everything about me, and I know nothing about you."

"And now I get to learn even more about you by asking five very personal questions," he said, raising his eyebrows up and down. He slid his chair very close to my side and rested his arms on the bed. One of his hands brushed mine, and I couldn't believe how much this thrilled me.

"First question," he said. "What's the most embarrassing thing that's ever happened to you?"

I only had to think for a moment. "Kissing you when I was five and getting a bloody nose in return." He snorted an amused *ha!* "Next question?"

His eyes drifted up to the ceiling. "Okay," he said, "if you could be any inanimate object, what would you be?"

Aside from your T-shirt? I repressed a smile. "I guess I'd want to be someone's favorite book."

"Why?"

"Because I love words. But I also need human companionship. If I were someone's favorite book, someone might pick me up off the shelf every night and flip through me."

He laughed a little, and all his features softened like something inside him had just melted. "What book would you want to be?"

"You realize that counts as another question."

"I know."

"*Jane Eyre,*" I said.

"That's the book my mom gave you for your birthday, right?" he said.

"You remember?"

"Of course I remember. She made me wrap the present."

I laughed. "I ended up writing an essay about it for school."

"I usually hate books I have to read for school."

"I know what you mean, but this book's sort of . . . special."

I wanted to tell him about the dream I'd had, to remind

him he'd been one of the reasons I'd fought so hard to pull myself out of it, but I didn't want him to think I was crazy. Gray began playing with the edge of my blanket, twisting a few loose threads in his hand.

"Two more questions, right?" he said.

"We could be here all night."

"That's okay. I don't sleep."

"Why not?" I asked.

"Hey, I'm the one asking the questions here," he said, leaning back in his chair and putting his arms behind his head in an exaggerated show of relaxation.

"This is a great song," I said as Coldplay's "Speed of Sound" came on.

"You like Coldplay?"

"I love them."

"What other music do you like?"

"If you reach down and grab my bag, you can find my iPod and see for yourself."

He found my bag on the floor, and I retrieved my iPod and handed it to him, letting him scroll through my songs. He shuffled through the list approvingly. "Barcelona, Embrace, the Perishers, Thirteen Senses," he said. "Good stuff."

"Thanks."

Then he unleashed a cocky smile. "Which song reminds you of me?"

My cheeks must have flushed bright red, especially when I recalled how often I'd been listening to the song Gray and I had danced to at the Snow Ball. The song about gravity and objects being drawn irresistibly toward one another.

"I do believe you've used up your five questions already, Mr. Newman."

"No way, I only asked three."

"One," I said, beginning to count off on my fingers, "most embarrassing moment. Two, inanimate object. Three, favorite book. Four, do I like Coldplay?"

"That didn't count!"

"Sure it did. Five. What other music do I like?"

"But we were just chatting."

"They were still questions. Anyway, you need to give me a chance to win some back. Let's play again."

He pretended to look angry, then indulged me with another game. This time we played nighttime baseball. I was so careful not to let my face show any emotion, to maintain a stoic façade so Gray couldn't see through me. It must have worked because I actually won. Either that, or Gray let me win. But I only got three questions out of it because I wasn't as bold with my betting.

I was about to ask him my first question when a nurse came in and told us Gray would have to go—she obviously wasn't as lenient as Dr. Richter. He grumbled, and we waited for her to leave so we could say good-bye.

"I thought we were going to get away with the late-night visits for one more day," he said.

"Me too."

He gathered up the cards and his laptop and came back over to the bed. "You really are a terrible poker player," he said, laughing. "You have the worst poker face I've ever seen." I frowned dramatically, and he came toward me. "Worst poker face," he said, "but the best face." He brushed a strand of hair off my forehead and leaned down very slowly, kissing my forehead so gently that his lips barely grazed the skin.

It might sound like a paternal gesture—kissing someone on the forehead like that—but it didn't feel paternal. Not at all. I found myself reaching for my necklace but stopped myself. I didn't want Gray knowing he made me so nervous. After he left, I let out the breath I'd been holding and fell onto my pillow, smiling a secret smile that even he couldn't see.

CHAPTER 23

The next day, I walked out of the hospital and into a different world. When I'd left Thornfield, it had been nearly summertime. All had been green and dewy, lush and blooming. Here, it was still February. The air was wet and cold, and frost glazed the edges of the lawn.

Even though I was anxious to get back to school, my dad insisted on taking me home for a few days to rest. We sat in silence for the first half of the drive until my dad could no longer restrain himself. "So, Gray Newman?" he said, a fatherly smirk on his face. "What's going on there?"

I shifted my gaze out the window, feeling self-conscious. How could I talk to my dad about boys? I didn't even understand them myself. "We're just friends," I said.

"Oh, really?" He took his eyes off the road just long enough to give me a skeptical arch of his eyebrow. "So friends come to visit you at the hospital every day?"

"Not some friends," I said. I had been feeling very hurt that Michelle and Owen hadn't stopped by.

"Oh, one of your friends did visit," he said. "A guy. With shaggy brown hair."

"Owen?"

"Yeah, that was him. He came to see you while you were

unconscious. He did say to pass along the message that Michelle couldn't make it. Something to do with the investigation."

"What investigation?"

"Oh, that's right, you don't know. There's a lot we haven't talked about."

I shifted in my seat so I was facing him. "What investigation, Dad?" I repeated.

"After the fire at the stables, your school conducted an arson investigation. They think Michelle might have been responsible for the fire."

"Michelle?"

"Apparently, she wrote some threatening poems in her journal?"

"Oh my God," I said. I thought back to the incriminating line in my poem: *Those who burn us soon will burn.* That must have been what he was talking about. "Dad, Michelle didn't write those poems."

"What are you talking about?"

"I wrote them. The journal is mine. Everyone thinks it's Michelle's, but it isn't. I have to go to school and clear her name."

"Emma, you just got out of the hospital. The last thing you need is to go to school right now. And if what you say is true, Michelle will be able to clear things up herself."

"Dad—"

"Emma, I'm not sending you into that hornet's nest. Dr. Overbrook said you had nothing to do with it. In fact, he was very impressed that you'd rescued all those horses. I'm sure they'll do a thorough investigation, and if Michelle is innocent, she should have nothing to worry about."

I wasn't so sure. My dad didn't know Overbrook like I did, and he didn't know his history with Michelle. I sat silently, mulling over my options. I couldn't let Michelle take the fall for me again. What had my mother said to me that night on the moors? *You cannot save me, but you can save your friends.* Perhaps this was what she'd meant.

It was funny, but I missed my mother. Our night together on the moors had given me a glimpse of who she was in a way that seemed far more real than any of my faded and unreliable memories. I had so many questions about her, so many questions I'd always been too afraid to ask my father. Now here he sat right beside me, a captive audience.

"Dad?" I said tentatively.

"Mmm-hmm?" I could tell he was concentrating on the road.

"Was Mom pregnant when she died?"

My dad veered off the lane slightly, then corrected his steering and cleared his throat. "What?"

"Was Mom pregnant when she died?"

He shook his head, annoyed. "Why would you ask that?"

"I'm just curious."

My dad's brow furrowed, and his mouth went rigid. I didn't want to push him for fear that he'd close off completely. My dad could be like that sometimes. He sighed wearily, rubbing his eyes with his right hand, then focused on the road once more. "Emma, there's a lot you don't know about your mom," he said. I kept quiet, wanting him to go on. We were pulling onto our street already.

He pulled the car into the driveway and shut off the motor. He sat there for a long time, staring at the steering wheel, then turned to me and said, "Are you sure you want to know?"

"Know what?"

"Everything."

I nodded. My dad got out of the car and placed his hands on the roof. I got out, too, and stared at him from across the car. "Let's take a walk," he said.

The sun was shining, but there was a bitter chill in the air.

I shivered and drew my coat tightly around me. We walked side by side to the end of the block, then ambled up the dune walk onto the beach and headed down toward the shoreline. We were about ten feet from the water's edge when my father stopped and put his hands on his hips, staring out at the sea.

"I need you to know that I didn't tell you because I thought it was best at the time. That doesn't make it right, but I was trying my hardest to do the right thing."

"Dad," I said, grabbing his arm. "Didn't tell me what?"

He escaped from my grasp and started walking up the beach, toward the curving spit of land. "How much do you remember about your mother?" he asked.

I pressed my lips together. "Not enough."

"Do you remember her disappearing into her bedroom for days at a time?"

I thought about this. I did remember her going on reading binges when she'd take a dozen books into her room and barely come out for days. I assumed this was where I'd gotten my love of books and stories. I also had a fuzzy recollection of my mother getting headaches, of my father warning me not to bother her when she felt sick. "Did she used to get migraines?" I asked.

He nodded. "Your mother was . . . sick, Emma. She . . ." I could tell he was trying to choose his words carefully so as not to shock me, but I just wanted him to come out with the truth, no matter how much it hurt. "She had bipolar disorder."

Bipolar disorder. I had heard of this before. It conjured up images of Dr. Jekyll and Mr. Hyde, dual personalities, unpredictable mood swings.

"I know I should have told you sooner," he went on. "And I would have, if that were the end of the story." He sighed again, and there was such emotion and regret in that sigh that I got a little scared. "When we were first married, it wasn't so bad. She had episodes every now and then, but most of the time, she was the most amazing woman in the world. She was so full of life. You remember how she was always singing or drawing or playing with you. She had this deep, deep reservoir of energy she could always draw from, and it was intoxicating to be around her. But then the depressions would hit," he said. "And she wouldn't want me around, and she wouldn't want you around. It was almost like she was ashamed of herself. One time she went into her room and slept for nearly a week, only waking up when I made her eat something. She could be very cruel then. Hostile, like it was my fault that she felt that way. I finally convinced her to see a doctor."

He was walking faster now, and I could barely keep up with him. "And what happened?"

"He diagnosed her with bipolar disorder. The doctor wanted her to go on lithium, but she didn't want to take any medication. She was afraid it would dull her senses, make her less creative. I kept trying to get her to reconsider. I was scared for her, Emma. Eventually she agreed to try it for me, but she hated the way it made her feel. Just . . . flat. She had none of that wonderful spark I'd fallen in love with, none of that boundless energy. We both agreed she should stop taking it. If I had known then, Emma . . ."

I'd never seen my father this way. He had always been so stoic, so practical, never one for emotional outpourings, but I could see now that he was fighting back tears.

"Dad, what happened?" I said, stopping him with my hand. He stood still for a moment.

"She was going through a really bad depressive state. She didn't want to do anything but sit in her room all day. She kept saying she couldn't do it anymore, couldn't be a wife, a mother. Then she started talking nonsense, and it scared me. I tried to talk some sense into her, but she was beyond reason. Looking back, I should have called the doctor. I'd never seen her that bad. I should have known that time was different."

"Why, Dad? Why was that time different?" The tension in my chest was ripping me apart.

He took a deep breath and stared out at the ocean again. "One night, she woke up and got out of bed. God, Emma, I heard her get up, but I just didn't think. I listened to her pad down the stairs. I thought she was getting a glass of water or something. I must have drifted back to sleep because I didn't hear her slip out of the house." A feeling of dread descended on me. Somehow, somewhere in the deep recesses of my mind, I think I had always known what my father was about to tell me. "She came here to this beach and she walked right into the ocean with her nightgown on." He was crying now, wiping fiercely at his face with his sleeve. Seeing him cry made tears spring to my eyes. I wanted to reach out and touch him, but I knew it might freeze him, and I needed him to go on. "You have to understand, she wasn't herself. Laura would never have done that. It was the disease."

"Are you saying she drowned herself?"

He swallowed something thick and heavy. Grief, I think. "Yes."

Blood roared in my ears. I didn't want to hear any of this. I didn't want to know any of this. "How do you know, Dad? It could have been an accident. She had a bad heart. Maybe she had a heart attack. Or was that a lie, too?"

"Emma—" my father said, putting a hand on my shoulder. I fell silent because his touch was so firm and calming, but mostly because it was my father's. "She did have a bad heart, I didn't lie about that. It was a side effect of her disease. But that wasn't what killed her. She left a note, Emma. It was in her journal, dated on her birthday. That's why I got so upset . . . last year, at your party . . . I thought it was the same thing. I thought you were . . ." My father slumped down to the sand and threw his hands to his face.

"Oh God, Dad, I'm so sorry." I knelt down on the sand and flung my arms around him, putting my face against his cheek. It felt frozen. "That's why you took me to a psychiatrist," I said. "You were scared I might be sick, too. Why didn't you just tell me?"

"I wanted to. I meant to," he said. "I guess I thought I was protecting you. I didn't want you to remember your mother like that. I thought I could handle it on my own. I guess I felt guilty, like I was to blame."

"Dad, you weren't," I said. "She was sick, like you said. No one was to blame."

He inhaled deeply and looked at me, his face streaked with tears. "I should have told you sooner. It wasn't right of me. But I didn't want you to hate her."

"Hate her?" I said. "Dad, why would I hate her?"

"For leaving you, and . . ."

And then I remembered the suspicion I'd had in the car, recalled the dream I'd had at Thornfield: wandering through the ruins carrying a child, one I knew I couldn't let go of. In the dream, the walls had crumbled, and I'd lost my hold, and the baby had tumbled to the ground. Just as Bertha had catapulted to her death. Just as my mother had killed herself on this beach.

"You thought I'd hate her for taking the baby with her," I said.

He looked at me, astonished. "How did you know?" he asked.

"I didn't. I just . . . had a feeling."

"I never told anyone. Not even Barbara. It was just too awful. It's haunted me all these years, the image of her walking out into the waves, knowing she had a life inside her. She'd kept the pregnancy a secret even from me."

"But why?"

"Maybe she knew all along what she was planning to do. Maybe she felt unfit to be a mother again, given her condition. I don't know. I only know I was shocked when Grandma

Mackie told me. She was the only one who knew the truth." He sniffled and wiped his eyes. "It was going to be a girl."

I sat for a moment, silently staring at the ocean that had stolen my mother from my father and me. Now I understood why he worried so much for me. Now I understood why I'd always felt something missing in my life beyond the obvious fact that I was missing a mother. I was also missing a sister. In some other version of the universe, a sister walked beside me on the beach, held my hand, played hopscotch and dug for sand crabs with me.

"Dad, how have you lived all these years with this? How could you not tell me?"

"Like I said, I didn't want you to hate your mother. For a while, I hated her. I couldn't forgive her for doing that to us. If she'd lived, I don't know that I would have ever been able to forgive her."

I was crying now, too, the tears streaming down my cheeks. "You would have, Dad. She was sick. Like you said, she didn't know what she was doing. She was sick, and you loved her. Tell me you've forgiven her. Tell me you forgive her now." I didn't know why it was so important that my father forgive my mother after all these years. It was almost as if in forgiving her, he might finally be able to look at me and not see my mother's sickness, not feel that bitterness over what she'd done to him. "You did love her, Dad. Didn't you?"

My dad started crying again. "Of course I did. But it wasn't a healthy love. It was all-consuming. She sucked all the life out of me because she needed every ounce of my strength. She drained me of everything I had."

A line went through my head, Mr. Mason saying of Bertha, *She sucked my blood. She said she'd drain my heart.* Maybe that was what he'd meant, not that she'd physically preyed on him like some monster, some vampire, but that she'd drained him of every ounce of his strength because she so desperately needed it for herself.

"I know you haven't liked Barbara over the years," my dad said. "But that's what attracted me to her. Her strength. She never seemed to need me; she just wanted to be with me." For the first time, I felt like I understood Barbara a little bit. Like Jane, Barbara had brought sunshine and lightness to a house too long filled with darkness. And like Jane, she'd been competing for my father's affection with a ghost in the attic.

"Do you love her more than Mom?" I said.

He closed his eyes and pursed his lips. "My love for Barbara is such a different kind of love. It doesn't consume me. From the first time I met her, I knew she'd do me some good, I knew she'd help me forget."

I suddenly felt defensive and angry for my mother, for the young woman who had felt so desperate and hopeless that she'd walked into the ocean and drowned herself. Even a new baby could not give her a sense of hope. And now my father sat here talking about the woman who had helped him forget her.

"But, Dad," I said, "you can't just forget about Mom. You can't lock all her stuff in the attic and pretend she never existed. Because she did exist, and you loved her! And I'm her daughter, and I'm still here!"

My dad looked at me, almost in shock, as if just realizing the truth in what I'd said. Yes, I was still here. His wife and his unborn child were gone, but he still had me. He embraced me and sobbed into my shoulder, rocking and hugging me, until we were clinging together for dear life, trying to make each other whole again.

When we got back to the house I asked my dad if I could go up to the attic to look through Mom's things. To my surprise, he offered to come up and help me. Unearthing relics that had the power to drown us in emotions was a task better tackled with a partner.

My father pulled down the attic stairs, and I followed him

up the narrow rungs, emerging into a dark and musty attic with a low-beamed ceiling, a third floor that had been closed off to the world. Walking through aisles of boxes in near-complete darkness and breathing in the stale, dry air gave me the impression of walking through a tomb. As soon as my dad pulled the ceiling chain, a naked blub washed the space in pale yellow light, revealing years of neglect—ceilings fringed with cobwebs, boxes upon boxes of forgotten artifacts, objects leaning against the walls covered in fabric.

At first we went through things slowly, reverently, like we were combing through items in a museum that shouldn't be touched. There was an oppressive heaviness in the air—guilt, unspoken emotion, grief. Finally, I couldn't take it anymore. I marched to the far window and cracked it, feeling fresh air invade the space like a tonic.

It was almost as if that burst of fresh air freed us, gave us permission to open boxes with abandon, to open our hearts again. My dad dumped the entire contents of one of the boxes onto the floor, spilling out photo albums, recipes, notebooks. I began opening another frantically, tearing off packing tape, throwing tarps off her old belongings, throwing off the old constraints, the heavy feelings, the things that had weighed us down for so many years.

We sat down in the middle of this maelstrom, studying the space, which looked as though it had been ransacked. It hadn't been an act of violence that had rent it asunder, but an act of compassion. We were setting free memories, letting them breathe. I sat down in front of one box and took out a leather notebook that was sitting on top. The moment I held it in my hands, I knew. This was my mother's journal.

I flipped through it breathlessly, reading fragments of poetry and prose, reflections about me and my father, entries capturing the beauty of a sunrise or the darkness of her mind. "Dad, why didn't you tell me Mom was a writer?" I said.

He looked up from the box he was sorting and cleared his

throat. "She was very private about her writing. She rarely showed me anything. I guess I didn't realize how alike you were in that way."

"But you did read her journal after she died, right?"

He nodded distractedly.

"So you know she loved us both very much. She wasn't trying to hurt us. She felt we'd be better off without her."

"I know," my father said. "But that wasn't her choice to make."

If this was her journal, her suicide note was somewhere in these pages. With my heart in my throat, I flipped through, searching for my mother's birthday. There on the page in quavering handwriting that looked very much like my own, I read her final journal entry:

> My mind is a tomb, empty of all hope and light. My insides are dead, unfit to give new life. Everything I touch withers and dies. I can't go on with this pain, and I refuse to be a burden. I have taken enough from you. I can only hope you'll forgive me. Though fate may sever us, parting will not last forever. I will love you always.

Where had I heard those lines before? *Though fate may sever us, parting will not last forever.* They were the lyrics of a song. A lullaby. The one my mother had sung to me as a child. The one Bertha sang to me the night after I helped her escape, the night we slept in the heather under the stars. My mother had been trying to tell me something after all.

My mother had killed herself, that much was clear. But she hadn't killed her baby. My father had gotten it wrong. My mother had had a miscarriage. That's why the note said her insides were dead, unfit to give new life. Her baby had already withered and died inside her. And just like Bertha, the loss had destroyed her.

I looked up at my father, tears stinging my eyes. "What, Emma?" he said. "What is it?"

"It's the note," I said through sobs. "Her suicide note."

"Oh, Em, this is why I didn't want you to come up here."

"No, Dad. She didn't kill her baby." I took the journal over to him and crouched down beside him, shoving the journal into his hands. "Look. She would never have willingly killed her baby. She loved us too much. Can't you see? She had a miscarriage."

I ran my finger along the lines as my father read the words to himself. The look on his face showed that he believed me. That he suddenly understood.

We wouldn't talk about that day again for a very long time, but I knew that was the moment my father forgave my mother, and more important, forgave himself. The knowledge freed him to love her again. And as we went through the rest of her things that afternoon, I couldn't help but think that my mother was right there with us, that in some way, we'd freed her, too.

CHAPTER 24

That night I dreamt of the fire. My skin singed, and my eyes burned until I couldn't see, could only hear the horses' whinnies and cries, their panicked stomps. I walked through the smoke until I came to Curry's pen, but it was empty. Numb to the heat, I ran through the stables looking for him, feeling a stampede of hooves all around me. I followed the cavalcade until I was outside, looking up at a sky lit up with flame, billowing with smoke. My feet took me to the tree by the Commons, and I saw something lying at its roots. As I approached, my heart wrenched in my chest as recognition hit me. Curry's dead body lay on its side, his body scorched, his eyes open and lifeless, his tongue lolling out of his mouth.

Shrieking, I collapsed onto his body, tugging at his mane, screaming his name, trying to get him to wake, to come back to life. And then my father was above me, shaking my shoulders, pleading with me to wake up. Several seconds passed as he tried to convince me it had only been a nightmare, that Curry was alive and well, that my actions had saved him.

Sweat poured from my face as my father consoled me, my father who hadn't touched me in years. His arms were tight around me for the second time that day, and I knew somehow that my mother was responsible for this miracle, too.

Just as she'd saved my life at the beach, now she was saving the two of us.

When Gray took me back to school the next day, I made him drive me down to the stables so I could revisit the scene. Even though I knew the horses had been taken to a local farm for safekeeping, when I caught sight of their pens, now reduced to a pile of black wood and cinders, I heard their terror all over again. Gray came up behind me and wrapped me in a bear hug. I didn't want him to leave me. I didn't want to face my classmates and their questions. I especially didn't want to face Michelle.

I needn't have worried about Michelle because when I got up to my room, she wasn't there. The room felt empty, bereft of her presence. Her things were still there—posters and pictures, clothes still in the closet—but her presence was missing.

I quickly discovered through the gossip mill that Michelle had been suspended, and that they'd taken my journal as evidence. There was going to be an expulsion hearing in three weeks. Even more astounding was that Michelle had gone to the Disciplinary Committee last week and implicated Elise Fairchild by telling them that Elise and her friends sometimes smoked pot down at the stables and that they probably started the fire. Her accusation unleashed a firestorm, and now Elise's parents were threatening to sue the school.

So that's why Michelle hadn't come to see me at the hospital. She'd been dealing with this arson investigation nonsense. And it was nonsense. There was no way Michelle had started the fire. She loved those horses more than anything. Yet with Overbrook heading the Disciplinary Committee, Michelle didn't stand much of a chance. Add to that the fact that Elise's parents probably had an arsenal of lawyers waiting in the wings to pounce on anybody who dared suggest that their dear, sweet, perfect daughter could have been smoking pot, and you had a recipe for disaster.

I called Michelle's cell phone several times, but kept getting bounced to her voicemail. I decided to call Owen to find out what I could from him. He sounded relieved to hear from me.

"Oh my God, Emma. How are you?" he said.

"I'm okay."

"I'm so sorry I didn't make it to the hospital again. This week's been crazy. I've been trying to run damage control with Michelle. You heard what happened?"

"Yeah. How is she?"

"Awful. She's won't talk to anyone, not even me. She's been acting crazy."

"Well, you can't really blame her. The situation is ridiculous."

"But you know Michelle. She's usually such a fighter, but now . . . it seems like she's given up. She's totally shut down. She even told me she's dropping out of the equestrian competition."

"Is she at home with her aunt?"

"I think so, but when I tried to go see her, her aunt wouldn't let me in."

"Don't give up," I said. "Michelle needs you, even if she's pushing you away right now. She just needs some time." Owen promised to keep trying, and I got off the phone feeling a little better. Of course, without Michelle there, I felt entirely alone, too.

The next day was one of the worst days of my high school memory. Everyone was talking about the impending hearing, and my sudden reappearance made me the subject of much speculation. How was I involved in all of this? Did I remember what had happened the night of the fire? Would I be testifying against Elise?

Elise and her crew glared at me all day while I sat through lecture after lecture. But my heart and mind were not focused on school. I was too busy worrying about Michelle, about my father, about the essay contest, about Gray. That night, I skulked back to my room, threw on some sweats, and had a dinner of Pop-Tarts and ramen noodles so I wouldn't have to go to the dining hall.

The next day I stayed after English class to talk to Mr. Gallagher about the expulsion hearing. It was incredible, but standing next to him alone in the classroom had absolutely no effect on me. It was like I'd suddenly woken up and realized the falseness in everything I'd dreamed. Mr. Gallagher was just a man, and an aging one at that. His hair had gotten grayer at the temples, and he'd even started to grow a little gut.

"How are you feeling, Emma?" Mr. Gallagher asked kindly, giving me the penetrating stare that used to leave me breathless. But I wasn't feeling it. And I didn't want to talk about me, not when my best friend's future was hanging in the balance. Ignoring his question, I said, "Mr. Gallagher, I have to talk to you and the Disciplinary Committee. I have some information that might be relevant."

"What is it?"

"It's about the poem."

"The poem?"

"You know, the one about revenge and burning? The one the committee is using as evidence? See, the thing is, I wrote it, not Michelle."

"You wrote it?"

"Yes."

He removed his glasses and began cleaning them with his handkerchief. "It's awfully noble of you to try to take the fall for your friend—"

"No, honestly, Mr. Gallagher. I'm not trying to take the fall. I actually wrote all the poems. The journal's mine."

He gave me a skeptical look and then sighed. "Even if it is yours, the poem is not the reason she's being suspended. It's just one piece of evidence. Her behavior toward the Disciplinary Committee has been entirely unacceptable."

"Please, let me talk to the committee. Ask Overbrook if he'll give me an audience."

He paused for a long time, then replaced his glasses and looked at me as if seeing me for the first time. "Because it's you, Emma, I'll try."

"Thank you, Mr. Gallagher. Really, thank you."

Gallagher was able to get me an appointment with Overbrook for that Thursday afternoon. I sprinted back to my room after class and changed into a nice blouse and skirt. When I arrived at the boardroom, Mr. Gallagher and Dr. Overbrook were seated at a long table at the front of the room, flanked by two board members. I had never addressed a group such as this, not even when I had interviewed for the scholarship. Even Mr. Gallagher looked harsh and unyielding. He resembled Rochester more than ever, but instead of inspiring my admiration and fear, he provoked only a cold resentment in me now.

I walked up the aisle of the boardroom, listening to my heels clack along the hardwood floor, and stood at a podium in front of their table. This room seemed designed to inspire terror in the presenter. *Come on, Jane, don't fail me now.*

I cleared my throat, about to speak, when Dr. Overbrook held out a peremptory palm. "Ms. Townsend, we appreciate the spirit in which you have come here today in an effort to provide information that may be useful to our investigation. Before we begin, let me remind you that you stand before members of the Disciplinary Committee. This board will serve as jury during Michelle's hearing, so anything you tell us today will become a part of our records."

Sweat was already beading along my forehead, my mouth was getting pasty, and I could feel the dampness under my armpits staining my blouse. "I understand, sir," I said. "I came here today because you have a journal with a poem that seems to implicate Michelle in the stable fire. But the journal is mine, not Michelle's."

I expected for the waters to part, for murmurs of relief to buzz through the boardroom as they realized they had accused the wrong person. But Dr. Overbrook simply said, "Yes, Mr. Gallagher has apprised us of your contention that the journal is yours. The fact of the matter is, the message in the poem is consistent with other behaviors observed in Ms. Dominguez throughout the year, and we feel your attempt to clear her name, while well-intentioned, is misguided."

"No, sir. I'm serious. The journal is mine. Every poem."

He glanced at Mr. Gallagher and, with an almost imperceptible roll of his eyes, said, "Ms. Townsend, you're telling us this is yours?" He held up my turquoise journal, the one containing my most private thoughts, my most secret fantasies.

"Yes, sir."

"Forgive me, but I find that impossible to believe," he said. It was clear he'd read the entire thing, not just the poem in question. The thought made me want to vomit.

One of the board members suggested, "Perhaps we should ask for a handwriting sample." I wanted to smack their heads together, they were being so stubborn and stupid.

"I don't think that will be necessary," Mr. Gallagher said. "But if it is her journal, surely she will know its contents, even without the pages in front of her. For instance, page twelve contains a poem called 'Noble Brow.' I wonder if you could recite it for us, Ms. Townsend, to the best of your recollection."

God, I hated him at that moment. He knew darn well what the poem was about, and now he wanted to humiliate me in front of the panel. The board members murmured to each other, still dubious but curious to see how this would pan out. I steeled myself for what I was about to do.

Before losing my nerve, I plunged in, reciting word for word the sonnet I'd written about Mr. Gallagher. The others were all craning their necks behind Gallagher's shoulders to see if my words matched those on the page, but Gallagher was staring down at me the entire time, listening with grave interest, his eyes weighted with a meaning I couldn't discern. When I finally finished, I was certain I would die on the spot.

Their glances flickered at each other. Stupidly, Dr. Overbrook said, "She could have memorized Michelle's poem."

But then Gallagher said, "I think it's pretty clear that Ms. Townsend did write this poem and, therefore, is probably the author of the incriminating poem as well."

Overbrook pursed his lips, annoyed. Things weren't going his way. "Unfortunately, that doesn't absolve Ms. Dominguez," he said. "Mr. Gallagher, you said yourself that you saw Michelle leave the dance just moments before Ms. Townsend left and found the stables ablaze. When we questioned some of the other girls, they said Ms. Dominguez was fond of spending time at the stables. She is a rider, yes?"

"Look," I said, feeling a strange power come over me, "Michelle is a rider and she does spend a lot of time at the stables. And yes, she did leave the dance that night. But Michelle loves those horses. Why would she want to harm them? Elise left the dance earlier that evening with some friends, and they were gone for a long time. Even her date said he thought she'd gone outside to smoke. Maybe she and her friends were smoking in the stables and accidentally started the fire. I've seen them there before, smoking marijuana."

Dr. Overbrook choked a little, then sat up in his chair. "That is a very serious accusation, Ms. Townsend," he said. "I warn you to be careful what you say. I am not dragging a girl like Elise Fairchild into some drug scandal based on the word of Ms. Dominguez's best friend. It is very clear your motivations in this case are not entirely based on a wholesome respect for the truth. It is interesting that Ms. Fairchild also saw Ms. Dominguez heading down to the stables that night."

"Sir," I said. "I'm sure Elise did claim to see Michelle going down to the stables, but given the circumstances, perhaps she also had motivations that weren't entirely based on a wholesome respect for the truth." I knew I was walking a tightrope between being strong and being stupid, but at that moment I didn't care.

Overbrook got the same red-faced expression he'd gotten when Michelle had challenged him in class about third-world countries. "In the past," he said, "Ms. Dominguez has displayed a fiery temper and a reckless disregard for the rules. Consider the night of the bonfire, when she dragged you out after hours and you ended up lying in a hospital for three weeks. Her behavior in my classroom has been consistently willful and disrespectful—"

"But none of that has any bearing on whether she did or did not set the stables on fire. You can't go into this situation with your mind already made up," I said. My calm and measured voice sounded foreign in my ears.

"Do not presume to tell me, Ms. Townsend, how I can or cannot run this investigation. May I remind you that you are here on the grace of a scholarship, one that is funded by the very family of the girl whose character you are trying to malign? Elise Fairchild is a model student respected by students and faculty alike. She has a stellar record of both scholarship and citizenship and is very likely headed toward an Ivy League education and a distinguished career. I see no reason why she would jeopardize all that for the sake of one night of smoking in a barn."

"Because she can!" I said. "She knows she won't get in trouble because you're all too afraid of her family to punish her. Why won't you even consider that it could have been Elise? You're willing to drag Michelle's name through the mud and ruin the chances for her future, but you're not—"

"Enough!" Overbrook said, shouting so loudly that even the board members recoiled. "You are treading on very thin ice, young lady. If it turns out that Ms. Dominguez is innocent, I will do what I can to be lenient and to make sure that Michelle is allowed to come back to Lockwood and finish her education here. But consider this. Ms. Fairchild's family is very generous to the school. They make it possible for you and your roommate to attend Lockwood. I have heard excellent things about you, Ms. Townsend, and if you play your cards right, you have every possibility of getting into an Ivy League school and launching a distinguished career of your own some day. I suggest you think very carefully on all of this and consider whether you really want to bring this damaging and far-fetched testimony to the hearing in April. We have heard what you have to say, and you are dismissed."

I glanced at Gallagher one more time, hoping he might soften and consider how unfair Overbrook was being, but he dropped his eyes. He knew this was a farce as much as I did. In the end, the rich would always win.

I walked out of the boardroom and into the cold February air. It was five o'clock. Months ago, it would have already been dark at this time, but the sun was still out, reminding me that spring would be here soon.

I was walking briskly back to the dorm hoping not to run into anyone when Mr. Gallagher came up behind me and grabbed my arm. "Emma," he said. "I'm so sorry about all of that. You must understand—"

I yanked my arm from his grasp. "I understand perfectly." His gaze fell to the ground with that same enigmatic expression I'd seen before.

"I wanted to ask you about the symposium," he said. "Given all that's happened, I hope you're still planning to enter your essay?"

At first I wasn't sure how to respond. What was the point in competing against someone like Elise? And yet, not competing seemed like giving up. I had been angry when I heard that Michelle had decided to drop out of the equestrian com petition. I would be a hypocrite if I quit the symposium now. "Yes," I said.

"Good. I hoped that all this"—he pointed back toward Easty Hall—"wouldn't change anything."

"It changes everything," I said. "But I'm still going to compete. I may, however, make a few changes to my essay."

"Oh?" he said.

"In the draft I gave to you, I say that Jane is a strong role model for women because she forgives Rochester for his failings, but at the same time, refuses to become his lover until he's redeemed himself. But now I disagree. I don't think she should have forgiven him at all. How could she go back to Rochester after discovering what he'd done? If she had been a true feminist, she would have looked out for Bertha." I realized my mind was muddled with all the events of the past few months: witnessing Bertha's suicide and not being able to stop it, learning the truth about my mother, losing my friendship with Michelle. But I did believe what I'd said about standing up for those who couldn't stand for themselves.

Mr. Gallagher wore a patronizing expression. "You are young," he said, "and you haven't experienced much of the world. I think you'll find that love does strange things to a person. We forgive much in love. Some day you will understand this."

I glared at him for a moment, my crush on him officially extinguished forever. How dare he condescend to me just because he was older and had seen more of the world? How dare he imply that I couldn't possibly understand the complexities of love because I was too young?

Maybe I hadn't experienced true love yet, but I was only sixteen. I understood love as much as anyone could at my age. At least, I think I was beginning to. And it was Gray Newman, not Mr. Gallagher, who had everything to do with it.

CHAPTER 25

The rest of the week was a miserable and agonizing blur as I waited for word about the hearing. I didn't hold out much hope that my "testimony" would make any difference. Michelle still hadn't called me back, and I was hurt that I'd gone to all this trouble for her and she still thought I was the bad guy.

That Sunday Gray was coming to take me out to a sushi restaurant in Waverly Falls, and we were finally going to get to finish our game of Poker Polygraph. Of course, with a father who was a fisherman, I'd eaten fish my entire life, but never raw fish. I was a little skeptical, but food was the last thing on my mind that day as I dressed in my favorite sweater—a fake cashmere in a soft violet color—with jeans and black boots. It had snowed overnight, so the campus was covered in a soft blanket of white and the trees looked like they'd been trimmed with lace.

I threw on my long black coat and ran downstairs, startled when I reached the lobby to see that Gray's hair had been nearly shaved to his skull.

"Wow," I said. "When did you do that?"

"Last night. The swim team just made Districts. The coach said this is more hydrodynamic." He ran a hand over his smooth scalp. "Do you hate it?"

I paused a second too long. "No, I just need a minute to get used to it."

Gray laughed and opened the door for me, and we walked across the quad. His navy Jeep Wrangler was parked in the lot, and I felt a little uncomfortable as I climbed into the passenger seat. Was this a date or just two friends hanging out? I still wasn't sure.

When we were in the car, Gray lifted his pant leg to show me that the coach had made the team shave their legs, too. He looked sleek and streamlined, like a dolphin. There was something oddly sexy about it.

Waverly Falls was a fifteen-minute drive through country roads, so I sat back in my seat and listened to a music mix Gray had made. It was liberating to leave the gates of Lockwood for a day, to wind down the road away from campus, surrounded by evergreens dusted with snow. Waverly was an old mill town that had been transformed into a quaint and trendy shopping destination. The mill still stood above the river, but it was just a burnt shell of itself, a museum relic that, for some reason, the town had left to rot on the hillside. We drove past the spot where the river was dammed to power the hydroelectric generator, and Gray pulled over to the side of the road and parked.

"I want to show you something," he said.

He walked around to my side of the Jeep and opened my door. I took his hand briefly then let go as we began walking uphill toward the falls. During dry seasons, people used to picnic on the rocks here and swim in the river. The water is clean, and the stones, smoothed by years of erosion, are striated with shades of beige, copper, pink, and white so they look like marble. A few years ago, a boy drowned when the dam opened unexpectedly, unleashing a surge of water that swept him downstream. That's when they stopped allowing swimming and built the four-foot stone wall that now separated us from the river.

When we reached the top, the mammoth iron gate that enclosed the hydroelectric plant partially obscured the view of the falls and the sixty-foot drop below. But we could certainly feel its presence. The air here was cool, moistened by spray, and the roar of the falls was almost deafening.

I pointed to a sign that hung on the gate near the drop-off. It said: RIVER LEVELS RISE AND FALL DAILY. STAY AWAY OR YOU WILL DIE.

"Not exactly subtle, is it?" I said. Gray laughed and shook his head. "So why did you want to show me this?"

"Because it's one of my favorite places," he said. "It's sort of peaceful here."

I scanned the industrial view of the dam and listened to the tumult of water, feeling more anxious than anything else. "How exactly is this peaceful?" I asked, laughing.

He paused for a second. "I can't think here. It's too loud. I imagine myself out there, in the thick of all that water and sound, and I can disappear. I come here when I need to get away from everybody."

"But you brought me here," I said, teasing him.

"You're not everybody." His eyes met mine for one charged moment, then flickered off into the distance. His hand gripped one of the slats of the gate, and I got the same feeling I'd gotten that day on the beach when I thought Gray was about to tell me something. Something important. I wanted him to open up to me, but I wasn't sure how to reach him. "Come on," he said, seeming like he was a little disappointed by my reaction to his special place. "Let's go eat."

I felt guilty, but his mood lightened as soon as we got into town. The hostess at the restaurant sat us at the sushi bar and brought us a little carafe of hot sake. Gray poured me a small cup but left his empty.

"Aren't you having any?" I said.

He shook his head. I took a sip and winced.

"You don't like it?" he said.

"It's an acquired taste."

"Like me." He smiled, and I wondered why one little flash of white teeth could rattle my brain like that.

We studied the menu, ordering a sampling of sushi, sashimi, and rolls. Once the waitress left us, Gray reached his arms across the bar and took my hands in his. I felt an electric shiver flutter through me. "You look really pretty today," he said, and I rolled my eyes, uncomfortable with flattery. "You realize that rolling your eyes like that only makes you look more adorable."

"Stop it," I said.

"Stop what?"

"Complimenting me. I liked it better when you were teasing me. Besides, how can you call me pretty after Elise Fairchild?"

His eyes narrowed like he was angry. "Emma, she may be pretty, but I'm not in love with Elise Fairchild, and I never was. Our friends set us up together, and it worked out for a while because we hung with the same crowd. But she's proven time and time again that she's phony and shallow and the complete opposite of you."

"Then why did you agree to go to the Snow Ball with her?"

He bit the inside of his cheek like he was considering whether to tell me or not. "Don't get mad," he said. My eyebrows rose expectantly. "I went with Elise to make you jealous."

"You what?" I let this sink in and found myself simultaneously annoyed and flattered. "Gray, that's horrible. Didn't you consider her feelings at all?"

"To be honest, I didn't. She doesn't worry about anyone else's feelings. That day at the beach, I asked you about the dance to see how you'd react. I thought you might be going with Owen, and the thought made me so jealous that I just blurted out that I was going with Elise."

"I can't believe you!"

"Don't be angry," he said.

I was angry, but it was hard to stay mad at him when his motivation had been to make me jealous. The waitress came and set down the sushi we'd ordered: tuna, salmon, red snapper, and unagi, which Gray said was just eel. I dutifully tried each one, but the only thing I liked was the pickled ginger.

"Based on our last game of poker," I said, hoping he wouldn't notice I wasn't eating very much, "I get to ask you some questions."

"Two, I think."

"Three, you big cheater!"

"I was hoping you were so out of it you wouldn't remember."

"Well, I do remember." He put a huge dollop of wasabi on a piece of sashimi and stuck the entire thing in his mouth. "Stuffing your mouth so you can't talk won't work," I said.

He swallowed dramatically. "All right, ask away."

"Okay, question number one," I said. "Who's your favorite author?"

He took a deep breath and sighed. "That's a dangerous question."

"Why?"

"Because my answer to this probably determines whether I get a second date with you."

"That's not true," I said, smiling at his use of the word *date*. "Come on, I'm not going to judge you."

"Girls always judge. You say you won't, but then I'll give my answer, and your face will get all weird, and I'll know you disapprove."

"Just answer the question," I said, laughing.

"Okay, fine. Hemingway."

"Ughhhh," I groaned.

"See? You're judging."

"I'm kidding!" I said. "But what is it with men and Hemingway?"

"I don't know," he said. "I guess I like the whole code hero thing. Like, in *The Sun Also Rises,* I love that Jake Barnes is this flawed hero who's so damaged that he can't connect with people."

"The strong, silent type," I said.

"Yeah."

"All right, moving on," I said. "And you have to tell the truth on this one. No telling me what I want to hear."

"You want the truth?" he said, standing up from his stool and doing his best Jack Nicholson impression. "You can't handle the truth!"

I cracked up. "You're pretty corny, you know that?"

"I know. It's my big secret." He sat down.

"I knew you had one. But stalling will get you nowhere. Here's my question: What do you want to do with your life?"

His mouth fell open, and he leaned back in his stool as far as it would go. "Has my mom been talking to you?" he said.

"No, I'm just curious."

"Aw, Em," he said, looking away from me. "I have no idea what I want to do. When I think about it, my stomach starts to hurt. Or maybe that's just the unagi talking." He picked up the last piece of eel with his chopsticks and wriggled it in front of me.

"Can you at least try to answer the question?"

"Okay," he said. "My dad wants me to go to Northeastern for business so I can take over All Naturals when I graduate. But when I think about doing that for the rest of my life, I want to kill myself. I used to want to study criminal justice at BU, but I don't think my grades are good enough to get in. I screwed up my freshman and sophomore years, and my GPA is pretty pathetic. I've thought about joining the military, but I'm not sure I want to do that right now, so . . . I don't know. I feel kind of aimless. I wish I had it all figured out like you."

"Believe me, I don't have it all figured out. But I know that I don't want you to join the military," I said, looking down at the bar.

"Why not?" He was watching me intently, waiting for my answer. I wanted to say something smart and political, like I was a pacifist or something. But the only reason I had at the moment was that I didn't want him to go far away.

"It seems dangerous," I said.

"It is dangerous. That's the point."

"You mean you want to put yourself in harm's way?"

"Kind of," he said.

"Why?"

We were no longer just joking around; I seemed to have opened some old wound. "I wouldn't mind dying if it meant saving someone else's life," he said. "Sometimes I feel like I have to do something dangerous, or I'll go crazy." He looked past me and out the window, and I was sort of sorry I'd brought the subject up. His eyes had gone all distant and sad. "Anyway," he said, "enough about that. What's your third question?"

For the moment, I couldn't remember what my third question was going to be. Before I could formulate my thoughts, I heard myself asking, "Did you sleep with Elise?" I was glad Gray didn't have food in his mouth because I think he would have spat it at me. Suddenly, I didn't want to know the answer.

"You know what?" I said, shaking my head. "Never mind. That was rude. I'll ask something else—"

"No, it's okay."

"No, really, Gray. You don't have to—"

"Yes."

"What?"

"Yes. I did. Sleep with Elise."

"Oh."

A surge of jealousy burned through me. What had I expected? That Gray Newman was a saint? That he was the only red-blooded eighteen-year-old in the world who could say no to Elise Fairchild?

"You've gone all quiet on me," he said, his head dipping to study my face.

"Hmm?" I couldn't look at him.

"I knew I shouldn't have told you."

"I was the one who asked."

"We did go out for six months, Em."

"I know. There's nothing wrong with it. I'm just . . ." I started compulsively straightening up our plates and glasses for the waitress. Gray stilled my hand.

"Hey," he said. "Let's not talk about Elise. She's out of my life. I want to talk about you. This day is about us. What do you want to do?"

"I don't know." I was kind of sulking.

"Let's go shopping," he suggested.

"What, you think shopping can heal a girl's wounds?" I said, insulted.

"No, I just think it'll be fun."

He paid our check, and we left the restaurant. I was still stewing a bit. The image of Gray and Elise physically entwined made me ill. We strolled down the street and passed an upscale dress shop. Gray threw his arm around my shoulder and steered me inside.

"Why are we going here?" I asked.

"Because."

"Is this some kinky high school boy fantasy? Get me to try on a bunch of sexy dresses while you sit outside the dressing room and watch?"

"Something like that," he said, flashing a ridiculously sexy smile.

He opened the shop door, which jingled as we entered. The

store was small but packed wall to wall with high-end dresses, accessories, and jewelry. I had never seen such nice gowns before—everything from little black cocktail dresses to stunning floor-length gowns. I walked through the aisles, running my hand along the different fabrics and textures.

"Choose a few to try on," he said.

"What for?"

"Just humor me."

I shopped around and chose two: a simple knee-length black dress with a sexy low back and a gray-blue chiffon dress with pretty beading and sequins.

I was heading for the dressing room when Gray said, "Take in a few more. Take this one." He held up an above-the-knee strapless red dress in a flouncy material that was gathered in a knot right where my cleavage should have been. The dress was daring and sexy and definitely not me.

"I don't think so," I said.

"Why not? You wore red to the Snow Ball, and you looked sexy as hell."

I felt vaguely uncomfortable, like I was playing dress-up for him. "That wasn't my dress," I said. "It was Michelle's."

"Well, you wore it well. I want to see you in red silk with roses in your hair and Tiffany diamonds around your neck."

"Gray, I don't want any of that stuff. I'd be far happier in this one," I said, holding up the plain black dress.

"I know, I know. I just want you to choose a dress that's going to make you feel the most beautiful when you come with me to my senior prom."

I stopped moving and gaped at him. "What?"

He got suddenly shy and took my hands in his own. "Emma, would you go to my prom with me?" My heart flipped once, and for a moment I thought I'd heard him wrong. Had Gray Newman just asked me to his prom? Despite all this internal combustion, my face must have remained expressionless because Gray began to frown. "Well, will you?"

I nodded, and the look of relief on his face was so adorable that I threw the dresses over one of the racks and flung my arms around him. I could feel his warm breath against my ear, his hands wrapping around my waist.

"I was worried," he said. "For a minute there, you looked like you hated me."

"It's called bluffing, Gray," I said, smiling. "You should try it some time."

"Oh, so now you're teasing me?"

"Maybe."

He bit his lower lip. "You know what's teasing me?" he said. "The thought of you in that red dress."

I shot him a playful look, then disappeared into the dressing room. Despite his numerous pleas, I did not model any of the dresses for him. It felt a little too voyeuristic, and besides, I didn't want him to know which dress I'd chosen.

Afterward, I told him to wait outside for me, but he insisted on slipping his credit card underneath the dressing room door. On the way home he kept trying to peek inside the bag, but I slapped his hand away. We arrived back at Lockwood around six, and I felt that familiar knot of dread forming in my stomach.

"Do I have to go back?" I said as he braked in front of Lockwood's gates.

"Not if you don't want to."

"Can't we just drive around for a little bit?"

"Sure," he said.

We drove right past Lockwood's gates and meandered through the wooded country roads until we came to a small grassy lot on the side of the road with just enough room for a few cars. The sign at the edge of the lot said, OAKWOOD LANE PARK.

"Do you want to stop here for a little while?" Gray said. My heart beat fast. "Okay."

He pulled into the lot and cut the motor, leaving the radio on. Then he leaned back in his seat and stared at me wistfully. I leaned back, too, our hands drifting toward one another until his knuckles were grazing mine. "Just brushing your hand makes me crazy," he said.

I took in a deep breath. "When can we see each other again?"

"How about Friday night? I'll take you out to dinner. Somewhere fancy. Your choice. No sushi this time."

"Gray, you really don't have to spoil me like this. I'm not like all those other girls you've dated."

"I know. And that's exactly why you deserve it," he said. "Come here." The huskiness in his voice made me tremble.

He took hold of my arms and pulled me toward him. I hovered awkwardly over the gearshift for a few seconds. Then, placing his hands firmly around my waist, he guided me over to where he was sitting, so I was straddled across his legs. I had never been this close to a guy in my life. Since there was so little headroom, I had to lean into him to avoid bumping my head. He smelled like salt and spice and ocean waves. His shirt was open a little, and I could see his dog tags lying across his still-tanned chest. I slipped my hand inside and pressed my palm against his heart, where his pulse beat hard and steady against my fingertips. He shifted in his seat, then pressed the seat release so I fell on top of him. I gasped a little and laughed nervously.

He laughed, too, but then his face grew serious as he clutched my hips and stared into my eyes. I ran a hand slowly across his close-cut scalp, enjoying the feel of stubble against my palm. He closed his eyes and made a soft sighing sound. His hands strayed from my jeans underneath my sweater to my lower back, making the blood rush to my head.

His chest felt so strong and warm beneath me, like our

bodies had been made to fit together. His hands came up to my face, and he gently drew my lips down to meet his. This time there was no pulling away. Waves of heat radiated through my body. The kiss grew deeper, warmer and wetter and more intense, until I wasn't thinking about anything other than this kiss, letting myself fall headfirst into the white-hot madness of it. I was tumbling into him, losing thought, losing time. Other parts of my body began to engage, and I was all heat and light, tugging at his shirt, digging into his back, burrowing myself in the hollow of his neck.

Gray was the one who pushed away first, looking breathless and flushed like he'd just swum the 100-meter freestyle. "Whoa," he said, panting.

I shook my head, unable to speak. I needed air, I needed water. I needed Gray. Even as he sat there looking worried about me, all I could focus on were his lips, seductively swollen from our kiss. "You're not going to hit me if I tell you we should stop, are you?" he said.

I exhaled a frustrated sigh. "I don't know," I breathed. "I might." Laughing, I collapsed onto his chest.

"God, you're a good kisser," he said. "Where'd you learn to do that?"

I sat up and flashed him a deadpan look. "Books," I said. He burst out laughing, dispelling all the pent-up tension in the air.

I crawled back over to my side of the car, still out of breath, and we sat and listened to music for a while as we waited for our heartbeats to return to normal. It was after seven o'clock by the time we got back to Lockwood. Gray parked his Jeep in the visitor lot, then leaned over and lightly bit my ear. Reflexively, I arched my back, loving the feel of his hot breath on my neck. He took this as an invitation to roam down my throat, his mouth parting slightly as he did, rendering me senseless. I might as well have been on morphine.

"I thought you said we should stop," I reminded him.

"Yeah, I don't know what I was thinking," he said teasingly, but pulling back. "Seriously, I don't want to mess things up with you by moving too fast."

"Okay," I said, not believing how much I wanted him. "Still, I wish you could come to my room."

"I know," he whispered. "It's probably a good thing I can't. I have a huge econ test tomorrow. I don't know how I'm going to concentrate." He reached his hand out to me, and I took it, drawing it up to my lips and kissing his wrist, delicately, like I was kissing a wound. "That's not helping," he said.

"Sorry." I grinned playfully. "Okay, I'm getting out of the car now. Until Friday."

"Until Friday."

He leaned over and kissed me one more time—a long, slow burn of a kiss—and I felt that intoxicating breathlessness again. I didn't want it to stop. Finally, I pulled away. Gray closed his eyes and made a frustrated moan, and I reluctantly got out of the Jeep and walked across the quad in a daze and up the stairs on a cloud of endorphins.

I was brought abruptly back to earth when I opened the door to my room and saw Michelle.

CHAPTER 26

"Hey," I said. "You're back!" I was still flushed from the kiss.

Michelle gave me a look as if to say, "No duh," but made no motion to get up or even change her position. We hadn't seen each other since the night of the Snow Ball, and I was sort of hurt that this was how she'd chosen to greet me.

"So how are you?" I said.

"How do you think I am?"

"Pretty pissed off, I'd imagine."

"Yeah, well, that's an understatement."

"I thought you were out for ten days' suspension," I said.

"Apparently they reconsidered. They said it's better if I'm here, not missing any more classes."

Silence fell between us, and it felt like the first day we'd met all over again. I sat down on my bed and tried to make small talk.

"How's Darlene?" I asked.

"Angry at the school, but fine otherwise."

"And Owen? Have you talked to Owen?"

"Sort of."

"What happened with you guys?"

"It's complicated." She sighed, sounding exhausted. "He's

mad at me because I dropped out of the competition, and I'm mad at him . . . well, for other reasons."

"You're really dropping out?"

She shrugged. "What's the point? The system is set up for them to win and for us to lose. It's easier to give up and accept the inevitable." This person who sat across from me wasn't Michelle. It was as if all the life had been sucked out of her.

"What's up with you and Gray?" she asked. "Chelsea told me you were out with him tonight. I guess that means Elise knows about you two."

"Good old Chelsea," I said, trying to engage Michelle in some harmless banter about Lockwood girls. But her face remained impassive. For a moment I just wanted to have my old friend back, someone to share in the excitement that I had just had my first official make-out session with a boy. "He asked me to his prom," I said.

"He did?" She made eye contact for the first time that night.

"He bought me a dress and everything." I kicked the shopping bag lightly, but she didn't ask to see it.

"Be careful with him," she said, averting her eyes.

"What do you mean?"

"Owen's heard things about him. He has a reputation. And not with girls like you." She slumped down onto her bed like she just wanted to go to sleep.

"Oh, right," I said. "He couldn't possibly be interested in a girl like me, is that it?"

"That's not what I said. You don't have to get so defensive. I was just trying to be a good friend." I hated her at that moment. She didn't know Gray, and she had no right to squelch all my enthusiasm with stupid rumors.

Something inside me snapped. "Oh, yeah, Michelle, you've been such a good friend that you haven't answered any of my phone calls and didn't even come to visit me in the hospital."

"If you haven't noticed, *Emma,* I've been suspended."

"I know, *Michelle,* but did they suspend your cell phone service, too?"

Her voice got very quiet. "I didn't want to talk to you."

"Why? I don't understand. Did I do something wrong? Am I missing something here?"

"You miss everything!" she said, lashing out at me. "How could you possibly understand what I've been going through? You haven't even been here."

"That's not fair," I said.

"You know what's not fair?" she said. "That I got blamed for sneaking out to Braeburn. That I got blamed for the fire at the stables. That I'm the only girl of color in a sea of white. Do you have any idea what that feels like?"

No, I didn't. And I never would. No matter how hard I tried to understand Michelle, there would always be some part of her I could never know. It was the part that had grown so shriveled and bitter and hard, she'd hidden it deep inside herself like a dormant seed that would only grow if she learned how to forgive people.

"Michelle, I'm not the enemy," I said. "I'm a scholarship kid, too. I've had it just as hard as you, and I don't appreciate being treated like Elise or one of the other Lockwood snobs."

"But you are like them," she shouted. My mouth fell as I tried to comprehend what she was saying to me. "People treat you differently than they treat me."

I stood up and approached her bed. "They do, Michelle, but not for the reason you think." I was so angry, but I knew what Michelle needed to hear. "It's because you speak your mind and I don't. You scare the crap out of these spoiled students and prissy teachers. They don't know what to do with you. I've always been timid and quiet, never one to make waves. That's why they treat me differently. But you know what? Your way is better. I realized that. Last fall when you covered for me about the journal, I thought you were the bravest person I'd ever met. And that's why I went to testify this week. On Thursday I stood before the disciplinary committee and told them the journal was mine, told them you were innocent. I even recited the Gallagher poem from memory in front of everybody—including him—to prove it was mine. I did that for you."

She stared at me in astonishment. "You did?"

"Yeah. I also told Overbrook that I'd seen Elise and her friends smoking pot at the stables, and he basically threatened that if I testified to that at the hearing, he'd see that I lost my scholarship and any chance of getting into a good college."

Michelle's defensiveness finally buckled. "God, Emma. I'm sorry. I'm sorry I dragged you into all this."

I pretended to slap her. "You didn't drag me into anything. I was already in it. It's my journal that started all this. My words. And I don't care about going to a stupid Ivy League school. You, on the other hand, are destined to go to MIT."

She dropped her eyes to the ground. "I'm so sorry I didn't come visit you in the hospital, Emma," she said. Her voice was muffled, ashamed. "I wanted to. But when this suspension thing happened, and you weren't there to help me through it, I felt like I was going to lose my mind. So I took off."

"What do you mean?"

"I went looking for my dad."

Her eyes filled with tears, and I went to sit next to her on the bed. "What happened?"

Michelle snorted. "Darlene called the cops and filed a missing persons report before I could find anything out."

"How did you even know where to look?" I said.

"Darlene forgot to tear up one of the envelopes with my monthly child support check, and I saw the postmark. I think my dad lives somewhere in Boston."

"Really?"

"Yeah, I never dreamed he'd be so close. All this time I thought he lived out in California or something."

"So what did you do?"

"I printed out the address of every post office in Boston and planned to go to each one and ask about their regular customers. I must have sounded like a lunatic. I didn't get very far before I realized how ridiculous it was."

I laughed. "Why didn't you ask Owen for help? He's been really worried about you."

"I couldn't go to Owen. He's one of the reasons I've been acting so weird around you for the past few months. It was nothing you did. I've been a jealous idiot."

"Jealous?"

"I thought that Owen had a crush on you, stupid."

For some reason, I felt guilty even though I had no reason to. "Well, he doesn't."

"But he did. It started the night of the bonfire. You went off with Gray, and all Owen could talk about for the rest of the night was where you'd gone and if you were okay. Later, he admitted that he liked you, and he was worried about you being alone with Gray. I was so mad at him, and I took it out on you. Then that night at the Snow Ball, when I saw the two of you dancing, I almost lost it. The champagne didn't help."

"But, Michelle, he likes you now. It's so obvious."

She fell back on the bed, her arms sprawled behind her. "I know. I screwed up. And now things are weird between us. Like they've been weird with you."

I lay down next to her so our elbows were touching. "It's okay," I said. "Jealousy does strange things to a person." I thought briefly about Elise and Gray, then shook the image from my mind. "It's been a crap year for both of us."

"Yup."

"But I've missed you."

She leaned up on her elbow. "I've missed you, too," she said. I propped myself up so I could look her in the eye.

"Why are you being so nice to me?" she said. "I've been such a bitch."

I directed my eyes to the ceiling as if deep in thought. "I'm loyal that way. Besides, you're pretty much all I've got."

She looked falsely outraged, then swatted my arm. It felt good to have the old Michelle back. To have an ally in this horrible place. "Emma," she said, "this hearing is no joke. If we both testify, Elise's lawyers are going to be all over this school, and they may target you next. It could get ugly. You sure you're ready for all that?"

"Bring it on," I said.

"Who are you, and what have you done with my room-mate?" she said, and we both fell forward, laughing at the absurdity of it all.

By the time we changed into our pajamas that night, things felt almost normal between us. But something still bothered me, some lingering doubts about Gray. I didn't know whether it had to do with Michelle's warnings or whether I just hadn't learned to trust my own happiness yet.

CHAPTER 27

*G*ray's lips move softy over my neck, his breath warm and spiced like a Caribbean beach. His hands, gentle yet firm, cup my face as he pulls my mouth toward his. There is a moment of unbearable tension as we hover mere centimeters from each other—waiting, wanting—and then pure release as our lips collide, sending sparks of heat and light through every limb down to our fingers and toes. He grabs my waist and draws me close, and my mind reels as he bends to kiss my ear, nuzzle my throat. . . .

"Ahem. Ms. Townsend, are you still with us today?"

Mr. Gallagher's booming voice rudely invaded my subconscious mind, jerking me abruptly and tragically out of my daydream.

"What?" I said, feeling blood rush immediately to my cheeks.

Elise and Amber snickered, and Michelle looked at me like I was pathetic, which I was.

"You seem to have your head in the clouds today," he said.

"It's just, *Mrs. Dalloway* sort of confuses me," I said, trying to recover.

"It should confuse you," he said. "It's a Woolf in sheep's clothing." He laughed at his own joke, and I felt embarrassed that I'd ever had a crush on him.

I was off the hook for the moment. I sighed and rested my head on my palm. A small part of me felt bad for Gallagher because generally, I was the only girl in class who got excited about literature, and even I could not be swayed by *Mrs. Dalloway*. After last weekend's date with Gray, it wasn't hard to see why.

I'd never been boy-crazy like other girls, had somehow avoided the pitiable fate of becoming a blathering idiot whenever a cute guy walked by. But now I was the living embodiment of a lovesick schoolgirl, watching the clock in agony, waiting for the minute hand to make its way around seven more times so I could be released from this prison, free to daydream about kissing a cute boy in peace.

Finally, the bell rang, and I hustled out of the room, not even waiting for Michelle. I was afraid that if I lingered, Gallagher would ask me to stay after to discuss my lack of focus, and I just couldn't deal with that right now. I was speed walking back to the dorm when I heard Elise's silky voice behind me. "Emma, I need to talk to you."

I stopped in my tracks. I should have ignored her and kept walking, but there was something in her tone that made me pause. It was . . . a kind of sincerity, a seriousness of purpose that made me believe that maybe she wanted to reconcile. She caught up to me, and I thought I saw a flicker of fear in her eyes, however briefly; then it was gone and I was standing in front of this formidable girl who had the power to expel Michelle and me in her back pocket.

"What is it, Elise?" I said.

"I just thought I should tell you something."

I folded my arms and waited for the inevitable power play. "What?"

"Look, I know you think I was responsible for that fire. And I know you told Overbrook that you'd seen me at the stables smoking pot. I also know he doesn't believe you."

"How do you know that, Elise? The two board members seemed quite interested when I told them."

"Whatever. It doesn't matter. It's your word against mine, and who are they going to believe? The girl whose daddy gives the school thousands of dollars every year? Or the girl who got struck by lightning and probably has brain damage? Think about it."

"Elise, you can't scare me into not testifying."

"I know that. But maybe I can convince you that testifying would be really stupid. I know about you and Gray. I can't believe he went from me to you, but there's no accounting for taste. Did he tell you his little secret yet?"

I was getting impatient. "What are you talking about, Elise?"

"Oh, he hasn't told you. Well, don't feel bad. He didn't tell me either. I had to hear it from one of his friends. Dan Brockman, remember him?"

"Stop playing games, Elise. You obviously want to tell me something, so just spit it out and stop wasting my time."

"Oh, no, that wouldn't be any fun. It would be much better coming from him. But I will give you a little preview." She paused and tilted her head up. "It's one of those things that would prevent him from getting into college. One of those secrets that destroys reputations. Do you want poor Gray to have to attend community college next year?"

"Elise, you're obviously making this up so I don't testify."

"Oh, really? Go and ask your boyfriend. Ask him what Dan Brockman knows that nobody else does, then come back and tell me I'm lying."

"So, what are you saying? That if I testify, you're going to spill his secret?"

"I always knew you were bright, Emma. Lots of brains, just not much common sense." She swiveled around and walked back toward the dorm, leaving me staring at the back of her head, wishing I had a blow dart. When Michelle approached me from behind, I nearly jumped out of my skin.

"What was that all about?" she said.

"She claims she has some dirt on Gray, and that if I testify, she's going to spread it all over and ruin him."

"I warned you about her. I've been dealing with this shit all year."

"Do you think she's telling the truth or just playing with my head?"

"I don't know," Michelle said, but she looked like she wanted to say more.

"What is it?" I stopped her with my arm.

"Nothing."

"Michelle, I know you. What do you want to say?"

She sighed. "I don't want you to get mad at me. The last time I even implied that Gray wasn't perfect, you nearly bit my head off."

"You're right. And I'm sorry. I promise I won't bite your head off this time."

"I meant it when I told you Owen's heard things. Probably rumors. But I wouldn't be surprised to find out some things you wish you didn't know." I was starting to feel a little queasy. "Then again, we might all be wrong, and Gray might be the only good guy left on the entire planet."

"Aside from Owen, of course," I said. "Has he forgiven you yet?"

"I think so," she said. "He wants to take me out Friday night. On a proper date. But we're going to take things slow this time. I'm not very good at that, if you haven't noticed."

"Me neither," I said.

"Oh, really?" She arched an eyebrow and smirked. "Do tell."

I could feel my cheeks getting hot. "Nothing. It's just . . . Gray is insanely sexy. When he kisses me, I melt."

"When he kisses you, you melt?" She doubled over in

laughter. "Oh, Gray, you're so hot, I'm melting . . . mellllt-ing," she said, imitating the Wicked Witch of the West.

"You're evil," I said, but she was too busy collapsing onto the ground in hysterics to hear me.

I tried to do some homework that afternoon, but I was so distracted, I couldn't even complete my very easy French worksheet on the conditional mood. "Si je témoigne, Elise va parler." *If I testify, Elise will talk.* "Si elle parle, je vais perdre Gray." *If she talks, I will lose Gray.*

The worst part was that Gray had his District swim meet that night, so I couldn't even call him. I desperately wanted to believe that Elise was just engaging in her usual scheming and plotting. Last week, I'd asked Gray three questions and he'd promised to tell the truth. Now I wasn't so sure the truth was what I wanted.

On Friday, I almost didn't get out of bed because the thought of sitting through classes with Elise and her toadies made me sick to my stomach. But not showing up seemed like admitting defeat. Somehow I made it through the day on autopilot. I don't think I spoke or glanced up all day, just stared out the window imagining scenarios, each one worse than the last.

Owen was waiting to pick up Michelle after school for their date. Part of me wished the four of us were going on a double date—two normal high school couples heading out for a Friday night of movies and mindless conversation. I didn't want to have this confrontation with Gray. Maybe I'd end up feeling foolish when Gray told me it was all lies, and we'd spend the rest of the night making out in his Jeep.

I ran back to the dorm and changed out of my school clothes and into jeans, black boots, and a sexy black top. Gray was coming around six, so all I could do for the next two hours was pace around my room waiting, willing the time to go faster. Finally, I saw his Jeep making its way down the main drive through the drizzle, so I flung on my coat and ran downstairs to meet him in the parking lot.

He hadn't even gotten out of the Jeep when I showed up at the passenger door, which was locked. He jumped when he saw me, then smiled and unlocked the door so I could climb in.

"Hi there," he said, smiling broadly.

Oh God. He looked so cute and unsuspecting; I wasn't sure I could do this.

My face was soaked with rain, and he wiped two damp streaks of hair off my face, then leaned in to kiss me. I'd been pining for him all week, and now that he was here in front of me, all I wanted to do was fall into his arms and spend an hour studying his face, kissing his lips. His right hand came around my neck, warm palm meeting cold skin, and he pulled me toward him and kissed me so deeply I thought sparks might shoot out of my fingertips. Our first kiss had started off achingly soft and cautious and had slowly intensified. Now we bypassed the slow seduction for an instantly mind-numbing, blisteringly hot kiss. That drug coursed through my veins again, and I worried I wouldn't be able to say what I'd come here to say unless I pushed his mouth off mine.

It took every ounce of my willpower to do so, and Gray looked at me like I was crazy. "What's wrong?" he said.

"We have to talk."

"Uh-oh," he said. "That's never good."

"Can we go somewhere?"

"Aren't we going out to dinner?"

"Dinner?"

"Yeah. You were supposed to pick the place."

He was right. I *was* supposed to pick the place, and once upon a time before Elise's insinuations had shattered my bliss, I would have planned a night to remember. But all I could think about now was what past deeds were following

Gray around, and what damage they might do to him and us now.

"I just want to go somewhere quiet where we can talk."

"How about the park?" he said. I knew he meant Oakwood Lane, where we'd stopped last Sunday. Somehow I didn't think that would be the best place for discussion, so I suggested we drive into Waverly Falls and get some coffee. I was mostly silent during the drive while Gray told me about his swim meet. They'd lost, but Gray had won the 100-meter freestyle, and the team had come in second place in the relay and third overall. "At least I can grow my hair again." He ran a hand across his scalp, and he looked so vulnerable that I felt a wave of affection for him that nearly knocked the air out of me.

When we got into town, we had to drive around for ten minutes until someone pulled out of a parking space. We ran the two blocks to the coffee shop, then clattered into the vestibule, soaking wet and breathless. As we waited for a table to open up, the silence was agonizing. Gray kept looking at me and smiling, and I felt so incredibly guilty.

Finally we sat down at a small two-top table and ordered coffee and biscotti. I kept playing with my biscotti until it broke apart in my hands. Gray smiled patiently and stilled my hands with his own. "What's going on?" he said.

I stared into his eyes and felt the most intense regret. "I don't know how to ask you this."

"Just ask me."

And so I did.

At first Gray deflected, saying something vague about Elise being an unreliable source. I felt a surge of relief. Elise was just up to her usual tricks, and in ten minutes we'd be at the Italian place next door arguing over appetizers. But then a realization seemed to sweep over him, and his face grew pale. He cast his eyes down toward the table.

"What is it, Gray?" I said. He didn't answer and he

wouldn't look at me. "Gray, you're scaring me. Say something."

"I knew it," he said finally.

"Knew what?" He stood up now, grabbing his coffee and throwing it into the trash can. I watched as he stalked toward the door. "Gray, wait!"

I gathered my coat and ran to follow him, but he was already outside, practically running down the street. I ran after him, the rain spitting icy darts at my face. He stopped at the curb as if trying to make up his mind which way to go.

"Would you please slow down?" I said when I'd caught up with him. I grabbed his arm, but he wrenched it away. "Why are you taking this out on me? Let's talk about this."

"I knew it," he said again. "I knew this was all an illusion. I knew I'd never be able to have you. You're too good for me."

"Gray, what are you talking about?"

He crossed the street, and I was off once again, chasing him through the rain. Thunder rumbled overhead, and I watched a streak of jagged lightning cut through the sky. I followed him, shivering, until we came to the bridge that spanned the river.

"Please, can we just stop here for a minute?" I said. "It's pouring out, and we're both soaked. Come in out of the rain." I tugged on his arm, and he followed me in a daze until we were standing under the cover of the bridge. The rain thudded on the wooden roof above us, pounding out a frantic rhythm.

A narrow window ran the length of the bridge so we could see the falls in the distance and the river that coursed below our feet. We stood side by side, looking out at the river, swollen from the heavy rains. Something red sailed by, and I recognized it as a tricycle. Someone must have left it too close to the riverbank.

Gray's cheeks were damp and pale as he turned toward me. "Emma, I'm a horrible person."

"No, you're not," I said. "I wouldn't like you if you were a horrible person." I tried to smile, but Gray's face was humorless.

"You don't know me. You don't know who I was."

"I don't care who you were. I only care who you are now." I reached for his hand, but again, he retreated from me.

"You know, all along I knew it couldn't last. I hoped. I think I believed you could redeem me or something." He laughed bitterly. "But I can't be redeemed."

"Gray, everyone can be redeemed."

He shook his head. "No."

"Gray, tell me what this is all about."

He inhaled deeply and ventured a glance in my direction. "You remember the night of the dance when you went down to the stables?"

"Of course."

"There was a guy there. With Amber."

"I remember. Dan Brockman."

He nodded. "We were best friends at Sheldrake. The end of my sophomore year, I went with his family to Jamaica for spring break. Dan had a sister, Samantha. She was older than us, and she'd always been gorgeous and wild, guys chasing her everywhere. Anyway, she used to flirt with me, tease me, but I never thought she took me seriously. But this one night in Jamaica, she got invited to a beach party and took Dan and me along."

He took a long, deep breath like he was preparing himself to go on. "Once we got to the beach, we were having a good time, playing drinking games and getting pretty buzzed. Dan went off with some girl and told me to keep an eye on his sister. Like I had any control over this girl. Hell, I'd already had four or five shots myself, and she'd been way ahead of us at the beginning of the night. I was practically senseless by that point. And then she suggested that we all go skinny-dipping." He fell silent, and I stared out at the river again, watching a lawn chair race by in the torrent. Lightning continued to pierce the sky, looking oddly like fireworks.

"Before I knew it, everybody was in the water, swimming around naked, diving and splashing, laughing."

"Were you swimming?"

"No. I told Sam that I swam every day during the year and I'd just watch instead. So she took off all her clothes, really slow, like this goddess or something standing there in the moonlight. I could barely stand or speak, but I knew I wanted this girl. She winked at me and turned around and dove into the water." I shook my head. I didn't want to hear any more.

He gripped the wooden sill of the window and kept his gaze forward. "I was out of my head drunk—just sitting on the beach watching like an idiot—and then some girl was yelling, 'Where is she?' 'Where'd she go?' My instincts told me it was Sam. I scanned the water for her, but it was so dark I couldn't see anything but silhouettes." His voice was trembling. I placed my hand on Gray's wrist to comfort him, or maybe to stop him from going on.

"I didn't know what to do, so I dove in after her. But it was chaos out there, and I was so drunk I could barely swim. Girls were screaming all around me, struggling to get out of the water. I looked for her for at least half an hour, diving under again and again, calling her name, but she was just . . . gone. I don't know what happened. And I knew I was going to drown if I didn't stop looking for her, and every day I sort of wish I had. When I came back to shore, I threw up about four times before I was able to walk. Dan was just sitting there in the sand in total shock, mumbling to himself. He kept saying, 'You have to find her. I told you to watch out for her. She can't be gone.' I finally had to leave him there so I could get the police." He stopped talking, like he'd run out of breath.

"So what happened?"

"They searched for her, but they never found her body. It was like she just disappeared." His head fell into his hands. "God, it was all my fault. I was supposed to be looking out for her!" He was crying now, unabashedly.

"Gray," I whispered. I wanted to comfort him, wanted to touch his cheeks and wipe his tears away, but something held me back.

When he finally pulled himself together, he said, "The night of the Snow Ball, Dan got drunk and told Elise what happened that night. That's why I didn't come down to the stables right away. He blamed me for everything right in front of Elise. I ended up hitting him in the face. I have no idea why, because I really wanted to hurt myself. And once Elise knew the truth, she thought of the worst possible way she could use it. She was looking for a way to hurt me."

"But why?"

A rumble of thunder rattled so close it shook the bridge. "Because of you. She was jealous."

"Because we danced together?" I said.

"No, it was more than that. She knew how I felt about you. You did what she couldn't do."

"What do you mean?"

"Last summer, I was so depressed, and Elise couldn't take it anymore. She knew she couldn't do anything to help me. No one could. Eventually she got tired of my moods and broke it off. That was my lowest point. I even thought about killing myself, but I couldn't go through with it. I couldn't do that to Anna. I think I might have done it, if it hadn't been for her. And for you."

"Me?"

He nodded. "Everything changed on your birthday. I didn't even want to go to your party, but my mom insisted it would mean something to you. And when I got there, we fell right into our banter like we always do. And then Elise called and we got into this huge fight, and you came outside, and, bam!

All the wind was knocked out of me. Suddenly I could see things clearly. I could see *you* clearly."

"How?"

"I could see that you were everything Elise wasn't. Sweet. Innocent. Good. Someone who didn't want anything from me, who wasn't always going to be dragging me to a party or getting me wasted." I felt myself reeling and gripped the window ledge to steady myself. "I knew you were the kind of girl I should have been with all along, not one of those self-destructive girls I always fell for," he said. "I knew I needed someone like you if I was ever going to pull myself together." He moved closer to me and put a hand on my shoulder.

I bristled, trying to absorb what he'd just told me. "So you decided that if you dated someone like me, I could fix you? Is that it?"

"No, no, you're misunderstanding me," he said. "I mean, I knew there was something different about you. Something I'd never appreciated before. I thought that if I had you by my side, I might be able to live with myself."

I stumbled away from him, feeling a little sick. "So I was, what, your atonement?"

"No!" he said. "That's not what I meant at all. I'm not explaining myself very well."

"So what exactly do you mean?"

"I don't know, Emma. I want to be with you, isn't that enough?"

Is it enough? Does Gray only like me because I make him feel better about himself? Am I just some tool he wants to use to redeem himself? "I want to go home," I said very quietly.

"Emma, listen to me—"

"Gray, I have listened to you, and I don't want to hear any more. I want to go home."

"Please don't do this."

"Do what?"

"Be angry with me."

"I'm not angry!"

The silence that followed was magnified by the pounding of the rain outside. I knew Gray was fragile, and I didn't want to wound him by saying something I'd regret later. But I couldn't process all that he'd told me. "I need time to think. Can you please just take me back to school? Please?"

Gray looked dejected but resigned, like a part of him had known all along this was how I'd react. We walked back to the car through the driving rain and drove back to Lockwood in silence. I was so torn in my feelings. His story was awful, tragic. I understood now the guilt that had haunted him all these years. But Samantha's death wasn't his fault. At least not entirely. He'd been stupid to get so drunk, but Sam was old enough to fend for herself. And Dan shouldn't have gone off and left his sister alone either. It was unfair that he blamed Gray because it was easier than admitting the truth to himself. Not to mention, a dozen other people had all watched it happen—why hadn't anyone else tried to save her?

As soon as I started feeling sympathy for him, I was reminded of his words: "I thought if I had you by my side, I might be able to live with myself." Like I was some penance for this terrible mistake he'd made. Like Rochester telling Jane that he'd wandered everywhere, seeking happiness in pleasure, and then he'd come home to find Jane, seeing in her all of the good and bright qualities he had sought in himself. He had asked Jane, "Is the sinful, but repentant man justified in daring the world's opinion, in order to attach to him forever this gentle, gracious creature?"

I didn't know the answer. But I knew I didn't want to be Gray's consolation prize. Anger and hurt tore through me, and I fought back tears.

Gray pulled his Jeep into Lockwood's parking lot and shut off the motor. "I have to go," I said immediately, not wanting to look at him for fear I'd lose my resolve.

"What about us?" he said.

There is no us, I wanted to shout. Instead, I muttered, "I don't know."

We sat there for a few seconds, staring at the windshield as the rain poured down, feeling the weight of our silence and the crushing mass of our disappointment bearing down on us. When he reached out and gently touched my face, something unfroze inside me. He leaned to rest his head on my shoulder, and as much as I wanted to comfort him, I knew I couldn't. I couldn't release him from his guilt. Not yet. Some dark part of me wanted him to suffer for it.

I pulled away and stared at him for a long time with a lump in my throat. Feeling sick at heart and tremendously sorry, I got out of the car and ran.

I couldn't go to an empty dorm room. And even if Michelle was back from her date, I couldn't face her right now. The last thing I needed was for her to say, "I told you so." I began running toward the stables, trying to drown out reality in a haze of rain and speed. It wasn't until I got to the bottom of the hill that I remembered: the stables were nothing but a burnt shell. I wanted to wrap my arms around Curry's neck and cry into his mane, but he wasn't here.

Drawing my coat tightly around me, I fought against the onslaught of rain and made my way up the hill, finding myself in front of the chapel. It seemed like the only safe haven on campus. I wasn't sure if it would be open this late at night, so I raced up to the door, blinded by rain and soaked to the bone. It was locked. I had nowhere to go. Even Papa Legba couldn't help me now. I was stuck, with no way of escaping my own life.

As I passed the Commons Building on the way back to the dorms, I watched as lightning tore through the sky and struck the giant chestnut tree.

It was split right in two.

CHAPTER 28

The morning of the hearing, Michelle and I both dressed in suits. Michelle wrapped her hair in a prim-looking bun, and I wove mine into a braid. We rehearsed what we were going to say, how we were going to respond to Elise's accusations and the committee's hard-hitting questions. Through it all Michelle behaved like a zombie, like someone going through the motions instead of taking responsibility for changing the outcome of her life. This was not the girl who had asked Sarkissian if he believed we could grow a new branch in the space-time continuum. This was someone who had accepted her fate as if it were predestined.

The morning was gusty, the sky threatening storms. Michelle and I braced ourselves against the wind as we walked in silence to Easty Hall. It was a closed hearing, so no other students or parents were allowed in the boardroom. Elise looked unflappable in her sleek gray skirt suit and four-inch heels, and the Disciplinary Committee appeared predictably stern at the raised boardroom table.

Michelle and I both testified to having seen Elise smoking in the barn on several occasions, and Michelle corroborated the fact that the incriminating journal was mine, not hers. When Overbrook asked Michelle why she had lied about the journal, Michelle claimed she had been trying to protect me.

I was expecting a barrage of questions and insinuations targeted against Michelle, but the committee seemed more concerned with clearing Elise's name than in sullying Michelle's.

In the end, Elise was cleared of all wrongdoing. But there wasn't enough evidence to prove that Michelle had started the fire either. Elise was still the golden girl, and Michelle and I had salvaged our scholarships by the skin of our teeth. But we were now on a watch list, forever suspect because we weren't part of the system. We hadn't inherited instant trust and respect because of our social status or connections.

"Should we go celebrate?" I asked as we left the courtroom, but the impulse to rejoice was short-lived. Elise's friends stood outside of Easty waiting to pounce on us, and we had to push our way through the crowd and make a run for the dorms to avoid the spiteful and malicious insults they were hurling at us. From our dorm window, we watched as Elise basked in all the attention.

"I want to celebrate anyway," I said. "You didn't get kicked out."

"It doesn't matter," Michelle said. "I'm not coming back to Lockwood next year."

"You have to!" I said. "You foiled Elise Fairchild's master plan, which was to get rid of you for good. If you leave now, you'll be giving her exactly what she wants."

"So what? Pride's no good if you're miserable all the time."

"Wouldn't you be miserable if you let her win? Wouldn't you be miserable without me?" I gave her a hopeful smile.

"It's over," Michelle said. "This stupid hearing. This horrible year. I want to put it all behind me."

"And we will. Together."

"You don't get it, Emma. They'll never let us do that, they'll never let us forget who we are and where we came from."

"So what? This place is your ticket to MIT. Two years of sacrifice for the rest of your life. Isn't it worth it?"

"I just want to feel normal," Michelle said. "Not like some outcast. I feel like no matter what I do, no matter how hard I work to earn respect, I'll never be accepted."

"Is that what you want? To be accepted?"

She bowed her head forlornly. "I know I make a good show of seeming like I don't care what anyone thinks of me. But the truth is, I want a normal teenage life. I don't always want to be fighting battles. It's tiring, Emma. I'm just so tired." She slumped onto her bed, and I saw a few tears slip down her cheeks. I sat down next to her and put my arm around her.

"It's going to be okay," I said. "We're going to get through this together."

Over the next few days, Elise was faithful to her word. Pretty soon, the campus was buzzing with the news that Gray Newman, Elise's ex and Emma Townsend's boyfriend, had let a girl drown on spring break two years ago. A part of me had not believed Elise would follow through with her threat. I should have known what she was capable of.

The story became more and more embellished as the days went on so that by the end of the week, just before we were about to go home for spring break, girls were spreading any combination of the following lies: Gray had raped Samantha; Sam had been pregnant; Gray had killed her and buried her body to destroy the evidence. And the worst part was, Elise and her friends were texting the rumors to their friends at Braeburn, so it was only a matter of time before all of this got back to Gray.

Even though Michelle had "won" her case, we all knew who had really won and who had lost. Michelle and I now walked on campus as social pariahs, people to be stared at and scorned. We kept to ourselves and went straight back to the dorms after class each day. Even Gallagher wouldn't make eye contact with us. I couldn't tell whether it was out of disgust or out of shame for the part he'd played in sealing our fates.

Each night before going to bed, I thought only of Gray, of what my testimony had done to his life and reputation. Telling the truth had done nothing to bring about justice; it had only served to increase Elise's power and to destroy my chances of ever finding happiness.

That Friday my dad came to pick me up for spring break. On the car ride home, he kept peeking at me from the corner of his eye, trying to make sense of my silence.

"Is everything okay?" he asked, finally.

"Fine," I lied. But I knew he didn't believe me. It occurred to me that as much as I liked to blame my dad for our emotional distance, I'd been just as guilty of putting up walls between us. But something had shifted that day at the beach when he'd told me the truth about my mom. I owed it to him to tell the truth now.

"Actually, Dad, no. Everything's not fine."

I told my father about Gray, about the awful incident during spring break, about Elise's threat, about my testimony in Michelle's hearing and how it would ruin Gray's reputation and future.

"Honey," he said, his voice taking on a soothing tone, "you stood up for what you believed in."

"And betrayed Gray! I shouldn't have done it, Dad. Elise got away with everything anyway. It didn't make any difference."

"It did to Michelle. What you did for her took courage, Emma. Look, Gray will make it through this. He's strong. The best thing you can do for him now is be understanding. Let him know you'll stick by him."

I shook my head. "We're not even talking."

"Why not?"

"Because, I'm . . . confused. He told me something I didn't want to know. And I don't know if I can forgive him for it,

Dad." My father drove in silence, letting me find my words. "I thought I was finally going to have a normal teenage life, you know? Boyfriend, dates, the prom."

"The prom?" he said.

I frowned. "Gray asked me to his prom a few weeks ago. But there's no way we're going now." I was almost crying.

"Emma, you need to talk to him."

"I don't know what to say."

"Tell him you forgive him. He needs people to believe in him now."

"But how can I forgive him?" I said.

My father fell silent, then stopped at a red light. "I don't know what he said that hurt you so much, but you have to forgive him. I forgave your mother, Emma. For a long time, all I could think about was how she'd abandoned us. But it ate me up inside not to forgive her. We forgive; we don't forget. But we have to forgive or it'll kill us."

Thoughts of Gray pressed in on me and made me ache in a way I'd never felt before. I remembered a line from *Jane Eyre*: "That I have wakened out of most glorious dreams, and found them all void and vain, is a horror I could bear and master; but that I must leave him decidedly, instantly, entirely, is intolerable. I cannot do it."

But Jane did do it. She discovered Rochester's past and found she could not reconcile it with her future happiness. What he had done was wrong, and no matter how much she loved him, she knew she must leave him and care for herself: "The more solitary, the more friendless I am, the more I will respect myself." I didn't know if I could be that strong.

When we got back to the house, Barbara, entirely unaware of all the drama that had unfolded at Lockwood over the past month, was her usual chipper self. She was setting the table for dinner, wearing a purple apron with Easter eggs on it.

"Emma, dear, how are you?" she said. A quick look at us

told her something had happened during the car ride home.
"Is everything all right?"

"We're fine, Barbara," my dad said, mercifully. I didn't feel
like talking about it, especially not with Barbara.

"Good. Then go upstairs and get cleaned up, honey," she
said. "We're using the nice china tonight. I'm making chateaubriand and slow-roasted potatoes."

I groaned inwardly and trudged upstairs to my room,
flinging my bags in the corner. I wasn't planning to unpack;
I'd just live out of my suitcase for the week. I couldn't imagine staying here for seven days, and yet I couldn't imagine
going back to school either.

I felt myself being drawn to Jane's world again, wanting to
surrender myself to another life, let someone else do the
thinking for me. But Thornfield was gone.

I came downstairs in the same jeans and T-shirt I'd been
wearing, and Barbara grimaced when she saw me. "Now
honey, I thought we'd have a special dinner tonight. To welcome you back home. Hurry up and change. Everything's almost ready."

"I'm not hungry," I said.

She shot a cryptic look at my father. "Look, your father
told me what happened. And I surely do sympathize. I've had
my share of heartache. But let's all sit down and have a nice
family dinner and chat about it."

"I don't want to chat about it," I said, gritting my teeth.

"You've got to talk about it," she said. "Your father and I
might be able to help."

"There's nothing to be done," I said. "Besides, what exactly do you think you can do to help me, Barbara?"

Her mouth went tight and she glanced again at my father.
"Maybe we should call Dr. Reese," she said.

"No!" I shouted. "You're going to have to deal with me
this time. You, Barbara! You want to be my mother? Well,
here's your chance!"

"Emma!" my father said, trying to intervene. "I know you're hurting, but don't take it out on Barbara. She's only trying to help."

"You always take her side, Dad. I'm upset, okay? I can't be like Barbara, turning my frown upside down and pretending everything's fine. I'm not built that way." For once Barbara kept silent, watching me like I was some wild creature whose behavior was not governed by the laws of nature. My father frowned, frustrated that the two women in his life could not bring themselves to get along. "I don't want to feel like every time I get depressed, you're both going to turn around and call the therapist. I get depressed sometimes, okay? So does everyone. Just because Mom was sick doesn't mean I am. Don't force me to sit and talk to some stranger in a padded room. If I want to talk about it, I'll talk about it. If I don't feel like talking, I won't!"

My father gaped at me, but Barbara stood up from her chair and took a step toward me. I was as angry and defensive as a feral cat; I didn't know what I'd do if she touched me. But she reached out and touched my chair instead.

"Sweetheart," she said in a soft, soothing tone. "I know I'm not your mother, and I could never fill the void left by her. And I also know I don't always say the right thing. But please know I'm here for you if you ever want to talk. Go ahead and be sad if that's how you need to feel right now. If you don't want to eat, don't eat. I'll make a plate for you in case you get hungry later." And then she walked quietly into the kitchen.

My eyes followed her, and I saw for the first time, not an interloper, not a conniving vixen trying to weasel her way into our lives, but a woman—perhaps with larger hair than anyone in New England had a right to, but still a woman just trying to find love and acceptance with a new family.

"I'm sorry," I said to my dad. "I've been so edgy lately."

He came and put his arms on my shoulders, then leaned

down and kissed me on the top of the head, like he used to do when I was little. "You've had a rough time," he said. "You can go on up to your room if you want."

I gave him a relieved half smile and turned to leave. When I was halfway up the stairs, I heard a scream. I ran back down and into the kitchen in time to see Barbara pulling a smoking pan out of the oven.

"My beautiful chateaubriand," she said like her heart was breaking. "It was going to be my masterpiece."

My father's mouth drew taut, and for some reason, I couldn't help myself. I started to laugh. And then my dad's shoulders started shaking, and even though his back was turned to me and he wasn't making any noise, I knew he was laughing, too.

"You've never liked my cooking," she said. My dad shook his head, unable to speak without losing it completely. I was bent over now, my stomach doing convulsions from laughter.

"Well, shit," Barbara said, letting the roast drop into the trash can with a loud clatter. "I guess we'll order pizza."

That night my father put on a Mozart CD to try to salvage the mood of Barbara's fancy dinner. We ate pepperoni pizza off the good china and talked about books and movies and summer plans the way I imagined real families did. Later that week, I even let Barbara take me shopping. She bought me a turquoise blouse that she said complemented my pale skin and a flouncy black skirt embroidered with turquoise ribbons. I didn't hate them.

I spent a lot of that week soul searching, walking the beach, thinking about what I'd do once I got back to school. The essay symposium was only three weeks away, and with everything else that had been going on, I hadn't given it much thought. But when I got back from the beach that afternoon, I opened my laptop and read the draft of the essay I'd sent to the qualifying panel.

Disgusted with it, I closed that file and opened a new one,

typing some ideas about Bertha, the mysterious woman in the attic who was loved by no one, abandoned by her husband and brother, and left in the care of a drunken servant, alone and terrified and trapped. Who wouldn't go mad under those circumstances? Bertha was a victim of society's propensity to marginalize anyone who was different, any woman who dared to speak her mind, any woman who was poor, downtrodden, or socially undesirable. Even though we lived in the twenty-first century, not much had changed.

With everything I'd witnessed this year, Bertha had emerged as a more fascinating study than Jane. Who had she been before society and Rochester had sucked the soul from her? What were her unfulfilled hopes and dreams? Why hadn't she escaped her situation instead of killing herself? What drove her to such an act of desperation? Maybe she'd been sick like my mother. Or maybe, with all that had been taken from her, she'd simply lost the will to live. Before I knew it, I had three pages written, then five, and in the end, a brand-new ten-page essay about Bertha Mason.

It wasn't that I didn't love Jane anymore; in fact, what I came to realize was that Bertha and Jane were two sides of the same coin. Bertha represented the wild and untamed side, the woman who lashed out in anger at anyone who tried to keep her down. Jane represented the socially acceptable side, the girl who obeyed the rules and tried to be good, even when it seemed society was out to destroy her.

Each of us was essentially incomplete, composed of multiple fragments that sometimes held us together, and other times, split us apart, leaving us lost and confused. Like my mother, we all had this duality—only with my mother, it had broken her completely. But we all felt this essential paradox in our natures. I was both reckless and careful, smart and foolish, strong and scared. I was Bertha, and I was Jane.

CHAPTER 29

When I got back to school, the campus was in a frenzy of activity with all the upcoming events and competitions scheduled for the final six weeks of school: the essay symposium, band and orchestra championships, the choral festival, lacrosse and softball playoffs, and of course, the usual chaos of final exam preparation and summer session registration.

On the morning of Michelle's equestrian competition, I woke at six and shuffled to the bathroom to shower. When I got back to the room, Michelle was already dressed in her riding outfit. She had tamed her curly hair into a tight braid and was holding her helmet in her hand.

"You look just like your mom," I said, pointing to the photo on her dresser.

"I know."

"Did you tell Aunt Darlene you were competing today?"

"Of course not."

"Don't you think you should?"

"You know how she feels about riding."

"I just think it's sad that she won't be there."

"It's fine," Michelle said, going into her impervious mode.

We met at the van in front of Easty. Michelle's trainer, May, was picking up Curry at the farm and taking him in her trailer, and Owen was going to meet us at the fairgrounds.

Elise looked fearsome in her sleek black outfit, like some beautiful evil princess. She gave us a cocky sneer, and we both tried our best to ignore her. Even though this was supposed to be a championship pitting school against school, we all knew what the outcome of this competition meant. Whoever won this competition would be the unspoken victor of an epic high school battle.

We piled into the van, Michelle taking the window seat and closing herself off from the world with her headphones. I took out the latest book assigned by Gallagher, *Lord of the Flies,* about a group of British schoolboys who get stuck on a desert island and try to govern themselves, with disastrous results. I read it hesitantly, hoping I'd never allow myself to slip into such a bleak story.

The drive to West Springfield took a little over an hour. When we arrived at the fairgrounds, the sight was a spectacle to behold. Trailers were lined up in the field behind the arena. Some of the horses were tethered to their trailers, still blanketed before judging. Others were being trotted around by their riders to get them accustomed to the ring. Michelle and I met May, who backed Curry out of the trailer. Curry seemed to know this was an important day. He looked anxious but regal, his muscles flexing against his harness, his nostrils flaring from the smell of the other horses, from the thrill of imminent competition.

I felt overwhelmed; there didn't seem to be any rhyme or reason to the goings-on, but Michelle assured me this was very much like all the other equestrian competitions she'd participated in. I was relieved when Owen arrived. He would be my only company on the bleachers all day. Owen greeted Michelle with a hug, but she was clearly rigid with nerves. I wished that Darlene had been there to give her some sense of grounding, some parental burst of confidence.

"Relax, Michelle," Owen said. "Remember what May said. Your strength is your connection to Curry. If you're nervous, Curry's going to pick up on it, and you guys aren't going to ride as well. When you two are in sync, there's no one who can beat you."

"I know, I know," she said, her voice tense. "I'll relax when I'm in the ring."

She turned from him and went to talk to May, and they saddled Curry and led him into the ring to warm up. I shrugged at Owen apologetically.

"She's right," Owen said. "She usually relaxes once she's in the ring."

"This must be hard for her. It's her first competition since her mom died."

"She's ready," he said.

We bought ourselves some soft pretzels and soda, then found a spot on the bleachers and waited for the first class to begin. Owen explained to me that some competitions judge the look of the horse more than the rider's skill. In those, Elise would have had the edge since Odin was a far more polished show horse than Curry. But this competition judged what the rider did—how well she sat and performed certain movements, how seamlessly she controlled her horse. During training sessions, I'd noticed Michelle and Curry's special synergy, a true partnership of minds and hearts.

Sixteen riders were taking part in the high school division. I watched the first few classes in a constant state of confusion, cheering whenever Michelle and Curry competed and sitting on the edge of my seat as Elise flawlessly went through her paces. Owen was tense; he kept grabbing my arm or involuntarily pushing against me, tapping his foot compulsively on the bleachers beneath us.

When Michelle finished in the jumping class, Owen stood up and grabbed me by the shoulders, shaking and whooping. This was the only way I knew that Michelle had performed well. I sensed someone staring at us and glanced over to see a petite blonde with a perfectly smooth bob and enormous sunglasses, immaculately dressed in a pastel green golf shirt and khakis. When she noticed me looking, she diverted her gaze back to the ring, but I'd registered her emotion. Pure hatred. Next to her was a tall, elegant-looking man with salt-and-pepper hair and piercing blue eyes punctuated by crow's feet. He looked kinder than the woman but every bit as aristocratic. He glanced over at me and smiled slightly, then continued watching the arena.

I nudged Owen and motioned to the couple. "The Fairchilds," he said.

"Ah."

"Who would have thought such attractive people could yield the spawn of Satan?"

I couldn't help but laugh. "Her mother looks so young."

"The magic of Botox and plastic surgery."

By noon, Elise seemed to be fulfilling her prophecy that this would be her year. She hadn't made a single mistake, whereas Michelle and Curry had taken a few events to hit their stride. Around three o'clock, I began to get antsy. We'd been sitting on the bleachers for hours, and my butt had long since gone numb. Owen told me the last event was coming up: reining. It was a solitary event, just one rider in the ring at a time.

We watched the other competitors enter the ring and go through the motions of the pattern, slow and steady. Elise and Odin handled the maneuvers like pros, both precise and poised. When it was Michelle's turn, she and Curry trotted into the ring, and Michelle peered out into the bleachers. I thought I saw her wink at us. Owen lifted his sunglasses and shot me a nervous look.

Michelle made a little motion with her feet, and suddenly, Curry sprang into action in a blur of dust. As they began to perform the pattern, every motion seemed faster and more dramatic than the last. In her red jacket, Michelle looked like a dancing flame. Horse and rider had truly found their rhythm, matching each other move for move like poetry in motion. After a spectacle of whirls and spins, they skidded to a dramatic stop, and the crowd erupted in applause. Even Mr. Fairchild was clapping, although his wife remained motionless.

We waited anxiously for the final scores to be tallied, and I felt sore and sunburned and a little sick from all the carnival food we'd eaten. Finally the judge's voice came over the loudspeaker and announced a ride-off.

"What's that?" I asked Owen.

"If the scores are too tight, they ask the riders to perform a final test to decide the winner."

We listened as the judge announced the three riders who would be called back: Anne Braithwaite from Newbury Academy, and Elise Fairchild and Michelle Dominguez from Lockwood Prep. Owen and I hugged each other and screamed Michelle's name at the top of our lungs.

The three riders would have to do a jump-off pattern that involved canters, counter canters, halts, and numerous jumps at various fences before returning to the lineup at the end of the ring. Owen and I watched breathlessly as the student from Newbury glided across the first few fences. On the third fence, her horse grazed the rail. He didn't knock it off completely but jostled it a little, which set off his gait ever so slightly on the landing. Owen leaned over and whispered, "She's out."

"Really? Just one rail?"

"When competition is this tight, that's all it takes."

Michelle was next. Her face was intense and determined, but Curry seemed relaxed now, almost exultant, like he was having fun. They set off over the first fence, gliding gracefully across without a hitch, then cantered to the next fence and put that behind them with ease. I got this strange jolt of confidence watching them out there gliding over rails like they were flying. They responded so artfully to one another's motions that they seemed to be a single creature riding as one, no longer a separate horse and rider. They sailed over the last fence to screeching applause.

Elise and Odin trotted to the starting point, and at the signal, launched into the canters and counter canters, moving like a well-oiled machine. Elise kept her head high and straight, looking supremely confident that she would nail each portion of the routine. Owen frowned when Odin cleared the first few jumps, looking imperial and powerful. Elise's face took on a fierce concentration as they neared the final jumps. And then, as if someone had whispered in Elise's ear, she shifted her head ever so slightly. She tried to correct herself, but the moment had flustered her. As they flew over the final fence, I watched with held breath as Odin's back hoof clipped the rail and knocked it off. Off! Elise's face collapsed immediately because she knew that something that had been right in front of her had veered infinitesimally and was now forever out of reach.

I smiled gleefully and clutched Owen's arm. Owen couldn't contain himself. He lifted me up and spun me, and as I twirled, I thought I caught Elise's mother's mouth dropping to the floor at our premature display of victory. Elise could still take the prize, particularly if she was the judges' favorite. Owen took my hand and led me down from the bleachers. We squeezed our way through the crowd and went to congratulate Michelle, who had been watching Elise's performance from the side of the arena.

When we got to the ring, Curry's sleek body glistened with sweat. Michelle's face was radiant as she took off her helmet, quickly unwinding the braid and shaking out her hair. The gesture had the effect of a supermodel removing her bikini top. I'd never seen Owen quite so enraptured as he looked then. He picked Michelle off the ground and swung her around, returning her to her feet and kissing her hard on the mouth. It was such a passionate kiss I had to look away.

Then Michelle and I did a victory dance, and all of us stood around marveling at the events of the day. So much adrenaline was pumping through our veins that we'd kind of forgotten the judges still needed to make a ruling. When we heard feedback from a microphone, Michelle shushed us all and we held hands as we awaited the verdict.

We listened intently as the head judge announced the results: Elise Fairchild in third place, Anne Braithwaite in second, and Michelle in first!

Michelle and Owen began hopping and screaming, but it took me a minute to realize that Michelle was going home with the gold medal and Elise had come in third! Michelle walked into the arena with Curry to accept her prize, and we cheered loudly from outside the fence. The judge also awarded Michelle a beautiful dressage saddle and a new bridle for Curry. Michelle kissed Curry on the snout as she laid the new saddle across his back. Curry seemed to know he was a victor because he neighed triumphantly and pawed the dust with his hoof.

After the excitement died down a bit, May took Curry back to the trailer, and Michelle went to change out of her riding outfit. While Owen and I waited for her by the parking lot, Elise and her parents walked past. We heard Mrs. Fairchild talking to Elise in clipped tones.

"We rehearsed those jumps thousands of times," she said. "How could you have missed the final one? You lost concentration for just a second, and look what happened. That piece of baggage took the prize from you. This was *your* year!"

"Apparently not," Elise said under her breath, and her mother slapped her hard and quick against the cheek. When she saw we had witnessed this, Elise's mother gripped her daughter by the arm and led her away toward their car. I hated to admit it, but at that moment, I actually felt sorry for Elise.

Michelle finally came out to meet us, looking comfortable and happy in jeans and a T-shirt. We were making our way to Owen's car when a booming voice stopped us all. "Michelle!"

We turned around to see Elise's father standing with a dozen red roses in his hands. "I'm Mr. Fairchild," he said, extending a hand to Michelle. She accepted his hand and stared at him like he was a ghost. "You did great out there today."

"Thanks," Michelle said, a bit stunned.

"These were meant for Elise, but I don't think she'd appreciate them at this time." He gave a sheepish nod back to his wife. "You deserve them anyway. Congratulations."

He handed her the bouquet, which she accepted and laid in the crook of her elbow, as one might cradle a newborn baby. "Thank you," she said softly.

"Is this your only cheering section?" Mr. Fairchild asked, referring to Owen and me.

"My aunt couldn't make it."

"That's a shame," he said. "I'm sure she'd be very proud of you." He smiled a little sadly, then turned and walked back toward Elise and his wife.

Michelle shook her head and knitted her brow. "That was weird," she said.

"But nice," I added.

"Mostly weird."

"Weird or not, let's go celebrate," said Owen. "I'm taking you guys out!"

We loaded into Owen's Prius, and he turned up his stereo, blasting out some celebratory Beatles. Owen asked Michelle where she wanted to go, and we were both shocked by the answer: Bec d'Or.

"You sure you want to tell Darlene about this?" I said.

Michelle smiled crookedly. "She's the only family I've got."

The next ninety minutes, we drove from Springfield to Boston with Owen's stereo cranked to full blast. Michelle was clearly on a high—I couldn't remember having seen her this happy for months. Now that the competition was over, her happiness seemed to have so much less to do with beating Elise Fairchild than we'd all thought. It was something personal, something Michelle had to prove to herself.

By the time we got to the bakery, it was almost six o'clock and the place was packed. Michelle walked around to the back of the counter, and as soon as Darlene spotted her, Michelle broke into tears.

"What's the matter, child?" Darlene said. But Michelle couldn't stop crying long enough to tell her.

Owen and I tentatively explained about the competition, worried Darlene was going to be angry. But Darlene just took Michelle into her arms. "Baby girl, you should have told me. It being your birthday and all."

"Her birthday?" Owen said, looking at me for confirmation.

"I didn't know either. Why didn't you tell us?" Michelle was bawling now, Darlene holding her tight against her chest, rocking her back and forth.

When she finally stopped crying, Owen approached her and wiped the tears from her face, then kissed her sweetly on the forehead. "Happy birthday, Michelle."

"Hey, everyone!" Darlene shouted from behind the counter. "It's my niece's sixteenth birthday. And she just won a horseback-riding championship. Isn't she something?"

Suddenly all the customers rallied around us, wishing Michelle a happy birthday and saying wasn't it wonderful, and shouldn't we celebrate by making Cremas and a fresh batch of banana fritters? And then Darlene was talking and baking so quickly one would never have guessed she might have been upset that Michelle was riding again. There was only joy and pride in her face, not a trace of fear.

We sat down at an ice cream parlor–style table, and

Michelle officially introduced Owen to Darlene as "her boyfriend."

"As if I couldn't have guessed," Darlene said. "So you're the one who's been callin' the house at all hours?"

"Yes, ma'am," Owen said.

"Michelle's been brooding over you all winter long," she said, making Owen blush.

"Aunt Dar," Michelle said. "Do you have to tell him everything?"

"And what about you, Miss Emma?" Darlene said. "Where's that boy Michelle's been telling me about?" Michelle shook her head and laughed as if she had no idea what her aunt was talking about. "You know," Darlene went on, "the silent swimmer?" Michelle shushed her aunt and continued laughing.

"Is that what you call him?" I said to Michelle. "The silent swimmer?"

"I might have mentioned Gray to my aunt once or twice," she admitted.

"Gray?" Darlene said. "That's his name? I thought that was a color." She laughed at herself, then gave me a conspiratorial look. "Gray and Emma. Two good, old-fashioned names. The names of people who will grow old together." I tried to smile at her comment, but it only made me sad. "Child, a shadow just crept right over your face," she said. "What's wrong?"

I clenched my jaw. The last thing I wanted to do right now was cry in front of Michelle and Owen. "Things with Gray are . . . complicated."

Darlene clicked her teeth. "Oh, you young ones complicate things that don't need complicating. You love the boy, don't you?" she said, and I felt my cheeks flush. Darlene had a way of seeing right through me.

"Why don't you call him?" Owen said.

"He doesn't want to see me now, believe me," I said. "That's why he hasn't called me."

"He just needs time to cool down," Owen said.

I had said these same words to Owen about Michelle. But now I shook my head. I knew Gray. He didn't bounce back as easily as some. "I know you're all just trying to help, but can we please change the subject?" I pleaded. They pouted in sympathy but complied.

Later, as we made our good-byes, Darlene came over to hug me. She pulled me close confidingly and whispered, "He doesn't need cooling down, child. He needs you." Tears sprang to my eyes because I so desperately wanted to believe this.

CHAPTER 30

That next week, it rained endlessly. Teachers were reviewing for final exams, but all I could do was stare out the window and watch rain batter the buildings. The wind blew the rain in sheets that followed one another in quick succession, looking like a row of dominoes collapsing. It felt like the whole world was falling apart.

Maybe I had been unfair to Gray. Perhaps I had taken his words and twisted them in my mind because I couldn't believe someone like Gray could love me. He'd told me the truth, and I'd rejected him when he needed me most. And now that his secret had been broadcast throughout our little corner of the world, Gray would blame me. I was certain of it.

On Wednesday I was making a futile attempt to organize my European History notes when Simona called. If I had recognized her number, I might not have answered. I felt guilty just hearing her voice.

After making some polite chitchat, she asked, "Did something happen between you and Gray?"

My shoulders stiffened and my gut wrenched. "Sort of," I said, my voice sounding strained.

"I thought something might have. Oh, Emma, I just don't know what to do anymore. He won't talk to anyone. Not to me, not his father. Not even to Anna. Will you please come talk to him?"

"I don't think he wants to talk to me right now," I said.

"Honey, I don't know what happened between you two, but he needs to talk to someone, and I'm at my wit's end. What if I picked you up Friday after your classes? Would you be willing to come to the house and try to talk some sense into him?"

I froze, hedging. What could I possibly say to him that would make any difference? And would he even agree to see me? Regardless, I felt like I owed it to him to try.

The Newmans lived on a historic estate in a home built from glacial boulders. I hadn't been to the house in years, but as soon as we stepped inside, I remembered coming here as a child. The house had reminded me then of a giant tree house perched on a hill with pale wood walls, tall banks of windows, and a central spiral staircase that seemed like something out of a fairy tale. Now, hovering in the shadow of the storm, it looked more like a tiny cathedral, its vast ceiling pierced by stained-glass windows and its dark recesses broken by shafts of eerie light.

Simona led me up the central staircase and along the atrium gallery and back hallway to Gray's bedroom, which was built inside the round stone turret.

"I'm not sure what he's going to be like," she said. "I didn't tell him you were coming." My heart seized, but I knew it was too late to run. She knocked lightly on his door, and I heard a gruff voice mumble.

"It's me, honey," Simona said. "You have a visitor."

When she opened the door, Gray was lying on his back in bed, his face toward the wall. When he turned and saw me, he shot up too fast and hit his head on the low ceiling of the peaked roof.

"Damn it," he said, rubbing his head. "What are you doing here?"

"I came to see how you were."

He laughed bitterly. "I'm fantastic."

Simona gave me an apologetic look, then closed the door behind her, abandoning me to my fate, whatever that might be. I had never been inside Gray's room before. It was surprisingly tidy and oddly impersonal, like the room of someone who thought he was only going to be staying temporarily. On the rounded walls were some posters of Michael Phelps, a few album covers, and a map of the world that was so large it wrapped around half the room. Opposite Gray's bed was a desk with a computer and a neat stack of books. On the far right was a door that led to a small balcony, a pair of crossed oars perched above the door frame.

I glanced from the balcony back to the bed. Gray looked like a shell of himself, and his voice was flat and lifeless. "Why did you really come? Did my mom make you?"

"I was worried about you."

"Since when?" He stared out the window at the gloom, refusing to meet my eyes. "You should probably just go. It was stupid of my mom to bring you here."

"Gray, I'm so sorry. I know you must be angry with me for testifying, but you have to know, I didn't think Elise would really do it." I waited for him to say something—anything—but he wouldn't look at me. "Gray, what I said to you that night. Under the bridge—"

"Don't, Emma."

"Don't what?"

"Apologize."

"But I overreacted. It's just, I was too insecure to believe you could really like me." I moved his desk chair to his bed and tried to take hold of his hand, but he jerked away. "Why are you punishing me?" I said.

"Punishing *you?*" he said, glaring at me, his eyes dark and unreflective, like there was no light in them anymore. "If you haven't noticed, I'm punishing myself." He lay back down and turned his face toward the wall.

"Gray, please don't do this. Don't shut me out. I can help you." I watched his back as he breathed, wondering what he could possibly be thinking. "Gray, what happened to Sam in Jamaica was an accident," I said. "It could have happened to anyone."

"No, Emma!" he said, sitting up to face me now, his eyes wild with anguish. "I was a lifeguard! And Dan's best friend. I should have been looking out for her. She was my responsibility."

"No, she wasn't. It's not your fault."

"It is my fault! Why won't you stop trying to help? Why won't you leave me alone?" he shouted, sounding almost delirious. "I just want it to go away."

"But you can't just hide out in your room and make it go away."

"No, you're right, Emma! I can't hide from what I did. It's something I have to live with for the rest of my life. Do you know what that's like?" He looked so beaten and anguished that all I wanted to do was reach out and touch his face. "And I don't know if I can live with it anymore. So before I give up on myself completely, I'm going to do something right for a change. I'm going to leave."

"What do you mean?"

"I'm joining the Coast Guard." My eyes roamed his face, searching for answers. "Emma, all I've ever wanted was to do something that matters. Maybe if I can save someone. . . ." His voice trailed off like he was incapable of thinking anymore. I gripped his shoulder, and he flinched like he was in pain. "I tried to save you once," he said.

"You did save me," I reminded him. "You dragged me out of a burning barn."

"That's not what I'm talking about. I'm talking about the day of your birthday party. I followed you to the beach that day. And when I saw all those people waving and calling at the point, I knew you were in trouble. I raced down to the water, and when I got close, I just froze. I kept flashing back to that awful night in Jamaica. All I could do was call your name."

"That was you?" I said, remembering so clearly that voice that had called to me, that silhouette with the halo around it. "Why didn't you tell me?"

"What, admit that I stood there and did nothing while you almost drowned?"

"Gray, I heard you calling me. I swam toward your voice."

"No, you didn't, Emma. Don't try to make me feel better."

"I'm not, Gray! I did hear you. Your voice pulled me out, just like it pulled me out of the coma. I don't know how else to explain it, Gray, but you and I are connected somehow."

He shook his head fiercely like he was shaking a nightmare away. "Emma, you don't want to be connected to me. Everything I touch gets ruined. That's why I need to get away. From you. From everyone."

I hadn't realized until that moment how much I wanted him near, how much his leaving would devastate me. "Don't leave, Gray," I said, hearing the desperation in my voice. "Not because of this. Let me help you."

"You can't help me!" he shouted. "No one can." The room went very still, and I sat there momentarily, staring into his sad, beautiful eyes, feeling helpless. I understood this need to push people away and refuse all help, even from those who loved you the most.

"I'm sorry," I said, finally, placing my hand gently on his temple and running my fingers softly across his cheek. "For what it's worth, I forgive you."

His jaw was set, like he was using all his willpower not to let my touch melt his defenses. Then he shut his eyes tightly and turned his body so he seemed irrevocably out of reach.

CHAPTER 31

Over the next few weeks, I did everything mechanically. I got up, showered, went to class, ate dinner, studied for finals, went to bed, tried to sleep. I was an automaton, going through the motions numbly for fear if I let my guard down, I might disintegrate on the spot. At night when I was finally able to remove my armor, I felt raw, like all of my organs had somehow migrated outside of my body. When I sat in front of my journal, I couldn't write a single word. My future seemed like an awful blank page, the way the world might look after being wiped clean in a flood.

On the Saturday morning before the essay symposium, Michelle stood behind me examining the outfit I'd chosen. It was gray and somber to match my mood.

"Looks a little boring," she said. "Want to borrow something of mine?" She whipped out a red blazer and held it up in front of her.

"I look terrible in red," I said, halfheartedly riffling through my own closet.

And then I spotted the outfit Barbara had bought me over Easter break, the turquoise blouse and the black skirt with ribbons running through it. I held the blouse to my face, and the color looked vibrant against my still-winter-pale skin.

"That's pretty," Michelle said. "Have I seen that before?"

"No. I've never worn it."

I quickly put it on, and then we went outside to wait for my dad and Barbara, who had picked up Grandma Mackie along the way. On the car ride to Middlebury, I practiced my essay from the backseat while Michelle and my grandma talked over me.

"Hey," Michelle said when we pulled into the parking lot of the college. "Overbrook's here."

I tore my eyes from my essay to see Overbrook, and a woman I could only assume was his wife, walking arm in arm to the auditorium.

"Who's Overbrook?" my grandmother asked.

"The repulsive headmaster of our school," Michelle told her.

"Oh, is he the one who—?" My father stopped short.

"Yeah, he's the one," I said.

"And isn't that—?" Michelle said.

She pointed in the direction of Mr. Gallagher. Any confidence I'd had shattered on the spot. How was I supposed to get onstage and read my essay in front of the two men who had questioned my motives, doubted my honesty, and mocked my words all year? How was I supposed to make my voice sing when all I wanted was to be swallowed up by the velvet curtains and sucked down the trapdoor?

Everyone took their seats in the auditorium while I went backstage to wait with the other participants. I sat in an uncomfortable folding chair, playing with the pieces of ribbon woven into my skirt. I didn't know a soul there, but Elise seemed to know several of the other girls and chatted casually with them like she was hanging out at a coffee shop. When her name was called, she shot me a toxic look that made me break out in a sweat. I sat among the remaining strangers and listened to her honeyed voice read her flawless essay with flawless poise.

Just as the applause died down, someone called my name.

My skin crawled with nerves, and my tongue went dry. For a moment, I thought I wasn't going to be able to get up. I'd just stay there in that cold metal folding chair until the whole thing was over. In sheer terror, I gripped the bottom of that chair like it was my best friend, thinking to myself or to God or to Papa Legba, *Please don't make me do this! Set the fire alarm off. Send a rat scurrying down the aisle. Do anything, but don't make me walk out on that stage and read my words to a sea of scary people.*

And then, it was as if a warm blanket was thrown over my shoulders. Suddenly I heard a soft and soothing murmur in my head, a familiar voice urging me on, telling me to trust myself, to trust what I had to say. And I knew it was my mother, just as I'd known it in the dream when Bertha crawled out from that corner and showed me her face. Now her voice came to me, so clear and reassuring, almost like the lullaby she'd sung to me in Jane's world. *Emma,* she seemed to say, *the sign of a true woman isn't the ability to recite French poetry or play the pianoforte or cook chateaubriand. The sign of a true woman is learning to listen to her own voice even when society does its best to drown it out.*

I summoned all of my strength and courage and walked out to the podium, placing my essay in front of me and gripping the sides for balance. It was a good thing the lights were so bright that I couldn't see anyone in the audience. If my eyes had fallen on Overbrook or Gallagher, I might have lost my nerve. Slowly and in a quivering voice, I read the first lines of my essay. But as I listened to myself making bold and controversial statements about characters I had come to know intimately, I knew that I had something important to say and that I deserved to be heard. My words were honest and heartfelt, and the conviction and confidence behind those words—my voice—was strong and true.

I took one last deep breath and finished my final sentences:

"To readers of *Jane Eyre,* Bertha Mason may just be the ghost in the attic, but only because society has made her invisible. Whether Charlotte Brontë intended it or not, Bertha represents every woman's unsung dreams, every girl's repressed emotions and squandered talents. She is the little girl lost, the woman drowning under society's expectations, the mother, the wife, the daughter—anyone who's ever been defined and limited by her role in society. She is even, on occasion, me."

When I finished reading, there was a moment of silence before the applause. Michelle let out a "Woot woot!" and I started laughing right there on the stage in front of the entire crowd. It didn't matter anymore; I had done it.

There was one more essay to be read after mine, so I walked into the wings and found a dressing room off a back hallway to wait in while the judges tallied the scores. When I heard applause again, I made my way out to the auditorium and found my family and Michelle. My dad gave me an uncharacteristic hug.

"You were fantastic!" he said. "I got a little choked up. My daughter, the scholar."

"I don't know about that," I said, blushing beneath my smile. I looked around and saw Elise basking in her family's adulation. Overbrook was there, too, no doubt kissing some blueblood tail. Gallagher must have slipped out early because I didn't see him.

Barbara took hold of both my elbows and shook them. "You were so calm up there. I would have been shaking in my shoes. Your mother would be so proud."

Grandma Mackie came over and hugged me as we waited to hear the winners, and Michelle held my hand as the head judge went to the podium. Two strangers' names were called for third and second place, and I held my breath as the first-place winner was declared.

"In first place, for her essay entitled 'Missteps and Mistakes: The Perils of Social Climbing in *Vanity Fair*,' Ms. Elise Fairchild from Lockwood Preparatory School!"

Disappointment bloomed on my face. I hadn't really thought I'd win, but I sort of thought I'd place. Elise glided to the stage and accepted her check for $500, along with a thick copy of *The Oxford Shakespeare*. My father put an arm around me and pulled me close. He'd heard me rail against Elise before, but the truth was, I wasn't as angry or jealous as I'd thought I'd be. I was far happier that Michelle had beaten Elise in the equestrian competition. My battle had not been with her anyway.

"Your essay should have won," Grandma Mackie said. "The others were so boring, I almost fell asleep. Come on, let's get out of here. I need a drink."

In the parking lot walking back to the car, I heard a familiar voice call my name. I knew who it was even with my back to him. Slowly, I turned around to face Gallagher. Michelle raised an eyebrow, then stepped away to let us have a moment.

"Emma," he said, a little breathlessly. "I just wanted to congratulate you."

I scrunched my brow. "Why? I didn't win."

"No, but you did something more important. You found your voice." I shouldn't have been so pleased to hear him say this—I was still nursing some serious wounds, not to mention harboring a massive grudge—but I couldn't help but smile. "I talked to one of the judges afterward to see why yours didn't place. He said he'd voted for yours but that some of the other judges thought the essay didn't demonstrate enough control. It seemed a little too risky."

"I wrote this one from the heart, not the head."

"Well, it showed. And I thought your essay was very . . . moving. And brave. Well done." He nodded humbly, then turned around and went to his car.

Michelle ran over to me. "What was that about?"

"He told me he liked my essay."

"Liked your essay? Man, I thought he was going to lean in and kiss you, that was so intense."

I blushed furiously and gave her a disbelieving snort. "Yeah, right," I said.

We all piled into the car and went to an Italian restaurant in town to celebrate my non-win, and then Barbara invited Michelle and Grandma to spend the night at our house. When we got home, I made up the pullout couch in the den for Grandma, and we stayed there to watch *Mr. Smith Goes to Washington* with her.

We all laughed and talked and ate a vat of buttered popcorn. After the movie, Michelle and I went up to my room. I let Michelle have my bed, placing a sleeping bag on the floor beside her. Michelle got all nestled into my comforter while I squirmed in the sleeping bag below, feeling like a moth trapped inside a cocoon.

Eventually, I nodded off for a while, but my eyes opened suddenly in the middle of the night. I bolted upright, listening closely for the sound that had woken me. All the house seemed still. Moonlight was streaming through my bedroom window, and I could see Michelle's sleeping profile. Her breathing was deep and rhythmic.

I lay there, unable to sleep, feeling my heart and mind race. Something in my chest clenched, as if my heart had made a fist. For a moment, I thought I was having a heart attack. And then it felt as though my heart stood still for just a second, like an electric current had shot through it, radiating outward toward my extremities. Blood raced cold through my veins, and my muscles tightened along the bones. Something seemed to snap inside me like a whip, and I felt an almost physical tugging, pulling me out of bed.

Adrenaline and instinct propelled me from the floor, and I threw on my robe and ran downstairs to the den. As silently as I could, I opened the door and recoiled in surprise when I saw a figure on the other side of it, hovering in a white nightgown.

The apparition jumped backward and gasped. I stumbled and searched the wall for the light switch and heard my grandmother cursing. "Jesus, Mary, and Joseph. What are you trying to do, Emma, give your grandmother a heart attack?"

"Sorry," I muttered, out of breath. "I was just coming to check on you."

"Did you think I'd died?"

"No, no. I just got a funny feeling. Go back to bed. I'm sorry I woke you."

"You didn't wake me. I was up already," she said.

"Oh, right." I stood staring blankly at her, that strange panic still tugging at my insides.

"What is it, Emma?" she said. "You seem upset."

"I must have had a bad dream or something."

She rubbed the sleep out of her eyes and put on her robe. "Well, since we're both up anyway," she said, "why don't you let me make you a cup of tea?"

I nodded blearily. Something about my grandma offering to make tea was infinitely soothing. She sat me down at the kitchen table while she put the kettle on and poured herself a shot of whiskey. I couldn't shake the feeling that something terrible had happened or was about to happen. It was almost as if someone had reached out from some other place and jolted me with a lightning rod.

My grandma took a sip of her drink, then pushed it in front of me. "Here, sweetheart. You need this more than I do."

I took a tiny sip and winced as the liquor burned down my throat. "Grandma," I said, my voice shaking. "Did you ever experience something you couldn't explain?"

Grandma laughed. "You mean, like Twitter? Or those

plastic ventilated shoes I see people wearing. What are they called?"

"Crocs, Grandma," I said, smiling. "No, I mean something stranger than that. Like, did you ever feel like someone was calling out to you? Someone far away whose voice shouldn't be able to reach you, but does?"

My grandmother slung the rest of her drink back and stared across the table at me, unblinking. "As a matter of fact, I have."

Relief surged through me. "Really?"

"Everyone thought I was crazy," she said, "but your mother called out to me the night she died. I don't know how, but somehow, her voice reached me."

"You knew she'd died?"

"Even before your father came to my apartment the next day and told me. And it's time you knew the truth, Emma. Your mother didn't die of a bad heart; she walked into the bloody ocean."

I drew in a sharp breath; it was a shock hearing her say it aloud. "I know. Dad told me."

"Well, it's about time."

"So you knew she had died, even before?"

"Well, I knew something was wrong. That night, I woke up with this panicked feeling, like someone had just taken out a giant chunk of my heart."

"I know the feeling," I said. That was how I felt now, only the piece wasn't gone yet. But someone was tugging on it furiously. "But how is that possible?"

"I don't know, Emma. Call it women's intuition, call it whatever you want. But I know what I felt. And there isn't a day that goes by that I don't wish I'd done something to stop her."

"Why didn't you?"

"I convinced myself I was dreaming. Otherwise, I would have been crazy, right?"

"And yet it happened."

Chills fell in waves across my body, and I felt the same hand squeezing around my chest, forcing the breath out of my lungs.

"Emma, what's wrong?" Grandma said.

"I don't know." And then a voice called out to me, very faintly. In it were traces of pain and sadness, with fear amplified above all.

"Grandma," I said, "how long has it been since you drove a car?"

"I still have my license, if that's what you mean."

"Do you know how to drive a stick?"

"Any self-respecting woman does." She was already walking back to the den to get her shoes and coat. "If I don't ask any questions, I can't be held liable, right?" she said, taking my father's car keys from the hook in the kitchen.

"Should we leave a note?" I asked.

"What on earth would it say?"

"Good point. What about the whiskey?" I said, pointing to her empty glass.

"Don't worry. One just steadies my nerves."

CHAPTER 32

Within ten minutes, the Volvo was plodding along the Massachusetts Turnpike, the windshield wipers moving faster than we were. Grandma was driving around thirty-five miles per hour, both hands on the steering wheel, and I was leaning forward in my seat trying to accelerate us by sheer force of will.

"Grandma," I said as politely as I could, given the circumstances. "Can you go any faster?"

"I can try," she said. "But I don't like driving in rain." I watched the speedometer rise from thirty-five to fifty. "Where are we going anyway?"

"Waverly Falls," I said. "I'll tell you when to get off the highway."

We finally made it to the exit, and I navigated us through the back roads that led into town. I told her to park near the bridge and wait for me.

"Emma," she said, just as I was about to exit the car. She gripped my arm as tightly as her frail hand could. "Be careful."

"I've always been careful," I said. "There are times for being something other than careful." She nodded and released my arm.

I ran through the rain to the middle of the bridge, listening as my feet echoed across the floorboards. Here I was again, where Gray and I had stood just a few weeks ago, only it was darker this time, so dark I could barely see my hand in front of me.

"Gray!" I shouted. I had no idea why I felt so certain he would be here. "Gray! Where are you?"

Gripped with a sudden fear, I peered through the long, narrow window that framed a view of the power plant, the falls, and the river below. Through the mist, I spotted a figure sitting on the stone wall inside the power plant, right at the spot where the river spilled over the falls, dropping into the churning white foam below.

"Gray!" I screamed, even though I knew he couldn't hear me.

I ran through to the opposite side of the bridge and started up the hill. When I reached the power plant, I peered through the slats of the iron gate and saw Gray sitting on the wall, casually almost, like one might sit at the end of a dock watching a sunset. My voice ripped through the thunder of the water, but still he couldn't hear me.

How had he gotten through the massive gate? I threaded my fingers through its metal slats as if I could rip them open with force.

The only way to reach him, I realized, was from below. I'd have to get to the bottom of the falls and try to get his attention. I ran downhill as fast as I could until the road flattened out. Without thinking, I scaled the waist-high wall that flanked the river, landing on a massive boulder and almost sliding right off. The rocks were slick and scattered at uneven heights. I tottered as I walked. Carefully, I treaded my way down to the rocky ledge below. The river raced mightily at my side, pent-up nature releasing its fury. Dread gripped me as I recalled that day in the ocean, how powerful the tide had been, how little control I'd had over my own destiny. I squatted down on the ledge to steady myself, clutching the ridges of the stone with both hands.

Terrified, I resumed my journey, moving faster now, feeling an urgency to reach Gray. I paused to see if he had spotted me yet, but his eyes were directed toward the middle of the dam. The rocky ledge inclined steadily, following the pitch of the street. The closer I got to the falls, the more steeply I had to climb. Wind and water whipped through my hair as the water from the falls catapulted in front of me, transforming into a writhing mass of white foam.

When I got as close as I was willing to go, I tilted my head back and called to Gray. He was standing now, looking straight ahead, his arms slightly back, like he was contemplating the unthinkable. He looked like a bird poised to fly.

A terror seized me as I recalled the dream I'd had at Thornfield—a child clinging round my neck as if to strangle me, a gust of wind blowing me off balance, stones rolling out from under my feet, the wall crumbling, the child falling through my fingertips, falling out of reach. My mother's body careening from the rooftop. Gray tumbling from the dam.

No. That wouldn't happen here.

"Gray!" I hollered again, fear bringing my voice to an unearthly pitch. "Don't jump! I'm here. I'm here!" I flailed my arms as much as I could without losing my balance.

I kept screaming, bellowing an incoherent stream of warnings, and then—a miracle!—Gray looked down. When his eyes met mine, his body went slack, and I thought he was going to fall, come toppling down and crash into the rocks right in front of me. Instead, he collapsed onto the wall, clutching it, turning his body away from open air and falling water, away from gravity and certain death.

I collapsed, too—in relief, in fatigue—and we both crouched there, hugging our separate life preservers of stone. I don't know how long we stayed like that. Eventually, Gray stood up and shouted something to me, but I couldn't hear through the din. I watched as he hopped off the wall and then shimmied up a tall tree that towered over the falls, its branches tangled in the slats of the gate that surrounded the generator. For a moment, he disappeared amid the leaves, and I held my breath until I saw him reappear on the other side. I exhaled and watched him fall unceremoniously to the ground, landing on his feet.

Content that he was safe, I turned around, intending to reverse my steps. But in the time it had taken for me to reach the falls, the water level had risen dramatically. The ledge I had walked here on had disappeared, submerged beneath the river. I descended as far as I could go. Gray called down to me from the stone wall above.

"Don't move!" he shouted. "I'm coming for you!"

"No!" I screamed, but he had already taken off down the street. I watched him climb over the wall about a hundred yards downriver and drop onto a large boulder. He only had about two feet of clearance before his feet would meet the river, and the water level was rising fast. He walked as far as he could to meet me, and when neither of us could go any farther, we stopped and stared at each other. There was a look of supreme tenderness and gratitude that passed between us as we stood there contemplating our next move. I only wanted to reach him, pull him toward me, tell him I was sorry, kiss him everywhere it hurt.

Like a surprise attack, the river surged and literally swept me off my feet. I felt like I was falling in slow motion, toppling from a great height, even though I must have met the water almost instantly. My body lurched into the frigid water and bobbed up again, swept along the currents like a piece of driftwood. The water pulled me downstream like a vacuum, sucking me toward its greedy mouth. My instinct was to fight against it, but my head kept dipping below the surface, water flooding my nostrils and lungs. I coughed and sputtered. I tried to swim again, to do anything, but my limbs were rubbery and chilled.

How long had I been in here? Minutes? Seconds? Water filled my lungs again, and I choked and flailed my arms. I was a pawn of Nature, being shuttled to a watery death.

And then something overtook me, something large and solid and powerful. It trapped my arms to my chest so I couldn't fight. My body thrashed instinctively, and my head hit something hard behind me. I was hurtling downriver on my back, headlong, floating on something, with icy river water streaming past me on all sides. I let myself be jettisoned downstream for several seconds, finally opening my eyes to see trails of red in the foamy wake behind. Blood. I shut my eyes, not wanting to trust my own senses.

My eyes shot open when my makeshift raft flung out from under me, and I found myself alone momentarily, splashing like mad amid the currents. I flipped onto my stomach, and my instinct to swim kicked in. And suddenly Gray was next to me, his hand on my arm, guiding me toward the riverbank. His face was bleeding.

"Stay above water," he shouted. "Go with the current."

I tried to answer him, but my mouth filled quickly with water, so I surrendered to the current and let it carry me down. My arms and legs and chest were burning, and I knew I couldn't last much longer. I was so tired. So very tired. Why wasn't I cold?

Maybe drowning isn't such a bad way to die. Maybe it's peaceful. After the gasping and choking are over, it's probably just like sleeping.

"Now!" Gray bellowed, yanking my arm with a powerful tug. My body lurched, and I tried to fight his momentum. "Swim, Emma! Swim. We can make it!"

"No," I said, resisting Gray's pull. I felt numb and drowsy. "Let me go. I can't do it."

"You can!" he said. "You're stronger than you think." His words echoed through my head.

Stronger than you think. Stronger than you believe. These had been my mother's words, and now they were Gray's. And the words had a power to them. I forced myself to swim toward him, following his voice, which kept calling to me and never wavered. It gave me the strength to keep going, to fight against the current until I was close enough to the riverbank I could almost touch it.

Spurred by a powerful surge of adrenaline, I began to swim, my arms wheeling in a desperate crawl until my hand struck stone. I scrabbled at it madly, finding purchase on the rough crags of the ledge. Gray had found it, too, and he was dragging his body up out of the river. I clambered onto the rock, trying to pull myself out, but I was too weak. The river rushed by, and I clung for dear life.

"Emma," Gray's voice said, breathlessly, as he extended a hand to me. His outstretched palm hovered just a few inches from mine. "Emma, you saved my life," he said.

With a transcendent effort, I reached out to grab his hand and let him return the favor.

CHAPTER 33

And so I ended up in the hospital for the fourth time that year. I was treated for mild trauma, but my injuries were nothing compared to Gray's. He'd suffered facial lacerations from the tree, a fractured tibia from the dive, and a broken nose from when I'd rammed his face with the back of my head. He had to stay overnight so they could set his nose and leg and treat him for tachycardia.

The doctor discharged me around five in the morning while Gray was still in the ICU, so I wasn't able to see him before I left. I called Gray's cell all day, but he didn't pick up. I was so worried. I slept for thirteen hours that night, and when I woke up I tried calling his house. Finally I reached his father, who told me Gray was doing much better and that they were releasing him that afternoon. Relieved, I asked if he could have Gray call me as soon as he was home. I was practically sobbing when I got off the phone.

Back at school, I called Gray all week, but he wouldn't answer or return my calls. He must have been angry with me, but I wasn't sure why. Maybe it was because I'd stopped him from following through on destroying himself at the falls. Or maybe he realized I'd been right after all, that the only reason he wanted to be with me was because he thought I could fix him. And when he found out I wasn't willing to do that, he'd given up on me completely. Whatever the case, it seemed that Gray and I were officially over.

Michelle stood by me throughout the entire ordeal, helping me study for finals when my mind could focus only on Gray. The gossip about his suicide attempt was uncharacteristically subdued by Lockwood standards. Some girls even had the good taste to stop talking about it when I entered a room. I was stunned when Jess Barrister approached me after our English exam and pulled me aside in the hallway.

I stared at her incredulously as she began to apologize for Elise's behavior. "She went too far this time," she said in her low throaty voice. "I mean, I know why she feels she has to do this shit, but it's getting so old. I just wanted to say I'm sorry. I like Gray, and it wasn't right what she did to him. Or to you." And with that, she left me standing there in astonishment, wondering where on earth that speck of decency had come from.

For the next few weeks, I sat through test after brutal test, filling in tiny bubbles on answer sheets and writing pointless essays on everything from Evolution Theory to Dystopian Literature. Then I'd skulk back to the solace of my room and watch the erratic spring weather wreak havoc on the quad. The wind was so wild, the rains so persistent, it felt like the campus was going to come unglued from the earth and slip quietly into the Atlantic.

It was the third Saturday of May when the skies finally cleared. The windows in our room were open for the first time in weeks, and when I came in from my shower, sunlight was streaming through the curtains, along with a cool breeze that smelled of roses. Michelle came in after me, kicked off her shower shoes, and flopped onto her bed. I could feel her eyes on me, so I turned toward the wall so I could sulk in peace.

"What's wrong?" she asked. I said nothing. "Emma, please talk to me."

I sat up and pulled my wet hair into a thick ponytail. "Tonight was supposed to be Gray's prom."

"Oh," she said. "I forgot. That sucks."

"Yeah, it does."

She came and sat next to me on the bed, putting a hand on my shoulder. "Where's the dress?" she said.

"What?"

"You know, the dress he bought you. I want to see it."

"Why?"

"Just humor me, will you?"

Reluctantly, I found the dress in my closet, removed it from its cellophane bag, and held it up to my body, watching the diaphanous material ripple in the breeze, changing colors from gray to blue to green.

"That's gorgeous!" she said.

"I know."

"Try it on. Right now."

"I don't want to."

"Do it for me. Please? Pretty please?"

I sighed, angrily stripping off my jeans and T-shirt and stepping carefully into the narrow sheath. It fit perfectly—slim but not too tight, the sequins at the bustline shimmering like sea glass, the sheer skirt draping elegantly from the empire waist so the material whispered against my skin.

"It looks even better on," she said. "At first I thought it was gray, but it changes color with the light. Sort of like the ocean." She stood behind me, playing with my hair, twisting it up and pulling down a few pieces to frame my face. "I know I've had my issues with Gray, and I haven't always been there for you when you needed to talk about him, but . . . maybe I was wrong. Maybe I misjudged him." I kept quiet, not wanting her to stop. "Look, I'm trying to apologize here. I think you're really good for Gray, and you've been so miserable these past weeks that he must be good for you, too."

Despite my horrid mood, I cracked a smile. Michelle's mouth broke into a mischievous grin. "So, I have an idea."

"That's never good," I said.

"Come on, it's a great idea. Dare I say it, an excellent idea?"

"You do remember that sneaking off to Braeburn was your idea, too. And drinking champagne in the limo before the Snow Ball?"

Michelle let out a devious laugh. "Yes, but this one's better," she said.

Before I knew it, she was on the phone in the hallway concocting some crazy scheme and leaving me out of the loop. When she came back in, she put some loud dance music on the stereo and got out her curling iron.

"Do you want to let me in on your plan?" I said.

"Just be quiet, hold still, and let me do your hair."

"If I do, will you tell me what's going on?"

"Soon enough," she said, holding a bobby pin in her mouth. She smoothed down an errant strand of my hair and inserted the bobby pin somewhere on my head. When she'd finished with my hair, she began dusting my face with a light bronzer and lining my eyes.

"Is this to compensate for the fact that you didn't have a Barbie as a kid?"

"I'll have you know, I did have a Barbie," she said. "Astronaut Barbie."

"You did not."

"Did too. She had glow-in-the-dark moon rocks. And anyway, I'm doing this because Owen's coming to pick us up in half an hour. We're taking you to Gray's house."

"Oh, no you're not," I said, grabbing the arm that was about to apply mascara to my eyelashes. "He hasn't called me back. He obviously doesn't want to see me."

"Oh, he wants to see you."

"Michelle, seriously, what's the point?"

"Emma, it's Gray's senior year, and he's missing the biggest event of his high school experience. So unless you can live with that on your conscience, you're bringing the prom to him."

"Michelle—"

"Emma, trust me," she said, sighing. "Okay, don't trust me. Trust Gray. He loves you. I know he does. And one look at you in that dress, he's going to forget all about being mad at you. Hell, he may forget his own name. Look at yourself. You're a goddess."

She dragged me in front of the full-length mirror and made me look at myself—really look. Who was this person? For sixteen years I had seen myself as plain and ordinary. The girl in the mirror was me, but a different version of me, one who had grown into her looks and seemed at peace with them. Michelle smiled at me through the mirror and said, "Now hold still and let me finish your curls. A goddess needs curls."

An hour later, we were standing in front of Easty waiting for Owen to show up. I chewed my lower lip while Michelle chastised me for messing up her Pink Nouveau lipstick. When Owen arrived, I crawled carefully into the backseat of his car, while Michelle hopped in front. I was a little jealous that they were both so relaxed and comfortable in their casual clothes while I sat stiffly upright, trying not to wrinkle my dress, trying not to breathe.

A half hour later, we arrived in front of Gray's enormous stone house. Owen helped me out of the car and handed me my purse. "You look beautiful," he said.

"You really do," Michelle agreed.

"We'll stay here for a little bit to make sure you're okay."

"What are you guys going to do while I'm here?" I asked.

"I don't know," Owen said. "Maybe catch a movie?"

"Or two," Michelle said, winking at me. "You have my cell if you need me."

"Okay," I said, feeling a thousand nervous flutters in my chest. "And, Michelle?"

"I know, I know," she said. "You're welcome."

I laughed and approached the front door on my heels, feeling like none of this was real, like I was walking through a stage set. Crickets were chirping and the sun was just dipping beyond the hills that lay behind Gray's house. I knocked on the front door and waited there, feeling a chill run under my sheer gown.

Finally, the door opened, and Anna was looking up at me with huge eyes. "Wow, Emma. You look like Mermaid Barbie."

"Thanks," I said, laughing. "Is Gray here?"

"Yeah. My parents went away for the weekend, and he's *supposed* to be babysitting, but he just stays up in his room all the time."

She led me inside and went running back to the couch to continue watching her TV show. Cautiously, I walked up that beautiful open staircase and along the corridor that led to Gray's room. I had a sudden feeling of panic. Maybe I shouldn't have come. What if he kicked me out? What if he wanted nothing to do with me?

But it was too late to do anything about it now. I was standing in front of his door, and my heels on the wooden floor had already given me away.

"Who's there?" I heard him shout.

I opened the door to his room and saw him sitting sideways on the bed, his feet splayed out on the floor, one in a cast. He glanced up at me, and his face dropped. I couldn't tell whether he was angry or happy or just surprised. Even though most of his lacerations had healed, his right hand went involuntarily to his face, touching the largest scar, which traversed his forehead and intersected one eyebrow.

"What are you doing here?" he asked.

"I came to see you." For a moment, my stomach plummeted. *I shouldn't have come. This is going to be a horrible repeat of last time. He doesn't want me here.*

"I thought you hated me," he said.

I froze in the doorway, stunned. "I called you, like, a million times."

"I lost my cell phone in the river that night."

"Oh," I said. I was so confused. "But I spoke with your dad. He promised to tell you I'd called."

"My dad's an idiot," he said. "He never told me. I assumed you didn't want to talk to me. I thought it was over."

"So did I."

Suddenly, I felt deliriously happy. Gray didn't hate me, and his parents were away for the weekend. I had as long as I wanted to make things up to him, to show him how much he meant to me. A part of me couldn't wait to get started. Another part of me felt nervous and uncertain. My body tingled with anticipation and fear, exhilaration and love. And Gray Newman, that beautiful boy, sat staring at me with those downturned eyes. He was just a few feet from me—unable to move, really—mine for the taking.

I walked over and sat down next to him on the bed. Reaching out my hand, I gently traced every scar on his face. I ran my fingertips along his almost-healed nose and kissed him softly, tenderly, on the forehead like he had once kissed me. He didn't move a muscle or say a word, but when I drew away, he was staring at me like he wasn't sure if I was real.

"Do I look awful?" he said, touching his scars again.

"Of course. You always did," I said, laughing. I took his hand and pressed his palm to my lips. "Your hands are freezing."

"I've been dead," he said, his voice choked with emotion.

I placed his cold hands on my flushed cheeks, and he pulled me toward him to kiss me. I wanted to, desperately, but I'd been holding in so much emotion for so long that everything felt too feverish, too rushed.

"Wait," I said, pulling away from him. His eyes followed me as I retrieved my iPod from my purse and hooked it up to his stereo. "I figured if you couldn't go to the prom, I'd bring the prom to you." I shuffled through my songs and selected one to play. "You remember that day when you asked me once which song reminded me of you? I never answered. This is the one."

As the piano chords of Embrace's "Gravity" filled the room, I walked to the bed and offered him my hand. "Gray Newman, will you dance with me?"

He shook his head. "Em, I can't."

"Why not?"

He nodded sadly toward his crutches. I grabbed them from the corner of the room and handed them to him. "Here. Now you're a Hemingway character," I said, and he laughed out loud. The sound was sweeter than anything I could imagine.

Offering him both my arms, I eased him off the bed and onto his crutches, then helped him to the balcony door. He hopped through, and I followed him over the threshold, so we were both standing on the now-darkened balcony, silvery stars just beginning to appear above our heads.

The music was faint out there, distant and haunting, like it was coming from another place and time. I placed my arms around his shoulders, and he gripped my waist for support. Leaning into him, I felt intoxicated by his nearness. His spicy sea-air scent made me dizzy with longing. I dropped my head against his chest and breathed him in.

"I can't do anything but move in circles," he said.

"That's okay."

And it was, because dancing requires little else. At one point I noticed Gray had stopped moving. I pulled back to find him looking down at me, a dazed expression on his face. "You're here," he said. "I can't believe it. . . . I was sure you . . ."

Before he could finish his thought, I placed a hand on the back of his neck and pulled his face down to kiss me. The moment our lips touched, it was like we'd been born to do only that. We stood out there on that balcony for hours, swaying and kissing, dancing under the laws of gravity, but feeling like our feet no longer touched ground.

CHAPTER 34

There are certain things I will never understand about that year. Did I dream myself into Jane's world? And if so, how do I account for my A in French class? Or the fact that Jane's voice still comes to me when I need her most? Although our voices are so similar now, it's hard to tell which is which.

Gray picked me up at school after final exams and drove me home. When we entered Hull's Cove, I welcomed the sight of the fishing marinas and crab traps, and even managed not to scowl at the new vacation homes that had sprung up on the waterfront. I was so glad to be home again.

Gray pulled into my driveway, but I wasn't ready to go inside. "Come for a walk with me," I said. "I want to see the beach."

We sat on the sand and undid our shoes, then went down to the water's edge and began walking along the surf. This was it—the beginning of our summer together—three months of bliss before Gray had to leave for Coast Guard training in September.

"I can't believe I won't be able to talk to you for eight weeks," I said. "I can't even call you?"

"Not during boot camp."

"But I can come to your graduation, right?"

"You better."

"I'm determined to get my license this summer so I can drive down myself."

"I'll teach you to drive stick."

"Really?" I raised an eyebrow teasingly, and he broke into laughter.

"Emma, you're making me blush."

We walked past the lighthouse until we'd reached the spit of land where Gray had called to me the afternoon of my birthday almost a year ago. The sun was starting to set, and I knew my father and Barbara would be waiting for us for dinner, so we decided to head back.

Just as we neared my street, an enormous black-and-white dog ran toward us. Gray moved in front of me, and as if in slow motion, the dog pounced on him. I screamed and lunged to pull the dog off, but instead of attacking, the dog pinned Gray down on the sand and began licking his face in a frenzy of kisses. I tried my hardest not to laugh as I reached out to help Gray stand up.

The dog crouched in play pose, tongue hanging out, begging for us to play. He seemed to know me. "Are you lost, little guy?" I gave him a solid scratch behind the ears and searched for a tag but found nothing. I couldn't shake the feeling that I'd seen him before. He pranced around us gleefully, even nipping the bottom of Gray's shorts. A name suddenly popped into my head.

"Pilot," I said. The dog's ears perked up, and he sat obediently.

"Pilot?" Gray asked. "How did you know his name?"

"I have no idea." But the truth was, I'd met this dog before. This was Rochester's dog, or at least a dog that looked very much like him. The world felt a little unhinged suddenly.

Gray brushed the sand off his pants and looked over at me. "You all right?" he said. "You look like you've just seen a ghost."

I crinkled my brow and shook my head. "No," I said. "It's just a coincidence."

The dog must have spied something more interesting down the beach—perhaps his master—because he went running off. I had to resist the urge to look around for signs of a man fitting Rochester's description. But the truth was, I had my own Rochester right here.

I looked up at Gray and caught him staring at me. For once, those hazel eyes didn't look sad. "Truth," I said. "What were you just thinking about?"

He hedged for a second, then replied, "Nothing," and bit his cheek.

"Oh my God!" I said. "That's it!"

"That's what?"

"Your tell! When you're bluffing, you bite your cheek."

"I do not."

"You do, too! Come on, tell me what you were thinking. Do I make you nervous?"

He laughed, but I could tell he was holding something back. "You really want to know what I was thinking?"

"Yes, I really want to know."

"Okay. I was thinking how lucky I am that you didn't give up on me."

"And . . . ?"

"And how I really hope you don't find some other guy while I'm away at boot camp."

"And . . . ?"

"And what?" he said.

"Tell me what you were really thinking."

He flashed me his devastating smile and raised an eyebrow. Now it was my turn to blush.

Gray laughed and reached for my hand. I thought back to that roller-coaster ride we took when we were little, the way Gray had grabbed my hand just before we went over the top. That was how I felt now, like wheels had been set in motion and we were about to plunge together into something terrifying and exhilarating and entirely unknown.

If you got lost in a book, which literary character would you be? Take the quiz to find out! As you answer the questions, keep a tally of your responses.

1. What is the most important principle to live by?
   A. Be kind to others.
   B. Be true to yourself.
   C. Embrace life's possibilities.
   D. Find love, no matter the cost.
   E. Have fun.

2. What is your dream job?
   A. A teacher or a nurse; a job where I can make a difference
   B. A challenging profession that requires brains and persistence, like a lawyer or journalist
   C. Something wild and outdoorsy where I'm my own boss; maybe a forest ranger or ski instructor
   D. A career requiring skill and creativity, like fashion or graphic design
   E. Job? What's a job?

3. Which song title best describes your love life?
   A. Beyoncé's "Broken-Hearted Girl"
   B. Taylor Swift's "Sparks Fly"
   C. Lady Gaga's "Bad Romance"
   D. Kelly Clarkson's "Beautiful Disaster"
   E. Rihanna's "Only Girl (In the World)"

4. Your dream vacation would be:
   A. A cozy chalet tucked into a mountainside
   B. A magnificent bed-and-breakfast overlooking the ocean
   C. A four-star hotel in exotic Marrakesh or Bali

D. A tropical oasis far away from everyone

E. An all-expense-paid cruise where I'm wined and dined 24/7

5. Your idea of the perfect date would be:
   A. Snowy walks by day; firelit conversation by night
   B. A romantic picnic by a lake; good food and good conversation
   C. An all-day adventure through museums, street fairs, and cobblestoned alleyways
   D. A secret rendezvous on the beach at night
   E. An expensive meal followed by dancing and nightlife

6. What are your thoughts on love?
   A. True love takes time, but it's worth the wait.
   B. Love happens when you're least expecting it.
   C. Love is intoxicating and dangerous, like a leap off a cliff.
   D. Love is a secret you hold close to your heart.
   E. Love is a ring on my finger and a house in the Hamptons.

7. What aspect of your life has given you the most trouble?
   A. My childhood
   B. My family; they can be so meddlesome
   C. My own recklessness
   D. A terrible mistake from my past
   E. My ambition

8. How would you describe your fashion sense?
   A. Simple and practical
   B. Tasteful and classic
   C. Flowy and romantic

D. I generally wear all black, but a hint of red is nice
E. Flirty and feminine

9. Your favorite romantic movie is:
   A. *Casablanca*
   B. *When Harry Met Sally*
   C. *The Phantom of the Opera*
   D. *Romeo and Juliet*
   E. *The Notebook*

10. People often describe you as:
    A. sensible
    B. smart
    C. free-spirited
    D. individualistic
    E. charming

11. Which animal is most like you?
    A. An optimistic songbird
    B. A clever fox
    C. A wild horse
    D. A fearless cat
    E. An elegant peacock

12. How do you react when you don't get what you want?
    A. I keep going after it; I'm nothing if not persistent.
    B. I pretend I didn't want it anyway—sour grapes and all that—but I'll secretly pine.
    C. I tend to pout and behave badly.
    D. I suffer in silence.
    E. I always get what I want.

If you got mostly A responses, you're:
Jane from *Jane Eyre*.

You are fiercely intelligent, independent, and loyal. You usually do the right thing, even when it goes against your own desires, and you always speak your mind. While you don't call attention to yourself, you have an inner poise and beauty that attracts men, particularly troubled souls who are drawn to your strength. You enjoy reading, deep conversation, and long walks in any kind of weather.

If you got mostly B responses, you're:
Elizabeth Bennet from *Pride and Prejudice*.

You have a quick wit and a sharp tongue that can sometimes put people off, but if they are able to get past your defenses, you make an incredibly passionate partner and a loyal friend. Your sense of humor and charm make you an excellent guest at any social gathering. You enjoy traveling, games of mental agility, and verbal sparring.

If you got mostly C responses, you're:
Catherine Linton from *Wuthering Heights*.

You are free-spirited, energetic, and prone to exuberant passions and deep emotional attachments. But with this passion comes a reckless nature and a fiery temper that frequently get you into trouble. You have a tendency to become listless if you don't get what you want. You adore extreme sports, romantic novels, and the outdoors.

If you got mostly D responses, you're:
Hester Prynne from *The Scarlet Letter*.

You are rebellious and proud by nature, with a vivacious beauty and sensuous nature that attracts men to you. Women, however, are threatened by your confidence and self-sufficiency and may attempt to sully your reputation. But those who know you best have witnessed your caring and compassionate side. You love creative pursuits, children, and private places by the sea.

If you got mostly E responses, you're:
Daisy Buchanan from *The Great Gatsby*.

You are beautiful, elegant, and poised, with a magnetic charm that draws people to you. You tend to flirt shamelessly, aware of the power you have over men. While you can be shallow and selfish at times, in your heart, you're a true romantic. You enjoy shopping, socializing, and the finer things in life.

If you enjoyed this quiz, come visit my website (www.evemariemont.com) for the follow-up quiz, "Who is your literary soul mate?" plus book trailers, playlists, an author Q&A, and much more!

Emma's adventures continue in
A Touch of Scarlet, by Eve Marie Mont.

Emma Townsend thought she had put the terrifying events of her sophomore year behind her—the lightning strike, the coma, the time she lost to a fantasy world in which she imagined she was Jane Eyre. But now she's living in the real world again—dating a gorgeous Coast Guard recruit, excelling in her classes, and making new friends at school. But when Emma makes a serious error in judgment, her relationships with both her boyfriend and her roommate begin to unravel, leaving her scorned and alone. As her isolation mounts, Emma lapses into her dreams once again, this time entering the world of Hester Prynne and *The Scarlet Letter.* And with her dreams come destructive impulses that threaten to alienate her from the people she loves most. Because each time Emma returns from Hester's world, she is increasingly torn between remaining the good girl she's always been and becoming the rebellious woman she longs to be.

Read on for a special excerpt and, like Emma, get lost in a good book . . . literally!

We drove to the lighthouse and parked along the beach road, tumbling out of the Jeep into a dusky violet night. The lighthouse sat on a crest of the beach a few hundred yards away, so we held hands as we walked the dune path to the lighthouse's base. A bronze placard showed the image of a Labrador retriever named Rex who had guarded the lighthouse for fourteen years, greeting visitors, providing companionship for the lighthouse keeper, and chasing off ghosts. This part of the Massachusetts Bay was known for being treacherous; there were dozens of tales of sailors and keepers who had lost their lives along this coast and still haunted the dunes where we stood. And nine years ago, my mother had killed herself on her birthday by walking into the ocean.

I shivered, pushing away the memory of my mother as we walked out onto the beach. The surf was pounding violently on the sand, moaning and hissing like a living creature. Coming to the lighthouse had sounded romantic when Gray suggested it, but now that we were here, I felt unsettled. Trying to quell my unease, I turned to face Gray, who was pulling something from his pocket.

He gazed at me sweetly. "Here," he said, handing me a small box. I glanced up at him eagerly and opened the clamshell lid. "I know you always wear your mother's dragonfly," he said nervously, "but I wanted you to wear a part of me, too."

I lifted up the necklace, a dog tag hanging from a silver chain. Gray always wore his uncle's dog tags, but I knew him well enough to know he'd never give those up, not even to give them to me. I brought the necklace closer and inspected the tag, which was etched with the small image of a scorpion.

"It's your zodiac sign," I said.

"Look at the other side."

I turned it over and read the inscription out loud: "'To Emma, the only antidote for my sting.'" Tears welled in my eyes before I could stop them.

"I'm wearing yours, too," he said, pulling his collar away to reveal a dog tag he'd added to his chain, this one showing the profile of a woman with wings.

"The Virgo angel," I said.

"I was hoping you'd be my guardian angel while I'm away."

This made me lose it completely, and then I was sobbing and sniffling into his shirt in a completely undignified manner. Gray pulled me into a hug, and I melted into him, inhaling the comforting scent of his skin mixed with cologne and laundry detergent. Gray's particular smell had always reminded me of the ocean, which was somehow fitting now that he had decided to spend the rest of his life on it.

"You okay?" he said after I'd finished my cry, wiping the last tears from my cheeks with his sleeve. Dizzy with how much I wanted him, I studied his downturned eyes and stubbled jaw.

He didn't even pause, he just cupped my face in his hands and brought his lips down on mine in that way that never failed to render me senseless. How could two pairs of lips fit together so perfectly, feel so sublime locked together that it made you forget where you were? His hands followed the contours of my summer dress, pausing at my hips, then gripping my waist.

I practically threw him onto the ground, not caring at all about the hard sand jabbing into my knees or the cold breeze creeping up my bare legs. Before I knew it, we'd switched places, and my dress was hitched up around my waist, Gray's body shifting on top of mine—all rock-hard 170 pounds of him. I tore at his shirt, trying to undo the buttons while he waited impatiently. If either of us had said a word, the moment might have dissolved, so I kept quiet and focused on his last button, pulling his shirt apart to reveal toned abs above faded jeans. A solar flare shot up from my core, radiating heat over every part of my body.

I traced the lines and curves of his chest and stomach as he arched above me. My body hummed with electricity. The button of his jeans was right beneath my fingertips. Just one more thing to unfasten, and there would be no holding back.

Part of me wanted to go for it—to lose myself in this moment and not think about tomorrow or the next day or the day after that. But the smallest reminder that a new day was coming—a day without Gray—paralyzed me.

And then he was moving off me and I was turning away from him, overcome with emotion, adrenaline, and a shrieking sense of doom. My breath was thick in my throat, my face and hair soaked with sweat and sea air. Gray collapsed onto the sand behind me, wrapping his arms around me and hugging me so tightly it hurt. His body was hard against my back.

"We don't have to do anything just because it's the last night," he said.

"I know."

"I don't want you to do anything you don't want to. Not ever."

I turned around to face him now, coming apart at the sight of his eyes, filled with concern. "Believe me, Gray, I want to. I just—"

"You don't have to explain. This has been a crazy day. I want the moment to be right."

I burrowed into his embrace, and we lay like that for a small eternity. With my ear pressed to his chest, I waited until our heartbeats synchronized, then pulled away, not wanting to feel mine rush past his. Finally, I propped myself up on an elbow, and he did the same, smiling a sexy grin. "It was fun, though, right?" he said.

"God, yeah."

His grin faded slowly, his eyebrows knitting together. "I want it to be me," he said.

"What?"

His eyes were closed, and when he opened them, they were glistening. "When the time is right, I want it to be me."

I laughed nervously. "What, you think I'm going to run off and have sex with the first guy who comes along?"

"No. It's just, we're going to be apart for a while, and the thought of some other guy being there for you when I can't be . . . it makes me sick."

"That's not going to happen."

"I'm just saying, don't do something with someone else because you miss me, you know? I want to be the first. Your first."

His face looked so vulnerable. "Gray, you will be my first."

"Promise?" he said, gripping my hands.

"Promise."

He collapsed onto his back and sighed in relief. I lay down next to him, one arm behind my head, the other resting on his chest as we stared at the stars.

"Hey, did you see that?" he asked a few minutes later, sitting up and pointing toward the sky. "The shooting star?"

I sat up and hugged my knees to my chest. "I missed it."

He leaned in and kissed me on the cheek. "Well, I'm giving you my wish," he said. "Go ahead, Emma. Wish for something."

I looked into his sad, lovely eyes and made a wish I knew could never come true.

When I crept into the house minutes later, fully expecting to tiptoe quietly up to my room, I nearly knocked the lamp over when I saw my father sitting on the sofa in a dim pool of light. His hands were knotted tensely in front of him. I looked down at my body self-consciously. In my damp and wrinkled dress, I felt crumpled and unmade, like a cupcake whose frosting had melted.

"Do you know it's two in the morning, Emma?"

Truthfully, I didn't. I'd been thinking it was closer to midnight. "I'm sorry," I said. "I lost track of time."

"The one thing I asked of you was not to stay out too late," he said, his voice cold.

"I know, Dad, but I figured since this was the last night I was going to see Gray, and it was my birthday party—"

"Can you think of any reason why I might be worried sick about you particularly because it *is* your birthday?"

Guilt washed over me like a toxic cloud. "God, Dad, I'm sorry. I forgot."

"You forgot?" His face was incredulous. Because I hadn't really forgotten. Some things, you never can.

"It seems like you've forgotten a lot this summer."

"What do you mean?"

He wrung his hands together and sat up like he was bracing for a fight. "Your relationship with Gray has taken over everything. I hardly remember seeing you this summer."

"Dad, we were here all the time."

"But you weren't really here. You were always taking off somewhere to be on your own. And even when you were here, it was like you were on your own planet. You were so wrapped up in each other, you couldn't see anything else."

"Well, what did you expect?" I said. "Last summer, you told me I should stop moping around the house and do normal teenage things, and now that I'm actually doing that, you can't handle it."

"It's you I'm worried about not being able to handle things."

"Dad, I'm fine."

"No, you're not." He ran both hands through his hair. "What's going to happen when Gray leaves? How are you going to go back to school when you can't go a day without seeing him? I don't like you being so . . . dependent on each other. I don't want you making yourself so vulnerable."

"But Dad, if you love someone, it makes you vulnerable. You, of all people, should know that."

He closed his eyes and blew air out his cheeks. "I'm not going to tell you that you don't love Gray, because I'm sure you think you do. But honey, you're seventeen years old. Gray's nineteen. Do you really think this is going to last? Gray's leaving for the Coast Guard, and you're going to be stuck here, pining for him. Without knowing it, you're going to let yourself get in deeper and deeper until you don't even know which way is up. Believe me, I know what I'm talking about. And I can't bear to see the same thing happen to you."

"Dad, you're wrong," I said, tears springing to my eyes. "Gray isn't Mom."

"I see the way he looks at you. Like you're the sun and moon. But you can't be everything to him. It's going to suck you dry."

"Dad, I'm not going to let that happen."

"I thought the same thing. I thought I was strong enough for your mother and me both. But I wasn't. I just wasn't. . . . " His voice trailed off, and he let his head fall into his hands.

All these years later, and my mother's suicide still haunted him. It still haunted me, too.

Ever since my father had told me the truth about her, I'd been having nightmares. Again and again in my dreams, I watched my mother disappear into the ocean, unable to say or do anything to stop her.

When I looked up, my father was crying a little. "Dad, I'm so sorry."

"I know," he said. "I'm sorry, too. I didn't mean to ruin your birthday."

"You didn't. I think we're both just upset and tired."

"Yeah," he said, wiping his face. "Why don't we get some sleep and talk about it in the morning?"

"All right."

I headed upstairs, feeling sick to my stomach. Because the thing was, we wouldn't talk about it tomorrow. We'd suppress it and then resent each other later. This had been our pattern all summer.

In my dreams that night, as expected, I found myself on the beach again. The ocean looked steely and wild, like an immense writhing creature that knows only greed, that takes and takes until all you love is gone. The moon was full and shining down on the waves, creating a path of shimmering light. Like always, my eyes followed the light until I saw her.

She was standing in the surf, wearing a white nightgown that billowed like a sail. Her black hair whipped around her head like feathers on a captive bird. For a moment, she cast a backward glance at me. I tried to run toward her, but my legs were stuck in the sand. She was already waist-deep, and I called out to her, but the roar of the waves drowned me out.

With every ounce of my strength, I willed my legs out of the sand and began running, crashing into the shallow surf behind her, the cold water hitting my legs like icy knives. I called her name again, but the word came out distorted, like an underwater voice. Panicked, I looked in every direction for a sign of her, but all I could see were whitecaps and inky blackness. She was gone already.

I shivered and gasped from the cold. Adrenaline pumped through my limbs, so they felt rubbery and slack. A wave toppled overhead, submerging me. Another wave battered me down. I plunged to the bottom, trying to dive under the tumult, but the waves kept careening over me, one after the other, flipping my body until I had no sense of where I was. Underwater, no sky, no idea which way was up.

Thinking was not possible. Instinct made me reach out for air, my lungs desperate for oxygen, and then, I felt not air but ice-cold flesh. Large hands grabbed me and pulled me out of the water like they were hauling out a large fish. Air detonated in my lungs. I coughed and sputtered, collapsing onto the shore.

I heard my father saying my name. "Emma, wake up. It's just a nightmare. Wake up!"

Just a nightmare. My damp pajamas clung to my chest and my goose-fleshed legs. I shivered uncontrollably, but I knew that if I sat up, I would find myself safe in bed but covered in sweat, my father's arms around me.

But this time when I sat up, I was still on the beach, drenched and cold, and my father was cradling me, rocking me back and forth, repeating, "It was just a nightmare, just a nightmare. . . ."

Only both of us knew this wasn't true.